More Praise for
Every Contact Leaves a Trace

"An intelligent literary mystery, featuring the kind of tormented narrator that Robert Browning himself might have relished."
—Maureen Corrigan, NPR

"Brings to mind . . . Ian McEwan, Ford Madox Ford and Donna Tartt. . . . This is a cunning, sharp first novel that revels in keeping one in the dark." —*Independent on Sunday*

"Dymott's debut novel offers a powerful meditation on grief, love and the nature of uncertainty." —*Sunday Times*

"Shrewdly plotted and elegantly written. . . . A narrative that is alert to life's unknowable randomness." —*Financial Times*

"A quite exceptional novel. . . . Beginning as a straightforward locked-room mystery, it develops into a delicate meditation on grief and revenge. . . . Dymott has contrived a plot that is deeply satisfying without being trite." —*Observer*

"An exquisite, creepy and unexpectedly sexy murder-mystery. . . . [*Every Contact*] gets under your skin from the first chapter and remains at the back of your mind for days after the final page. Read this novel now before everyone else starts talking about it." —*Elle*

"This is more than a murder mystery. It's an examination of the subjectivity of accounts of truth. It's a desperately moving love story about a lonely man who finds salvation in another only to have the idyll destroyed. Finally, it's a tale of revenge, served cold and deadly."
—*Independent*

Every
Contact
Leaves
A Trace

Elanor Dymott

W. W. NORTON & COMPANY

NEW YORK LONDON

For information about permission to reproduce selections from this book,
write to Permissions, W. W. Norton & Company, Inc.,
500 Fifth Avenue, New York, NY 10110

For information about special discounts for bulk purchases, please contact
W. W. Norton Special Sales at specialsales@wwnorton.com or 800-233-4830

Manufacturing by RR Donnelley, Harrisonburg, VA
Book design by Ellen Cipriano
Production manager: Anna Oler

Library of Congress Cataloging-in-Publication Data

Dymott, Elanor, 1973-
Every contact leaves a trace / Elanor Dymott. — First American edition.
 pages ; cm.
ISBN 978-0-393-23977-5 (hardcover)
1. Murder—Fiction. 2. Grief—Fiction. 3. Oxford (England)—Fiction. I. Title.
PR6104.Y58E94 2013
823'.92—dc23
 2013001706

ISBN 978-0-393-34827-9 pbk.

W. W. Norton & Company, Inc.
500 Fifth Avenue, New York, N.Y. 10110
www.wwnorton.com

W. W. Norton & Company Ltd.
Castle House, 75/76 Wells Street, London W1T 3QT

1 2 3 4 5 6 7 8 9 0

Have you seen the white lily grow
Before rude hands have touched it?
Have you marked the fall of the snow
Before the soil hath smutched it?
Have you felt the wool of beaver,
Or swan's down ever?
Or have smelt o' the bud o' the brier,
Or the nard in the fire?
Or have tasted the bag of the bee?
O so white, O so soft, O so sweet is she!

<div align="right">Ben Jonson, The Devil is an Ass</div>

Il est impossible au malfaiteur d'agir, et surtout d'agir avec l'intensité que suppose l'action criminelle sans laisser des traces de son passage. Ces traces sont extrêmement diverses: il faut avoir présent à l'esprit que, dans chaque affaire, on peut en trouver d'une sorte différente.

<div align="right">Edmond Locard, Manuel de Technique Policière</div>

BENVOLIO

I do but keep the peace. Put up thy sword,
Or manage it to part these men with me.

<div align="right">William Shakespeare,

The Most Excellent and Lamentable Tragedy of

Romeo and Juliet, Act 1, Scene i</div>

Every
Contact
Leaves
A Trace

PROLOGUE

London, Friday 21 December 2007

Early Morning

I f you were to ask me to tell you about my wife, I would have to warn you at the outset that I don't know a great deal about her.

Or at least, not as much as I thought I did.

And I would go on to say that reaching such a conclusion, if I can call it that, has been, for me, a process of discovery: I went into a dark room with my camera for a time, and I came out with a photograph of a woman I had never seen before.

It is perhaps because of these fluctuating states of knowing and un-knowing that, when I am asked that sort of a question, I find it a little difficult to decide where to start.

She died six months ago, almost to the hour. On Midsummer Night in Oxford, underneath a great and spreading plane that grows in the gardens of Worcester College as you walk down to the lake, the bridge to the Provost's garden somewhere on your right hand side and a new moon rising. That was where I found her body. It is, as a place to begin, as good as any other. Or, I suppose, as a place to die. As a place to have your head stoven in by someone bringing a stone, lifted from

the lake and still covered in weed and scum, down onto your skull six or seven times as you crouch to the grass, your face getting closer to it with each blow until at the fourth you give up and sink into it, smelling memories there, and the moistness of the evening, and wishing things had turned out differently.

I do not think she would have minded being brought this close to the ground when she died. Had the choice been left to her she would doubtless have selected some other method. But the grass itself, the fact that it was damp and that it stained her dress in the way that it did; that would not have troubled her. She was the sort of person who would sit down on a lawn whatever she was wearing, or kneel on damp earth if she wanted to. And after all, that was exactly what she did the night I met her at Richard's wedding, the night before the morning she agreed to become my wife.

PART 1

London, Friday 30 November 2007

Late Evening

1

It would not be inaccurate of me to describe Richard as my closest friend, although I doubt it would occur to him to refer to me in quite the same way. Oldest friend then, rather than closest, and I can say that with confidence since our first meeting took place within hours of our arriving at Oxford, over a tea given by our tutor. It is those initial meetings that stick in the mind. The hands I shook in the first few days of the Michaelmas term are the ones I can almost feel against my palm still. If I try to, that is; if I think back.

'The study of law,' Charles Haddon said to us as we stood in his drawing room, 'will only disappoint those of you who approach it with anything other than the expectation that, in order to succeed, you will have to work phenomenally hard. There will be one or two of you who think, erroneously, that the really challenging work is behind you. That the small modicum of success you have garnered in your little clutch of A's at A level was what mattered. There may even be some among your number who are under the illusion that by having won your place here, you have won also the right to enjoy yourselves. Let

me assure you that such an assumption would be the gravest of errors, and one not without consequences. That is all I have to say, for now. There are scones behind you, and tea in the urn by the window.'

If this speech made me want to melt into the curtains and remain there, it seemed to have the opposite effect on Richard, who sprang forward and started a debate with Haddon about an article of his that he'd read in *The Times*. We were to be tutorial partners for the next three years, Richard and I, and this pattern would continue throughout that time without either of us much minding: me observing almost without comment while Richard and Haddon battled things out between them. We did as well as one another in the end, each of us sticking to Haddon's advice. We breakfasted together in Hall every morning before going to lectures and having lunch in the faculty. Then we came back to College and stayed at our desks in the Old Library until the supper bell rang, breaking only for tea in the Buttery and a stroll around the lake, and of course for our Friday afternoon sessions with Haddon.

It wasn't until after supper each day that we parted company. Richard announced at the outset that he intended to be well-read by the time he was called to the Bar, so he strolled back to the library every evening at eight and, having started by reading the complete works of William Shakespeare, worked his way chronologically through the shelves of English Literature. As he read, I pulled pints and opened bottles in the Buttery bar, glad to be earning some cash and being in company in a way I could control. Within weeks I knew everyone by sight, and, through overhearing conversations and witnessing greetings again and again as I worked, most of them by name.

Richard stayed on at the end of our three years to do some research while I went straight to law school, and I did wonder once or twice whether it was because he hadn't yet reached the shelves that held the twentieth century. He joined me in London eventually, taking up a pupillage in Middle Temple while I was qualifying as a solicitor in

the City. My work was purely litigious in the first few years, so that our paths crossed fairly regularly, either because my own firm had instructed him on a case, or because we would bump into one another in the commercial corridors of the Royal Courts of Justice at the end of a day and find time for a drink or two. But as I began to spend more time negotiating deals and drafting contracts, and both of us became far busier professionally, I saw less of him each year than I had done the one before. Still, it was a rare month that passed without one of us lunching the other. We had never, to my mind, been competitive in our studies, each of us accepting that we were evenly matched and predicting, from the moment I became the audience to Richard's performance at Haddon's tea party, the divergent paths our careers would take. Where there was no competition to speak of professionally, there was perhaps a little too much of it in those lunches, each of us trying to outdo the other every time with our choice of venue, or, if we couldn't do that, with our largesse on ordering the wine. It reached the point one month when my turn came around again and I couldn't stand it any more. I was almost tempted to cancel the booking I had made and take him instead for liver and bacon in Leadenhall Market, which would have been sure to have brought the whole thing to a close. But then he met Lucinda, who told him he had to do something about his weight, so it was all over anyway.

He informed me of his intention to approach his physical transformation in the same way that he had approached the canon of English Literature almost a decade earlier, and I wasn't at all surprised when he announced six months later that he had been successful. I saw him next at his stag weekend in Paris. Lucinda had suggested he take her to the Seychelles to propose, and it was his tan, I think, rather than his shrunken waistline, that made it so difficult to recognise him in the hotel foyer. He told me over the weekend that she had planned the wedding with a similar exactitude, and so it was with a degree of reluctance that I made my way to Temple Church that sweltering

August afternoon two summers ago. We had always shared a certain ineptitude when it came to relationships, and the speed and skill with which Richard had extricated himself from his single state had surprised me. Because Lucinda had decided Richard's brother should be his best man, I had no duties to perform. I left nowhere near enough time to walk down to Temple from my apartment in Islington and it was too hot to hurry in morning dress. In the end I was really quite late, turning the corner to see the final inch of Lucinda's train sweeping into the church, the bridesmaids stooping to lift it over the threshold before pulling the door shut behind them. I stood for a minute or two, wondering whether it would be intrusive of me to push it open and follow them. In the end I decided against it and strolled on beyond the church to lie on the Inner Temple lawns in the sun. I reckoned I had about an hour before I would have to go and make an appearance at the drinks in the Middle Temple rose garden; any earlier and I'd risk bumping into Richard and Lucinda as they emerged from the church.

I was only mildly disappointed to find, on opening my eyes a little while later and looking at my watch, that I had been asleep for quite some time. The drinks were almost over when I arrived. It was the usual sort of affair, overdressed guests helping themselves to as much champagne as possible either through thirst, or desperation, or both; the canapés wilting slightly in the sun; children becoming bored and beginning to quarrel. Everyone looked worn out, apart from Lucinda. She was by my side almost immediately, demanding to know what I had made of the chaplain's address, and of the choristers. 'Weren't they just divine?' she said, with what looked to be tears in her eyes. I was halfway through what I thought was a passable attempt at covering my tracks when Richard appeared behind her. 'Didn't see you at the line-up old chap. Shame. Where the bloody hell were you?' 'Richard darling, don't swear,' Lucinda said. 'And don't interrupt. Why don't you go and see if your mother needs anything?' She told me not to worry about Richard, that he'd become almost unbearably pompous

since discovering that he was tipped to become the youngest Silk at the Bar, and that she hoped I wouldn't mind but she'd put me opposite an old school friend of hers who, from what Richard had told her about me, she thought I might like. 'I'm sure you will, really I am,' she said, gripping my forearm and speaking so quickly I struggled to keep up with her as she carried on, saying, 'She's a total brainbox, terribly high-flying academic at UCL actually, always makes me feel like a complete twit. But she's really lovely, honestly! Talk to her about poetry, that's her thing. Yes, ask her about poets and you'll be absolutely fine.' And then she smiled in a sympathetic kind of a way and said she would have asked me what sort of law I did but that Richard had told her it was far too complicated for her to understand so she wasn't going to after all, and come to think of it, if she was me, she'd probably steer clear of that particular topic of conversation altogether over dinner, if I could bear it, and then she laughed, and I laughed, and the gong sounded and we were going in to eat.

I look back to that evening sometimes and think how strange it was that I chose not to scrutinise the seating plan in the way that I usually do at weddings. Perhaps it was the heat, or the champagne, or the awkwardness of my conversation with Lucinda. In any case, when I arrived at the entrance to the Hall and saw the crowd of people gathering around the board searching for their places, I looked over their shoulders only for long enough to see my own name before going downstairs to the cloakroom to throw some water on my face. And so it was that when I set off across the Hall to find my seat, I knew only that the woman opposite me would be someone who'd been at school with Lucinda. As I came closer and spotted the empty space that was waiting for me on the far side of the table I saw the back of her, this woman Lucinda thought I might like, and I will admit to taking a fairly careful look at what I saw. She was small, which I supposed was why she was wearing such high heels, and her dress clung to her body, showing clearly the shape of her. And her hair. It was long and dark

and as I walked past her she swung it to one side and revealed her back, almost entirely bare, her dress cut away to the waist. The bride and groom made their entrance at the moment I reached my seat and because she turned to applaud them I had to wait to see her face. I looked instead at her back once more, following it down to where her body became clothed again and resting my gaze there. As soon as everyone stopped clapping, the woman on my right started to introduce herself. Only then was I able to lean across the table and shake Lucinda's school friend's hand, becoming aware of an extraordinary sensation spreading across my chest and down towards my stomach as I realised who I was looking at. 'Rachel Cardanine,' she said, and smiled at me, and for a moment I thought she hadn't recognised me, that she had forgotten me altogether and that I was, for her, no more than a perfect stranger. But then she laughed a little through her smile, and I understood. She was playing some kind of a game with me, and so, as had been my habit all those years ago whenever she did something like this, I began to play it with her, smiling in return and saying, 'Alex. Alex Petersen,' not letting go of her hand until she pulled it away from mine.

Before I could say anything else the man to her left was announcing a proposal to reorganise our end of the table. The woman on my right was his wife and he didn't see why he shouldn't sit next to her. 'D'you mind, love, what's your name, Rachel? Do you mind, Rachel?' He placed his hand on her bare back and steered her away from the chair she'd been about to sit down on. 'I like to have my princess right beside me. I'm sure you'll understand.' I looked down and saw that the woman was pregnant, and then I looked back at her husband. He loomed above the rest of us, almost as wide as he was tall, with his hair shaved close to his head and rings on three of his fingers. As I started to move, Richard was behind me suddenly. 'Sorry old man, didn't get a chance to tell you about any of this.' He looked across at Rachel, coming round the table towards us, and then at the pregnant

woman and her husband. 'Those two?' he whispered into my ear, his breath thick with alcohol. 'Distant relations of Lucinda's. Don't blame me. She did the seating plan. Bit of a rum chap, but apparently he's rolling in it. And her—' He looked at Rachel, taking her seat beside me. 'Sorry. Should have said.'

Then he was gone and Rachel and I were listening as Adrian, the man with the rings on his fingers, asked the waitress her name. He repeated it back to her as she poured his wine and, leaning across the table towards us, said, 'Makes them feel valued that does, learning their names. Doesn't it, princess?' and he turned to his wife and started to stroke her belly.

It was for the most part a fairly awful evening. After telling us he knew everyone else at the table and there wasn't one of them who couldn't realise assets of at least 'one mill', Adrian pulled out his keys and talked about his car and showed us the fob. He picked up the menu and read out the information on the back about the history of the Hall. When the waitress came back he addressed her by her name as many times as possible and when Rachel said no thanks, she didn't want any more potatoes, he told the woman that Rachel was shy and she did want some really. Then he told Rachel that she was never going to grow any taller if she didn't eat a proper diet. Rachel said nothing until the waitress had gone, at which point she stood and tipped her potatoes on to Adrian's plate. He was silent for a moment but then he turned to his wife and whispered something to her and Rachel leaned in towards me and pressed her hand onto my thigh and said, 'Do you think he fucks her in the arse?' and I felt her lips touch my ear and for a moment I could smell her.

Before I can reply Adrian suddenly raises his voice and I become aware that he and his wife are having a disagreement. It looks for a moment as though it might escalate, and Rachel presses her hand, which she has left resting on my thigh, harder into me. But then princess draws things to a close by saying, 'You don't want me to get upset

do you?' and she lifts Adrian's hand up and places it on her belly and they start to rub noses. Rachel pours some wine for us both and raises her glass and, turning her head so that neither of them can hear, says, 'Here's to fucking awful weddings. Don't worry, I'm not going to ask you to rub noses.'

Just as I am beginning to feel uncomfortable about the course the evening is taking the best man stands up and taps his glass with a spoon. Whilst the speeches given by Richard's brother and Lucinda's father are exactly as I expect them to be, Richard's takes me by surprise. He has lost his usual bombast, and displays none of the pomposity Lucinda had felt it necessary to warn me about. He sounds almost nervous, and although at first I wonder whether this is because he has drunk far more than he ought and is struggling to keep things under control, there is in his voice a tenderness I am not sure I have ever heard before. He turns to Lucinda and looks at her as if nobody else is present and then, tentatively, he declares his love and thanks her for allowing him to love her in the way that he does. And then he looks at us all and makes a joke about her mother and he is himself again, and Lucinda's face becomes composed and she turns to whisper something to her father.

Adrian and his princess leave immediately after the toasts. Rachel and I stand together in silence as the tables are moved back to the sides of the room. Then she says 'What a hideous couple' before excusing herself, telling me she'll come straight back. 'I promise,' and she takes my hand briefly in hers as she walks away. But of course she doesn't come back, and I realise eventually that she has gone. I watch Richard and Lucinda dance the first dance and start to calculate when it will be acceptable for me also to leave. I am standing alone as the applause for the dance dies down when I feel somebody behind me. They press themselves against me and put their arms around me and I turn to see it is Rachel and suddenly we are dancing to the next song, slowly, uncertainly. I lower my head down towards hers and I can smell her

again. I move my hands onto the bareness of her back. To my embarrassment I feel myself become hard almost immediately and so, it seems, does she. More out of panic than anything else I hold her even closer and sense that she is laughing. She's trying to hide it by burying her face into my chest but I can feel her whole body shaking with it. And the more she laughs the harder I become. She takes my hand and says, 'Shall we get some air?' and she leads me out of the Hall into the night, keeping herself close in front of me all the way so that, I suppose, nobody can see what is happening.

We half ran around the Hall and down the steps and slipped in through a gate to the rose garden. Here she kissed me and undid my zip and put her hand inside and touched me. Then she pulled me further in among the roses and there was a bench and she sat me on it and knelt on the grass in front of me. I cried out when I came. She wiped her hand across her mouth and then she stood and pulled me up and held me for a time.

'Come on cry-baby. Let's get you home,' she said then, and she led me out of the garden, bending over once to say 'Oh god look what I've done to my bloody dress the grass must have been soaking.'

It is evening now and the darkness is spreading out against the sky as though something viscous has been spilt there. This is the time of day I have come to dislike the most, when I start to reflect on the loneliness of the hours that have passed, at the same time as sensing the unease that accompanies my drift towards sleep. I dream of Rachel every night, almost to the exclusion of anything else. I understand this to be quite normal in my situation, though I would have expected the frequency of these dreams to have decreased a little by now, or their content to have begun to vary more than it does, or that I might at least have started to hear something in them: since Rachel's death, my dreams are all in silence.

The one that recurs most often is of the night I found her body. I am not surprised by this, but I do find it strange that what seems to surface most often is not the moment I actually ran to her and found her, but instead, a brief episode that took place shortly after that. The first of the policemen have arrived in response to the porter's call and I sit on the grass and listen as one of them asks me questions

and I don't answer because instead I am hearing the other policeman attempt to resuscitate Rachel. I look across and see him raising his head and shouting out numbers and then lowering his head and pressing his face onto hers and raising his head and shouting his numbers again and then I realise the first policeman has started to shout at me because I am not answering so I turn back to him and focus on what he is saying and I have answered one or two of his questions when I become aware that I can't hear the other policeman shouting out his numbers any more and then I realise that this is because he has stopped and we all fall silent.

I hear him saying into his radio to cancel the ambulance and I am shouting now and I ask my policeman why they are cancelling it and he says, 'No need sir, we're calling for a doctor' and I say 'Why?' and he looks away from me and says 'To verify the death sir.' And then I see that the other policeman has started to place something around Rachel that looks like a short white fence but it is made of cloth. I am watching him do this and I think to myself that it looks like the windbreak my father used to hammer into the sand each summer in Cornwall to keep my mother warm and then I realise I can't see Rachel any more and I stand and start to move towards her and I am shouting at the man to stop what he is doing and to let me see her but I can't move and my policeman is holding me and talking to me quite gently now and putting handcuffs on me and explaining that he is arresting me.

In my dream I hear none of the speech, and none of the shouting. I see our lips move and I know what we are saying but I hear nothing. It is somehow more than silence, this absence of speech: it is a space devoid even of the idea of sound, as though hearing has become a sense not yet thought of.

The dream continues. I turn away from the cloth fence that has been put up around Rachel and I look up the lawns in the other direction and it is an October morning fifteen years ago and I am watching another moment unfold, the moment I have come to think of

as being the precise point from which I can say that I knew her. Of course, by the time we found ourselves looking at one another across the table at Richard's wedding we'd known each other for years already; it was just that there had been what you might call a long pause in our acquaintance, until that night in Middle Temple Hall when Lucinda's seating plan brought us together again.

In my dream, a man with a megaphone stands under a tree and calls out to us to Go quietly and Be careful and Get a move on, except that in my dream he only holds the megaphone to his mouth and watches as we file silently on to the stands and face him. Another man is standing beside him, hunched over a camera. And then a woman appears behind them, the figure of a woman running, and we all turn to look at her instead of at the camera.

And then the dream is over.

When I say that I think of that moment as being the point in time from which I can say I knew Rachel, I mean that in a qualified way of course. So that if someone were to ask me how long I'd known my wife before she died, that is the point from which I would count the days. But in truth, I would have to explain that I knew her then only in the sense that a lot of people did: she was the sort of person that a lot of people knew. We went up to Oxford together in the autumn of 1992, Richard and Rachel and I, and it was as Richard and I stood waiting to be photographed in honour of that occasion that she made herself known to us, running towards the great plane tree we stood beside.

The stands had been erected just beneath my window early one morning in the first week of October. It can't have been more than one or two days into the term. I had been allocated a room up in the eaves of the Nuffield Building, a 1930s block standing alone in the gardens just to the south of the main quad. It was a tiny space, with a low door and a ceiling that slanted on one side of the room, right down to the ground. There was a narrow iron bed just inside the door and beyond the bed was a desk pushed into an alcove formed by one of the win-

dows. The window emerged from the roof, jutting out into the sky, so that when I sat at my desk I was afforded a view of the whole of the lawns stretching down to the lake, dotted about with those enormous trees that I would come to see swaying in night breezes like ships at sea. At the other end of the room was another window looking down towards the lake, and behind that, on the opposite wall, a tiny basin with a mirror above it.

On the day I arrived in College I found a letter waiting for me in my pigeonhole in the porter's lodge. I had been addressed on the envelope with an 'Esq.' after my surname, the first time I'd ever been given one. I saw from the signature that the person who had done this thing was Mr H. P. Gardner, Senior Tutor and Fellow in English Literature. His letter instructed me to be on the lawns in front of the Nuffield Building by eight a.m., dressed in what he called subfusc, so that the picture could be taken before we went over to the Sheldonian for the matriculation ceremony that would make us members of the University. It was the choreography that would take the time, the letter said. Getting all of us up on to the stands in the right height order and then off again without injury or mishap; that was why we had to be there so early. When it came to it I was woken at six by the sound of men laughing and the clanking of metal poles beneath my window. I remember feeling strangely nervous, so much so that instead of going over to Hall for breakfast, which I had promised myself I would do every day regardless of how I felt about being with people, I took a bowl of cereal with me into my bath and ate with the steam filling the room and sweat running into my mouth. Afterwards, my face flushed red, I stood in front of the mirror trying to do up my white bow tie, second-hand and slightly marked, and thought to myself that I would have preferred a new one. And then I swung round and looked out of the window.

The leaves were turning and there was a mist hanging over the lake, spreading a little way up the lawns towards the students who

were gathering in groups around the tree just to the right of my building. Suddenly I didn't want to go down. I didn't want to be among them, having to think of something to say. I felt that if I could stay in my room, with my books, I would be alright. I had a sense then that I would remain like this for the whole of my time at Worcester College: looking on groups from the outside. To a certain extent that was exactly what happened, and thinking about it now, I realise that is how I have felt for most of my life, the way I did that October morning. On the edge of things, apart from people, not wanting to be among them. For most of my life, that is, apart from the months that passed between the night of Richard's wedding and the night when Rachel died. The months when I was finally with her, and loved by her.

I went out when a man with a megaphone, who later became known to me as the Harry P. Gardner who had sent me my letter, started to organise the groups, now grown larger, into height order. I nodded in acknowledgement to a few of the students I had met at Haddon's tea, Richard included, and then we were being filed up on to the stands. The mist had cleared and Harry was standing beside the camera now, watching as the photographer raised his hand in the air to count down to the moment we would be captured forever. And then she appeared, running from one of the passageways that cut through from the main quad. She cried out as she ran, 'Wait! Oh please wait for me oh bloody hell I'm so unbelievably sorry I got the wrong lawns!' and everybody laughed, the whole of the stands laughed as she ran towards us in her black and white, pulling up one of her stockings and fixing her hair back with a clip. She had that ability, my wife, to make a whole crowd of people laugh, almost unintentionally. And then she laughed as well and said, 'I did! I really did! I thought it was on the quad and then there was nobody there so I went round to the playing fields through the Sainsbury Building and I had to run all the way back again and—' 'Miss,' the photographer said. 'Quieten down miss. Stand there. Smile. That'll do. And, one!', as Rachel, smaller than the rest of us, took her

place in the middle of the first row, directly in front of me. 'Two!', the photographer called out. And then he had to stop again while she fixed another clip in her hair. She lifted it all back behind her and it fanned out in the air, long and dark. It flicked into my face, catching me in both my eyes. I must have reacted in some way, out loud. 'Oh god I'm so sorry!' she said and turned round and I caught the scent of her perfume as she did, and she put her hand on my arm. 'I'm so sorry are you OK? I'm being utterly hopeless this morning.' 'I'm fine,' I said, wiping my eyes and feeling embarrassed. 'I'm fine.' 'Oh god,' she said again, still looking at me. 'You're not are you? Tell you what, could you just hold this a minute?' and she passed me a black ribbon and leaned forward and shook up her collar to straighten it and as she did her shirt fell open and I could see that she wasn't wearing a bra. Her breasts were small, her nipples pointed and dark. She stood back up and looked at me and said 'Thanks' and took her ribbon and tied it under her collar in a sort of a half-knot and pulled on her gown and turned back round. 'One! Two! Three!' And it was over.

We would not speak again on such intimate terms, Rachel and I, until the end of our second year, when we both found ourselves staying up in College for the summer vacation. I had assumed, as the shutter clicked again and again, that the photograph represented no more than a pause in our conversation, but Rachel disappeared immediately and I was left alone on the stands, looking around, confused about where she had gone and why she hadn't waited for me to go with her. I felt pretty foolish when she ignored me on the way over to the ceremony. Richard told me that the group she was with were the English students. He said that this explained why they were making so much noise. 'As natural attention-seekers,' he went on, in what I would come to know as his customary tone, 'they will labour throughout their sojourn at Worcester under the perpetual misconception that whatever they choose to say will be of the utmost interest to the rest of us, and that we, in contrast, will have nothing whatever about us

that might be of interest to them. And that is how things will remain for at least a decade or so, until they realise that the rest of the world finds them far less fascinating than they thought themselves to be and they'll start to seek us out and marry us.'

'Why?' I asked him. 'Why us?'

'Because by that point old man,' he replied, 'we'll be stinking bloody rich.'

Unlike Richard, I did come to find them interesting, the group that Rachel walked with that October morning, the group who were louder than the rest of us and seemed to notice no one but themselves. As far as I could make out, they did very little work as such. In the winter, if they came anywhere near the library at all it was not to sit inside at the desks, but outside on the spiral staircase, talking so loudly that I sometimes gave up trying to concentrate and took my books back to my room instead. When the summer term arrived Richard and I used to see them on our strolls around the lake, and then they seemed to do nothing other than lie all afternoon on the lawns, smoking and passing novels between themselves and arguing, or telling each other the plot to save them having to read everything for Harry Gardner.

I have described them as a group, but it was one that split fairly soon into smaller units. Rachel's was made up of only three. The other two were her tutorial partners: a smallish and slightly effeminate northerner called Anthony Trelissick, and an American woman, Cissy Craig, who had whiter teeth than the rest of us and coxed for the college Boat Club.

I was especially interested in Rachel herself. Of course she was known to us all from the moment she ran towards the stands for the photograph, from the moment we turned collectively to look at her, but there were plenty of other things that brought her to everyone's attention. In addition to the way she chose to make her entrance that morning there was the matter of her appearance, a topic that came to be much discussed in the Buttery bar. And then there was her reputa-

tion as a pricktease, a title given to her by the men she came to reject. It was a word I first heard used with reference to Rachel one evening at the start of the Hilary term of our first year. Richard had surprised me by giving up on his reading and coming to sit at the bar. I noticed he was drinking a lot, keeping up with the man he sat next to, Philip Towneley, who himself had announced his intention to drown his sorrows before closing time. Towneley had, it seemed, thought he stood a chance with Rachel until earlier on that evening when she'd asked him to leave the set of rooms she and Cissy shared, 'just', he said, 'as things were getting interesting.' And that was when Richard, nodding into his pint and drawing the corners of his mouth down into an upside down 'U', said the word pricktease. 'That's what the story is,' he went on. 'Shouldn't take it personally if I were you.' And then I remember seeing Anthony, who had been sitting at a side table reading a novel all evening, look up at Richard and frown. He seemed always to be frowning, Anthony, but where it was usually a frown that suggested puzzlement, or, with his eyebrows creased together just a little and the beginnings of a lopsided kind of a smile breaking out across his face, something like bewilderment, there was no doubt about the fact that he was angry that night as he watched Richard. 'Women like Rachel Cardanine,' Richard continued, not noticing Anthony, who by now had put down his book and was walking across the bar towards him, 'tend eventually to get what it is they seem to be asking for, whether they like it or not.' He picked up his pint at this point and started to gesticulate with it, beating time to the rhythm of his own speech, the volume of which was beginning to rise. 'And if she continues to go about the place treating men in the way that she does, there won't be a lot of sympathy for her when it happens, I can—'

He broke off when Anthony punched him in the side of the head. He fell from his stool, more because he was drunk than because Anthony had hit him particularly hard, but as he did so his hand hit the bar and his glass flew through the air and smashed against the

wall, so it seemed a little more dramatic than it actually was and a few hopeful chants rose up from across the room. Richard pulled himself up from the floor and said straight away, 'I don't fight I'm afraid. Terribly sorry.' He brushed off his trousers and pressed his hand against the side of his head where Anthony had punched him. 'Well I don't insult women when they aren't around to defend themselves,' Anthony replied, rubbing his hand, 'I mean, it's just not on mate.' 'Look here Anthony, you and I both know I'm not your mate.' Richard was smiling now, and I could tell he was beginning to enjoy himself. 'Stood you up this evening has she? Is that why you're in here all alone? Feeling a bit rejected are we? And where's your little American friend? Getting sweaty somewhere with her crew?'

I think, looking back, that Anthony almost regained a kind of a moral high ground by saying nothing in response. He walked over to his table and collected his things and came and put some money on the bar and said to me, 'For the glass. Sorry mate,' before walking out and leaving Richard and Towneley in silence as I started to sweep up the mess and fill out an incident form for Haddon, who, being more than zealous in his performance of his duties as Dean, insisted on these things being done properly.

The thing people talked about most frequently though, and the thing that allowed the persona we created for Rachel to command a certain degree of sympathy from us all, was her near-legendary status as an orphan. There were plenty of students I came across who, like me, had lost one parent, my mother having died shortly before I went up to Oxford, but to have lost both lent her a kind of mystique. This was further enhanced by the story that went round that it had happened when she was very young and that since then, she had been supported, if not quite adopted, by her godmother, a woman said to be an art dealer who, because she spent most of her time in Italy, gave Rachel the run of her house in Chelsea. 'Godmother Evie', Rachel called her when she talked about her in the bar with Anthony and Cissy. Never

just 'my godmother', or 'Evie', but always both at once. I found myself wishing sometimes when I was at Oxford that I had a Godmother Evie. I suppose every one of us is capable of falling for a notion like that, the idea that there might be someone out there other than our parents, someone who will look after us and lend us vast houses and send us money when we need it.

I heard from time to time that Rachel gave weekend parties at Godmother Evie's house, a house said to be so tall it had its own lift and so grand it came with a butler. There were stories about these parties, and it was rumoured that Rachel gave them names. For Menagerie Night, everyone was instructed to wear fancy dress, and Rachel herself appeared at the head of the staircase as a cat, her naked body spray-painted black. She wore only stilettos, with whiskers drawn wide across her face and a feather boa attached to a piece of ribbon about her waist so that it hung from the base of her spine. And at the party she called Anti-Orgy, the men were invited to compete in turn to see how long they could withhold an erection, Rachel and Cissy stroking them and licking them, Anthony standing by with a stopwatch. Because my source for these stories was usually Richard, who in turn heard them from Towneley, I never took them particularly seriously. She was just that sort of a woman, I used to think. The sort of woman people made up stories about.

As an undergraduate I saw the house in Chelsea only once. It was at the very end of the Michaelmas term of my second year. I had caught sight of a parcel one day in the porter's lodge. Because it was too big to fit into a pigeonhole it had been left out on the side to be collected. I noticed Rachel's name on the label and took a closer look. The original address had been crossed through and it had been sent on to her at Worcester. That was how I found out where the Chelsea house was. I didn't set out to remember the address, as such, but it stuck in my mind somehow. There was something about the name of the street, I suppose, that must have been familiar to me, and when at the end of

that term I found myself in Sloane Square, I thought I would look it out. I had been in Peter Jones, as it happened, picking something up for my father. I was due to spend Christmas with him in Hampshire and he'd ordered an electric blanket or a mattress cover or something like that and hadn't wanted to pay for the postage. Because I found it more quickly than I thought I would, I had a bit of time to spare before catching the train back to Oxford.

The street when I reached it was empty. It was growing dark and the frost that had fallen crunched under my feet as I walked. It was a much smaller house than I had been led to expect; more of a cottage really. Rather than the steps I'd imagined I would see leading up to a huge front door, perhaps with a lion's head for a knocker, there was in front of me a path, lined with a box hedge on either side and so short I could have passed up it in no more than a couple of strides. The curtains were closed and lights shone from behind them, a lamp burning low over the door, so that the whole cottage glowed against the evening. I put my parcel down on the pavement and rested my hands on the gate, wondering whether it was Godmother Evie who was inside, or Rachel, or if in fact there was nobody there at all, the curtains closed each day by a neighbour and the lights switched on by timers. And then I saw someone looking down at me from an upstairs window so I picked up my parcel and walked away without once looking back at the house.

3

Had I known that night beside the lake that I would never see Rachel again, I would have struggled more than I did. Fought, even, to break free of the man who was restraining me; to run to her and lie down beside her and hold her and burrow my face into her neck. These are some of the things I want to do now and can't. It simply didn't occur to me that we would not at some point be reunited. I don't mean that I thought in any coherent or logical sense that we would be together again. I knew, to the extent I knew anything clearly that night, or in the weeks that followed, that she was dead. But I had no idea of the finality represented by the fence that was put up around her in the minutes before I was led across the lawns and driven away.

It was Godmother Evie who identified Rachel's body the next morning, while I was in custody, and much later on, when the police had finished with her, I allowed myself in my grief to be persuaded that it wouldn't help me to see her. They had tried to put her back together again, they said, but the injuries she had sustained and the

work they had had to do on her head meant that she was no longer herself.

I looked back just once as we walked towards the college gates, the policeman and I. The whole area had been cordoned off with tape sweeping wide around the tree and forming a barrier across the path up from the lake. More people had arrived and yet more were walking down towards the cordon carrying bags, floodlights, ladders even. A line of figures dressed in white boiler suits was strung out across the lawns and moved as one, each of them waving a torch back and forth across the grass in front of them as they went so that they looked like some sort of alien landing craft newly come to earth. I could see the porter standing under the tree and talking to the policeman who had stayed behind with Rachel. He sat on the ground and put his head in his hands and the policeman sat down beside him. I know now the story that he started to tell. I have been told by my lawyer, and in some cases, by the authors themselves, all of the stories of all of the people who were there that night. I know something also of the tales told by the cameras at the college doors and across the road; by the blood on my clothes; by the stone that was found beside the lake with tiny pieces of Rachel's skin still stuck to it. In some places they fit with one another, these stories, and with my own, but in other places they do not.

As for the porter's tale, he'd been puzzled not to have seen us on his tiny TV screen leaving the college. He'd heard us standing outside his lodge saying our last goodbyes to Harry and thanking him for dinner and telling him we'd always wondered what it was like to dine on High Table and now we knew, and how kind he was and how good the food and the wine and the company and how glad we were to have been invited back. So he'd decided to go on his rounds a little early, just to make sure we hadn't slipped in again.

I remember that when we'd arrived that evening for dinner and reported in at the lodge and signed the Old Members' Visitors Book

he'd asked us whether we'd be staying the night and when we told him we weren't he said, 'Well then, you'll be gone by midnight please. No creeping around or I shall have to ask you to leave. Old members do that sometimes,' he carried on. 'They come over all nostalgic and think they can linger and no one will mind letting them out at three in the morning when they remember they have to go to work the next day and realise they'd rather be sleeping in a bed than on the grass.' He told us he'd found them down by the lake more often than he'd like, reliving their student days. Had to get quite shirty with some of them once, throw them out more or less. 'Of course,' we promised, and we laughed, and I really believed that was a promise we would keep, Rachel and I.

He told the police that when it came to it he'd thought he ought to check, just to be sure, especially since he hadn't actually seen us leave. And it seems that as he set off from his lodge and turned from the alcove before walking to the right, past the chapel doors and on towards the terrace forming the north face of the quad, he hadn't seen me sitting in the shadows of the library staircase, waiting for Rachel to come back.

'Actually, can you wait just a moment?', she had said suddenly, placing her hand on my arm as I was about to duck out through the little wicket door on to Beaumont Street so that we could walk back to our hotel and I could take her to bed, which was what I'd been wanting to do all evening. 'I'm going to run down to the lake before we leave. I want to see it in the moonlight. No, please don't come. Wait here for me. I always used to love that, walking past it at night on my own.' We discuss it for a few minutes, almost arguing I suppose. I say that she didn't always do it on her own, that we walked there together once and doesn't she remember, and why can't we do it again, like we did that summer night, but of course she goes, and I'm left looking at the notice boards and remembering doing exactly this over a decade ago: standing around on my own after the Buttery bar had closed, wish-

ing I was in bed with Rachel. When I have read all the notices, twice, I realise how tired I am. I turn around and see through the doorway immediately opposite the porter's lodge the staircase spiralling up to the Old Library that overlooks the quad. I slip into the shadows and sit on the coldness of the stone, leaning against the banisters. I put my head in my hands and, having drunk too much over dinner, I doze off almost immediately.

It seems from the porter's story that by the time I woke with a jolt and looked around me, feeling puzzled as to why Rachel hadn't come back yet, and wondering why she wanted to do this thing alone, he had already trodden his path through the orchards, on past the student blocks that sit at the northern edge of the lake, and was starting to swing back round again, making for the lodge. I see myself standing up slowly and stretching my arms above my head, yawning, hoping she hasn't walked straight past and gone back to the hotel on her own thinking I've given up waiting for her and done the same. And then, as I stand there, I realise that I am not only puzzled but also a little hurt that she hadn't wanted me to be with her. Placing the porter's story against my own, I can see him skirting the edge of the playing fields as I am on the stairs thinking these things. He checks for us beneath the trees and as he walks back up towards the point at which the path starts to follow the line of the canal, he stoops slightly under low-hanging branches, shooing away the geese he has woken.

And that is the point at which I hear it. Just as I am considering whether to leave my shadowy corner to find out where Rachel has got to. It is the sound of her screaming. I jump down the stairs two or three at a time and start to run and my mind becomes strangely calm. Sufficiently so for the thought to occur to me that it is a curious thing, my immediate and unquestioning knowledge that it is Rachel who is screaming. Rachel, who I have never heard scream in all the time that I have known her. I run faster than I am really able to and I stumble slightly on the steps that lead down into the quad so that my glasses

fall from my face. As I reach to pick them up I manage instead to kick them further away and then to fall forward, landing hard and fumbling around for what seems an age until I find them. At the same time as being terribly afraid, I am somehow elated. There is in my recognition of Rachel's scream something immensely reassuring, joyful even: it seems suddenly that the connection we share has become something elemental, overwhelming. I think all this as I stumble, fall forward, pick up my glasses and take a quicker route than the porter, running through the first of the passageways that cut through the cottages forming the south side of the quad.

All at once she is there in the distance, stretched out on the grass near the lake at the foot of one of the plane trees. I have scratched my glasses when I dropped them and I cannot see entirely clearly and it looks at first as though she is lying gazing up at the moon with her arms flung out on the ground behind her head. I slow my run to a jog. There is, it seems, nothing whatever the matter. Either I have imagined the scream altogether, or the powers of recognition that so excited me were not so accurate after all and I was simply mistaken. Had there been a scream it must have come from the street outside the college walls; it must have issued from the lips of a perfect stranger. I am afraid she will find me ridiculous in having run to her rescue. And then I become aware that I am a little angry with her for abandoning me like this in favour of some romantic notion of lying around on the college lawns looking up at the night sky, and that tomorrow, she will complain about having spoiled her dress.

But as I get closer I see that she is not on her back looking up at the moon. She is positioned with her face down and her knees tucked underneath her and her arms flung out before her as if she is praying but her head seems to be pressed right into the ground so I start to run again and when I reach her I see in the half-light that her hair is spread about her and it looks wet and I fall to her and touch it and say Rachel Rachel and she says nothing and I lift up my hands in front of

my face and there is something on them and I look at her again and I see that there is blood everywhere and she is covered in it, the whole of her back is covered in it and it is seeping still from her head and I shake her and I can't breathe and I can't say her name any more but then I can and I shout it over and over and I lean forward and down onto her and I hold her and she is very still and then I sit back and I am shaking, my whole body is shaking, and I slide one of my hands under her forehead and I lift up her head and I press my other hand down onto the back of it and I try to stop the blood but I can't and that is how the porter finds me: I am kneeling on the ground holding her head in my hands.

4

I was released from custody the following evening on the condition that I would return for a further interview in a fortnight's time, and that I would inform the police if I was planning to leave the country. I know now that my release was delayed by the lack of security cameras around the lake. That, and the absence of the porter from his lodge when I decided to come out from the shadows of the library steps. Until Harry Gardner had been tracked down, the police had been unable to find anyone who had seen me leave. Nobody could confirm the time at which I had done so nor whether it was before, or after, the screaming. The camera trained on the inside of the college doors had caught Rachel and me making as if to leave after saying our goodbyes to Harry. In a slightly later frame we are seen kissing each other before she disappears in one direction and I move out of sight in the other. The porter had pinpointed the moment he heard the scream to exactly midnight, and I had no way of proving that I had been sitting on the library steps when I also heard it and began to run towards Rachel's body. There would easily have been time, apparently, for me

to have left my hiding place, as one of the policemen insisted on call-
ing it, and run down to the lake to kill her, all before the porter found
us under the tree.

After I was arrested, after I'd been checked in at the station and
had everything taken from me, I was allowed to make a phone call.
Godmother Evie wasn't at home and when I tried her mobile it was
switched off, so I decided to wait and try again the following morn-
ing. I lay on the bed in my cell and I felt half certain Rachel might be
shown in at any moment, all apologies and explanations, telling me
it was someone else's blood that had stained the shirt the police had
taken from me, that it was someone else's head I had cradled in my
hands, rather than her own. And I was sure that my being held there
was little more than a formality, that there was no question of my
being seriously considered a suspect for more than a few hours. When
the duty lawyer had been to see me and we had discussed what I would
and wouldn't say in my interview, they told me I should try to get
some sleep. There was no hurry, the police said, and there were things
that had to be attended to before they spoke to me properly. Even with
the brightness of the light from the corridor and the faces looking in
on me every ten minutes, I managed eventually to do as they said:
when they called me at eight and gave me something to eat, they told
me I'd been asleep for hours.

I wasn't especially troubled by the first interview, despite its length
and the resigned manner in which the detectives were asking their
questions, their conclusions obviously drawn before they entered the
room and read out their caution again. Nor was I concerned by the
youthfulness of the duty lawyer who sat beside me in a shiny suit, his
face flushed from sleep and, presumably, excitement. I assumed the
police were in all likelihood, still only at the stage of gathering infor-
mation, of collecting stories, and that mine would be one of many that
was being told. It was clear that what they actually knew amounted
to very little, and I was quite certain that in the hours to come, as

the facts settled into some kind of order, something would emerge to make them question the assumptions they had made about me.

Throughout the whole experience of telling and retelling my tale, of sidestepping their tricks and their feints, I felt nothing but the coldness which had seeped into my chest and my stomach at the moment I'd first realised there was something odd about the position of Rachel's body. I remember having a sense somehow, as we sat around the table talking into the tape recorder, that what was happening was not in fact happening. It was as though we were all pretending; as though we were playing a game and performing our roles and marking out time until someone opened the door to tell us we could stop, she had been found, it was over. In fact, looking back and thinking through the days I spent in Oxford after her death, my overriding memory is of feeling that I was elsewhere, or that elements of my cognitive functioning had been frozen, so that I couldn't keep up with what was happening around me, and nor could I see or hear or understand it properly.

What seems to be happening now, particularly over the last few days and nights, is that my perspective is growing clearer. Something, or someone, is twisting the lens on the camera that is my memory, so that as the focus sharpens, questions are beginning to occur to me that did not then and should have done. I realise now that it wasn't until the second interview that I began to feel uncomfortable, the one that took place in the late afternoon of the same day. It quickly became apparent that someone had provided me with an alibi, and that if I gave the right answers, I would be released for the time being. There were certain things about it that didn't feel quite right, and something in the approach the police were taking that didn't strike me as being entirely sensible. I can't pretend that I was aware of anything more than a vague sense of unease or confusion. And perhaps that is what anyone would have felt in such a situation; I'm sure it's possible that another man might even have felt it much sooner than I did. But the

more I think about Rachel's murder and the days that followed, what was then no more than a hazy sense of disquiet is growing into something more troublesome than that.

I was aware from the start of that second interview that there were stories circulating in the room which were not my own. I knew that these stories would already have been divided into parts and shared out between people all over the building who would have been busy all night and all day checking facts and calculating timings. I knew also that the college, shut down to the outside world from the moment the police had arrived, would have been full of people knocking on doors and asking questions, or moving slowly across the lawns on their hands and knees, or swimming across the bottom of the lake looking for something, anything. Whatever they had discovered, I realised, would have been woven together with whatever had been found in our hotel room and whatever had been taken from our apartment in London, and the stories flying around the room would have been made from all of these things. I was aware also that the men interviewing me were throwing their theories like fishing nets and testing my responses against them, and that in so doing, they were inviting me to incriminate myself. So I answered their questions as fully as I could, whilst trying to relate only the sequence of events that I intended to, despite what seemed like several attempts to persuade me I was mistaken in my recollection.

For my part, I received very few answers to the questions I asked in return. They said they couldn't tell me who they'd spoken to during the night, or who they would be speaking to in the coming hours or days, or even if they had arrested anyone else. Nor would they tell me what had happened to Rachel's body; where she had been taken or whether any part of her was injured apart from her head. I didn't realise how badly I wanted to know these things until it became obvious that I wouldn't find out, however I framed my enquiries. 'I just want to know if there is somebody with her, that's all,' I said. 'I just want to

know where she is. Has she been left on her own? Did someone stay with her, through the night?' I've learned since that as I lay in my cell waiting for my second interview, she was also lying in a small room, somewhere on the other side of the city, waiting on a gurney to be sliced into pieces and weighed and measured and photographed, and that parts of her had already been sent away in unmarked vans to be measured all over again.

Whilst they would say nothing directly, it was clear by the end of the afternoon, after they had gone away and discussed my answers and come back again, that their stance towards me had shifted. Only slightly, but enough for me to realise that they considered it likely, or at least possible, that by the end of my fortnight on bail I would become their chief witness rather than their prime suspect.

From what my lawyer was able to gather, and from what Harry himself told me the following morning, I discovered it was Harry I had to thank for my release. After he had said goodbye to Rachel and me the night before, we'd turned to let ourselves out of the wicket door. At the same time, or so we'd thought, he'd set off in the other direction to go back to his rooms. He'd told us he had to collect something, and that otherwise he'd have come with us and crossed over the road to catch a taxi to his house on the Woodstock Road, leaving us to walk back to our hotel on St Giles. However, instead of returning to his rooms immediately, he had changed his mind and, out of sight behind us, taken the steps up to the Old Library. It seems that Rachel had asked him a question over dinner that he hadn't been able to answer, and that her obvious surprise at finding him without a response had irked him somewhat. Not being entirely insensitive to the assumptions he thought people were making as he approached his retirement, quite unfounded assumptions about his memory not being what it had once so famously been, he had wanted to look up the answer to her question straight away, thinking that he might write out his findings on a card and drop it into our hotel first thing in the

morning so she could read it over breakfast. A poet, my lawyer told me. Something to do with a poet. I hadn't heard the exchange Harry was referring to, the one in which Rachel had asked him a question he couldn't answer, occupied as I was with the woman on my other side who spent the evening telling me about where I should go when I was next in New York, or what I should have seen when I'd been there last. Whatever Rachel's question was, it had so perturbed Harry that by the time she had finished persuading me to wait for her while she went to look at the lake, he was already standing in front of one of the window tables in the library directly above me, the volume he needed lying open in his hands.

As Harry stood there puzzling out his answer and switching his gaze between the pages in front of him and the view of the quad from the library window, he saw two things. First, a woman who looked like Rachel, although he told the police that it hadn't occurred to him at the time that the likeness was anything other than a coincidence, walked quickly down the steps from Hall and on along the path running in front of the cottages on the south side of the quad.

The last in this line of cottages, their grey and rose-clad exteriors little changed since the sixteenth century but for the chalked and rechalked boating ephemera etched above their doorways, was where Haddon had taught Richard and me every Friday afternoon. Our tutorials took place in his study on the ground floor and he lived in a small flat laid out above. It was in what he referred to as the drawing room of this flat that he hosted his welcome tea every year for newly arrived undergraduates; the tea that had been the occasion of my first meeting with Richard. French doors opened from the drawing room on to what everyone in College called the secret garden. Sitting as it did at the height of the first floor, this tiny garden was suspended on top of an arched passageway, the inside walls of which were lined with doors opening into a series of sheds where the gardeners stored their mowers and their tools, so that the only access to the garden was

either from the drawing room or by way of a tiny set of steps built into the wall and running up from the flower bed beneath. The path that ran down the side of the quad passed in front of Haddon's cottage, at which point one could choose either to turn to the right and continue walking around the quad, or sharply to the left, passing into the passageway that ran beneath the secret garden.

Harry, watching from the library window, saw the woman he'd thought looked like Rachel pass in front of Haddon's cottage and duck left into the passageway. Had she turned right from the other end of it and continued walking, she would soon have found herself looking on the lake in the moonlight.

The second thing that Harry saw was the porter emerging from the alcove beneath the library. The man stood on the north terrace of the quad looking about himself, sniffing the air as if for a scent before glancing back up at the clock which sat on the wall immediately beneath where Harry was standing. This, Harry said, made him think of pulling his own watch from his pocket. It was 11.42 precisely. He turned back to his reading for a few moments. When he looked up again he saw the man disappearing into staircase number 6, exactly as he had described his route to the police. This would have taken him through to the orchards and down towards the student blocks at the northern end of the lake.

At what Harry notices is 11.55, he finds the answer to Rachel's question about the poet and leaves the library. He passes me, sitting on the staircase with my head in my hands, and, hearing me snore, realises I have fallen asleep whilst, he presumes, waiting for Rachel to come back from wherever she has gone. Choosing not to disturb me, he leaves the alcove and follows in the porter's footsteps, intending at last to collect whatever it was that he had left in his rooms on staircase number 5.

Harry is halfway along the north terrace when he hears the scream. He turns to face the direction the sound has come from and

looks across the quad towards the lake. He stands stock still on hearing it; he makes no attempt to move. And then he sees me, running like a wild thing from the alcove and virtually throwing myself down the steps. He sees me stumble, sees my glasses fall from my face, and sees me fall forwards and fumble about before jumping up again and dragging myself through the passageway at the top of the south side of the quad. At the moment at which I drop my glasses and retrieve them, which I do, he says, in a single slow-motion movement, a sort of a balletic dive followed almost immediately by my leaping back up again, so that it is as though I don't really stop, as such, he notices a movement in the right of his peripheral vision. He turns to see a figure running up the path from the passageway underneath Haddon's secret garden. It is a small figure, perhaps that of a woman, or a teenage boy. It wears dark clothing, a hood pulled forward and down, tight around its head. Because of the hood, and because it is hurtling towards me at an extraordinary speed, its torso thrown so far in front of itself that it looks like a sprinter just off the blocks, he doesn't see any part of the face and is unable to provide a description. He says that this little figure dressed in black is moving so fast that it reaches the top of the quad in an instant and passes me as I stumble and fall, and that by the time I have picked myself up and carried on, it has gained the top of the steps behind me and is away. The police have told my lawyer that if my glasses hadn't fallen from my face when they did, I would undoubtedly have seen this running figure, just as Harry had done. As things turned out, I was entirely unaware of its presence.

Partway through my second interview the detectives began to focus with some intensity on the figure Harry had seen. I remember thinking at the time that it had caught their attention in a way that seemed to be somewhat disproportionate. Had I been more alert, or more engaged with what was going on around me, I think it likely I would have suggested there was perhaps a danger in the approach they appeared to be taking, in that it might prevent them from see-

ing other strands emerging. As it turned out I made no such com-
ment, and in the weeks that followed I allowed myself to be reassured
by my lawyer that this was merely one of many lines of enquiry that
were being pursued, and that, in any event, it was possible they had
not been misguided by their instincts. It seemed that they had been
able to eliminate from their enquiries almost everyone who had been
recorded as entering or leaving the college during the forty-eight
hours before and after Rachel's murder. Every entrance and every exit
was covered by CCTV, and the tapes had been scrutinised and a list of
individuals compiled and worked through exhaustively. There were,
my lawyer said, only one or two points on the tapes that were prov-
ing to be problematic. The end of the academic year was a busier than
usual time in the porter's lodge and there were a couple of moments,
each of them lasting no more than a minute or two, when the num-
ber of people gathering in such a small space meant, inevitably, that
some of them remained, as yet, unidentified. The police were com-
fortable though that they had all that they needed on those tapes, and
they were comfortable also that there was very little chance that any-
one could have got in, or out, by any other route. Following a major
rebuilding programme five years ago, my lawyer told me, the college
had been made impenetrable apart from these entrances, the height
of the walls having been raised and the levels of deterrent increased.
Metal spikes and pieces of broken glass were everywhere, and anyone
exiting by an unofficial route would have left some trace of their pres-
ence. The only weak point, apparently, was the path that ran alongside
the south-west side of the lake and followed the line of the canal, the
boundary there being formed only by a border of trees and hedges, at
the back of which was a low brick wall. However, anyone running that
way from Rachel's body would, first, have passed the porter coming in
the opposite direction and, second, have had to jump down from the
wall directly into the canal.

I wonder now at my inertia that afternoon, and am coming to

think of it as a very serious error on my part. Despite the months that have passed, the police have been unable to track down the person Harry saw that night, and, despite their repeated assurances that it is only a matter of time, I am beginning to doubt their chances of doing so. I don't think of myself as someone who is of a mindset capable of accepting this kind of uncertainty. Indeed I have begun, in recent weeks, to find it very difficult to accommodate. It has occurred to me once or twice that if I had only said something that afternoon, things might be quite different. But I have been told that to think such things is entirely normal, given the situation in which I find myself, and that I should not allow myself to follow such trains of thought too frequently, for fear of indulging what is no more than the forlorn but inevitable fantasy of a man who has lost his wife.

Towards the end of the interview, when it became apparent that I was sticking to my story that I hadn't seen anyone running past me on the steps, I was taken to another room and shown the CCTV playbacks. The footage from the camera trained on the inside of the college doors shows the figure with its hood still pulled down and its head bowed low. It reaches out its hand and opens the wicket door at exactly the same time as the camera on the street outside captures a group of students arriving. Some of this group change their minds at the last moment and go back the way they have come. Apparently drunk as well as indecisive, they appear not to notice the diminutive figure that is new to their number and huddles among them as they stand in the full glare of the street lights. They provided nothing in the way of assistance in their interviews, their memories of the incident being blurred by alcohol and their thoughts being only of the exams that had ended and the summer that was beginning. The group was recorded again five minutes later by the camera positioned at the north-west corner of Gloucester Green, the square lying diagonally opposite the college entrance. The hooded figure is no longer among them.

I watched those sequences of grainy images several times that

afternoon, but still it does not sit well with me, the idea that this figure ever really existed. After they had been played to me once or twice, I began to have the strangest of senses that I'd seen it all before some-where; the whole of Harry's description of the running figure, and the footage of it slipping out of college, began to seem to me an echo, as it were, of something I had already experienced. I set the thought aside, realising it was probable that anyone in my position would have felt the same, it being a well-documented phenomenon that a person without any recollection of a certain sequence of events, if they are told enough times that it has happened, and shown some visual record of it, will come to believe not only that it did, but also that they have actually experienced it, or witnessed it, for themselves. And in any case, there was never any real doubt in my mind. Not only had I not seen anyone run past me on the steps, but nor had I even so much as sensed them. Of course I can't think of a reason why Harry should have fabricated such a story, but nevertheless, I am uneasy about it. He said that the entire episode had lasted no more than twenty or thirty seconds, and the police have established from their repeated recon-structions that it is entirely possible for someone to have run from the passageway under the secret garden to the top of the quad and on up the steps within that time frame.

My undergraduate knowledge of the law of evidence was at best rudimentary and is now no more than sketchy, but that which I have retained is sufficiently clear to mean that I must accept, in principle, the fallibility of the human eye. And I know that even a person of sound mind who claims to have observed a sequence of events from a reasonable distance in daylight hours can have their statement entirely undermined by a competent advocate who elicits the appar-ently unremarkable fact that the witness occasionally wears reading glasses, albeit only after a particularly long day and only when they find themselves to be unusually tired. The doubt he needs to establish has been introduced; his long assault is safely underway.

Were I to take to a stand and swear to a jury that I had been alone in the quad as I ran to find Rachel's body that night, and to swear that there had been no running figure, I am quite aware that a barrister would have no difficulty in persuading that jury to discount my evidence in its entirety on account of my glasses having fallen from my face as I stumbled down the steps, and of my mind having been so firmly focused on the path ahead and on my desire to run faster than I had ever run in my life.

The police have staged their reconstructions so carefully I cannot fault them. As well as the ones they carried out for themselves the morning after Rachel's death, the ones with runners and clocks and watchers at the library windows and tapes marking off sight lines, they staged more lifelike versions later in the summer, with actors playing the parts, in case there were memories already buried that could be jogged. They have made this story as true as it can be. My lawyer has told me that they have even gone so far as to visit my opticians to verify my prescription. Yet despite all this, despite knowing that I could not ask for more in the way of reasons for believing it, I find that I am unable even now to accept the narrative that has been presented to me.

Reflecting this evening on my reluctance in this regard I was reminded of my father experiencing a similar difficulty one summer in Cornwall. For a moment I was almost entertained by the memory, but only for a moment, realising as soon as it began to surface that it must have taken place on one of the last of the summer holidays that we took together as a family, perhaps even the very last one before my father stopped coming with us, my mother and me.

And as it flits now across the inside of my mind I am there again, cold at the end of the day, so cold that the tips of my fingers are starting to turn dark blue and I am hoping in my eight-year-old way that somebody will tell me it is time for Final Swims before we head back to the cottage for tea and a bath, at the same time as hoping

this announcement will never be made, so that instead we will stay out into the evening, all night even, and build a fire on the clifftop to keep us warm as we sleep. My friend Robbie has come on holiday with us, my parents giving in to my badgering and seeing that I needed someone to play with, and to talk nonsense with, and that his coming would give them more time to themselves. And although Robbie, who is almost a year younger than me and far smaller, has noticed that his fingers also are turning blue, we keep our mutual blue-fingeredness to ourselves, knowing that to share this extraordinary phenomenon would make my mother shriek with horror and be certain to bring the day to a close immediately. But because we are beginning to feel quite uncomfortable in our coldness, when the call does eventually come for Final Swims we demur, claiming that we would prefer instead to remain on the side and watch my father take his. And so we stand with the children from the other cottages who have dried and dressed themselves and are ready to climb back up the cliff path for their tea but have persuaded their parents to let them stay just to watch Dr Petersen's final swim.

My father, delighted by his audience, stands as a prizefighter might, draping his towel around his neck and clenching his hands into fists and raising and lowering each arm in turn as if flexing his muscles, and as he does so we all jump up and down and clap our hands and my mother tries to take a photograph but she's laughing too hard to keep the camera still for long enough. At last he drops his towel and strides to the place we have dived from all day long. It stands at the edge of a tidal pool formed by a perfect ring of rock which protrudes high enough to mean that the water never drains from it. The tide is come back in again now and the ring of rocks is submerged, the water deep and dark and churning and the boundaries between pool and sea blurred in a way that we children find exciting and terrifying at the same time. My father is everyone's hero as he swings his arms round and round before launching himself into a perfect arc and slipping

into the sea. He rises up again almost immediately to holler and shout and say My God Georgie it's cold and to laugh as my mother shouts Oh Love don't swear, the children. And then suddenly he is swimming hard and fast and straight and this is when it happens, this extraordinary occurrence that he would never believe had taken place, even though we all saw it, all of us children and all of our mothers.

He has struck out from the side and has reached the pool's halfway point when two things happen simultaneously that make us children stop mid-jump and thud back down to the ground our hands clasped over our mouths our laughs and whoops and cries silenced so that we all hear my mother shout Oh Jesus Oh Jesus as the body of a bull seal, all eight feet of its length and all three feet of its girth trembling, rears up from the water and towers above my father's head which is half-submerged in his front-crawl endeavour. At precisely the moment at which the bull seal emerges my father executes a perfect underwater turn and starts the swim back to the diving place, moving twice as fast as he had been. He drags himself up on the side and we run towards him, expecting him perhaps to fall to the ground in terror. Instead, he only reaches for his towel and bends over to rub his hair before looking up and smiling. His smile becomes a frown as he sees that our faces are white and realises that we are jumping up and down screaming and that my mother is in tears. When we are calm enough to tell him what we saw he laughs again and says don't be silly, there was nothing there. But why did you turn and swim back when you did, we all ask, incredulous. I'd had enough, that's all, he says, shaking the water from his ears. I'd had enough, and so have you two, it's time for your tea you're turning blue. But why did you swim twice as fast on your way back, my mother asks, it was because you'd seen the seal, it must have been. It was because I was hungry, he replies, pulling on his clothes. I would have seen it, there was nothing there, I would have seen it, and he says this all the way back up the cliff path to anyone who tries to talk to him about it.

The only fact the crowd of witnesses to this extraordinary event came to debate in their telling and retelling of the tale, the only strand of the story over which there was any doubt, was as to whether the bull seal had roared as it rose from the water. We were unanimous in our verdict that it had thrown its head back and opened its jaws wide before looking down on my swimming father, and that it had snapped its jaws shut as it did so, but we were almost evenly divided among our number as to whether this action had been accompanied by any kind of a roar. As to the tale in its entirety being a fabrication, my father was resolute. You're liars the lot of you, he said eventually, on the last night of our holiday. My mother and Robbie and I had re-enacted the event for him again in front of the fire after supper, Robbie and I taking it in turns to play my father, and my mother playing the seal and adding, or so I objected after my father had gone up to bed early and left the three of us watching the last of the embers die in the grate, the emission of a roar from the mouth of her seal as it towered above me where I lay face-down, my head pressed into the carpet as my father's had been under the water. I thought at the time that this was a little unkind of him and so did my mother and so did she say to him, pointing out that to call his own wife and son liars wasn't a nice thing to do, not when they were telling the same story as everyone else and they'd seen it with their very own eyes.

On the journey home though, when we'd been driving for hours and both of them thought I was asleep, I heard my father say to my mother that he supposed he might have sensed something, maybe just the water becoming darker for a second, and maybe it was because of that that he'd turned and swum back so much faster than he'd swum out. But he changed his mind a moment later and said he didn't want to talk about it any more, he'd had enough, and then I moved and he looked at me and saw that I was awake and they never spoke of it again in front of me.

And then the memory has run its course and I am left with the

hollowness that comes when I think of what happened to Robbie at the end of that summer, and the fact that my father never came to Cornwall with us again, my mother and me.

I turn my thoughts back to my second interview with the police. It is on my mind now as the evening draws in about me, largely because it was that which kept me awake last night. I had fallen asleep with relative ease, despite feeling more than a little unsettled by the events that had taken place during the day, and by the letter that had come from Harry and lay beside me on the bedside table. I must have slept quite heavily for several hours before waking suddenly, convinced I had heard a noise in the apartment, or from the balcony, or on the roof. My heart was pounding in quite a ridiculous way, and when eventually my breathing began to relax I found I was thinking of the moment in the interview when I realised it was Harry whose story was emerging from the detective's questions and offering me a way out. I closed my eyes and tried to ignore the thudding in my chest, which was becoming less rapid, and I replayed for myself the CCTV footage I had seen. And then I remembered telephoning the college from my hotel the morning after I had been released, and asking to be put through to Harry's room.

I hadn't really expected him to be there, it being a Saturday, but it was the only number I had for him. I told myself I was calling because I wanted to hear his story in his own words, but as soon as I heard his voice I realised that my desire had another motivation: this was the man who had shared with me the final hours of Rachel's life and I needed to see him.

He answered straight away, his hello ringing out loud as if to say, 'At last! I thought you'd never call.' When he realised who he was speaking to, he sounded a little shocked and apologised profusely for the exuberance of his tone, telling me that of course, he had heard

the terrible news, and whilst he couldn't find words that were in any way appropriate to express the depths of his sadness, he wanted me to know how deeply sorry he was for my loss. He said in explanation of the way in which he had greeted my call that he'd been expecting someone to phone. The lodge had told him only that I'd said I was a former student and had declined to give my name. When I asked if I could meet with him he hesitated before saying, in a tone of voice that implied he was surprised by my suggestion, and not entirely pleased, 'Yes, of course. I've time on my hands, as it happens. The person I mistook you for was due here an hour ago and has obviously thought better of it. I imagine you'd prefer it if I came to you though?' And so he did and, wanting to avoid the press who were gathering in the lobby downstairs, we sat in the bay window of my hotel room, drinking coffee and talking of the events of Thursday evening.

As I lay awake last night running through what I remembered of the night Rachel died, and what I knew of Harry's story, and what my lawyer had told me in the weeks that followed, a fact that had never occurred to me before somehow worked its way out of my memory and into the front of my mind and as it did I felt my stomach tense and I became aware of something rising cold in my throat and feeling as though it was running across the inside of my chest.

It was only a tiny detail that occurred to me, but it was one which had never made itself apparent before last night. Harry had told the police that he'd heard the scream from the lake as he was walking along the north terrace of the quad on the way back to his rooms from the library, and that he'd stood entirely still on hearing it, making no attempt to run towards the sound as I had done. This had come up in our conversation in my hotel room, but only in passing. I didn't specifically ask him about it, and we moved on to other things too quickly for me to wonder about it then in any precise way. But as I thought through our conversation last night, his words came back to me as clearly as though he'd been lying beside me with his head on Rachel's

pillow. He told me that he froze on hearing the scream because he was afraid. 'Scared out of my wits,' he said in response to my telling him about the way I had known it was Rachel, without a doubt, despite never having heard her scream before. 'It wasn't that I didn't want to move,' he said. 'You see I couldn't. I was quite paralysed by fear.'

One might suppose such a sound to be a not infrequent occurrence late at night in a college situated in a city centre. I am quite prepared to accept that a man of a certain sensitivity might feel curiosity, or even alarm, on hearing it. But unless there was some particular feature about this scream, or about the circumstances in which he came to hear it, I cannot understand Harry's reaction. He professed at the time to have had no idea that Rachel was down by the lake, no idea whatsoever. Unless, like me, he had recognised the scream as having been voiced by someone in particular, by someone known to him, or unless it had signalled to him the occurrence of an event which he had already entertained in his consciousness as a possibility, why should it have made him so very afraid?

It's quite possible that I have attributed an undue significance to the realisation that occurred to me last night, and to my wakefulness. It was unrealistic of me to have expected to sleep at all. I'd been aware when I went to work in the morning that the day would not be uneventful, but even so, I was surprised by how things turned out.

I could very well be said to have brought the situation on myself, in that it was the decision I made two days ago that led to my having to take a taxi home yesterday, burdened as I was with the box of things I'd cleared from my office. Even as I made it, I knew it was the sort of decision Haddon would have described as one unlikely to be without consequences: I was, for the first time in my career, acting against the wishes of my partners at the firm.

In the months after Rachel died I found in my job a kind of a refuge; a forum in which I was required not to think, but simply to function. I didn't go back straight away of course, although on the first morning after I got home I did try to. I'd rung and cleared it with my senior partner before setting off from Oxford on the Tuesday lunch-

time. He insisted that there should be no client contact initially, and certainly not while I was still on bail. I agreed to this eventually, saying I was content to work only with my colleagues for a period of time, at least until the press interest had died down. There was no question in my mind: I needed to be there, to be doing something, in whatever capacity they would have me. I needed to be busy.

I remember getting ready that Wednesday morning. I put on my suit and tie, picked up my keys and my wallet and my phone, and I went to open the front door of the apartment. As I let myself out I felt suddenly sick. My legs became completely hollow, and I sat on the floor and lowered my head into my hands and stayed like that for some time until I realised the feeling wasn't going to pass and I couldn't face seeing anyone.

For the rest of the following fortnight I stayed at home, waiting out the days until I could go back to Oxford for my third interview, the one in which I found out I was being released from bail without charge. There was the occasional visit from a detective, coming with queries about Rachel, or bringing letters to see if I could shed any light on them, or photos, to see if I could identify faces, and situations. But apart from that, nobody came to the apartment; I had told everyone who asked that I would rather, for the time being, keep myself to myself. I tried to go out once or twice but I found it difficult. It wasn't just the lack of any sense of purpose or structure to my day, but also that I felt a strange and horrible sense of vulnerability. My grief at that time was a very violent one, so that, for example, when I walked along the canal on the first afternoon, I could feel an almost real physical sensation that someone was kicking and beating me as I walked. On the second day I tried again, and while the precise sensation of being beaten was no longer there, it had been replaced by a fear of being attacked, so that when I reached the point where the towpath passed underneath the first bridge I had to turn back, feeling sure there was someone waiting at the other end ready to assault me.

On abandoning my walk I went back and spent hours on the balcony, digging furiously and repotting plants, weeding the raised beds, tying back the jasmine and sweeping the boards clean of the mess I had created. When there was nothing left to do, I crawled into bed and gave in to an overwhelming sense of exhaustion. In the days that followed I did little more than sleep. In the evenings, when I woke, I wrapped myself in my duvet and crept out on to the balcony and sat watching the sky and thinking of Rachel and the times that we'd spent out there, until it grew too cold, or too dark, and I had to get back into bed. I lay awake most nights thinking of her, and of how the police would be taking her life to pieces, and mine, and lining up what they found and examining it, and how it was very likely that by the end of it, they would know far more about Rachel than I had ever known, or ever would. I longed for her to be there those nights, so that she could lie beside me and listen while I told her these things as they occurred to me, and so that she could hold me as I cried myself back to sleep.

Returning to work was an escape, of a sort. The tension and suspense of managing the kind of deals we were doing then, the value of which ran to sums so excessive as to be almost absurd, was sufficient to shut me off from what had been so difficult in the fortnight I'd spent in the apartment. I had let it be known beforehand that I didn't want to talk to anyone about what had happened. I was grateful for the cards and letters that I'd found when I arrived back from Oxford, I said, but I didn't feel able to discuss it in person. And, of course, my colleagues were more than happy to respect this wish, their relief being almost palpable from the minute I'd walked into the office on the first morning. Their silence on the subject made it possible, almost, to forget that anything unusual had happened while I'd been away. I hadn't watched the news or read a paper whilst I'd been at home, and the information I needed to know in order to keep up with the commercial world was, as it always had been, filtered for me each day by my secretary and lay waiting on my desk when I got in. Those small

things that did seep through were so slight, and so remote, as to make me feel rather like an Arctic explorer, striding across an icy wilderness hundreds of thousands of miles away from the newspapers that were reporting on my journey. For the hours I was at work I functioned almost as a machine, feeling very little in the way of emotion, apart from anger or frustration if things went wrong or if people fell short of my expectations.

It was inevitable, I suppose, that thoughts of her death would eventually start to encroach upon that territory, and that I would come to operate less successfully as they did so. I was surprised though by the sort of mistakes I began to make. There were enough people around me whose desire to create a good impression meant that not only did they pick up on what became a series of little omissions, but also that they were able to reclassify these episodes of inattentiveness as nothing more than calculated tests of their own competence.

And then one day in August, in the week following Rachel's funeral, I made a mistake that couldn't be disguised in such a way. When it was drawn to my attention, I was more than a little sceptical that I would have missed such a thing as that. But there, in the client file, was the copy of the letter that had gone out, printed on green paper with my signature in the top left-hand corner, and there was the relief on the face of the lawyer presenting me with this evidence of my approval of her work. The comparatively minor scale of the transaction concerned, combined with the relative slimness of the client's contribution to the previous year's turnover, meant that I was able to convince myself that what had occurred demanded no more than a letter of apology and a waiving of my fee on the file for the foreseeable future. Until a month ago, that is, when I was asked, as I am every year, to fill in a form for the purposes of notifying our insurers of potential liabilities arising by way of third parties seeking redress against the firm. The letter accompanying the form invites me to declare any errors or omissions that I have made, or that I think I

might have made, or that I suspect might have been made by others, and it was as I sat at my desk staring at the line on which I was about to write my signature that I realised I had to make a confession. The error itself was a small one, but I could no longer pretend that the potential ramifications were anything other than enormous.

My partners, on considering the issue, found themselves able to allow me a certain latitude, given, as they put it in their letter to me, the delicacy of my situation. The compromise that was negotiated with our insurers that week permitted me to retain my partnership on the condition that I agreed to be referred to a psychotherapist. My grief, though entirely understandable, was having a not insignificant effect on my performance and it had been decided, as was usual in cases such as this, that I should undergo a course of treatment designed to bring about a resolution to my situation in such a way as to avoid the risk of further negligence on my part.

I have little doubt that my partners had no choice but to ask this of me, but after the session I attended on Wednesday I made up my mind not to see him again, the man deemed capable of resolving my situation. And having made my decision, the prediction I'd imagined Haddon making turned out to be even more accurate than I had anticipated.

I met with my senior partner first thing yesterday morning to tell him face to face. The fact that a letter arrived at my desk within two hours of our meeting suggested to me that it was a development that had not been unforeseen. Of course, the letter said, my feelings about the appropriateness or otherwise of the idea that a complete stranger might be able to bring about a resolution to my grief were feelings that the partnership, as a whole, respected, and this was something they did unreservedly and with one voice. But equally, I must appreciate his position. Whilst he acknowledged that only five months had passed since the occurrence of that undoubtedly tragic event, he hoped I would not find him insensitive in making the observation that it was felt by the partnership that it was not unreasonable to expect me to

have progressed somewhat further than I appeared to have done with what they referred to as my mourning process. It was noted that it had been my own choice to return to work so promptly, and it was noted further that I had done so rather sooner than might have been wise. In recent weeks, feedback received in relation to my pitches to prospective clients had made it apparent that it was no longer simply the matter of my one-off act of negligence that had to be considered. I must understand that it was no single event in particular that was being relied on by the partnership in justification of the decision they had reached, but rather, the combination of factors they found themselves facing. As it was, they were able to offer me a compromise: I could retain my equity stake for the time being on the condition that I agreed to take a sabbatical, the duration of which was negotiable but would not be less than three months. During that time I would take whatever measures I thought appropriate to recover sufficiently in order to return to work, and I would come back only when I felt able to fulfil my partnership duties and maintain the same standards of professionalism that I had demonstrated prior to the unfortunate death of my wife.

And that is why I have spent much of today looking down on the canal from Rachel's desk, rather than looking out from my office at the dome of St Paul's. As the evening falls, I realise with some unhappiness that I don't know how I will spend the next three months, this being the first time in my adult life that I have faced the prospect of having to endure more than a week or so with time on my hands and the absence of any immediately obvious way to spend it. I may take the tube to Hampstead and walk on the Heath, though I am not sure I want to do this without Rachel, having so often been there with her. There are exhibitions to be seen and museums to be visited. I don't remember the last time I went to the cinema. I might leave London altogether and visit the coast, or go further than that and travel properly in the way that people do who want to forget their past, or to bury it, by changing their environment for a time. I suppose I could just

start with a weekend, having lost count of the number of times Richard and Lucinda have invited me away.

Or I may do none of these things and accept instead the invitation that awaited me on my return from the City yesterday. It was a strange coincidence that Harry should have sent it when he did; it must have crossed in the post with the card I wrote to him on Tuesday night telling him about the colour of the leaves that are gathering in the square where my psychotherapist lives. I sometimes find myself at a loss for what to write to Harry about, in much the same way that I could never think of what to say in my letters to my father after he left us at the end of that summer, even though I wanted so much to tell him every detail of my life since I had seen him last, and about how it felt to walk around the house longing for him to come back and announce that everything was forgiven, everything could be forgotten. It was, then, almost for the want of anything else to write that I had told Harry about the square. After what happened there on Wednesday morning as I sat waiting for what turned out to be my final appointment, and having seen what I saw on the wall of one of the houses as I left, I shall have to write again and correct the errors in my description.

I'd arrived a little early so I wandered through the square and sat on a bench to wait. After a moment or two a boy ran past me, carrying a balloon. He moved awkwardly, holding the balloon low down in front of him, and I realised it was full of water. I know this boy, I think to myself, and then I remember that I saw him last week as I sat on the same bench waiting. He can be no more than twelve years old and he has an unusual face, his eyes set wide apart and slanting slightly downwards. His hair is long, but in an artful rather than a neglectful sort of a way, and there is a brightness and a cleverness in his gaze when it rests on me. When he disappears with his balloon I close my eyes. He is there again when I open them, running past me at full pelt. His hair and his T-shirt are soaking wet and he is shaking water from his hands and his arms. A fight, I think. He is engaged in a

water fight somewhere around the square. He reappears with a friend, a boy smaller than himself and smarter in his appearance, and they are laughing and excited. The balloon he is carrying this time is bigger and fuller than the one before, and he turns his head from side to side as he walks, looking at the people sitting on the benches smoking cigarettes, or making phone calls, or, like me, just watching.

Everyone has begun to notice them now, the boys and their water bomb. A few people laugh at what they see, but others frown and put their things away in bags and start to leave the square. At this point I also become uncomfortable, and it occurs to me that it would be inconvenient to find myself soaking wet minutes before I am due to knock on my psychotherapist's door and take my seat in his hallway underneath the coat rack and opposite the children's buggy that is propped against the stairs and festooned with tiny cardigans and picture books on strings.

The boys are standing on the path in front of me. They face away from one another, their backs together, as if in preparation for a duel. Then, walking in opposite directions, they count out five or six paces before they stop and turn to face each other. The smarter friend, I think to myself, has volunteered himself as some sort of a practice target. But then he shouts out, 'Do it!' and the long-haired boy bends his knees and lowers the balloon almost to the ground and hurls it up in the air and positions himself underneath it so that when it falls it bursts open on his own head and soaks him utterly. His friend is laughing, bending over and laughing and holding his sides and clapping and they are both laughing and they run towards me and disappear. As they go, shouting out words that are indistinguishable, I realise suddenly that the thing they have disappeared behind, the thing that the long-haired boy must also have been running around the first time I saw him, the thing looming white and wooden and enormous from the centre of the square in front of me, is a bandstand.

I thought to myself, as I sat there looking at the bandstand and

reflecting on how extraordinary it was that it should be there, that I might begin my session by talking about what I had seen. And that if I was asked why I found it so extraordinary, the bandstand at the centre of the square, I would begin by saying that it was only the night before that I had sat at Rachel's desk after dinner, watching the heron that sometimes visits my balcony. And then I would say that after I had seen it drift down the canal into the setting of the sun, I wrote a postcard to Harry Gardner about the leaves gathering in the square, and about how it seemed to me to be exactly the sort of square one would expect to see a bandstand in and how strange I found it that there wasn't one. And then I would have told him that I'd realised as I waited on the bench that I must have seen this bandstand every time I had walked through the square, but that until that morning, I had never so much as noticed it.

That was not how the session began after all. I found, as I had done every time I'd visited him, that I didn't know what to say after he had asked me to come through from his hallway and had closed the door and sat on the chair in front of the desk and wheeled himself across the room to where I sat, my back up against his bookcase. 'So,' he says, as he does each time we begin. And my mind becomes a perfect blank. That is to say, it becomes a perfect blank after an intense flurry of thoughts and images and things I want to say have launched themselves momentarily across it, each one more important than the other, so that in the end I short-circuit and find myself unable to speak. We smile at one another, him raising his eyebrows in expectation, me desperately hoping he will ask me a question, any question, thus restoring to me the power of speech. Eventually he does, but only after I have admitted defeat and told him I don't know where to start.

'Tell me about your family history,' he says.

'How far back do you want me to go? Where do you want me to begin?' I ask, feeling only panic, sensing the impossibility of meeting his request with any kind of order, or helpful information, thinking it

unlikely I will be able to tell him what it is he wants to know, and wanting instead to talk to him about my grief now, about how I wake in the mornings sometimes and forget that Rachel has died and about how I feel when I remember. He only shrugs in response, so I speak to him of the old vicarage I grew up in in Hampshire, the front half of the downstairs converted into a doctor's surgery for my father's patients, the key to the medicine cabinet kept on a string about my mother's neck, and I go on to tell him in answer to his questions that no, I have no siblings, and nor did I ever have, but that for a time I had Robbie, my friend Robbie, and that I was eight years old at the time of the accident.

But I talk without talking, because I am thinking only of Rachel, on whom I have been allowed to dwell for the duration of each of my sessions thus far, piecing together how we'd first met, the night of her murder, the way I felt when I was with her, and I am thinking about the fact that although I sometimes feel I hardly knew her, it seems at times as if she was the only person ever to have loved me.

After the man had closed his door behind me I heaved out a sigh and turnèd and walked away. And it was at that moment, knowing I was incapable of having such a conversation again, that I decided never to return. As I reached the other side of the square I looked up and saw its name, Exeter Square, embossed on a white sign tacked to the front of one of the houses. I realised then that when I'd written to Harry the previous evening, I'd told him it was called something quite different, and the name I had given it by mistake was my own inadvertent fabrication, an amalgamation of other street names I must have seen nearby. So that if he were ever to look for it, say, on a map of London, he would never be able to find it. It would be, for him, as though it did not exist, this square with a bandstand at its centre.

Sitting here this evening with Harry's invitation on the desk in front of me, it strikes me that apart from the day of Rachel's memorial, I

haven't seen him since the morning after I was released, the morning he came and drank coffee with me in my hotel room. I saw a lot of people in the few days that passed between her murder and my returning to London, but I'm not sure I'd be able to say exactly who, if someone were to ask me. Friends of Rachel's seemed suddenly to appear, asking if they could help, almost demanding to know if there was anything they could do, as if by going to the supermarket for me, or speaking to the funeral directors on my behalf, they could make things more bearable. I see now that it was not for me that they offered to do these things, but for themselves; for the assuaging of their own private grief at what had happened, or at other things that had happened to them at other times in quite unrelated ways.

Some of them surprised me by their visits, being people I'd barely met, so that I became confused, I think, about who I knew and who I didn't. On the Saturday afternoon, the day after I was released, I had a fairly long conversation with a woman who showed up in the hotel, only to discover partway through that she was a reporter, rather than a friend of Rachel's. Richard and Lucinda checked into the hotel just after this and they took it upon themselves from that point on to be my representatives, taking charge of me utterly and telling me to speak to nobody but them. Richard, whose anger on my behalf seemed a little disproportionate, and somehow misplaced, stayed downstairs in the lobby to discuss with the hotel manager the security arrangements he said would be necessary for the remainder of my stay, and Lucinda came with me to my room. She apologised for Richard's temper. 'He was really very fond of her you know, whatever he might have said about her.' She carried on talking for a while, saying something about Richard having found out that he hadn't made Silk again and it really bothering him even though it would have been unheard of at his age, and that he'd even been talking of doing a rush job on the New York Bar exams and 'getting the hell out of here' for a couple of years. And then she realised I wasn't really listening and she came and sat by me

on the bed and held me for a time, and she cried and said that I would too, eventually.

When Richard reappeared and announced he was taking me out for a walk, Lucinda went to lie down, having told me not to worry, I wouldn't be on my own for a single second now that they were there. That evening, after the three of us had finished our room-service dinner and they'd left me to myself, I saw that Richard had forgotten his newspaper. I picked it up intending to go after them and give it back to him but then I noticed there was a book underneath it, *On Death and Dying*, or *On Grief and Grieving*, or something like that, and I realised they'd done it deliberately. They stayed in the hotel with me until I went back to London the following Tuesday and I was glad of it, although I have yet to read their book.

And then there was Evie. Not having managed to get hold of her on the Thursday night when I'd called her from the police station, I'd been allowed to try her again as soon as I'd woken the following morning. When she answered her mobile it turned out she was in Oxford already. 'Just for the weekend,' she said. 'Fundraiser at the Ashmolean. Terrible bore. Godawful guests. Godawful wine. There we are.' And then she surprised me by saying that Rachel had known this. They'd talked on Thursday morning and discovered the coincidence. She'd even invited us for cocktails at Browns before our dinner at Worcester that evening, but Rachel had left a message saying she'd checked with me and I didn't want to. 'How is she anyway? She sounded in an awful mood when she rang yesterday. Will you have tea with me today do you think? Is that why you're calling? You don't both have to come you know.'

And then I told her. She said nothing, nothing at all. I listened to her silence for a time and then I said that when it came to my release I would need her to bring me some clothes and some shoes, and I listed for her all of the things she would have to do. She still hadn't spoken by the time I said goodbye, and I put down the phone without being entirely sure whether she was still there. She had appeared at

the police station later on though, almost as soon as I'd been told I was to be released on bail. I hadn't expected her to do as other people might have, to come forward and embrace me or even to take my hand in hers, but I suppose I had thought she would at least look at me. Instead, when the door was closed behind her she stayed where she was and fumbled for something in her jacket pocket before checking, two or three times, the contents of the bag she had placed on the floor. It wasn't until after all of this, and after she'd reached into her jacket pocket once more, taken her phone out and put it back again, that she looked across at me sitting on the other side of the room watching her. At first I could detect nothing in her face that could tell me what she might be feeling, nothing at all. But then she took off her sunglasses and I could see the redness around her eyes and I noticed the muscles in her cheeks moving as she clenched and unclenched her jaw. She pushed the bag across the floor towards me. 'The clothes you asked for.' I opened my mouth to speak but she raised her hands up in front of her chest, palms outward. 'I'm not sure we should talk at this stage, Alex. It's just too complicated isn't it? You can be in touch by email, I think that's best for now,' and she walked away and left me there.

I put on the clothes she'd brought me and I signed the forms I had to sign before leaving the station by a back entrance and being driven back to the hotel in an unmarked car. When I let myself into our room I could see straight away that it had been searched by the police; the wardrobe door was wide open and some of our things were missing, just as they had warned me they would be. I sat down on the bed. The card that would have been put there while we were having dinner with Harry lay still on one of the pillows, telling us that the forecast was for sun and reminding us the hotel could provide bicycles and a picnic, or book us a punt if we wanted one. I picked it up and put it in my jacket pocket. Then I took the bag Evie had given me and held it upside down to see if she had put anything else in it apart from the clothes. A single A4 envelope fell on to the bed beside me. Inside was a note

from Evie and some photographs and a smaller envelope, addressed in Rachel's writing to her godmother. I put the photographs on one side and picked up the note.

> *Alex, I'm writing this because I know we shan't really talk when we meet. You'll be tired and I don't suppose I shall feel like it anyway. You know I've never liked you – didn't think Rachel should have married you, couldn't believe it that night when I found out she was going to. And I know you don't care for me either. But Rachel loved you, and I want you to be in no doubt about that. She loved you very much, in fact, and I'm giving you the letter she sent me last year after your wedding in case you should ever come to question her. And I thought you might like to have the photos. Sorry I never got round to giving you them before now. There will be plenty to arrange between the two of us but I'd rather we kept to email for now. I'm sure we'll speak before too long but I simply can't face it at the moment.*
>
> *Evie.*

I put all the things she had given me away in my case and I drew a bath and lay in it for hours. I ran it a little too hot so that it hurt when I got in, and I lowered my head under the water and up again. I felt my face burning and I shut my eyes and pretended I was dreaming everything that had happened; that none of it was real. I lay there until I realised I had fallen asleep and the water was completely cold. I don't think I did anything else that night other than phone Richard and ask him to speak to my senior partner for me. And then I ordered room service and climbed afterwards into bed.

The next few days merged into one; Richard took me on walks and Lucinda sat with me in my room, each of them taking it in turns to go with me to see the people I had to see and Lucinda starting a file

of all the things I would have to deal with, collecting phone numbers and addresses and making lists. I overheard her saying to Richard at breakfast on the Tuesday morning, when she thought I was still at the bar ordering more coffee, 'Do you know darling I haven't done anything like this since the wedding, isn't that amazing! I think I'm quite good at it really, don't you?' And she was right, she was good at it, so good in fact that by lunchtime that day it had become apparent I could achieve nothing by staying in Oxford any longer, and I said goodbye and left.

I thought about Evie as I drove. Until the moment when she had taken off her sunglasses and I had seen her eyes, she had looked that day as she always did. As far as I could recall, I had seen her without those glasses only once or twice in all the time that I had known her. They always struck me as being a little too large for her face, which is small and clipped somehow; her hair cropped short at the back, her chin pointed and much of her forehead hidden by a fringe cut in a sharp diagonal so that it covers the upper part of her right cheek as well. That she had chosen to wear red that day seemed almost inappropriate at the time, given the reason for our meeting, but that also was something she always did.

I asked Rachel about this once, Evie's choice of colour, and about whether it was the same jacket each time or whether she'd had several made to an identical design: cut from a blooded silk that looked thick and quilted and was traced about with some kind of an oriental pattern, they hung stiffly from her shoulders and almost hovered about her body so that I was never quite sure of the size of her torso; of whether she was squat or slight above her waist and tiny legs. This was something I could have ascertained were I ever to have held her in any kind of embrace, even for a moment. The sleeves of the jackets were shaped so that they were far wider at the bottom than they were at the shoulder, the material folded back to form oversized cuffs sitting only a couple of inches below her elbows and allowing for her wrists and forearms to emerge bird-like and wiry. These little arms of hers

suggest to me each time I see them that the frame lying beneath her jackets is a diminutive one, but I cannot be certain of this.

Rachel ignored my question about Evie's jackets. She laughed at me and said she didn't know why I was so interested and then she changed the subject. Talking about her godmother was something she did only when I pushed her to, and even then reluctantly. 'I suppose you'd better meet her at some point,' she'd said to me in bed one morning when we were talking about who to invite to our wedding. In the end we both agreed we'd rather not invite anyone at all, but that since we had to have witnesses, Richard and Lucinda would do as well as anyone else. And then I said, at the same time as running my hand up and down her back again and again so softly that I wasn't sure whether I was actually touching her, 'Don't you think Evie should come?' 'That's nice,' she said. 'Can you do it a bit harder? And a bit lower down?' 'Answer my question,' I said. 'You're not going to distract me from the fact that you haven't.' 'What question?' she said, taking my hand and pulling it across herself and putting it between her legs. 'Evie. Shoot. Tell me why on earth you wouldn't want her to come to your own wedding.' But then she did distract me and it wasn't until later on that she said, 'I suppose you'd better meet her,' by which time I'd forgotten who she was talking about and said so. 'Evie,' she said. 'Evie bloody Evie. Dinner or something. But can we invite Richard and Lucinda as well? That should lessen the impact a little.'

And so we did. Our engagement celebration, such as it was, took place a couple of weeks later. It was left to me to make the call to invite Evie, Rachel finding a seemingly endless list of reasons not to do it herself. The phone rang and rang, so that by the time it was finally answered I had become mesmerised by the sound of it and had to remind myself who I'd wanted to speak to. Just as soon as it had been picked up, the connection was cut and I was left listening to the dialling tone. I rang back straight away and this time I got through immediately. A woman's voice said only 'Yes,' without even so much as an

inflection suggesting that a response might be welcomed. I told Rachel about this when I got in that evening and she said it was nothing to do with the fact that I had let it ring and ring the time before; it was just the way Evie answered the phone.

'I suppose so,' she'd said when I told her we wanted to take her out for a meal. 'I mean yes, of course Alex, of course. You could have given me a little more notice, that's all. I'm so sorry I really have to go now I'm working. If you ring again and I don't pick up, don't ring back will you? It either means I'm out or I don't want to talk to anyone. Alright?' 'Alright,' I said. 'Goodbye, Evie. I look forward to meeting you.' 'Yes,' she said again, as bluntly as before, and then she hung up before I could tell her where or when, or even why it was that we were meeting, so I asked Rachel that evening if she could email her.

As it turned out, Rachel made no mention to Evie of what it was that we were celebrating. She said to me some time later on, after the dinner was over, that it was something she hadn't wanted to put in an email, and when she'd called to try to talk about it, Evie had said she was busy, couldn't it wait, whatever it was, and did it really matter why we were meeting she'd said she'd be there and she would. She was the last to arrive at the restaurant. By the time she walked in, half an hour or more after everyone else, Rachel had become agitated, checking her phone for messages every few minutes and looking over to the door whenever someone arrived. When I asked her what was the matter she spoke to me quite unkindly, the first time she'd ever done so. 'We should never have invited her should we? It's just so bloody rude, don't you think? And don't tell me she's been held up.' 'Rachel,' I said, but she carried on. 'You always make excuses for people don't you? Always want to see their good side. Well you know what Alex, some people just don't have a good side.' 'It's OK,' I said. 'It's OK,' and I put my hands over hers. She pulled away from me and turned to speak to Lucinda so I went to look for Richard, who'd got up and left as soon as Rachel had started to snap at me. I found him standing on the balcony

smoking a cigar, and felt suddenly that the evening was beginning to
unravel before it had even begun. 'Still a bit of a crazy tern, eh?' he
said to me, clapping me on the back. 'Rachel Cardanine,' he carried
on, nodding his head and turning his mouth into the upside down
'U' shape he used when he wanted to look serious. I thought he was
about to say something else, but instead he only held his breath for a
moment, and then he laughed and clapped me on the back again, and
we started to talk about the wine list and what we should move on to
after the champagne. As we went back to our table a woman walked
into the restaurant. The instant I saw her I knew it was Evie. Rachel,
to my surprise, got up from her seat and almost ran towards her and
embraced her. The strange thing was that as they held one another,
which they did for slightly longer than one might have expected them
to, I had a sense for an instant that the woman I was looking at could
have been Rachel, twenty years on. And then Evie detached herself
and made a fuss about her coat and whether it would be hung prop-
erly, in a closet, and didn't they have such a thing as a coat hanger,
and the idea seemed suddenly ridiculous. Apart from the slightness
of their build, and the colour of their hair, they were entirely unalike.

The evening was, for the most part, uneventful. Lucinda and Rich-
ard spoke of the house they were hoping to buy, and of their honey-
moon and how the other couples in the safari lodge had been awful,
really dreadful, but that there was no other way to have done it really,
and that at least they'd had their own beach on Zanzibar so they'd been
able to have some time to themselves. Lucinda and Rachel exchanged
news of old school friends, Rachel masking her indifference, I thought,
with considerable skill and Richard going outside again at that point,
saying he had to join a conference call from the US.

Evie said hardly a word, as I recollect, until right at the end of the
dinner. We had finished our dessert and I was beginning to feel a little
drunk and quite relieved about the way the whole thing had turned
out when someone, Lucinda I think it was, asked her a question about

her work. She started to talk about a project she'd been asked to advise on in Oxford, something to do with some kind of chest that had been purchased by the Ashmolean and needed to be restored. There had been terrible delays already, she said, some sort of row going on with the Japanese government about the materials that were going to be used for the restoration. I couldn't follow what she was talking about, or rather, I didn't want to, so instead I asked her to tell us more about the chest. It was a wedding casket, she said, a tiny thing really, but terribly significant in its context and a great mystery in terms of how it had come to be owned by the family who'd sold it to the museum. 'Some Italians had it originally. Phenomenally wealthy of course. Merchants at some point, travelling salesmen really. Wanted it for a gift, as it happens,' she said. 'A wedding present, or perhaps a form of payment, something to seal a betrothal.'

I had stopped listening to Evie altogether and was wondering whether I should say a few words, something about Rachel, and about our engagement, when Lucinda stood up and said 'Of course of course I almost forgot! We've all been having such an incredibly lovely time just chatting but we absolutely have to play a game before we go.'

'Oh for god's sake,' Evie said. 'Don't be ridiculous. I'll go if you do.'

'Oh come on!' Lucinda said, clapping her hands together. 'We have to.'

'No we don't Lucinda,' Evie said. 'I don't do games. And I think I shall go now anyhow. It's late, and I'm lecturing in Oxford tomorrow.'

Lucinda sat down again and said 'Oh come on everyone, it's the engagement game! Richard and I had to at our dinner and there were horribly loads of people there so I don't see why you two should get away without doing it. Don't be a bore Evie, really. Anyway you absolutely have to stay, you know more about Rachel than the rest of us put together I should think. Come on. Me first. Right. What shall I ask?'

Evie had put on her sunglasses and was already standing up but then she sat back down and took them off and said, 'What do you mean the engagement game?' And then she said it again, exactly

the same thing, 'What do you mean the engagement game?' 'Well,' Lucinda said. 'We take it in turns to ask Alex and Rachel questions. About themselves. About each other. They both have to answer the same questions and we get to compare the answers. It's a kind of cross-examination. Richard's always brilliant at it as I am sure you can imagine! You know, wheedling out people's secret thoughts. Fantasies. Should they really be marrying one another. That sort of thing.' Rachel had turned away from the table and was gripping my hand in hers and Evie was staring at her. And then Evie spoke, so quietly I could hardly hear her. 'You might have told me Rachel. You might have told me. Don't you think?'

Rachel said nothing. Eventually she turned to look at Evie. She pulled a tissue from her pocket and offered it to her and I saw that there were tears running down Evie's cheeks. Evie shook her head and turned and stared at me instead. There was something angry in her gaze and I didn't know what to say. Neither, it seemed, did she, until at the last she turned back to Rachel, her face composed again, and said, 'There's still time to change your mind darling. You always were a little impulsive.' She reached out and took the tissue. 'Grasping even, I used to think.' She was smiling now, but I noticed that her hands were playing in her lap and she was tearing at the skin around her fingernails. 'I remember when you were very small, if there was something you wanted, something you were told you couldn't have, you used to—' 'Evie,' Rachel interrupted. 'Don't you think you ought to go now?' And Evie stood, quite suddenly, and did exactly that. Richard leaned over and whispered something to Lucinda and then they said they ought to go as well, and we were left alone, Rachel and I, waiting for the bill and not speaking to one another.

At the halfway point on the drive back to London on the Tuesday after Rachel died, I found myself starting to cry, just as Lucinda had said I

would. I stopped being able to see the road ahead so I pulled over on the hard shoulder and got out. I was sick, kneeling on the grass verge and wishing Rachel was there, knowing she would have stroked my back as I knelt. She would have laughed at me a little, but she'd have said it would be alright and given me some water and she would have offered to drive the rest of the way home and when we got there she would have carried our things in and put me to bed and told me I'd be better in the morning.

I sat on the ground for a while longer until someone pulled over and stopped. They wound down their window and asked if I was alright and did I need help? 'No,' I said. 'No, I just felt unwell. It's passed now.' I picked myself up and brushed myself down and got back in the car and set off for home again, going more slowly than I had been before. But when I got into London and reached the turning for my road I panicked, feeling unable to face the apartment alone, and instead I carried on, driving all the way down through Moorgate and the City and swinging west towards Strand, thinking I would go to see the river.

Waterloo Bridge was heaving with people fresh from the West End. Walking in pairs, they held hands and moved with a certainty that seemed somehow misguided. I parked when I reached the half-way point and got out, walking a little further across the bridge and leaning against the wall looking down into the water, disappointed to have found the place so busy, wondering at the same time why I should have expected otherwise. When I was tapped on the shoulder and asked to take a photograph of a couple against the backdrop of Big Ben, I realised I'd had enough. I found my car and drove off again, looping once around the IMAX and back over the bridge, and as I started to head east the crowds thinned out. Instead of couples there were groups of men in suits, their ties undone, leaving the City behind. An old man with a beard and a briefcase, his rain jacket stretched over his suit, struggled along hurrying to make his train, and a woman sat

opposite St Clement Danes waiting for a bus. I found myself slow-
ing down and looking back over my shoulder at her, trying to see her
face more clearly, and I became aware then that I'd been doing this
all evening: looking for Rachel without realising it, hoping she might
emerge from among the bodies and run towards me and shout out my
name and say it's alright Alex, it's alright. I'm here. For goodness' sake
don't be such a cry-baby.

As I drove home that night I remembered doing the same thing
pretty much constantly throughout the years that fell between our
graduating and our meeting again at Richard's wedding, this look-
ing for Rachel and hoping she might emerge from among a crowd
of strangers. And in all that time I never saw her, not once. At every
street corner, in every underground station, I thought there might
be a chance. On every park bench I walked past, at every neighbour-
ing table in every restaurant I ever ate in. Occasionally I would hear
from mutual acquaintances how she spent her time, and I knew where
in town she was working, so I thought it was possible, theoretically
at least, that we might meet. And I saw plenty of other people from
Oxford in this way. It was the sort of thing that would happen in an
interval at the Wigmore Hall, or in the queue for an exhibition, and
would lead inevitably to the exchange of news and telephone num-
bers and insincere promises to meet on purpose the next time. There
was a time, a few years after I moved to London, when it seemed to
happen with an uncanny frequency, so much so that I started to see
these meetings as precursors of a greater event to come. But I never
saw Rachel. Of course, I didn't actually try to find her as such, but if I
happened to be in a part of London that I knew or thought she might
frequent, particularly if I came to be walking along the street where
she worked, I suppose I did look more closely than I might have done
at passers-by, or at women in cafés, in case she was among them.

Every now and again I wondered if this behaviour was a little
absurd. While I lived with a constant hope that we might meet by

accident and start to talk, there was also something slightly comforting in the improbability of it actually happening. And perhaps it was that improbability that allowed me to indulge in this speculative keeping an eye out for her. I never seriously thought anything would come of it, and at no time did I plan for what I would do if we met. Well, not seriously plan. Fantasise maybe, but never strategise.

To have spent so many years looking at women as they approached me, hoping to see only the particular set of her shoulders, only the precise rhythm of her walk, only the way she smiled or turned her head, was a wearing sort of a business. I imagine it would be no trouble then, for someone to guess the effect it had on me when I looked across the table at Richard's wedding to see her standing there, smiling. It was a kind of a physical shock, like the jolt of the body when one is dropping off to sleep and dreams of suddenly falling.

That night, after looking back at the bus stop and realising it wasn't Rachel sitting there, I picked up speed again, but only briefly. The lights at the bottom of Ludgate Hill were broken and the traffic moved slowly, edging on to the crossroads with no guidance as to who should go first and who should wait. I hung back, gazing out through the rain that had started to fall and feeling the slow thud and suck of the windscreen wipers' lull. I sat for an age without moving until I realised everyone else had gone, and then I drove on up towards the dome of St Paul's, white against the night.

6

When I woke this morning and came through from the bedroom the sun was already slanting in and the whole of my apartment was filled with a filtering light. I sat at Rachel's desk and looked down at the canal. There were streams of cyclists making their way to work: the nine a.m. towpath rush hour Rachel used to talk about. As I watched, the heron rose up from the water and flew straight towards me. It positioned itself on my balcony wall, looking away to the east, a perfect silhouette. That first morning she was here with me, the morning after Richard's wedding, Rachel had thought it was a sculpture. 'It's so still,' she said when I told her. 'It can't be! I don't believe you.'

I had walked through from the kitchen and found her naked, standing with her back towards me. I wasn't sure if she knew I was there until she said 'I like your pretend heron' and she leaned forward and placed her hands flat on the glass, one either side of her face. After I told her it was real and she said it couldn't be she made a fist and knocked with it and the bird rose up startled and heavy in the morn-

ing light and Rachel gasped and turned to face me. 'That's amazing! It's just amazing I thought it wasn't real!' And then she said 'I'm sorry for making it fly away' and she covered her mouth with her hands and because she looked as if she might start to cry I walked over and folded her into me and held her there.

There had been no hesitancy in her desire that first night. None. She had stared and stared at my body, reaching out to me almost like a child might, greedy, hungry, touching me and rubbing my chest and my back and licking me until I was so hard I asked if I could be inside her and she said yes, and pressed me into her, and no, I wasn't being too rough, and she bit into my neck as I came. And later on, when I tasted her, she pushed herself against my mouth and lifted her hips up from the bed and moved as I moved and then she said I can't I can't wait and she turned me onto my back and she was there looking down at me and moving so quick and saying jesus fuck and then it was over and she was in my arms and we slept. When I woke and buried my face in between her legs the scent was of oranges and something sharper and she opened her eyes. Later on she took me in her mouth again, all the way in, holding me there and moving her tongue around the tip of me and drawing me back out and back in and I pressed both my hands onto the back of her head and afterwards she sat up and stared at me again, licking my slick from her lips.

She liked it here. That first morning she said she would have preferred one of the outside walls to be made of something other than glass, but when the evening came and it went dark we sat in the middle of the living room looking out across London and she saw how beautiful it is.

The apartment covers the whole of the top of the building and has at its core a cluster of three central rooms: my bedroom, my bathroom and my study. Each of these rooms has a window hung with a slatted blind and a sliding panel in the wall so that they can

either be made entirely open to the views beyond them, or instead, completely private. The little cluster they form is surrounded by a series of open spaces that flow from one another to make up the rest of the apartment. These spaces are loosely divided so that the kitchen and the living room look out to the south-west while the north-east end is much emptier, holding only a piano and a table and chairs for reading.

When she had been living here for a few months Rachel persuaded me to have the pictures removed from the outer walls so that nothing interrupted her view. I held out for some time but I could see what it was that she wanted, and in any case, she could do a lot of her work at home and would come to spend more time here than I did. She told me that she loved the apartment most of all when it was warm enough to push the panels in the outer walls right across as far as they would go, and that when we did it felt as though we were living outside rather than in. One summer night as we sat holding one another in the half-light, she said that we were a pair of travellers making camp in a desert of sky: our very own airborne oasis.

The balcony walls are made of a kind of Perspex. I had a line of apple trees espaliered low against the south-west end. Honeysuckle climbs among their branches and lavender runs along beneath them. Jasmine grows on a trellised arch that straddles the balcony and a series of troughs is strung out between the apple trees and the kitchen, raised up from the ground and filled with the herbs and flowers that my mother and I used to grow in the garden in Hampshire, so that in the summer months, when the panels are left open, the scent of all these things sweeps in with the breeze.

I told the architect that I envisaged a glass box placed over a series of rooms and open spaces, so that I could walk unimpeded around its periphery and look out at the city on one side and the greener reaches of north London on the other. And that is what Rachel used to do sometimes, walking round and round reciting the landmarks

she could see and watching the planes passing. She told me that on nights when I was due back from one of my trips abroad, if she knew the time of my flight, she would sit on the sofa at the south-west end watching for me and checking the clock and staring and staring to see if she could guess which plane I was on. I remember calling from the airport one evening to say that I had landed and she said she was quite sure she'd worked it out, so sure that she'd actually jumped up and run to the glass and pulled the panel across and stood on the balcony and leaned out into the night and stared and stared to see if she could see my face at one of the windows of the plane, knowing all the time that such a thing would have been impossible. When I arrived back at the apartment she was standing just inside the door smiling and she said I saw you I saw you I'm sure I did and I had hardly put my bags down on the floor before she was tugging at my coat and kissing me and taking my hand and walking me through to the bedroom saying fuck me fuck me right this minute and don't ever go away again I hate it when you're gone.

I have a very clear memory of the first night I ever spent here. I didn't sleep at all. It was only a week after it had been finished and the smell of paint was fresh in the air. I slid the panels in my bedroom wall right back so I could see out to the space beyond and on through the glass, right across the night. I lay with my head propped up on the pillows and I thought about the fact that there was nothing above me apart from endless sky. And as I lay I had a sense that there was nothing beneath me either. It was as though I was floating in mid-air, my bed a Zeppelin cut loose from its mooring. The feeling I had then, that the whole apartment might take off at any moment and drift wherever the breeze sent it, is one that has never quite left me in all the time I have lived here.

Now that Rachel has gone and it is only me again, I will sometimes spend a night sitting on the sofa at the south-west end, wrapped in my duvet and looking out at the lights of the planes passing. I will follow

the paths they trace across the blackness of the sky and I will wonder where they are going, or where they have been, and I will imagine the people sitting up there full of the anticipation of homecoming.

A few weeks after that first morning, when Rachel moved her things in and came to live with me, she asked if she could put her desk up against the glass where she'd seen the heron. I offered to share my study with her, or even to have it partitioned so she could have a room of her own, somewhere she could be alone, but she said she wanted to be closer to the outside, and to sit and watch the heron when it came. And this is where I am sitting now at the close of the day while the evening settles outside and everything becomes still. There is no sound apart from the occasional wail of the buses as they pass along the New North Road, like dinosaurs roaring, Rachel used to say, or whales turning in the ocean.

When she wasn't in the library, or teaching at the university, she would work here at her desk most days, looking out at the canal with her books on the shelves behind her. She slotted them into the spaces that she found amongst my own so that now, when I am searching for an old textbook or browsing for one of my mother's gardening books to read in the silence of my weekday breakfasts, I am from time to time surprised by a volume of Shelley, or Keats, or by a run of novels. And sometimes I will open one of those instead and see an inscription, 'To Rachel, My Love', without a signature, and I will begin to read and find myself rushing through an open weir, carried away by a current that is strange to me and new. And when I am halfway through and utterly lost to myself, no longer in London but far away in Italy, a fifth person in an abandoned hillside villa lit only by candlelight and now and then the light from a storm, I will turn a page and come across a postcard covered in a script too faded to read, or a photograph of Rachel with someone I do not recognise, and I will remember what

she used to say about the sort of person who went to the trouble of using an actual bookmark to keep their place.

'Are you really sure you don't want a space for yourself?' I asked her one evening as I lay on the sofa marking up a contract and she sat typing, and she said no thank you, honestly, she'd already told me it was fine. It was enough that she could lock the drawers of her desk and know that I'd never be able to look in them. Sometimes when she was out, or asleep, I would walk past her desk and look at the drawers and wonder whether she'd been joking when she'd said that, or whether they were actually locked, and if they were, where she kept the key. I never thought of trying them, not until the Tuesday after she died when I got home from Oxford to find a message on the machine from Evie. She wanted me to look for a document wallet of Rachel's and courier it to her at her house in Chelsea the next morning. It was black, she said, black leather, zipped up around its sides. And if I didn't find it straight away, she said, I should carry on looking until I did because she absolutely had to have it. I couldn't see it immediately and I noticed that the desk drawers were probably big enough for it to be in one of them. They were locked after all, every single one, but then I looked on the shelves again and found it so there was no need search for the key. Even if I had, I wouldn't have found it; the police had taken it away with them, as it turned out, having carried out their first search on the night of Rachel's murder. They were to return often, in the weeks that followed, and the first of those occasions took place the day after I got back from Oxford. The search they had done on the night of Rachel's murder was only a brief one, they said; they had come back again to look more thoroughly, and to take some things away with them.

After they had finished, and a couple of officers had bagged up Rachel's things and carried them downstairs, the detective came and sat with me on the balcony. He explained that they'd found very little of interest when going through the emails in her Hotmail account,

and none to speak of in her university account. There didn't seem to be much that was particularly personal, hardly anything at all in fact; the only emails she'd kept were ones relating to research, or holiday or theatre bookings. They weren't particularly surprised by the lack of personal correspondence in her university account, but when it came to her Hotmail they had to assume one of two explanations: either she was someone who deleted almost everything she received, and everything she sent, as a matter of course, or someone else had hacked into her account and done it for her, knowing that the content would be incriminatory. I told him she would never have been so fastidious, describing the state of her desk in her department office the few times I'd visited her there, and her tendency to leave her mail unopened for days. In that case, the detective said, did I think she might have printed off her correspondence and kept it somewhere, and could I think of anywhere they hadn't looked yet, since nothing much seemed to have emerged from their search that afternoon? No, I said. No I couldn't. And I explained then that although we'd been careful with our boundaries, Rachel and I, and that I'd respected hers to the extent that there may well have been personal correspondences she'd kept from me, I was sure she would have said if anything had been troubling her. He asked one or two more questions about my relationship with Rachel then and I told him I'd had that conversation already, in the police station, and that we'd been very much in love, and if he was suggesting that there might have been someone else he was mistaken. He made a note of our conversation and said they'd carry on looking, and that something would be bound to show up, it usually did. If anything occurred to me, though, I must let them know immediately, and I should expect another visit in the next week or so, once they'd looked through everything properly.

They took several of Rachel's things away with them that day, including the contents of her desk, and it wasn't until a few weeks ago that it all arrived back, packed into two cardboard boxes labelled

'CARDANINE – DEC'D. DESK DRAWERS'. They were delivered in person by the woman who has been appointed as what is called my Family Liaison Officer, a woman I have met no more than a few times. Because I can never remember her name, I have come to think of her as Flo, reverting to the lawyerly habit I have of thinking of things in acronyms wherever possible. Flo seemed extremely upset when she came to the apartment this time. I made her a cup of tea and she sat on the sofa at the south-west end and recited pretty much the same script as she had the first time I'd met her, all about Rachel, and about how sorry she was. When I didn't respond she raised her eyebrows and grimaced and said, 'Let's get down to business then Mr Petersen.' She turned to the boxes I'd helped her bring in from her car. The first thing she handed me was a smaller box marked 'CARDANINE – DEC'D. PERSONAL EFFECTS'. She explained that it really only contained Rachel's wedding ring and her engagement ring, and the necklace she had been wearing that night. She carried on, biting her lip and closing her eyes in between each sentence for longer than was really necessary, telling me they'd never been able to find the bag I'd told them Rachel was carrying when she went down to the lake, and nor did they think they'd be able to trace it now. She told me that certain things would have to be kept, and then she gave me a letter explaining what had and hadn't been returned and informing me that the reason the two larger boxes contained a number of photocopies was because the originals of Rachel's papers and documents had to be retained for the remainder of the investigation. When I asked her how long she thought that might be, she made quite a lengthy attempt to answer me until she realised my question had been sarcastic. After that she got up to leave, saying, 'I'm very sorry for you but I'm only doing my job, surely you can see that.'

It was several days before I felt able to open them, those larger boxes. I was hesitant about discovering what it was that Rachel had wanted to keep from me, and I felt that it would constitute such a very

great intrusion on her privacy, even in her absence. When eventually
I did, one evening last week, it was almost too much to bear, looking
through the things that I found there. There was no one thing in par-
ticular that was worse than any other for the way it made me feel, and
nor was there anything of any great significance, or at least, not that I
could fathom; it was, instead, by way of their accumulation that they
made their assault upon me and left a pain across my chest that was
so real I thought I should have to gouge at it with something sharp
to make it go away. I had pulled the boxes through to the north-east
end of the apartment and I sat beside them on the floor in front of
the piano and emptied the things out, one by one. I didn't look at any
of them until everything was sitting in little piles like tiny sandcas-
tles springing up across the floorboards, spreading out towards the
glass and the night sky beyond. And only then did I kneel and crawl
among them, lifting them and holding them, reading them and look-
ing, slowly, at everything I found there, before placing them all in turn
back in the boxes they had come from.

How does one describe a life?

Hers was there that night, in bits across my floor: in swimming
pool membership cards bearing images of her face; in letters from
libraries fining her for overdue books; in examination certificates and
ancient school reports; in scribbled phone numbers and postcards
from friends of hers I'd never met or even knew existed; in loyalty
cards from coffee shops; in dry-cleaning tickets and bank statements
and insurance policies and booklets listing her vaccinations and in
a letter summoning her for cervical surgery she'd never so much as
mentioned.

And then there were the photographs. One of them showed her
and Lucinda holding hockey sticks and standing in a line with their
teammates, so young as to be almost boyish. There were other photo-
graphs also, and some of them were of me, gardening on the balcony,
or walking on Hampstead Heath, or sitting reading at the other end

of the apartment, caught in an evening sun. The first thing that struck me about the next few I came to, the ones of Rachel as a child, was how like her adult self she looked in all of them. And the second was the fact that not a single one of them showed her smiling. There were other photos in which she was smiling, though she was older in all of those. They must have been taken at around the time we were students together, she looked so similar in them to the way I remembered her looking then.

Most of the ones of her smiling had been taken on a holiday, somewhere sunny. Evie is there too in some of them, standing next to Rachel on a tiny jetty, and I wonder who took them, these shots of the two of them together. The boat they are standing in front of looks similar to some Rachel had shown me once on the internet. It was in the early spring of this year, when we were talking about where we might go in her summer vacation, and she'd shown me the website and told me about a holiday she'd taken a long time ago in Turkey, when she'd spent a fortnight on a boat she called a gulet, and she'd said that she would like the two of us to do the same.

I carry on through the pile, finding more pictures of Rachel at school jumbled in with a sheet of passport photos and one she'd asked me to take for her profile on the department website. The last few are of the boat again and I see that they weren't alone on this holiday that they took, Rachel and Evie. Some of their group seem familiar to me. I look more closely and I think I recognise them as people from Worcester, people who Rachel had known but I had not, but because they are either slightly out of focus or have been taken from so far away that their faces are too small for me to make out clearly, I can't be entirely sure. I linger over the last of them. The photographer must have been right in front of Rachel and the woman who stands beside her. They are caught from the waist up. Each of them is wearing a bikini and Rachel is smiling, though less broadly than her companion, who has her arms wrapped around Rachel's waist. This woman is wearing a

sunhat, and because of the way she is resting her head on Rachel's shoulder, the brim of it covers part of her face. My attention is drawn to this photograph not by the image itself, as such, but rather because of the fact that it has been cut in two down the middle, separating the women from one another. It has been taped back together again, and I am curious as to why Rachel would have done such a thing.

As well as all of these things, there was the letter the police had already spoken to me about. Twice in the fortnight after Rachel's death they had brought it to me, when I had stayed at home falling apart as I waited to return to Oxford to discover whether I was going to be released from bail or not. They had found it buried among the documents they'd taken from her desk drawers, and they said, both times, how important they thought it was, almost begging me to tell them something about it, anything at all, but I couldn't help them. And as I sat on the floor of my apartment I read it through over and over, thinking that when they'd shown it to me previously I must simply have been so distracted that something had passed me by, something I would be able to spot this time, if I looked more closely. I remembered that the original had been written on airmail paper, in a hand I was quite sure I had never seen before, and nor did I recognise it when I read it this time.

> We spoke of love once, you and I, when we fell on the grass and held each other. And I really thought you meant it when you told me that you cared for me.
>
> I found out last night just how wrong I was.
>
> Like I said, I'll never forget you, whatever happens, and I don't think you'll forget me either, not for a long time anyway. You might think now that you will one day, but this much I know for sure: you won't be able to, however hard you try.
>
> So long then. I'm going this afternoon and I won't be coming back. I guess that's the way you wanted it.

And because it meant no more to me that night than it had done before, I put it away again and moved on to the next thing. The detectives had seemed disappointed when I'd been unable to tell them anything about it, but they'd agreed with me that they had perhaps been optimistic in their expectations of my being able to do so, given the absence of either a date, or a signature, or even so much as an envelope bearing a postmark. That it was a love letter was clear enough, but when they realised I could tell them nothing else, they had taken it away again and added it to the rest of the contents of her desk to be photocopied and returned to me, eventually, in those boxes.

I sit quite often at her desk, now that she does not use it. I find that it has become one of the ways in which I am able to be near her in her absence. I have developed other methods besides this, such as sleeping on her side of our bed instead of mine. Or occasionally, when I am out, phoning the apartment and hearing her voice telling me that we are busy and can't take my call right now and that I can leave a message after the tone but not a long one. The strange thing is that Rachel used to do this too when she was alive. Sit at my desk instead of hers, I mean. Despite her protestations that she had no need for a room of her own, I would find signs sometimes that she had been using my study. Little signs, the sort of things that a less observant man might perhaps have missed, but unmistakable ones nevertheless. There would be an impression in the cushion on my chair, as though a cat had curled itself up and slept there all afternoon. Or I might notice that a stack of papers had been moved to one side and not replaced. Once or twice I found an apple core in the bin, or biscuit crumbs and a half-drunk mug of tea on the bookcase. And my desk drawers, which it wouldn't have occurred to me to lock, were sometimes left ajar. I never said anything to her about these things, and she never once mentioned that she used my room. It was no trouble to me, and there was something endearing about the way she made so little effort to cover the tracks she left on my desk at the same time as insisting that she worked

every day at her own. They never felt like any kind of intrusion, these incursions into my territory that she made and pretended not to. I find I miss them very much.

I look up from Rachel's desk now and I see through the darkness that the heron has come back to the balcony. It is difficult to be completely sure from this angle, but I think it might be asleep. The lights are coming on across London and it is the time of the evening when Rachel and I would normally have started to think about going to bed. I know I ought to do the same, but it feels odd to think of sleep after a day in which I have done precisely nothing. The desk in front of me is covered in things I could have seen to but didn't. There are the photographs Evie gave me at the police station, still sealed tight in their envelope. And there is also the letter that she gave to me then, the one that Rachel wrote to her after our wedding. I have developed a habit of allowing myself to read this letter once, and then to let a few weeks pass until I read it again. This method is starting to work less successfully now that I have it by heart, but there is still that sense of surprise every time, that happiness on reading the things Rachel said about me, and about us. Beside that is the bundle of correspondence from Rachel's friends and colleagues and students that I keep meaning to reply to, and of course there are the boxes of things from her desk that I know I should have gone through again, more closely this time, to see if I might have missed anything, anything that could trigger some memory that would assist the police in their investigation.

I haven't even managed to dress myself, having had no good reason to do so. I have, in fact, done nothing more than wander aimlessly from one part of the apartment to the other, making cups of tea and failing to drink them, finding them cold and abandoned on a bookcase before washing them up and starting all over again. I took blankets and a woollen hat and ate my lunch on the balcony, sitting like a tramp beside the raised beds, looking at them and imagining my mother pausing in her digging and sitting back on her heels and say-

ing to me, 'Now really come on Alex this is silly isn't it? What would your father say if he was here, hmmm lovey? Come on, chop chop, get dressed and we'll think of something fun to do together, just you and me eh?'

In any case, I know I won't sleep until I make up my mind about Harry's invitation. He has written often since her death, but until yesterday, and apart from the letter offering his condolences, he has sent me only postcards, or occasionally the briefest of notes enclosing a cutting from the *Oxford Times* about Rachel, or about the investigation. The postcards arrive in a steady stream, the message always linked in a careful way to the image. Some describe exhibitions he has seen and thinks I might like to know about, others carry quotations he has come across and considers pertinent. Once or twice a card has come without any message at all, bearing instead a pasted-on clip from *Private Eye* of his most recent contribution to Pseuds Corner. They are all, though inconsequential in their way, strangely comforting. Before her death it was Rachel he sent them to, these postcards of his. I assume that he sends them to me not for my own sake but for the sake of her absence, in a kind of continuing acknowledgement of it, and of my sorrow.

Harry's letter of condolence arrived in early October, almost four months after she died. I remember him describing its timing as intentional, rather than negligent. He explained that the correspondence he had received in the immediate aftermath of the death of his own wife, an event he had grieved bitterly, made no impact on him, numbed as he was to sensation of any kind. As I read his letter, I remembered coming back from the Christmas vacation of my second year at Worcester and seeing the notice that had gone up outside the porter's lodge, and how it carried the most perfunctory of announcements about her death, stating the request that nobody should speak to him of it directly. It

was not until much later on, he wrote, that he was able to reread those letters and have any sense of what it was that people had intended to convey with their clichés and their expressions of sympathy, always clumsy, always inept. Because of this, he said, he had developed a custom of delaying the sending of such letters until the initial period of numbness, as he referred to it, might have passed, or might at least have begun to lessen. He wrote further that he hoped to avoid the risk of cliché himself by allowing another to speak for him, and he set out a quotation from Tennyson, something about wheat and chaff, something that meant little to me.

When I opened Harry's parcel last night I found that he had sent me poetry again: a whole volume of Browning this time. It was the poetry that had accounted for the weight of the thing when I'd picked it up from outside my door. I'd stood looking at the label, noting the fact that he still gave me the Esq. after my surname and feeling happy that he'd written. The letter itself, which I'd expected to be pages and pages long given the weight of the parcel, was, as it turned out, no more than a single side of paper.

Worc. Coll.
27.xi.MMVII

Dear Alex,

There was a hoar frost around the lake this morning. Ordinarily there would be nothing noteworthy in its presence; this year's winter is far colder than last, and we are late in November. I write of it only because I have never known it to be so beautiful, nor so thick as this.

You said when last we met that you would like to visit again at some point, and I wondered whether this might be as good a time as any, now that the frost is here? The students go down next week and there will be rooms at your disposal in College.

*You may stay for as long as you like; there are Christmas con-
certs, and there will doubtless be fine weather for walking.*

*I have begun the great task of preparing the contents of my
own rooms for the embarkation I must face in the summer
and, in so doing, I have come across some things of Rachel's
that I thought you might like to see, or even have. They are not
the sort of things I felt it necessary to give to the police, despite
the fact that their work remains undone, but nor would I want
to dispose of them without at least letting you look at them
first.*

*If you find that what I suggest is amenable to you, do please
telephone to let me know whether you will be able to arrive
next Friday afternoon in time for tea. The enclosed was among
the things I found; you could perhaps read it before you come.*

Yrs. ever,

Harry

It is a smallish sort of a book, and it has sat on the desk all day
inviting me to open it. I think I will take it to bed with me tonight. I
feel certain there is something familiar about the volume. Its cover is a
faded pink, part of the front of it darker than the rest as though some-
one has left it in the sun for months, half-hidden by another book.
And the heft of it sitting in my hand: it is a book I am sure I have held
before.

And then, all of a sudden, as I bring it to my face and inhale its
scent, holding the cloth cover right against my nose and breathing
in deep, I turn and see Rachel lying on the sofa behind me. It is early
June and the setting sun has made the room pink and everything in
it. Rachel glows with it, the light finding orange and golden swathes in
her hair, and she closes her eyes, not so much to avoid its brightness
as to bask in it more deeply. A few moments later I look up again from
where I am sitting and I see that she is asleep. Her mouth is slightly

open and one of her legs has fallen to one side so that I can see she is wearing nothing beneath her skirt. I stand up and walk over to her and I kneel in front of her. Her arms slip away and the book she is holding starts to drop from her hands. I catch it as it falls and I sit back on my heels and decide not to touch her. Instead I hold the book to my face and breathe it in to myself and as I watch her I know what it is to be content.

I remember her waking a few moments later and saying 'What are you doing? Why are you sitting there? What time is it?' and I told her she had been asleep and she smiled and said 'Let me read to you. Go and sit down again and stop staring at me like that.' I handed it to her, the book with part of its pink cloth cover faded by the sun, the book that I am holding now, and as the sky grew darker she read one and then another of the poems and it was I who closed my eyes. The evening had fallen and the first scent of jasmine was drifting in from the balcony when she said, 'One more then I have to eat. What do you want? Something spooky?' 'Yes,' I said, 'something spooky,' thinking to myself that I didn't much mind what she read as long as she carried on.

And now as I sit at her desk in the darkness without her, it falls open at the poem she read me then, the last poem, and I hear her voice again.

> *The rain set early in tonight,*
> *The sullen wind was soon awake,*
> *It tore the elm-tops down for spite,*
> *And did its worst to vex the lake:*
> *I listened with heart fit to break.*
> *When glided in Porphyria; straight*
> *She shut the cold out and the storm,*
> *And kneeled and made the cheerless grate*
> *Blaze up, and all the cottage warm;*
> *Which done, she rose, and from her form*

Withdrew the dripping cloak and shawl,
* And laid her soiled gloves by, untied*
Her hat and let the damp hair fall,
* And, last, she sat down by my side*
* And called me. When no voice replied,*
She put my arm about her waist,
* And made her smooth white shoulder bare,*
And all her yellow hair displaced,
* And, stooping, made my cheek lie there,*
* And spread, o'er all, her yellow hair,*
Murmuring how she loved me – she
* Too weak, for all her heart's endeavour,*
To set its struggling passion free
* From pride, and vainer ties dissever,*
* And give herself to me forever.*
But passion sometimes would prevail,
* Nor could tonight's gay feast restrain*
A sudden thought of one so pale
* For love of her, and all in vain:*
* So, she was come through wind and rain.*
Be sure I looked up at her eyes
* Happy and proud; at last I knew*
Porphyria worshipped me; surprise
* Made my heart swell, and still it grew*
* While I debated what to do.*
That moment she was mine, mine, fair,
* Perfectly pure and good—*

She broke off there I think, right in the middle of the line.

'God Alex I'm so sorry did you hear my tummy rumbling? I'm ravenous.'

'Rachel you can't!'

'Can't what?'

'You can't stop there! You can't start the last one and not finish it! I can't believe it!'

'Oh. I'm sorry. I wasn't even sure if you were listening. I mean you looked like you were asleep.'

'Of course I wasn't asleep. I just had my eyes shut. I was concentrating.'

'You fibber!'

'I'm not. I was really listening!'

'Oh. Well, I'm sorry. But if I don't eat something right this minute I think I might die of starvation. Anyway, it's not such a great ending.'

'Rachel! That's so unfair.'

'Alright. Alright, I'll finish it after we've eaten. You must be hungry too, it's so late. Come on.'

We had supper outside and stayed up for hours and hours. She didn't finish the poem in the end, but she did tell me more about poetry and how it worked and said I should read some for myself and it wouldn't hurt me and what was I scared of? I said I wasn't scared of it, I'd just rather she carried on reading to me, that was all, and she said alright, she would, another time. And it was then that she said, 'I think we should go back.'

'Where?' I said. 'Go back where?'

'To Oxford, silly,' she said. 'Where do you think? I'll write and ask Harry. He's always going on about it, especially now I've married a Worcester man. It'll be fun. We'll get to wear our gowns and drink sherry and sit on High Table and pretend we're Fellows. Come on, I'm sleepy,' and she stood and carried the things through to the kitchen.

I stayed on the balcony and looked across the night for a time and when I came in she was in bed already and fast asleep. The book lay on her chest where it had fallen. In the days that followed she seemed to read nothing other than this little pink book, and I realise now that she must have taken it with her when we went to Oxford later that

month, and somehow ended up leaving it with Harry, who has sent it back to me without any explanation of how he came to have it.

And that is the question that is troubling me as I stand up from the desk and pull my dressing gown tighter around me, clasping the book to my chest. While there is nothing of any certainty about the half-formed answers that begin to occur to me, beyond the fact that each of them is accompanied by a similarly undefined sense of disquiet, I realise as I go through to my bedroom that I have decided what to do. I'd normally prefer to take a more considered approach to this kind of question, and certainly a lengthier and a more systematic one. I suspect this may well be the first time in my life that I have resolved to do something purely because of the absence of a good enough reason not to. In any case, I have made up my mind: I will go to Oxford, and I will see what it is that Harry has to show me, and I will ask him if there is anything he can tell me about Rachel, anything I don't already know.

PART II

London, Friday 21 December 2007

Early Morning

7

I miss her. That's the long and the short of it.

I missed her before I took my trip to Oxford to visit Harry, and I missed her on my return, and this last week or so since I've been back, trying to work out what to do with myself, I have felt her absence more keenly still. And it is because I can't be with her that I've decided to leave London, and to start again elsewhere.

I have booked a car to the airport and I have a few hours to pass until it is due to arrive. I've done everything there is to be done, or at least, everything that I can think of. Until it is time, I shall stand out here on the balcony, wrapped up against the cold, looking out across the city I'm leaving behind.

It wasn't difficult to arrange in the end: my senior partner spoke with the New York office and Richard pulled all of the strings he'd been promising to pull since he and Lucinda had relocated there at the beginning of December. They'd started trying to talk me into joining them almost as soon as they'd arrived, saying it wasn't going to be the same without me around, it just wasn't, for either of them. Lucinda has

taken the credit for having won me over in the end, and she did put her all into the task. She told me first that neither of them wanted one of their as yet unborn sons' godfathers on the wrong side of the Atlantic, and then, when that didn't work, she asked what Rachel would have said if she'd known I was hanging around in London pretending she might come back at any minute. Until he's finished the New York Bar exams Richard's own work will be in an advisory capacity, and so many of the projects he is working on involve clients I've been instructed by in London that his wanting me on board made perfect sense to everyone involved. Once he'd garnered enough support for my transfer, things happened very quickly.

I had some work to do initially, convincing people I'd moved on sufficiently to take the step I was proposing. And I won't be able to start work until the end of January, having managed to negotiate only a partial reduction in the agreed term of my sabbatical. I had to visit the man in Exeter Square again, and when he reported back to the partnership that he was satisfied with the progress I'd made, and that my visit to Oxford seemed to have brought about the necessary shift in my behaviour and in my thinking, I was relieved, assuming the worst was over. But then the New Yorkers had their own requirements, insisting I take part in an hour-long conference call with a psychologist. The woman fired question after question at me, working her way through a list of what she called 'depression indicators' and ticking boxes until she realised she had nothing more to ask and said she'd file a report in a couple of days. And of course I've had to agree to a short-term contract, renewable only on my meeting certain performance targets; anything more permanent is a distant prospect until the Americans are quite content I'm no longer what they refer to as a loose cannon. I have a sense also that my exposure to clients will be restricted, to a certain extent, for some time, and that I'll start off working only with the ones that already know me. I don't think I'll mind a great deal though, being kept back from the front line proper in this way. I am

perhaps better suited to the role they've put together for me, it being more in my nature to remain almost behind the scenes and to be only listening, advising, correcting and suggesting, rather than performing and touting for business in the way that Richard seems to relish.

When I had packed the last of my things this morning and booked my car, I sat at Rachel's desk and wrote a note to the tenant who will take over my apartment tomorrow. Afterwards, I stood in the bathroom and looked at myself in the mirror and as I did I saw that Rachel was there also, standing in front of me and leaning towards the glass. 'You can come in if you like,' she'd said, hearing me waiting on the other side of the bathroom door, not sure whether she was inside or not, not wanting to disturb her if she was. It was in the early days, before we knew each other's boundaries, or at least before our curiosity in one another had subsided enough for us to be able to see them clearly and abide by them.

'I'm cleaning them. It's so dull. Can you believe it's taken me this long to get them pierced! I should've done it when I was a teenager. God knows why Evie wouldn't let me.' I was barely listening to what she said, I was just watching. And then she stopped talking and I put my arms around her and held myself to her as she cleaned first one earring and then the other before twisting them and turning them and snapping them back into place and I pressed my face into her neck and she wriggled away from me for a moment and back again.

I miss the way her neck smelt that day, and I miss the ease of our silence, and I miss the fact that she wanted me to be with her.

8

I travelled to Oxford by train when I went to visit Harry earlier this month, and it was as we pulled out of Paddington that the snow began to fall. I had intended to drive but when it came to it I doubted my ability to concentrate for long enough. It struck me, though, as I pulled my case across the station concourse, that it was somehow right that I was doing as I had at the start of every term all those years ago, especially since it was in answer to Harry's summons that I was making my winter journey. And I found myself doing the same as I'd always done, standing in front of the announcement boards waiting to find out my platform and looking around for a face that was familiar. Feeling the same slight sense of disappointment that I had each time on realising there was nobody I knew, I was reminded of the occasion at the start of my second term when, having resigned myself to that fact, I'd gone to the platform and boarded the train only to see Rachel sitting partway down the carriage I'd chosen. She was wrapped in an enormous scarf and half buried in a book and the place opposite her was empty and for one ridiculous moment I con-

sidered tapping her on the shoulder and asking her if I might take it but instead I walked straight past, pretending I hadn't seen her, assuming that this would be precisely what she was doing in return.

The train this time was only half full, and I managed to find two places to myself. I took the seat by the window and put my bags on the other. As London fell away the sun sat almost at eye level, so I closed my eyes and felt its warmth on my face and I slept for a while. When I woke it was still just as bright, slanting across meadows that spread into the far distance, wide and rimed like salt flats. For much of that part of the journey a plane flew just ahead of us, marking out our course, but as the landscape opened out and the light began to flash from patches of water round about, it veered off and left us to find our way alone and I closed my eyes and slept again.

When I woke we had gone past Reading and the view was bosky and deep and a mist lingered in the hollows of the fields and everything was spiked with frost. The landscape was utterly blank, every branch of every tree looking as though it had been coated by hand with thick white paint. And then suddenly we were dipping down into a hollow and the air became white also, as though we had flown into a cloud, as though we were lost, as though, almost, we had stopped existing. We skimmed along, passing in and out of that cloud of frozen mist. A figure loomed out of the whiteness alongside the train, close enough for me to have thought we might hit him at any moment. He was surrounded by dogs and he skirted the edge of the field as if floating through the air until he was gone again, as suddenly as he had appeared. All at once there was a church spire, conjured by the mist a moment later into rugby posts rising from a playing field and clad in red wraps as though they were horses' legs, and then they were hidden from us, and we from them, and there was nothing to see except the whiteness and we were hurtling once more through time without leaving so much as the ghost of an impression of ourselves.

Shortly before the end of our journey an inspector came through

the carriage and I reached into my jacket pocket for my ticket. What I pulled out with it meant that I almost missed my stop, so absorbed was I in what I'd found. I thought at first, before the inspector went and I looked at it again more closely, that it was nothing more note-worthy than the parking ticket I'd come across just minutes before leaving my apartment earlier that day. I had been closing all of the blinds when the one behind Rachel's desk, the one that had always been a little difficult to operate, fell too quickly and shot down behind the radiator instead of in front of it, getting stuck there. I moved the desk forwards and knelt on the floor and tried as carefully as I could to release the blind and as I did so, the parking ticket was dislodged and fell to the floor beside me. I picked it up and read the car registra-tion number printed on it and saw that it was one of Rachel's and I smiled as I knelt there, thinking it was exactly like her to have put it at the back of her desk and let it fall without noticing, and, when it had disappeared from view, to have forgotten about it entirely. I stopped smiling when I saw the date, working out that she must have received it about five weeks before she was killed, and feeling suddenly, bleakly alone. And then I realised I would be late if I lingered any longer, so I stuffed it in my jacket pocket and finished closing the blinds and locked up the apartment and left for the station.

When the inspector had gone I looked down again at the park-ing ticket and noticed for the first time that it was folded in two. I unfolded it to find a reproduction of an image that had been taken by a traffic camera. And there was Rachel, photographed for what must have been the last time before she died. It was a shock to see her face. I had started to find myself unable to recall what she looked like in any precise way. It had happened only occasionally, but it upset me, distressed me even. I was still perfectly able to hear her voice in my mind, particularly her laugh, but her face had begun to slip away from my memory and I had taken to looking more frequently at the photo-graphs that I had of her, determined to learn it again more carefully,

so that I wouldn't be able to forget it. But this photograph had taken me by surprise, and I think it was that more than anything else which caused the jolt that went through my body when I saw her looking back at me.

She was sitting behind the wheel of her car and caught in close up, her face as clearly depicted as one might wish it to be were one looking to identify her. In the passenger seat beside her was a man who looked strangely familiar, though I couldn't immediately place him. Printed beneath the photograph was an address, as well as a record of the time and a note of the particular offence for which Rachel had been fined. It seemed to have been taken early one morning in the middle of May, on the red route at the eastern end of the Euston Road, and from the tiny thumbnail of a map that was printed beside the address, I worked out that the precise location was just outside the entrance to the British Library, where she sometimes used to work.

I looked back at the photograph, gazing first at her face and then at the man again. Just as I was wondering whether perhaps he was a colleague of hers I'd met at one of her department drinks, or at some sort of a university function, I realised I knew who he was, and as his name came into my mind, I felt as though someone had hit me, hard, right in the stomach.

He had come up in conversation that day in the summer, when Rachel and I sat in the sun of the late afternoon and she read Browning to me. I asked her at one point about those poetry tutorials. Which of the poems had they studied with Harry, the three of them? What had they actually talked about? And she said she couldn't really remember, it was so long ago. When I asked her what it had been like to study with Cissy and Anthony, and whether she had preferred it to the final year when she had been all on her own with Harry, all she would say was that it hadn't made a great deal of difference really and why was I so interested anyway? Then I asked what they were doing now, the two of them, and Rachel told me that she had a vague notion that Cissy had

gone professional with her rowing, or with some other sport, or that maybe she had become a coach at one of the big American universities, but that she couldn't be sure and nor did she really care anyway. As for Anthony, she said she had no idea whatsoever what had happened to him, and that she had lost touch with him almost as soon as he'd been sent down at the end of our second year and that she hoped it would remain like that. I think I asked whether it wasn't perhaps a little extreme to have broken off contact with him altogether, but she started to say something about the fact that, while she didn't see that it was any of my business who she was or wasn't in touch with, that was perhaps the essential difference between us. I asked her what she meant and she said she was referring to my tendency to put up with someone whatever they might have done. I stopped listening then, thinking only of Richard, and of how I was glad that we had managed to keep our friendship ticking over in the way that we had. And then I think I asked her to read another poem and she did.

I looked more closely at the photograph and at Anthony sitting beside her in the passenger seat, and I felt only confused, rather than shocked, realising that of course there would be some sort of an explanation, something innocuous, and rational. I resolved that as soon as I got back to London I'd look him up somehow and ask him what they were doing there, the two of them.

Of the fact that it was Anthony I had no doubt, although he looked to have dyed his hair since our student days. Thinking back and trying to recall when I'd last seen him, I remembered having caught sight of him, or of someone who looked very like him, at the memorial service I held for Rachel in the college chapel. Harry had offered to assist with anything he could, anything at all. In the end, as well as liaising on my behalf with the chaplain and the kitchens, and writing a piece about Rachel for the college magazine, he had volunteered his services for the particular task of contacting all of the students from the time that we had studied there, saying that the college secretary would be

more than happy to help with that sort of thing. So I had accepted his offer and simply sent him a stack of invitations. Harry, assiduous as ever, sent me a list of people he'd invited on my behalf, noting who had RSVP'd and who hadn't. Anthony appeared on the list as one of the latter, as did Cissy. When I'd asked Harry about it he said that he was half expecting Cissy to come, despite the length of the journey, and that it was always possible she'd never received the invitation, not having kept the college up to date with her address. She didn't though, and nor did she ever respond.

As for Anthony, he said that the RSVP had probably just gone missing, or that he'd forgotten to send one, and that he was bound to be there when it came to it. I can't say with any certainty whether Harry was proved right in his assumption in the end, but I think he might have been. The person I'd seen, the person I'd thought at the time was Anthony, arrived late that day, stepping in alone through the chapel door just after the start of the service. I didn't get a chance to approach him then, and when later on I looked around the room where the drinks and food were being served, he wasn't there. Some-how, the fact that I thought I'd seen him slipped my mind and I forgot to ask Harry about it when it was all over; there were so many people to talk to that day, or rather to listen to, it seeming in the end to be an occasion that was more about other people, and about their own experience of loss, than one about Rachel, or about me. He had been no friend of mine, and, Rachel having told me she wasn't in touch with him, I suppose there would have been no particular reason for me to have followed it up.

The train began to slow and I saw that we were pulling into Oxford. Just as I was about to fold the photograph back up again I noticed something I hadn't registered before. Caught in the upper corner of the image was an arm reaching in towards the back door of the car, either just about to open it, or just having closed it. I looked more closely and saw that the arm, along with the upper part of the torso to

which it was attached, was clad in the unmistakable red silk of what had to be one of Evie's jackets, so similar was the shape of the sleeve, and so wiry was the tiny wrist emerging from it. And then we arrived and I put the ticket back in my jacket pocket and grabbed my bags and ran to get off before it was too late. I looked at my watch and saw that if I hurried, I would be in time for tea, just as Harry had asked me to be.

I had no dealings with Harry at Worcester apart from once, when I think he may have done me a very great favour. I was never certain whether he did what he did out of a particular desire to show kindness towards me, or merely in the course of the ordinary discharge of his duties. In any event, there was a problem over the settling of my college bill at the end of my second year. My father had become unwell. Or he had become of unsound mind. Or perhaps it was nothing more complicated than drink. Whatever it was, he had neglected to sign the necessary forms and the local authority had withheld my grant cheque. The Bursar took a dim view of my explanation and told me I had two weeks to pay or he'd have no choice but to send me down. When still I didn't pay up he referred the matter to Harry who, as Senior Tutor, summoned me to see him immediately. It was the only time I had cause to go into his rooms while I was a student at Worcester. I had been once before to his staircase and seen his name painted on the board there, but having gone up to the second floor and stood for a while outside his door, I had walked away without having knocked.

That earlier occasion took place in the first few weeks of the summer term of my first year. Richard and I had finished a stint in the Old Library one Friday afternoon and were packing up our things when he'd said, looking out of the window to the quad, 'Here she comes, Jordan Baker, late as ever.'

'Jordan who?' I said, and I looked down to see Cissy strolling along the bottom of the quad towards Rachel and Anthony, who were sitting

waiting for her on the steps leading up to the north terrace. 'Why did you call her that?'

'Oh come on Alex. I know you haven't read much but surely there are limits even to your literary ignorance.'

'Shut up, Richard. How far have you got anyway? What century are you up to?' I asked, wondering if there was a chance I could work it out that way.

'Sort of gave up on the chronological approach actually. Doing it geographically now. I'm in America at the moment, the jazz age. I'm perfectly prepared to accept in principle that Jordan Baker is beyond you, but I have to say I'm surprised—'

'Richard, I've seen the film,' I said as the penny dropped. 'I know who you're talking about so you can stop showing off. I don't quite see the link though, apart from her being American. And a bit sporty.'

'And her tan? Come on. All that golden skin everywhere. Haven't you seen her legs?'

'Of course I have.'

'You and everyone else,' he replied, and he was right. From as long ago as March, Cissy had gone back to wearing the same sort of shorts she'd arrived in in Freshers' Week, and she'd stuck to them as spring went on, however cold it got, sometimes adding an extra jersey beneath the little cropped jackets she wore on top, with a thick scarf piled onto her shoulders and wrapped around her neck. But always the shorts, and her legs had attracted as much attention as might be expected, since her thighs appeared to be as firm as wood, and the same deep shade of brown that her face always was. The tan came from the summers she'd spent sailing with her father, year on year since she was a girl. She talked about them all the time in the Buttery bar, these trips they would go on, her father taking time off work and the two of them staying out on the ocean for weeks. I told Richard about them when he started to make sarcastic comments about her footwear, and to ask why did she wear those stupid sailor shoes all the time, such an

affectation? He seemed quite disappointed when I'd explained, say-ing, 'She's not on a bloody boat now though, is she? Attractive enough woman, I'll give you that,' and he began to walk out of the library. 'Shame about that bloody ugly scar though, don't you think?'

It was an ugly scar, he was right about that as well. Gouged into her forehead, it was about an inch long and ran straight down from her hairline so that it was usually covered up by her fringe. But it wasn't so much of a shame, I used to think. It made her almost more beauti-ful, rather than less, by its contrast with the softness of her features, her dark eyes fringed with lashes so long as to be slightly comic, her golden cheeks almost babyish in their fullness. I supposed that was why she kept her hair cropped short in the way that it was, dark and tousled on her forehead so that most of the time it tended to half fall across that scar and hide it. And although I'd seen it clearly only once, I was able to tell Richard how she'd got it.

My sighting took place in the bar one night. I was wandering around the room, clearing glasses and listening in to conversations, when Towneley suddenly left the group he was drinking with and walked over to the table where Cissy was sitting with Rachel and Anthony. 'Excuse me,' he said to Cissy, swaying slightly, and because I could tell that he was drunk, I prepared myself for an altercation. But when Cissy looked up at him he simply reached forward and prodded her once, sharply, in her thigh, before turning around and walking away again.

'What the fuck?' Cissy said, standing from her stool and following him and yanking his arm so he turned back round. 'What the fuck?'

He had reached his table again and his friends were patting him on the back, laughing.

'Oh jesus I'm sorry. Please don't be offended.'

'Of course I fucking am. Weirdo.'

'Sorry, sorry. It was a bet.'

'A bet? About what?'

'About your legs.'

'And? What about them?'

'Oh god. It's quite embarrassing really,' Towneley said, taking a step towards her. 'Sorry, can I just buy you a drink to apologise? It's not worth explaining, honestly.'

'Shoot. I'm not going anywhere till you do. And right now I can't make up my mind whether to laugh at you or report you.'

'OK, OK, sorry. Well, I think it's more of a laughing thing than a reporting thing, actually. In fact, you should take it as a compliment. The guys said your legs couldn't be as hard as they looked. You know, your muscles. And I said I thought they probably were. So we had a bet.'

'And?'

'So I had to find out.'

'And were they?' she said, and she was grinning at him now.

'They were,' he said, smiling back at her. 'Rock hard, as a matter of fact.'

'So what d'you win anyway, you jerk?'

'Um. A pint.'

'A fucking pint? You walked over there and did that to me and all you won was a goddam drink?'

'Look, I said I'm sorry. It was stupid OK? I've been drinking. We all have. Sorry. I'll buy you a drink, I'll buy you a drink. Please don't report me.'

Cissy laughed then, shaking her head and saying, 'You're on. But you're a jerk. You know that don't you?' and she turned and walked over to the bar. Towneley followed her, glancing back at his group, raising his eyebrows and grinning again, and Rachel and Anthony got up abruptly and left. Cissy saw neither of these things; she was already sitting on a stool, drumming on the bar with her fingernails, so I came back over and poured them their drinks and within an hour or so, when the two of them were as drunk as one another, Towneley

felt comfortable enough to reach over and sweep back her fringe and say, 'So how'd'you get the famous scar then?'

And that was how I discovered it had happened out at sea, with her father, on one of their sailing holidays. They were a week or so off finishing the trip, she said, when, one stormy afternoon, she'd forgotten to duck as the boom swung round. It hit her so hard she passed out. She came round to find that her father had patched her up as best he could and put her to bed down below with a bandage tight around her head. She slept it off and when later that night she came back up on deck, he took the view it was hardly worth calling sea rescue over something like that, so it wasn't until she got back to shore that she went to hospital and had it stitched. It had been open for so long an infection had set in and it didn't heal well, not for a while. And still, years later, it sat a bright white patch against the brownness of her face. I saw it properly that night in the Buttery bar, and it looked as though it had been scraped from her forehead with a spoon, so marked was the hollow in her skin. And then Towneley let her hair back down again and it was hidden.

We left the library then, Richard and I, after I'd told him this story, and when he suggested a stroll around the lake before our tutorial I said no thanks, and let him go alone. Instead I walked around the quad a few times, keeping half an eye on Rachel, who was still sitting on the steps with Cissy and Anthony, waiting, I supposed, for their tutorial with Harry. When the half-past bell rang out, a minute or two later, the three of them stood and turned to walk on up to the terrace. A piece of paper slipped from the pile Rachel was carrying. It floated back down the steps behind her and landed on the grass. She didn't notice, so I called out, but none of them heard me. I jogged round the quad and picked up the piece of paper and followed them. I stood for a moment at the bottom of the steps and read the page I was holding. I was surprised, not having seen Rachel's handwriting before. I don't know what I had expected. Something grandiose, perhaps, or striking,

and in purple ink rather than black maybe. What I saw instead was written in a tiny crabbed hand, perfectly even and readable but tiny nonetheless, and all in pencil. There seemed to be no paragraphing, as such, just one long stream of prose answering the question written across the top line. I'd read only the first few sentences of Rachel's essay when a couple of students came out of Harry's staircase talking about the tutorial they'd just had, so I let them pass and rushed up, taking the steps two at a time. And that was how I came to stand outside his door for the first time, and how I came to be too late to enter. The outer of the two doors was open, indicating Harry's presence, but the inner door was closed on the tutorial that had already begun. The wooden panels in front of me were covered in postcards, political cartoons cut from newspapers, poems and songs and posters advertising London exhibitions. There were black and white photographs of the lake, and snatches of what looked like medieval English but could have been in any language, it was so strange to me.

As I stood there looking at the door I had a very great longing to be inside the room with the others. I thought of the door to Haddon's study, the wood bare apart from lecture lists, or photocopies of the most recent amendments he had made to the 'Dean's Rules and Regulations as Currently Enacted', a document he kept always posted there. I was about to knock on Harry's door, to interrupt and hand over Rachel's work and explain about having seen her drop it, when I heard the sound of laughter from inside, Rachel's laughter, and then the others joining her, uncontrollably it seemed. Harry's laugh rang louder than the rest, and I went back down the stairs and walked round to the porter's lodge and put the piece of paper in Rachel's pigeonhole.

Towards the end of the summer term of my second year though, I did knock on the door and go inside, in answer to Harry's summons. It was early June, late on a Friday afternoon. He didn't have long, he apologised, taking from his jacket pocket a gold watch on a chain and raising his glasses for a moment to look at it before gesturing to me

that I should sit in the armchair facing the window. However far I went into the chair, which sat so low on the ground that I had half stumbled as I sat down, I couldn't seem to reach the back. I panicked slightly until I felt the cushion behind me, and then I panicked again as I sensed that, in reaching it, my feet had lifted from the ground and were hovering in mid-air. I pulled myself up and perched on the edge, hunching forward so as to avoid starting the inexorable slide back again. And then I realised that because the sun was falling directly in my eyes I was unable to make out Harry's expression, being able to see only his silhouette against the window.

'I wonder if I might ask you to shut the curtain a little,' I asked. He moved into the shadows on the other side of the room and said, with a half-smile that I could see clearly now he was out of the light, 'I tend not to when I am with a student. I hope you don't mind.' And so we sat, the sun streaming through the glass and me holding up my hand to shield my eyes, Harry standing partly in the shadows and looking down at me, while I told him, in the most abstract terms I could think of, about my difficulties. I was acutely embarrassed. He said barely anything until I finished, when he asked me what it was like at home, in the holidays, living with my father. Was I able to work in the house with him in that state? Humiliated now to the point of positive discomfort, I said that it was something of a challenge and that, on occasions, I had felt the strain of it more than I would have wished to. He nodded, and pulled out his watch again and raised his glasses for a moment to look at it, before disappearing into a side room. He came back holding his gown and started to put it on, signalling the end of our interview. 'Thank you for coming,' he said. 'I'll be in touch.'

I heard nothing for three days, and I never found out exactly what it was that had shaken my father from his torpor, but by the end of the week my grant cheque had arrived and I was able to pay my bill. And then, on the last day of term, I received another letter in my pigeonhole addressing me with the 'Esq.' that Harry had used before,

informing me that the college had considered my request for vacation accommodation and decided I was a suitable candidate. I could keep my room on through the summer, without charge. I was amazed, not having made such a request, and not having admitted to myself how much I was dreading having to spend two months in Hampshire with my father, and his drink, and his rages.

A couple of days after he'd sent me the letter, Harry put an identical one in Rachel's pigeonhole. Because there were only a few of us staying up in College that summer, no more than a handful, Rachel and I became aware of one another's presence almost immediately. On the very first morning she interrupted my solitary breakfast by walking into Hall and, to my surprise, sitting down beside me. 'Hello,' she said. When I said nothing in response, she smiled and carried on. 'Looks like you'll have to make do with me if you want any company this summer.'

I said hardly anything that day, being uncertain what to make of her approach. On the second morning I assumed she'd think better of it and go for breakfast at another time, or that perhaps she'd make a point of sitting on the other side of Hall and ignoring me. But she did the same thing again, and the next day, and the day after that, and eventually I grew comfortable in her presence, and realised they would continue to happen, these breakfast conversations, and that Rachel was enjoying them as much as I was. At that stage, I knew nothing of the circumstances which had led to her needing accommodation over the vacation, and despite the amount of time we ended up spending together that summer, and the intimacy that grew up between us, the opportunity somehow never arose for me to ask her why she was there, and why she hadn't gone home to Evie instead.

And that was a question I never did put to her. At the very beginning of October, as soon as the Michaelmas term began, Rachel dropped me just as suddenly as she had picked me up. I was shocked of course, and hurt. Devastated, even. Richard only laughed when I told him,

asking me why I had thought she would treat me any differently from the way she treated everyone else, and going on to make sure that as many people as possible knew that I had been 'Cardanined'. I took my consolation, such as it was, not from his rather brutal attempts to align me with what he described as most of the male population of the college, but from the fact that Rachel, from that point on, seemed to lead an almost entirely solitary life. Cissy had gone back to America at the end of what had apparently only ever been a two-year exchange programme, although I was sure I had heard her in the Buttery bar talking about which authors she'd chosen to study for her Finals at the end of the third year. And Anthony, to everyone's amazement, had been sent down, never to return and never to take his degree. The story went round that he had failed his college exams, or that he hadn't met some sort of a minimum performance standard that Harry was said to have imposed on him during that summer term in response to a generally poor work record. We were surprised though, all of us, given the amount of time he had always spent in the library, and the reputation he enjoyed for being obsessively intellectual. Still, he was gone, and Rachel took her tutorials with Harry on her own after that. She seemed to spend most of her time working, or away from College altogether, staying, or so we all presumed, in Chelsea with Godmother Evie.

Of course I know now that that wasn't the case, and that Evie, having cut Rachel off on account of what happened at the end of that summer term, refused to have her in the Chelsea house, thus beginning an estrangement that would last for several years. That was one of a number of mysteries that Harry solved for me earlier this month when I visited him in Oxford. His invitation had, as it turned out, been almost entirely disingenuous, its only accuracy being with regard to the presence of a hoar frost around the lake. The motivation that lay behind it was not, as he had written, to give me some things of Rachel's that he thought I might like to have, but instead to

reveal to me the circumstances of her death. And he wanted to seek to persuade me, even as he revealed it, that there was no purpose to be served by the story's wider disclosure. I stayed for only a few days in the end, our business together being concluded more quickly than he had anticipated. In the series of meetings that we had during my visit, as we sat together in his rooms with the fire crackling in the grate and a cold wind blowing outside, he told me two tales. The first concerned the sequence of events that had led to Rachel's long estrangement from her godmother; to Anthony's disgrace and Cissy's return to America; to Rachel and me spending our summer together before she so abruptly ended our relationship; and, a long time later, to her death and my great sadness. The second story he told me was that of the weeks that had led up to her murder, and of what had happened beside the lake on Midsummer Night as I sat on the library steps waiting for her to come back.

It is because of those stories that I am standing here now on my balcony, in the dark of a December morning. There is nothing left for me here, and no one who needs me to stay. Richard and Lucinda had no trouble persuading me in the end to relocate as they have done, and I didn't mind letting Lucinda think she was right about the swiftness of my decision being entirely due to their having asked me to be godfather to one of the twins born to them this week. She wrote in her email that she hoped the baby's arrival might give me some sense of a future which would hold meaning for me. There was a kindness in her sentiment, and I felt no need to contradict her, nor to tell her that I am going only because I have a need for new surroundings, and a longing to be away from the places Rachel and I shared. It is for the want of her that I am going, and in the hope that that want may fade a little, eventually, by reason of my being elsewhere.

The air about me is harsh and I have grown cold as I wait for the car, cold in a way that I don't remember feeling in Oxford, despite the snow that fell then. There is a pain in the tips of my fingers, and I

wonder about whether to put a brazier out here, but as soon as I do, I remember that I am leaving. I stop thinking about the cold and I wonder instead whether the tenant who will come tomorrow to live in my apartment will think, as Rachel did that first morning, that the heron sitting beside me is a sculpture, because it is so still.

By the time my taxi pulled up at the gates on Worcester Street it was snowing even more heavily than it had been all day, so heavily in fact that I could barely make out the shape of the facade that lay behind those gates, looming out at me from the whiteness before disappearing again almost immediately. In the moments in which it was visible it triggered in me the same feelings that it had at the beginning of each new term when, as a student, I had stood there and sensed something like fear, or anticipation, I was never quite sure which.

It was precisely the sensation I remember feeling for the first time on the September afternoon when, shortly after Robbie and I had our accident, I was sent away to school. I had come in from the garden one Sunday morning to find my mother in tears, kneeling on my bedroom floor and packing all my things into a trunk. When she had finished I helped her to carry it down the stairs. I stood in the driveway and watched, amazed, as she loaded it into the back of our car and turned to me and announced that later that day she would be taking me away

from our home, and away from her. The feeling came back every year after that, presaged by the first cooling of the air and the rain feeling cold rather than warm, and by spiky globes appearing in amongst the leaves of the horse chestnut trees.

The intensity of the sensation always increased on the actual journey. As soon as we set off my stomach would start a leaping motion, jumping almost into my chest and falling again. On nearing the town itself the pace of that movement would accelerate, so that by the time we pulled into the avenue of beech trees forming the approach to the school, it had become almost unbearable.

The first time she took me there, just as we had stopped outside the boarding house and she was reaching to turn off the ignition, the housemaster appeared on the steps leading down from his front door. He was dressed in a pinstriped suit, somewhat inappropriately it seemed to me at the time, and even more so now I come to think of it. He had his hands behind his back and his chin was lifted slightly and there was something that looked like a grimace on his face, as if he was saying to me, 'Come on, buck up old boy, this is no fun for either of us so we may as well make the best of it.' I remember closing my eyes and slowing my breathing, planning to stay like that until I felt calm enough to get out of the car. But when I did feel ready, I opened them again to find that there were tears pouring down my cheeks, literally pouring, like little waterfalls hot against my skin and so far beyond my control it was as though it was somebody else entirely who was crying, somebody utterly unknown to me.

I realised I had to say something to my mother, to explain that I was alright really and she mustn't worry. I started to try to speak but she just held me then and kissed my eyelids and began to cry herself and said, 'I know I know but we have to lovey, we have to' and the man had come down from the steps and was standing beside our car, bending over and tapping on the window. Suddenly, so suddenly that I flinched, he opened the car door and looked in at us and laughed

before uttering some platitude or other which I couldn't hear properly because my mother had her mouth to my ear and was saying, 'I love you I love you my little one.' I couldn't stop crying then, not until the man had got me out of the car and told my mother to wait outside while he took me into the house. 'We find it's better that way, Mrs Petersen,' he said, and she obeyed him and some boys had carried my trunk into the house and it was all over and I realised I wasn't crying any more and suddenly I felt nothing, absolutely nothing, as if my stomach was no longer there and I was not a physical body but only a part of the air.

It started all over again though, as soon as the matron told me that my mother, instead of waiting outside in the car to say a final goodbye as I thought she must have done, had driven away. The woman told me to stay where I was, sitting on a bench in an empty corridor, while she went to sort through my things. Because there was nobody looking I cried properly then, and bit into my hand. The thought occurred to me that I hadn't asked my mother when she'd be coming back, and that I had no idea when I'd see her again, and an emptiness opened up inside me and I stopped thinking about her. And that was an emptiness that would remain until the months that Rachel and I spent together before she died, when she held me at night and sometimes slept with her hand curled against my neck, and sometimes woke and breathed into my closed eyes that she loved me.

I never told my mother about the way my stomach turned each time she drove me to school. Eventually, after the first year or so, the crying stopped, and I was able to smile and wave as she drove away, as though I was perfectly happy with the whole situation and hadn't noticed the fact that she herself had been weeping since the moment we'd set off from home.

On the October afternoon that I arrived in Oxford to begin my degree, I stood outside the college gates with my old school trunk beside me, my initials painted in black capitals across its side, and the

feeling began again. I thought of my mother then, and how if she'd still been alive, I would perhaps have telephoned her that night and found a way to tell her about it, and we would have laughed together and agreed how silly it was really that it was still happening, even after all this time. I remember looking up at the darkness of the stone rising above me and feeling certain there would be no place for me there, that I would be unwelcome. And then I looked up at the huge wooden doors that formed the main entrance to the college and was wondering how on earth I would open them, or who would do it for me, when a small wicket door that was cut into the bottom half of one of them swung inwards and the person standing just inside stood back and held it ajar for me so I had no choice but to lift the handle of the trunk and pull it towards them. They helped me in with it and suddenly I was inside, and the porters were giving me a key to my room and pointing it out on a map of the college and showing me my pigeonhole with my name on it and there was Harry's letter about the matriculation photograph waiting for me.

When I found myself there this time, standing in the snow and glancing at my watch and hoping I wouldn't be late for tea with Harry, I looked up and saw a window in the wall of the spiral staircase that ran down from the Old Library. Because of the effect of the flakes swirling about in little clouds and half-clouds, the window itself seemed somehow isolated from the building, as if floating in mid-air. As I looked more closely, and as the window appeared and disappeared and reappeared above me, I could just make out a figure standing there and it looked as though it was raising a hand in greeting. I turned to see who they were waving at but the path behind me was empty. When I looked back, the window had been obscured once more by a flurry of snow and the figure was no longer there.

I let myself in through the little doorway and went through to the porter's lodge, half expecting to find there the person who had been standing at the spiral staircase window, but there was only the porter,

leaning on his counter. I introduced myself, realising from the way he stared that there had been no need for me to do so. He said nothing in response, only handing me my key, and with it, an envelope. I opened the envelope and took out the piece of paper that was inside and saw that it was just a note of when breakfast would be served each day, and of the times at which College would be locked up at night and opened again in the morning. Then the porter pushed an open book towards me and handed me a pen, pointing to where I should sign. I think I was growing impatient by this point, so I asked whether it was really necessary, but he nodded and, having looked at the front cover and seen the words 'Old Members' Visitors Book' embossed in gold letters, I did as I'd been told, noticing that mine was the first entry for several days. I looked back at the man, who was still staring. 'Could you phone through to Mr Gardner please, and let him know I'm here?' I said. 'He's expecting me for tea so I'll go straight over to his rooms.'

Still the porter didn't speak, but he reached forward and picked up the telephone, and as I turned to walk from the lodge I heard him say the words, 'He's here, Mr Gardner. Says he's coming to you now.'

Looking back to that first meeting I can see that Harry knew enough then to have told me the whole of the story, and that the essentials of the narrative had been in his possession even when he invited me to Oxford, when he sent me Rachel's little book of Browning and suggested it was something I might like to read. I realise now that when I walked into his rooms and took off my jacket and sank into his armchair, he could simply have placed it before me then, barring a few minor details, for my consideration. And had he done so, I could have got up and gone straight to the police with what he had told me. And that is why he chose instead to hold his fire, and to let me find things out little by little and to infer things hint by hint. I suppose it was his hope that once he had begun, I would be so transfixed I could not

choose but stay and hear him out, and that by the end of my visit, when I had heard the stories he had told me, I would be able to see things as he did, and to agree to his suggestion that we should keep them to ourselves.

On arriving at his staircase that afternoon I'd felt nervous, horribly so in fact, but when he opened the door and welcomed me in and asked me if I had my tea with milk, the feeling dissolved immediately. It was warm inside those rooms of his; he had a fire burning low in the grate and there was a soft glow from a standard lamp behind the sofa, and he took my hand in his and said, 'Welcome, Alex. I am so glad you felt able to come.' And then I remembered Rachel telling me, after we were married, about Harry welcoming her into his rooms like this, with a handshake and the offer of a cup of tea, on the December day she'd travelled from London to be interviewed for her place at Worcester. She said that as she'd stood outside the door waiting to be called in, she'd cried a little with nerves, and with the exhaustion brought on by having spent every night of the previous week reading novels and learning quotes and rehearsing answers to the questions she thought she'd be asked. And then the door opened and there was Harry, smiling at her, and he said her name and she said 'Yes, that is who I am,' and he stood back to let her pass. As she stepped across his threshold she felt as though she was entering another world and escaping from the one in which she'd been living, and that, having done so, she was changed forever. In the end she needed none of the answers she'd rehearsed. It was just a conversation, she said, between her and Harry and the other two tutors she found inside, the youngest one sitting cross-legged on the floor by the fire and buttering himself a crumpet. It was just a conversation about stories and how to tell them.

In return, I had to tell Rachel that there was nothing interesting to say about my interview and that, were I to describe it, the trade would only short-change her. There were no logs burning in the grate and no buttered crumpets, nor anything approaching the warmth of Harry's

welcome. Come to think of it, I'm not sure Haddon even shook my hand. The conversation I had with him strayed beyond an athletic working through of the hard facts of my history and politics A levels only once. It was, I suppose, utterly predictable that he should want to test my ability to construct an argument off the top of my head and, moreover, that he should need to ascertain whether I was able to withstand his opposition to it. Nevertheless, I was taken aback by the question itself. Up until that point in the interview Haddon had said very little, leaving the bulk of the work to his junior colleague. Haddon looked away, taking a note of almost everything I said. He seemed once or twice to lose interest altogether, gazing out of the French doors into the garden I'd caught a glimpse of on coming in. But at a certain point I looked over and saw that he was continuing to take his notes even as he did this, his hand moving steadily across the page and back again to start another line.

When his colleague reached the end of her questions he closed the file that had been on his lap throughout and I relaxed my shoulders, thinking we had finished, and it was then that he chose to stand from his chair and walk over to where I was sitting. He looked down at me and fixed me with a gaze that seemed entirely hostile and then he said, 'Define for me, if you will, Mr Petersen, a white lie. Quick as you like.'

'A what?' I said, wishing immediately that I hadn't, realising that he would see straight through my prevarication and discount me out of hand as a no-hoper. But he repeated himself, humouring me in my gaucheness.

'A white lie, Mr Petersen. A. White. Lie. You have heard the expression, I presume?'

I nodded and, as he turned and glanced at the clock behind him, I began. We argued back and forth for a time, and eventually I settled on my preferred definition. Haddon, having asked me whether it was my best offer, sat in his chair and opened his file and wrote down what I had said. He shook his head as he did so and I thought it was

all over, but at the last he looked up and asked me if I could come up with an example that would prove my case. I think it was only because I assumed I had failed utterly that I did what I did next, and offered up for him the anecdote of a mother telling her son that she and the boy's father, who was a doctor, had fallen out of love, and decided to live apart, and that she had told the boy this in order to spare him the emotional anguish that would surely have been occasioned by the truth of the matter: that because of a game gone wrong, a game the boy and his friend had played without thinking one summer afternoon, in the way that boys do, the father had been barred from his profession, and, this having ruined him, had lost his mind for a time, so that until he had recovered, it had been necessary for him to live elsewhere.

When I had finished, Haddon got up from his seat and walked over to the French doors and looked out on the garden. And then, without turning back to face me, he said, 'Thank you very much, Mr Petersen. We shall be pleased to see you in October. And now Miss Templeton will show you out. Tempus fugit.'

Rachel had told me about Harry's rooms after we were married, and about what I would have seen as I'd sat there talking about my father, had I not been blinded by the sun. And of course, I had seen them once again when Harry had invited us there for a drink before we dined with him on Midsummer Night, but still, I was surprised when I came in from the cold and looked around me. There seemed not to be a single inch of wall that wasn't covered by a picture, or a postcard. A long thin map of the world, large swathes of it coloured red, had along its base the line 'How Did We Get Away With It?' and cartoons of Ronald Reagan hung beside a photograph of Harry as a young man kneeling with a pack of beagles somewhere in a wild English countryside. Coffee mugs carrying US election slogans stood amongst tins of Turkish Delight, and to the right of the bookcases holding row upon row of

dictionaries was a poster, a few feet high, of an American footballer. Half turning round on himself with a ball held in both his hands, up and away from his body, he wore a red shirt with MONTANA written in large white capitals across his back, and the number 16 below.

'The man of many moments,' Harry said, noticing me looking at it. And he stood and looked at it himself, taking off his glasses and folding his arms across his chest.

'It was as if he was running around in a playground,' he said, 'simply having fun. They called him a surgeon, though. A surgeon on the football field. I always thought of it more as a kind of poetry, what he did out there. It would be the very last second of the whole thing, all hope gone, and then, right then, there would be one wonderful pass and the game would be turned on its head. He said he only did it for the love of it. And because every down was different. There we are,' he finished, smiling at me and putting his glasses back on. When he'd walked over and taken his seat on the sofa, I smiled back at him, unable not to share something of his enthusiasm for this man I knew nothing of, but because I could think of nothing to say, I kept silent and carried on looking around.

Perhaps strangest of all the things I saw in those rooms of his were the red squirrels. Everywhere I looked there were paintings of them, postcards of them, and even, as I saw when turning to put my tea down on the side table next to me, a stuffed one in a glass case, its see-through eyes staring out at me where I sat. Other than that, the stretches of wall in between all of these things were lined with books, and those that couldn't fit on the shelves were stacked on every remaining inch of the floor. Up against one wall was a blackboard, words in a language I didn't recognise written across it in a careful script inscribed in fading chalk. In amongst everything was an old record player, half hidden behind a stack of cushions, and when I saw it I remembered Rachel telling me about how Harry had played recordings sometimes, of Tolkien reciting medieval poetry, or of someone

proclaiming verse in Anglo-Saxon, or of long-dead actors hollering out Shakespeare's soliloquies.

I am not sure I focused at all well on the conversation that afternoon, there being so many things to look at. There was one photograph in particular that distracted me again and again from the thread of whatever it was that Harry was saying. Its location was in part responsible, in that it hung just to the left of where he sat on the sofa, so that every time I looked at him, I looked also at the black and white image next to him. It sat so directly in my line of vision, in fact, that it could almost have been placed there deliberately, had my reaction to it been something he'd wanted to observe. It was of a group of students who were gathered together with Harry at their centre. They all seemed to be holding glasses of champagne, and they were positioned on what looked to be the steps down from the Provost's drawing room, the ones that led directly into his rose garden, a private space ordinarily out of bounds to students.

There was something slightly haphazard about the group, as though they had none of them been quite ready for the photographer. Harry was standing in the middle, more as if by accident than by design, his arms half folded in front of him and his head slightly bowed so that I couldn't quite read the look on his face; if it was a grin, it was a sardonic one, though it could just as well have been a grimace. The other reason for my being drawn to the picture provided a much more obvious explanation for my fascination with it: standing beside Harry, with her hair falling slightly across her face and a half-smile just beginning to break out across it, was Rachel, and because she had been caught at precisely the moment at which she had turned her head towards the photographer, it was, from where I sat in Harry's armchair, as though she was looking right at me.

Apart from Harry, they are all either wearing evening dress, or some form of costume, as though they are characters in a play. And as is sometimes the way of black and white photographs, every one

of them appears to be more beautiful than they might otherwise be. As Harry talks on I think to myself that their dress, and the austerity of the lines of the building that provides the backdrop to the image, combined with the fact that it is clearly an evening sunlight that falls on them, lends the whole thing something of an aristocratic air, something of a peculiarly English kind of romance. I try to work out the occasion on which it would have been taken. Because Cissy is in it, standing on the other side of Rachel from Harry, with one of her arms draped across Rachel's shoulders in a lazy kind of a way, I know that it must have been before my third year, when she was no longer there. And because there are other students there as well as Rachel and Cissy, I know it was a college event rather than one just for the English students, and one of some significance for them all to have been dressed as they were and allowed into the Provost's rose garden. I had wondered at first why I wasn't there also, but only for a moment, knowing that I would have been somewhere behind the scenes, as I always was when those people were gathered together.

As I sit and try to remember, at the same time as attempting to appear interested in Harry's conversation, I hear him say my name, and then I hear him say it again, and I am suddenly aware that he has asked me a question I haven't heard. Unable to hide my embarrassment, I feel my face flush red and I apologise.

'It was the photograph,' I say, hoping this will be enough of an explanation for my having completely ignored whatever it was that he'd asked me. He turns his head to look at it and seems surprised, somehow, to see it hanging so close to him. And then he turns back and stares at me again, as though waiting for me to say something. When I don't, he starts to tell me about the former student who took it, and how she had gone on to become quite a successful photographer. I sip my tea again, only half listening to what he is saying. My gaze has wandered back again to the photograph, and I realise suddenly what it is that I am looking at.

I suppose I must have known all along that it had been taken at the Commemoration Ball that had been held on Midsummer Night at the end of our second year, when the whole place became Casablanca and a fire pit was dug beside the lake, and next to it a snake charmer writhed about partly in darkness and partly in the flickering brightness thrown on him by the flames he sat beside, and the Buttery bar became Rick's Bar, serving martinis and cosmopolitans instead of pints of lager, and there seemed to be jazz everywhere you went. The huge wooden doors of College, opened only rarely, had been drawn right back on their hinges and a red carpet appeared on the flagstones and the green grass of the quad, usually out of bounds, became strewn with men clutching programmes and women looking uncomfortable in the newness of their shoes. Somebody had the idea at the last moment of rigging up a projector at the bottom of the quad and playing a reel of the film itself up onto the Old Library, all night long and magnified a hundred times, so that shortly after Rachel and Harry had been photographed toasting one another with champagne on the steps down from the Provost's drawing room, Ingrid Bergman and Humphrey Bogart appeared, spread up across the whole of the old stone building, their silent twenty-foot-high heads entwined in a black and white kiss that seemed as though it would never end. Of course it did end, eventually, but only when the dawn broke and the Survivors' Photograph was taken and breakfast was served beside the lake and, with an uncertain sunlight filtering through the trees round about, the cleaning staff appeared, strung out across the lawns like a line of beaters crossing a moor, bags at their waists for the litter.

'It was an extraordinary night, wasn't it, Harry?' I ask. I turn to look at him again only to see that he is frowning at me, and I realise that he was in the middle of saying something and I have interrupted him. He doesn't answer my question, and so I try again. 'You didn't think so? Don't you remember everyone talking about it afterwards? Wasn't it the most expensive college Ball ever held?'

Harry, still frowning, looks away. 'I couldn't say, Alex. I remember little of such talk, if indeed there was any.'

There is something peculiar in the way that he says this, and I am puzzled by it until he tells me that he would doubtless have attended, had his wife still been alive, it being exactly the sort of thing she would have enjoyed, but that it was not the sort of thing to go to on one's own. I remember then, too late, that the year the Ball had been held was also the year in which Harry's wife had died, and I realise that my clumsy questions have offended him.

'I'm sorry, Harry,' I say. 'I— Of course. I mean, I hadn't realised. I thought—', and I look back at the photograph, feeling confused by what I am seeing, 'I thought you were there also.'

'There is no need to apologise, Alex,' he says, shaking his head. 'It was a long time ago.' He explains that he'd been given no choice about making an appearance at the Provost's drinks beforehand, and that that was where the photograph had been taken. 'Three-line whip, you know how these things are. It was fairly brief, as his parties go. But the Ball proper was, by all accounts, as you say, an extraordinary night,' and he pauses, looking at the photograph again before looking back at me and asking, 'You remember it well, I take it?'

'Yes,' I say, and I tell him that I remember a certain amount, but that because I had Richard as my companion throughout and kept pace with him on the alcohol front, those memories are perhaps more fragmented than they might otherwise be. Harry holds my gaze for a moment, saying nothing, before putting his cup back on its saucer and pulling out his pocket watch. He flips it open for a moment and stands then from the sofa, and it is apparent that we have reached the end of our conversation.

I stand also, and we arrange what time I should arrive in the Old Bursary for drinks before dinner. Harry runs through the sort of people I can expect to meet on High Table over the next few days, and when I ask after Haddon and whether he will be among them, I'm

not at all disappointed to discover that he's undertaken his annual pilgrimage to visit his aunt in New South Wales. Harry says he's fairly sure there won't be anyone at all who I know, as a matter of fact, and that if I find the assorted company of visiting academics and elderly Emeritus Fellows too much at any point, he can arrange for me to have some food sent up to my room instead. 'It might be just the thing though Alex,' he says. 'For both of us, I mean. To take us a little out of ourselves at the close of a day?' I weigh the thought of my empty room against the potential comfort of strangers and say yes, why not, and he asks me to wait a moment while he fetches a gown for me to try, saying as he goes through to his other room that he presumes I haven't brought my own. No, I say, no, I haven't, remembering that he'd put exactly the same question to Rachel and me as we'd stood there on the Midsummer Night of her death. He comes back and holds one out and I am a little slower than I might be in taking it from him, stuck as I am with this memory that has surfaced. Mistaking what he sees as hesitation, he begins to help me on with the gown, standing behind me and holding out first one sleeve and then the other. I put my arms in in turn, but the second one becomes stuck so that he has to reach his hand in and search for my own and there is a moment then when we touch one another that makes me feel somehow uncomfortable.

After a certain amount of struggling, it becomes apparent that the only way I will secure my release from the gown is to relax my arm completely and let him guide me out of it from where he stands behind me, and as I do so we both laugh, and finally I emerge and take it from him and my feeling of discomfort has passed. We've exchanged what I think are our goodbyes when Harry says suddenly, catching me unawares after the awkwardness of the gown, 'And the Browning? How did you find it?'

I don't know what to say. I've been intending to read it since he sent it to me, but somehow I haven't found the time. In fact, I haven't so much as looked at it again since the day I opened his parcel and

held the book up to my face and relived the memory of Rachel read-
ing to me from it so soon before she died. I look at him standing there
frowning and it occurs to me that I could simply come out with it
and ask him how he came to have it in his possession, and tell him I
know that Rachel took it with her to Oxford that weekend, and that
I know that what he'd written in his letter about having come across
it in the course of sorting through the contents of his rooms simply
wasn't true.

And then, suddenly, realising how much I want to say these things
but being unable to think of a way of doing so, something like anger
rushes over me, irrational anger towards Harry for having thought
that I would have had the time to sit about reading poetry. I wonder
to myself whether he has any idea of the impact of Rachel's death,
and of the difficulties I have begun to experience in carrying out what
would once have been the simplest of tasks. And so instead of ask-
ing him why he had the book, which is what I want to do, I tell him
that I haven't had time to look at it on account of the fact that I've
spent most of the previous week engaged in an unsuccessful attempt
to locate the original of her death certificate, it having gone missing in
the post. He says nothing in response, so I go on to describe for him in
detail, aware that my tone is growing more acerbic with every word,
precisely how difficult it has been to convince either the register office
or the post office of its importance to me. I tell him then how it felt to
make phone call after phone call to one nameless administrator after
another trying to explain that a copy would not satisfy the insurers,
who were refusing to pay out on her life policy without it. And when
still he says nothing, I infer from his silence that he is wondering why
I need the money, so I go on to explain that it is not for me, but for
the charities that Rachel listed in her will. 'Do you see?' I say. 'It is my
duty. Can you see that? Can you imagine?'

And then all at once, even before he lays his hand on my arm again
and says the words, 'I do see, Alex, I do. Remember that I too know

what it is to grieve,' I recall the letter he wrote to me after Rachel died, and the things he said in it about his wife. But before I can begin to apologise for my outburst, he is holding open the door for me. 'Six forty-five,' he says. 'That should give you plenty of time to change.'

I arrived in the Old Bursary for drinks that evening to discover that Harry was busy arranging a seating plan and introducing people to one another. He didn't so much as allow me to catch his eye until we were filing into Hall, and even then, when I made an attempt to express how very sorry I was for what I had said, he only nodded at me. I tried again over coffee but he was busy once more, and when I looked around towards the end of the evening and found he wasn't there, I was told by one of the staff that he had left quite some time ago. On my way back to my room I walked a couple of times around the quad, wondering whether he had gone back to his own rooms and whether perhaps I should go to him there and apologise properly. When I reached the bottom corner for the second time I stood beside the passageway that ran beneath the secret garden and I looked up and saw the windows of the Old Library, each one more than twenty feet high and lit from their base with lamps that glowed red against the night. And there was Harry, standing at the middle window.

I didn't think he'd be able to see me in the shadows so I stood and watched him for a while until eventually he turned and walked away. As he did so, I remembered that that was where he'd stood on the night of Rachel's murder, and the thought occurred to me then that if someone had known Rachel was going to be walking down to the lake at the time that she did, and if they had wanted to observe her as she walked, they couldn't have chosen a better place to do it.

When I got back to my room I undressed straight away, too tired even to have a bath. My bed was raised up as though on a tomb, mattress after mattress stacked beneath me and long drawers forming a

kind of a plinth underneath them. 'Like the princess and the pea,' I heard Rachel whisper in my ear as I climbed into it, and then she laughed, and then her laugh faded. I reached over and took the little book of Browning from the bedside table, wondering why it was that Harry had been so insistent I should read it. I looked at a couple of the shorter poems and then I flicked through the book again until I found the final one that Rachel had read that summer night in London, and I read up to where I had got to the last time I had looked at it. As I read I saw the man, lonely in his cottage. I heard the storm that he had heard, howling loud enough to tear down the trees and vex the lake. As his lover came through the door I saw her make the fire rise in the grate and I saw the room lighting up around them as she took off her wet things and sat beside him. I felt her take his head in her hands and place it on her shoulder and I listened to her murmur that she loved him. And then, turning onto my front and pulling the covers up around my shoulders, I read on.

> Be sure I looked up at her eyes
> Happy and proud; at last I knew
> Porphyria worshipped me; surprise
> Made my heart swell, and still it grew
> While I debated what to do.
> That moment she was mine, mine, fair,
> Perfectly pure and good: I found
> A thing to do, and all her hair
> In one long yellow string I wound
> Three times her little throat around,
> And strangled her. No pain felt she;
> I am quite sure she felt no pain.
> As a shut bud that holds a bee,
> I warily oped her lids: again
> Laughed the blue eyes without a stain.

And I untightened next the tress
About her neck; her cheek once more
Blushed bright beneath my burning kiss:
I propped her head up as before,
Only, this time my shoulder bore
Her head, which droops upon it still:
The smiling rosy little head,
So glad that it has its utmost will,
That all it scorned at once is fled,
And I, its love, am gained instead!
Porphyria's love: she guessed not how
Her darling one wish would be heard.
And thus we sit together now,
And all night long we have not stirred,
And yet God has not said a word!

I closed the book and got out of bed again and walked across to the window. The view was the one I'd enjoyed as an undergraduate from my room up in the eaves of the Nuffield Building, but from sideways on and slightly lower down. I looked across to the plane tree we'd all been photographed beside that October morning, and then I wrapped my dressing gown more tightly around myself and leaned further out. Gnarled branches of some kind of creeper climbed down from the window and I could see as far as the lake. I could just make out in the pale moonlight the trees rising up around it, and as I stared out across the blankness of the lawns that lay clad deep in the snow that had fallen throughout my journey from London, I heard the hooting of an owl.

When I woke the next morning I pulled back the curtains and looked out on the lawns. I saw that a new snow had fallen and that if I was quick enough I would be the first to break a path across it. I breakfasted alone in Hall and wrapped myself back up again before heading straight out around the quad towards the orchard. A couple of gardeners were clearing paths and scattering grit in front of the cottages and because the sound was muffled by the snow it was as though they worked in silence. As far as I could tell I was the only person about apart from them. I walked across the orchard and cut through the Sainsbury Building, opening the tiny gate that led down to the lake and striking out along the path skirting its north-west side.

The snow lay almost a foot deep, and the hoar frost that Harry had written about held fast to the trunks of the trees. There was no sound apart from the occasional easy sweep of wind past my ear as I walked and I moved awkwardly, sinking my feet one after the other into the snow and having to pull them back out again before carry-

ing on. The branches that sat just at eye level were coated in a blanket of spikes and coarse hair-like growth, and because I was focusing on them so intently it was only when I felt my body shift suddenly, almost as though I had tripped, that I looked down and realised I had stepped into a footprint. I looked up and saw a whole path of them strung out in the snow before me and I abandoned my notion of trailblazing, stepping instead from one to another of these hollows. Before long it became too difficult to do so, the walker obviously having picked up his pace so that his stride had become far longer than my own. I paused and stood for a while at the side of the lake. The playing fields were spread out behind me undisturbed in their whiteness and I looked across to the south-east side, towards the tree that Rachel had died beside, and I wondered whose route I was tracking. The water had frozen hard and deep so that the low-hanging branches had been caught at their mid points beneath the ice. They emerged again above its surface as if struggling, as though their entrapment had happened all at once, without warning. A few of the college geese skated about, pecking here and there before huddling together and swaying slightly for warmth.

I walked on around the lake and as I reached the place where I had found Rachel's body I remembered the time the two of us had met there on another summer night, the one that fell partway through the long summer vacation we spent in College at the end of our second year. We had taken a pair of seats at the top of the stand that had been placed there, Rachel having asked me to see *The Tempest* with her. I'd seen it once already, earlier in the week, and would far rather have spent the time lying on the lawns listening to Rachel talk about nothing in particular, which was what I'd done every other evening so far. Because of that, I didn't complain when, twenty minutes or so into the first half, she tugged at my sleeve and whispered in my ear that it was quite hopeless wasn't it, and why didn't we abandon ship now rather than later and do something more interesting. I remember cringing

slightly as we climbed down from the top of the stands, Rachel apologising profusely all the way, her mock whisper audible to all of the audience and all of the cast.

Her next suggestion was tennis, but she kept calling out the score as loudly as she could even though the courts were just the other side of the lake, so that the actors would have been able to hear her words ringing out across the water as clearly as we could theirs, and eventually I said I'd rather do something else. She called me a coward but she agreed to stop, and we strolled fairly aimlessly around the gardens instead, Rachel trailing her racquet on the grass and complaining from time to time that she was bored.

'I know. Let's stay out all night,' she said eventually, just as I was wondering whether this was the moment for me to summon up the courage to ask her back to my room. 'It's so beautiful,' she carried on, 'we have to see the sunrise.' So we crossed over to Gloucester Green and got some food and some bottles of wine and sat in the middle of the playing fields, not talking much, just eating and drinking and looking at the sky. At midnight she stood and said she'd thought of a plan, but that I had to agree to it before she would tell me what it was. I'd drunk enough to say yes straight away, and what was it? But then she said she wouldn't tell me until we got there, so I followed her back around the lake and across the lawns and I remember thinking how strange it was that the play had finished without our noticing; I was sure I hadn't heard any applause. Even stranger was the fact that because it was the last night of the run, the stage and the seating and the lighting towers had been taken away and not a trace of them remained: it was as though it had never happened.

We were halfway up the lawns when I turned back towards the plane tree again. I stood there for a minute or two, swaying slightly in my drunkenness and wondering whether in fact we had imagined it all. But then a breeze disturbed the lake and I caught a glimpse of the duckboards lying just beneath its surface, laid there so that Ariel,

happy in his release at last, could appear each night to be running sprite-like on the water, and I knew it had been for real. By the time I turned back round again, Rachel had disappeared.

'Rachel,' I called out. 'Rachel, where are you? Wait for me,' and I started to jog up the path, thinking she had run on ahead and left me there. And then suddenly, I hear her voice from right beside me in the flower bed, speaking in a half-whisper.

'Shut up you idiot. This is it. This is the plan.'

I am so disorientated by now, and so drunk, that for one wild moment I think she is propositioning me, but when I have clambered through the plants to where she is crouching she says straight away, 'Follow me. And be quiet for goodness' sake.' She pushes on ahead and I realise what she is intending to do. Immediately in front of her are some tiny steps set into the wall that rises up from the back of the flower bed. They lead to an old gate that is suspended halfway up and opens into the secret garden, the one that Haddon's drawing room looks out on. Before I have time to speak, or at least before I have time to say anything at the kind of volume that won't risk waking Haddon up, Rachel has reached the top of the steps and is attempting, unsuccessfully, to pull open the gate. I grab hold of her foot, meaning to try to persuade her to come back down. 'Don't be a wimp Alex,' she whispers, and the gate opens and she pulls herself up and into the garden. What else can I do but follow her, so that a moment later we are both there, sitting on the tiny lawn right outside Haddon's drawing room. There is no light coming from the French doors, which means, or so I assume, he is already asleep in the room above. I look up at the bedroom window and see with relief that the curtains are closed and the window is shut, and then finally I relax, laughing at the absurdity of the situation.

Standing there this time in the early morning snow and playing the scene back for myself, I have a sudden urge to climb the steps again. I scan the lawns and see that I am still alone; whoever provided my path

of footprints has disappeared altogether. I know from what Harry said over tea that Haddon is in Australia for the Christmas vacation, so I step into the flower bed and walk up to the base of the wall. It had been difficult enough that summer night with Rachel to gain any purchase on the steps and I assume the snow will make it even trickier. But as it turns out, the soft cushion that has fallen and set on each of them provides a kind of support as I climb, and before long I am at the top, standing on the tips of my toes and peering in through the iron gate.

As I do so, it seems as though I am looking in on the two of us and what we did that night, watching our summer trespass unfold again before my eyes. The scene I am observing is exactly as it was, apart from the curious fact that we are all in snow the two of us, so that our movements are slower, and the sound of our voices is dampened slightly. I feel faint as I watch, and a little dizzy, and I wonder whether I am experiencing some kind of half-hallucination. I realise I should perhaps have eaten my breakfast more slowly, and more of it, and I decide then that I have been out in the cold for long enough and should probably go back in. But I am transfixed, and I stay, and the two of us grow clearer in front of me. We are dressed for a summer night but I see that the lawn we are sitting on has become a strip of white leading up to Haddon's French doors and the boughs of the trees are bending over above us under the weight of the snow that has fallen. A soft clump of it slips down and drops silently on to Rachel's head, and she laughs and brushes it off and says to me, 'What are they Alex? What are all these plants? That's just the sort of thing you'd know. I have no idea whatsoever about plants. Tell me tell me tell me, right this minute, or I'll never speak to you again.' And I feel once more the foolish relief that I'd felt then, knowing that I was able to do what she'd asked.

I see myself get up from the grass, a little unsteadily, and I pull her up with me. I lead her about the garden brushing snow from one plant after another to reveal its leaves or its flowers, pleased to find that so

many of them are the ones my mother grew in the years after Robbie's accident, when my father had gone and I had been sent away to school. And because they are the same, I am able to do for Rachel what my mother always used to do on my first night home at the beginning of my summer holidays. After we had unpacked my trunk and eaten our supper and I was all ready for bed, she would wrap me in my dressing gown and open up the French doors and lead me out into the half-light and hold my hand and walk me round and round and breathe to me all of the names of all of the plants. She would listen to me naming them back to her, and she would tell me how they had fared in my absence. There was snowy woodrush, and bleeding heart, and solomon's seal and lamium, and if they were ready she would pick wild strawberries for me and crush them into my mouth and kiss away the juice that ran sticky down my chin. There were goat's rue and phlox and night-scented stocks, and gillyflowers and marigolds, and then we would get to the top of the lawns and find ourselves at the herb garden. We would walk right into the middle of it and kneel on the ground side by side and she would reach in and cup both her hands around a great clump of lavender and rub her palms together again and again and hold them straight up to my face. And I would breathe in deep and know that I was home, and safe.

Rachel laughs when I find the herbs at the top of Haddon's garden and say that I want to do this for her, but she follows my instructions and kneels beside me and I hold my hands up to her face. She breathes in and I can feel her skin against my palms, and I can smell the scent of the lavender, and I want her then more than I have ever wanted anything. But she takes my hands from her face, telling me that I am hurting her, and she gets up from the ground and walks away into the shadows. She goes once around the garden and then over to the wall again, and looks across to the plane tree that stands beside the lake, and the tone with which she speaks has changed and it's as though what has just happened has never happened. 'The perfect viewpoint,'

she says. 'Best seat in the house. I wonder whether he saw the play tonight? What do you think Alex? Does he like his Shakespeare, your man Haddon? Or is he just a boring old lawyer?'

I stand on my tiptoes on the step looking in, remembering the sense of disappointment I felt then. I realise suddenly how uncomfortable I am, clinging to the iron railings with both hands, my hat pulled so low on my head that I am barely able to see through the snow that has begun to fall again, and I consider once more whether I have been there long enough, whether it is time to go back to my room. But then I remember what happened next that night, and so I stay, wanting to experience again the sense of surprise that I felt when it did. As I stand there, my calves beginning to go numb with the awkwardness of my position, the whiteness that is in front of me melts and the garden becomes green and soft, and it is June rather than December, and I am watching myself lying on grass not on snow, and Rachel has come back from the wall and is lying right beside me and she says we are going to play a game. The sky has retained a kind of a brightness long into the night and we can see clouds floating past and she says we have to take it in turns to tell each other what they are. First, I see a shark, and then the hull of an enormous boat looms vast against the night and then no, Rachel says, it is not the hull of a boat it is the tail of an aeroplane, and then it is a whale turning in the ocean, a great jet of spray spouting above it, and then it disappears and a newborn lamb skips past, chased by a whole cloud of butterflies which, Rachel says straight away, isn't a cloud of butterflies but a herd of wildebeest stampeding, can't I see it? Look, there!

And then we grow tired of the game and Rachel turns away from me and lies not on her back but on her side, so I turn also, and I place my arm across her body and hold her against myself. And because she doesn't resist me, I move my hands up and put them on her head and feel the warmth of her beneath her hair, and I am amazed that she is allowing me to do this. 'Your head is so small,' I say, my face almost

touching the nape of her neck. 'So small.' And I find that because I am somehow unable to make a proper sound, I have sighed the words rather than spoken them.

'Not like yours,' she says, reaching her hands up behind herself and placing them on my head and moving them back and forth through my hair a few times before letting them rest where they are and saying, 'You are like a lion.' And then she moves her hands again and trails her fingers across my face, barely touching me, until I can't stand it any more and I catch them in my own and she turns to me and suddenly we are kissing and my heart is thudding inside me, really thudding, at a pace that actually alarms me a little, and I hold Rachel into me and we turn and turn in the grass as we kiss, and then we come to rest. There is nothing then, no more movement, and no sound apart from the soft murmur of my voice, and I am watching us and craning my neck to try to hear what I am saying, knowing very well what it is but longing to hear the actual words again, when all of a sudden I hear a shout that seems to come from in front of me and behind me both at once, and the snow reappears around us and I am no longer lying there, I am only standing outside the garden and looking in, clinging to the gate and watching the two bodies that lie buried again in whiteness, and the shouting carries on and two things happen at once.

The first is that the French doors burst open and there is Haddon, holding what looks like a cricket bat and roaring at us to get out, get out immediately, what the bloody hell do you think you're doing and don't you know it's trespass and I know who you are Petersen and I'll see you in my study first thing in the morning get out and take her with you. And I see us jump up from the ground and run and Haddon disappears back into his drawing room and closes the French doors but the shouting carries on and the second thing that happens is that I turn to see a man at the foot of the steps beneath me, a man who seems from this angle to be improbably tall. He is shouting at me to get down sir, the steps aren't safe sir, you'd better come down, you shouldn't

be up there, and as I look at him, wondering who he is and trying to see his face but not being able to because he is so well wrapped up against the snow, I slip from the step I am on and I am falling, fast, and he half catches me and we both crash to the ground together and everything starts to become dark and I realise I can't move so I stop trying and I lie there in this man's arms and the thought occurs to me that I still cannot say with any certainty, no matter how many times I have thought on it, which of us it was, Rachel or me, that began that kiss. It was a kiss that had not begun, and then suddenly it had, and it was soft, and gentle, and huge and small all at once, and from time to time we were kissing necks instead of lips, and we turned and turned in the grass and then we were still, not kissing any more, just holding one another.

And then someone is shaking me and slapping my cheeks, gently, and I am being pulled up from the ground and a plastic cup of hot sweet tea is being put into my hands. When I have drunk from it, and when the porter has screwed it back on the flask he'd been carrying with him on his morning rounds, I look up and notice that the wall has started to bulge out in its middle, and that it is held in place by great iron bars fixed across it, and that the steps are crumbling away in places, and it becomes apparent that what I did by climbing them was perhaps more foolhardy than I'd realised.

The whole escapade is one I come to regret even more when, longing for a bath and some dry clothes, I arrive back at my room only to find I have lost my key. I check all of my pockets again and again but it isn't there, and I make my way to the porter's lodge to ask him for another. 'We'd prefer to try to find the original, sir, if it's all the same to you. Cleaners'll be in tomorrow and they'll need the spare. Costs money you know, cutting a new one. Round about where you fell, I imagine. I'll help you; got a little time on my hands as it happens.' I am slightly irritated that I can't at least borrow one so that I can change first, and am about to suggest this when I think better of it, relieved

that he seems to have calmed down since shouting at me earlier on. I follow him down the steps into the quad and we take the route I took on the night of Rachel's murder, when I ran down to the lake and found her body. As we walk across the lawns I sense the porter quickening his pace and see from the prints he is leaving in the snow that it must have been him whose route I'd been following that morning. We reach the spot where I fell from the steps and we dig around a bit in between the plants but our search is as fruitless as I'd expected it to be. He steps back out of the flower bed and looks down at the snow around his feet. 'Wouldn't have made much of a sound in snow like this would it.' Seeing my frown, he explains himself further. 'When it dropped, sir, from your pocket. Nobody would have heard it, would they? It'll turn up, when everything melts. Can't be helped.'

He seems positively friendly now, and he starts to talk about the things he has found on the lawns over the years, things that people drop, or forget, things you'd never imagine would get left behind, he says. And so I ask him about his work, and about whether he had walked around the lake that morning, and when he says yes, he had, I asked him whether he did that every morning.

'And every night, sir. Got to keep an eye on things.' And he tells me then that his father did the same before him, and that for a time, when he started in the job, they shared the rounds together. He knew the college already though, he says to me, after a fashion. He'd been at St Barnabas School as a boy, in Jericho, and they had been allowed in to use the playing fields. He'd never forget the first time, he said. 'It was like entering another world. Our very own Narnia. One minute we were outside, all of us, holding our football boots in our hands, and then the gate was opened and we were in, and it was like nothing I'd ever seen before. It was so big, that was the thing,' he carried on. 'I remember the gate opening and all of us filing in and seeing only the green of the playing fields, stretching on and on ahead of us.'

I was confused by his description and said so, suggesting that

surely the view they'd have seen first on coming into College would have been of the quad, rather than the one he'd described. And then I apologised for my pedantry, explaining it away as an occupational hazard of my profession. He only nodded, and carried on, so lost in his childhood reverie that it was almost as though he'd forgotten I was there. It seemed from what he said that they had come in through a back gate, directly from the Jericho street St Barnabas stood on. I didn't know you could get out that way, I said, puzzled, and he said no, nobody goes that way any more, haven't done for years and years, not since the paths were rerouted and the old gate at the bottom was forgotten. 'I'd forgotten it myself until now. It'll still be there,' he said. 'It's just not used any more, that's all. It will have been overgrown long ago. Completely hidden from view. You wouldn't have any idea it was there unless somebody told you about it. Or unless you already knew about it. Which I don't suppose anybody does, apart from me, and some of the older tutors,' he carried on. And then he looked at me in a way that made me feel uncomfortable. 'And you,' he said, 'now that I've told you.'

I didn't know what to say then, so I thanked him for his help and apologised again about the key. I asked if I might trouble him for a spare, and after we'd gone to the lodge and found one, I went straight back to my rooms to change.

As Harry opens the door to me later on that afternoon I see that he has his pocket watch in his hand and I realise I am late. He snaps it shut and says, 'You have been busy?' Because I can't tell whether the frown on his face is irritation or simply puzzlement, I tell him about my walk around the lake, and the hoar frost, and the depth of the snow that was there. I stop when I get to the part about my climbing up the steps to Haddon's garden, sensing somehow that I should withhold this transgression from him. And then he pours our tea and tells me that the last time the lake had frozen as hard as this was more than twenty years ago, just after he had arrived at the college to take up his post. 'There seems to be something of the valedictory in its return this last week,' he says. 'As though it is telling me it is time to go elsewhere.'

And then he talks about the fact that he is approaching his retirement, saying he will miss his students most of all. 'One never knows,' he says, 'at the start of every new year, quite what to expect. Of course I have met them all once already, in their admissions interviews. But

only the once, and they change, in the time between. I am sometimes a little surprised by the people who walk through my door. I shall miss the luxury of their conversation, and of their company.' And I remember again Rachel saying to me, when I had asked her about what actually happened in a poetry tutorial, that there was nothing to it, studying English. That it was just sitting around having conversations about books, and stories, and the ways there were to tell them. When I ask Harry how he will spend his time, he only jokes about obtaining a string bag and visiting the supermarket on a daily basis to buy a tin of beans, or a loaf of bread. He'll carry on taking his visits to London, he says, keeping up with exhibitions, seeing his man at Trumper's and continuing with his research. He intends to make a habit of dining as often as possible on veal and brandy sauce with whomsoever he should find at the O&C's club table, safe in the guarantee that whatever they might lack in personality will be more than compensated for by the sharpness of their intellect. He will be, he says smiling, a man about town.

'So you see,' he continues, 'I shall have no shortage of things to do. That is not my worry, Alex.' And then he stops his jokes and tells me that the real difficulty, the thing that is really troubling him, is the need to confront the fact that he will no longer be needed, that his opinion will no longer count, and nor will it be something after which people seek. The signs are already there, he says, despite his having another six months in his post. He has sensed it in the meetings of the Governing Body, where his powers of persuasion seem to hold less sway than they used to, and he is beginning to feel that there is no further purpose to be served by remaining. 'My replacement was appointed over a year ago and he seems to be here more regularly now, preparing himself,' he says. 'Before the funeral meats are even slightly tepid.' And then he smiles and looks at the piles of books lined up against the wall and says there are too many practical matters to be attended to for him to become seriously melancholy for any signifi-

cant length of time, and that he will be given a desk in the Emeritus
Fellows' room which, as things stand, is little used, so that he will be
far from evicted when it comes to it. 'It is a shock though,' he says, 'to
become aware of the idea of one's own absence.'

I don't respond to this last comment, thinking suddenly of my sec-
retary ordering me a box up from storage on the last day before my
sabbatical, and the embarrassment I'd felt when I saw the looks on the
faces of the security guards as I left that evening. And then I become
aware that Harry is speaking again and it seems that his topic of con-
versation has shifted to a discussion of various contemporaries of mine
with whom he is still in touch and I think, all at once, of the photo-
graph of Anthony sitting beside Rachel in her car, the one that was
attached to the parking ticket I'd found just before leaving London.

'I never heard from Anthony, you know, nor Cissy, after Rachel
died,' I say when Harry asks me who I am in touch with from among
my peers. 'I don't suppose I had any reason to be surprised, not really,
but I was. I mean, neither of them showed up for the memorial, that
was one thing. Or at least, I don't think they did. I saw someone who
I thought looked a bit like Anthony. He came in alone, after the start,
and stood right at the back. I couldn't see him afterwards though, he
must have gone straight away. But it can't have been can it? He would
have said something to me, don't you think?'

And then I realise that Harry is saying nothing. When I stop and
wait for a reply, he only shrugs his shoulders in response. I have no
idea what he means by this gesture and it occurs to me that I might as
well be talking to myself, but still I persist, saying that I hadn't even
had so much as a letter from either one of them, and didn't that strike
him as strange?

The silence I am met with again makes me feel uncomfortable,
somehow, but I stumble on, asking Harry whether he himself had
heard anything. 'They were so close the three of them, weren't they,

Harry?' I ask him. 'You must have seen that, when you taught them?' And it is only then, finally, that he speaks, choosing his words so carefully that he almost pauses between each one.

'Theirs was a closeness that had about it the ephemeral quality that is, I think, evident in many such student liaisons, whatever their precise nature might be. But yes, I was a little surprised myself by their absence, and by their failure to communicate. On the other hand,' and he takes his glasses from his face and looks down at them in his lap, before pulling a case from his pocket and taking out a cloth and starting to clean them, 'people do drift apart, over time, don't you find?'

And I tell him then what Rachel had said to me that day in June, about having lost touch with them both after our second year, and I say yes, people do drift apart, of course they do, but that she'd seemed somehow bitter when she'd spoken of it, and that I'd never understood why, or known what lay behind it all, if anything. 'She never said,' I tell Harry, 'but it had seemed strange to me that they should go their separate ways like that, so suddenly.'

Harry cuts me off then, saying, 'I suppose it is being back here that has made you think of it, Alex, that is all. The directions our memories take us in are so easily swayed, are they not, by our surroundings?' He asks me instead about Richard, saying that he understands that he has been a good friend to me these last months, and I tell him about them moving to New York, and the fact that Lucinda is expecting twins, and that I will miss them when they are gone.

And then Harry changes tack again and we are speaking of Evie, and he asks me whether I have heard from her since her move to Tokyo, and did I know if she had made any progress in her negotiations with the Japanese government about the mess into which the restoration project had descended? I say that I haven't, but that she'd told me not to expect to for a while, not until after she had settled and established herself in the museum.

'But she was Rachel's godmother,' Harry says to me then, almost combatively. 'And Rachel had no other family.'

'"Ferociously busy" was the phrase she used,' is all I can think of to say by way of explanation, feeling somehow reluctant to be entirely open about quite how precarious my relationship with Evie actually is. 'I'm sure we'll be in touch before too long,' I carry on, not knowing how to tell Harry that we were never close, Evie and I, and that her relocation had made little difference to either of us in those terms, and that I had emailed asking how she was getting on, but when she'd finally replied it had been in a way that hadn't invited any kind of a correspondence, nor had she returned any of the calls I had made to her since.

And then suddenly it seems that Harry has run out of questions, and I start to wonder when he is intending to give me the things of Rachel's that he'd found. I half expect that at any moment he will raise the question of the Browning again but he doesn't, and I think to myself that it is fair enough if he has decided to leave it to me to bring this up, given the way I'd responded to his enquiry the day before. In the absence of this, there seems to be little else to speak of, and our tea having been drunk, I am not surprised when Harry gets to his feet and says that he will see me later on for drinks before dinner.

I stand also and I pat about in my pockets to make sure I have my key. 'I lost it this morning,' I say, and for no other reason than to fill the silence I tell him about it falling into the snow and disappearing without trace and how the porter had insisted on our searching for it before he would give me a spare. I told him about the conversation we'd had afterwards, and how the man had told me about his father doing the job before him, and about how, as a boy from St Barnabas, he had imagined he was entering Narnia when he'd come through the gate and seen the playing fields for the first time. And then Harry did as I had and questioned his description, saying that the view the porter would have seen first on coming into College would have been

of the quad, not of the playing fields, and that he must have been mistaken in his recollection. I start to explain but he interrupts me. 'He was very young at the time,' he says, looking at his pocket watch again. 'Childhood is another country, Alex, and we are none of us as clear in our memories as we like to think.' But then I tell him what the porter had said when I'd questioned him, and I describe for Harry the old gate, forgotten since the paths were rerouted years ago, overgrown and unused and completely hidden now.

Harry lets go his hold on the door and it swings shut again and he goes over to the armchair and sinks into it, sighing as he does so an almost guttural sigh, as though it has come right from the depths of his stomach. He brings his hands together as if in prayer and he holds them up so that his chin comes to rest on the tips of his fingers and he closes his eyes.

'Harry,' I say, but he doesn't seem to hear me. 'Harry,' I say again, and I am about to ask him what is the matter when he speaks, almost too quietly for me to hear him.

'So. That is how.'

And then he is silent again, for at least a minute or two, until he opens his eyes and says, looking not at me but at the floor, 'I wasn't sure.' He gets up from the chair and walks over to the window and looks across to the other side of the quad, to Haddon's secret garden and the trees beyond, and then, his back still turned, says, 'Six forty-five, Alex. Do be on time.' I go to let myself out, and as the door closes behind me I think I hear him say to himself, 'Of course. I had forgotten.'

12

The gathering in the Old Bursary for drinks before dinner was no different from the night before in that Harry and I barely spoke, he was so busy about his work. When we went into Hall I found that he had arranged the seating plan so that I was some way down the table from him, and whilst I managed to catch him over coffee afterwards, it was only for a moment. He told me straight away that he had been called unexpectedly to London the next day, and I might like to consider a walk on Boars Hill, or in Wytham Woods, which would be quite magical in the snow. And then he said that there was always Evie's collection of inrō to be looked at in the Ashmolean should I find it too cold for walking. He couldn't be sure he'd be back in time for dinner, he said, but that shouldn't stop me from going to Hall; he would see to it that I was expected.

I got up early to make a start on one of the walks Harry had suggested, and I went to the lodge after breakfast to ask for a map. The porter said yes, of course, but just as he was reaching up to the shelf behind him, the phone began to ring. As he took the call I looked

around me at the pigeonholes that lined the walls of the lodge, amazed to see that nothing, as far as I could tell, had changed since the time when one of them bore my name. It seemed that the call the porter had taken wouldn't be a short one, so I started then to flick through the books on the counter in front of me. Eventually I found myself looking at the Old Members' Visitors Book that I'd signed when I'd arrived, and turned the page to see if anyone else had come since then. They hadn't, so I looked back to the week before and read down the list. There was someone from Nepal, who from his date of matricu-lation seemed to be in his early eighties, and another name, a Ger-man one, and that was all. And then, while the porter was still on the phone, I flicked back through until I found it: 21 June 2007, the night of Rachel's murder. The page fell open easily and I saw that there were crosses in pencil beside each name, written down the left-hand side. There we were, Rachel and I, partway down the list, and I felt sick as I read in her hand this record of our visit: 'Mr and Mrs Alexander Petersen, London N1, 1992'.

Rachel had never actually taken my name but she did this some-times, for a joke, this calling herself Mrs Alexander Petersen, and I remembered her laughing that evening as she'd written it, and I remembered our holding hands as we'd walked from the lodge and gone over to Harry's rooms before dinner. I looked down the rest of the list and saw the name of the American woman I'd ended up sit-ting beside that evening, her home town listed just as NY, NY, USA. There were other names, and other countries, and as I read them all, each of the people I'd met that night had come back to me in a vague sort of a way. And then I saw a name that had nothing written beside it in the address column, and nor did it have a note of the year of matriculation. I noticed also that the name was written in pencil, and that it had two crosses beside it rather than one. I had read it again, 'B. Volio, Esq.', and was wondering what kind of a name Volio was, when I realised the porter was holding out a map and telling me the bus

number for Wytham. I shut the book and took the map and thanked him, putting on my gloves and leaving the lodge.

I walked first across Boars Hill that day, turning back to see the city spread out beneath me, and then I made my way to Cumnor and over to Wytham. The woods were as magical as Harry had said they would be, and this time I really did seem to be entirely alone. I walked for half an hour or so, soaking up the quietness and wondering about Harry and what it was that had taken him so suddenly to London, and as I did it occurred to me that if I had been made to feel comfortable on the day of my arrival, when he had welcomed me into his rooms and my nerves had dissolved almost immediately, it was only on account of the warmth of his fire and the kindness I had inferred from the simplest of things, like the way he had poured me my tea. Any sense of rapport between us had gone utterly by the end of that first meeting, when we had spoken so awkwardly about the Browning and he had reminded me about his own grief. It was entirely possible, I supposed, that the awkwardness had lingered into our second meeting, and that was what lay behind the sense of discomfort I felt now. That, and the fact that I'd had on my mind from the moment I arrived in Oxford the parking ticket I'd found just before I'd left London, and the question of why Rachel might have been lying to me about being in touch with Anthony, and what Evie was doing getting into the car with them. But it struck me that there was more to it than either of those things: I could not make Harry out, and it was becoming less and less clear why exactly he'd invited me, it being obvious that he was in no hurry to divest himself of the things he had of Rachel's, the things he'd said he would give me.

The previous day's discourse had been shot through, for my part, with a sense that I was being led by the hand through a series of quite pointless conversations. I began to wonder whether perhaps my visit was something he had conceived of entirely for his own benefit, because he was lonely and wanted to carry out some kind of mourn-

ing ritual for Rachel, in the same way that he'd begun to send me post-cards after her death simply because he could no longer send them to her. But there was something odder about it than that, this need he had to be involved still. As I walked on, I wondered why he'd been quite so interested in my relationship with Evie, and it occurred to me that I should perhaps have asked some questions of him in return: how it was that he knew about her move to Tokyo, and about the work she was doing there, and why he was suggesting that I go to see her inrō. Such was my unease about the way the conversation had gone, and my embarrassment about Evie and I getting on so badly, on top of the confusion I had felt when I'd asked question after question about Anthony only to be met with a complete lack of responsiveness from Harry, that when it came to the end of our meeting I'd neglected to ask him about how he'd come to have Rachel's book in his possession, feeling pressurised instead to justify myself for not having read it.

I was looking up at the canopy formed by the branches above my head, hearing only the steady tread of my boots and thinking of how Harry had reacted so strangely to what I'd said about the old gate at the bottom of the playing fields, when I stumbled suddenly and fell, landing awkwardly on my right shoulder. I picked myself up and brushed myself off, and when I looked back to see what it was that I had tripped on, I saw the body of a woodpigeon lying right in the mid-dle of the path, mangled and bloody and red against the snow.

I had seen a bird fallen in the snow once before, when I was a child. It happened right at the beginning of my first Christmas holiday home from school. After lunch one day, having decorated the tree together, my mother and I went through to the kitchen to make some scones for our tea. We'd put them in the oven and set the timer and their scent was already seeping out around us. I stood on a chair at her side so that I could reach the sink and we did the washing-up together, and then she swept the flour from the floor where I had spilt it. After that she took off her apron and told me that she had to make a phone call,

and that I mustn't listen. I asked her why not and she held my face in both her hands and said, 'I have to talk to Daddy. It's just a conversation for grown-ups, that's all.' And she kissed me and I ran and put on my boots and my scarf and I went outside and wished that Robbie was there to see the snow. I ran round to the back of the house and started to throw snowballs against the wall. I was beginning to become bored, and a little too cold, when suddenly, without any warning whatsoever, a bird hurled itself from out of the sky just above my head and flew directly into the wall of the house. I watched, amazed, as it fell straight and heavy to the ground. I looked in through the sitting room window and I saw my mother sitting in her armchair, holding the phone to her ear and talking to my father.

She had already told me that he wouldn't be coming home for Christmas, and that it would just be the two of us, so I thought to myself that perhaps they were discussing what he wanted her to give me as a present from him. I looked across to where the bird had fallen and I wanted at that moment to run in and tell her what I had seen, and to describe for her the speed with which the bird had appeared, as if from nowhere, or as though somebody had been standing behind me and had thrown it against the wall, straight into the hardness of the brick. And I wanted to ask her why the bird had done such a thing, but I knew she would be cross if I did this while she was still having her conversation with my father. So instead I walked over to the bird and knelt down to look at it. It was trembling slightly, no more than tiny shudders really, and blood was seeping slowly from its broken neck, melting out a circular hollow from the snow and collecting there, a little steaming pool of redness. And suddenly I began to cry and I got up and ran inside to my mother and when she saw me she put down the telephone and started shouting at me. I was so surprised I stopped crying immediately and I heard her say that she had told me not to listen, she had known it would only upset me, and couldn't I just have waited and did I have any idea how difficult the decision

had been, and then she told me to go to my room immediately and not to come down until supper time. So I turned and ran upstairs and I climbed under my bedclothes and closed my eyes. I thought about the scones and wondered whether they were still in the oven and whether she would remember them, and I thought about how nice it would have been if she had cut one of them open for me while it was still warm and how she would have turned to ask me if I would rather have jam or honey. I wrapped my arms about myself and began to cry again, imagining the bird lying outside in the snow and wondering whether, if only I had picked it up and brought it inside, my mother would have known that I hadn't been listening to her conversation, and then I thought about whether we could perhaps have bathed it and bandaged it and put it into the bottom of the Aga and that if we had, it might have come back to life.

Standing in Wytham Woods that afternoon I looked down at the woodpigeon that had fallen in my path and I nudged it with the toe of my boot. It had frozen solid where it lay. I kicked it once, and then again, harder the second time, so that it lifted into the air and landed some way away, in amongst the trees. And then I walked on and out of the woods as fast as I was able to.

I went straight to the Ashmolean when I got back. Apart from the shop, which was full of people buying Christmas cards, the museum was almost empty. Evie's inrō were strung out in a line of glass cabinets on the second floor. Each of the tiny laquered boxes hung from a string or a short length of rope that would originally have been tied onto the sash of a kimono. Gold, or red, or both of these and black, every one was a different shape, some of them taking the form of an animal, a tortoise or a tiny rabbit, and none of them bigger than a cigarette case or a tin of travel sweets. I read on the display boards that the collection had come almost as a whole, its original owners

an Edwardian couple who, honeymooning in Japan, had purchased one after another of these little caskets as souvenirs and brought them home to England.

Rachel had told me about Evie's work during the summer vacation of our second year. We were halfway round the lake on one of our evening strolls when, trying to think of a topic of conversation that would keep her talking, I asked her whether her godmother was an Italian art dealer or a dealer in Italian art. She laughed and said, 'She's English, Alex. And it's Japanese stuff, not Italian. And she's a curator, not a dealer. There's a difference you know. There's nothing remotely commercial about what she does. She's an academic basically, if you really are interested. She's got one post in London and another in Oxford. Where do you get your information from anyway?' I told her that lots of the stories I heard about Evie, and about Rachel herself, came from Towneley, via Richard, and she stopped laughing then and said that I shouldn't listen to a word Towneley said about anyone, not ever, and especially not about her. I realised I'd said completely the wrong thing and, keen to get her talking again, I asked her what exactly a curator did, and whether it meant that Evie looked after things. 'I wouldn't say looking after, no,' Rachel said. 'That's not Evie's bag, looking after things. More like preserving things. Keeping things as they are. Wrapping them up and hiding them and making sure they'll never change.' 'Tell me about Japanese art,' I said, glad that I seemed to have retrieved the situation a little. 'It's not art really, Evie's stuff,' Rachel said. 'I mean it's not paintings. It's lacquerware. Boxes. Chests. Caskets. Things to keep secrets in.' But then she said 'Jesus Alex she's so boring why do you want to know about her anyway? Can't we talk about something other than my bloody godmother?'

Standing there that afternoon in the Ashmolean, looking at the inrō hanging in a line in front of me, I remembered the time I'd found some of them on the mantelpiece of the bedroom Rachel and I had slept in when we'd stayed in Evie's house at Chelsea. Harry had

described them to me as 'Evie's inrō' only because she had procured them on the museum's behalf, and overseen their restoration, but she'd purchased some of them for herself and the Chelsea house was where she kept them. We'd visited her there only once, when she'd given a party on the Boxing Day after we were married. She'd asked us to help her prepare for it, saying that it was the least we could do given that it was in our honour that it was happening, and whilst the two of us agreed that this was slightly absurd, since neither of us had ever met a single one of the people she'd invited, we turned up in the afternoon anyway. There wasn't much for me to do when it came to it: whilst Rachel and Evie were in the kitchen, cooking and talking and writing place cards, I was sent to pick up the wine. When I came back they said they didn't need me, so I went upstairs to the sitting room I'd seen earlier, intending to read the paper. I think I fell asleep in my chair fairly quickly, and when I woke later on and went downstairs I found a note on the kitchen table saying that everything was ready and they'd gone for a walk, they wouldn't be long.

Finding myself alone I wandered through the rooms, toying with the idea that I would come across something interesting about Evie that I could share with Rachel on the way home, thinking I might impress her with my detective work. As it turned out, there was very little to be discovered. The whole place was immaculate and furnished sparely. It was almost as though nobody actually lived there, so little was there to be seen of a personal nature. Most of the furniture was in a Japanese style, and the walls were either covered in screen prints, or simply left bare in a cold sort of a white. There were thick rugs stretched across polished wooden floors, and I was beginning to think the house was improbably anonymous when I came to the bathroom and opened the cabinet and found a packet of contraceptive pills, almost finished. I don't know why this should have surprised me but it did, and I wondered who Evie was sleeping with, and whether we'd meet him that night. And then I heard the key

turning in the front door so I closed the cabinet and stepped out of the bathroom, slipping down the stairs just before Rachel and Evie came in from the street.

When the evening was over we helped Evie clear everything away and we put the room back to how it had been before we started. Evie and I were standing in the hall, waiting for Rachel to come back downstairs with our coats, when she said we may as well stay if we wanted to, and that Rachel's old room was all made up as it always was, just in case anyone came. It seemed a perfectly sensible suggestion to me so I said yes, why not, given that it was so late and we had no plans for the following day. 'Fine,' was all Rachel said when she came back downstairs and I told her what had been agreed. And when she turned then and went upstairs without saying another word, I followed her. Having drunk more than I should have done over dinner, and being fairly shattered from the deal I'd closed on Christmas Eve, I fell asleep almost immediately. Rachel, on the other hand, couldn't sleep, turning and turning so much that eventually she woke me up. I groaned at her I think, and she said she couldn't help it, she could never sleep in Evie's house, and that if I'd even so much as asked her whether she actually wanted to stay there she would have told me that. Eventually she said she'd get up and go downstairs if she was keeping me awake, but after she'd gone I couldn't get back to sleep again. The room was slightly too hot, and the hangover I would have for the whole of the next day was already beginning to make itself felt. I went to the bathroom for a glass of water and when I came back I opened the curtains and pulled up the window and stood looking out, wondering if I should go downstairs and tell Rachel to come back up so that we could console one another in our sleeplessness.

I didn't in the end, walking over to the mantelpiece instead and seeing the inrō that had been placed there. There were three of them, all in a line and quite beautiful in the beam of the street light that fell on them. I picked one of them up meaning simply to feel the weight of

it, sensing somehow that I shouldn't be, Rachel having told me when we'd put our coats in the room that afternoon how valuable they were. But there it was in front of me, and there I was on my own and in the half-light. As I turned it over in my hand there was a rattle and I felt something moving about inside. I put it down and picked up the next one and did the same thing. This time there was no rattle, but instead, the soft and almost imperceptible thud of something shifting against the sides of the casket. I wasn't surprised to feel that there was something inside the third one as well; it was lighter, and scratchier somehow, but there was certainly something there.

Suddenly feeling wide awake, I picked up all three of the inrō and took them back over to the bed. I sat with my legs crossed under the covers and lined them up in front of me, trying to decide which one to open first. I stayed still and listened for a while, in case Rachel was coming upstairs again, but when all I heard was the ticking of the clock in the hall I turned back to my task. I was bored I suppose; bored and still a little drunk. And so, having picked up the first one and shaken it again, hearing whatever was inside rattling like tiny dice against its sides, I opened it and tipped it upside down, emptying the contents into the palm of my hand. I couldn't quite make out what it was that I was looking at at first, so tiny were they, so I closed my hand into a fist to make sure I didn't lose any of them and I stretched over to switch on the bedside lamp, feeling them pressing sharp against my palm as I did so and wondering whether perhaps I had happened upon a stash of rough-cut diamonds. When I unfurled my hand I saw that it wasn't diamonds I was holding but teeth. They were tiny, the teeth of a child, and there were perhaps six or seven of them nestling there. The sharp points that I'd felt as I squeezed them were the little roots of the things, and as I held them up closer, moving the lamp so that it shone on them, I saw that there were a few small pieces of flesh still attached to them, darkened with time and grown hard where they clung to the bone. I stared at

them, thinking of tooth fairies and five-pence pieces and the fact that when I was a child, I had never even thought to wonder about what had happened to the teeth that were taken from under my pillow at night by my mother, or by Matron, but that I was quite sure I had never seen them again.

Hearing what sounded like a floorboard creaking outside my door, I cupped my palm and poured the teeth back into their casket and quickly pulled the covers over all three of the inrō. But it was nothing, I had imagined it, and so I took them all out again and picked up the second one, shaking it gently and hearing something shift lightly against the sides. I opened it with slightly less enthusiasm than I had the first, uncertain now whether I actually wanted to know what was in it. I brought the lamp closer and tipped up the casket and what fell out was a lock of hair, thick and dark and shiny, tied with a little velvet ribbon attaching a tiny label, yellowing with age. I stroked the hair with my fingers and found it to be soft, and I turned the label over and saw the initials, in thick black ink, R.C., and a date, September 1981. I brought the lock of hair to my face and inhaled its scent, and after that I held it against my mouth, feeling it silky against my lips, and I wondered what Rachel would have looked like as a child.

The contents of the last of the inrō was perhaps the most intriguing, if only because I was interrupted before I'd finished looking at it properly. I held the casket upside down and shook it but whatever was inside became caught, so I reached in two of my fingers. What I pulled out was a piece of paper, folded and folded so it would fit. I could sense its age as soon as I began to unfold it, and the fact that the ink had faded and the handwriting was rambling and uneven meant it was quite difficult to make out the script I found myself looking at. I got up and took my glasses from my jacket pocket and sat back down on the edge of the bed, holding the piece of paper right up under the lamp and beginning to read as best as I could.

Iona, June 21, 1981

My darling Rachel,

I know this last month has been so very difficult for you, and so very sad. Before Daddy died he asked me to tell you as often as I could, and always, how very much he loved you. You were his only little girl, his best lady, that's what he always said, and I sometimes even thought he loved you more than me he spoke of you so often towards the end!

I am so sorry that I left when I did, but I have a need to be on my own, and in some wide open spaces. I hope you can understand. And I hope she is looking after you; I told her she had to. I'll be back soon my darling, I promise, and I ask only this of you: you must be strong for me when I return from this time away. I know you are little still, but you were Daddy's best lady and I'm only writing to you like this because I know you're grown up enough to understand what it is that I am asking of you.

Some of these nights on the island I have stayed awake until dawn thinking of you, and remembering when you were a tiny baby, and what it was like to hold you for the very first time. And I can only begin to fall asleep when I feel certain that I will come back to you soon and hold you in my arms—

And then there is the very definite sound of someone coming up the stairs, and fast, so I fold the letter up as best I can and slip it back inside its casket and run over to the mantelpiece and put them all back in what I think is the right order and I am jumping back into bed again just as Rachel opens the door. 'Alex what are you doing? You're awake! You've got the lamp on and the window open and it's freezing in here! Why didn't you come and get me if you weren't sleeping either? You're such a weirdo do you know that?' And she switches off the lamp and pulls the curtain across and climbs into bed and I

hold her and tell her I was too hot, and that I'd only just woken up that minute, and I'd needed some air, and I start to stroke her head where it rests on my chest and soon she has fallen asleep and I think about the letter and wonder what the rest of it said. I knew by then, of course, about Rachel's father's illness, and about how her mother had gone away to Iona for the whole of the summer that followed, leaving Rachel in London with Evie, and that she'd returned in the September only to go to Oxford Street on her first morning back and walk straight under a bus, and that the inquest had returned an open verdict. But having told me the bare facts once when I'd asked her, Rachel wouldn't talk about it again, saying she'd rather not, and that there were some things it wasn't necessary to discuss, and that if I couldn't handle that I could just walk away there and then.

And then I fell asleep as well, wishing as I drifted off that she could talk to me about those things, and thinking that if she would let me I might perhaps be able to help her, or to comfort her in her sadness.

Harry, as he had anticipated, didn't make an appearance at dinner that night, and when I went to the porter's lodge the next morning I found he'd left me a note apologising for his absence and saying he'd be pleased to see me for tea at the usual time. In the afternoon, he welcomed me in and took my jacket and I sat back in my chair and said nothing, thinking he might begin by offering some sort of explanation for his trip to London, but he only asked me how I had spent the previous day. It wasn't until after I'd told him about my walk in the woods at Wytham, and the Ashmolean, that he made any reference to it, and even then it was only in passing. He told me he'd got back early enough to make it to dinner, but only just, and that because he tended to find the journey tiring these days, he'd ordered a quiet supper in his rooms. He'd spent the evening alone, sorting through some of his things and continuing the slow process of deciding what he would keep and what he would let go when it came to his retirement.

He gestures then to a stack of pictures resting in their frames

against the sofa, saying that the cataloguing of his collection is something he is actually quite enjoying. He reaches forward and takes one from the top of the pile and passes it to me. The photograph I am looking at is about half a foot square and printed in black and white. There is a boy in this photograph, a small boy of no more than eight or nine years old. He is standing in front of one of the lions on Trafalgar Square and is wearing a winter coat and a scarf. He is flanked by two adults, each of them clasping one of his hands so that they are strung out in a line like figures cut from folded paper. The photograph is slightly faded, and from the way the three of them are dressed it appears to have been taken some time in the 1950s. The boy is wearing glasses, and when I look up at Harry and see that he has brought his glasses back down from his forehead, I realise that the photograph is of him. 'These are your parents?' I ask, and he says yes, and he tells me that what I am holding is the only picture he has of them, and how relieved he was to have come across the negative when sorting through the contents of their house after his mother's death. 'Until I found it I had to make do with my memory of the day. It was vivid enough, but it is good to see them there, all the same,' he says, and he tells me about the three of them catching the train from Hull and tracking the banks of the Humber, heading west towards Goole before swinging south, and what it was like to arrive in London and find themselves among crowds suddenly. And how they had stopped a policeman on Trafalgar Square who, having given them the directions they wanted, had offered to take their picture and suggested they stand in front of one of the lions, and hold hands, and how as he'd stood there he'd been quite sure that his father wouldn't have wanted to be photographed holding hands, not in public, and that it was only because it was the policeman's idea that he had allowed it.

He talks then about his childhood in Hessle, his mother's voice always singing, and how she had longed to become a pianist until her own mother had sold the piano one day, saying it took up too much

space in the drawing room, and that it was because she had never recovered from this dashing of her hopes that she hadn't let him learn a musical instrument, not wanting him to know what it was to experience something wonderful only to have it taken away. As he talks I stop listening properly, looking once more at the photograph that sits just to the left of Harry's head, the one of the group of students standing on the Provost's steps with Rachel in their midst, standing next to Harry, and it occurs to me that had I been in Harry's position, I am not entirely sure I would have left it hanging there, knowing that I was coming to visit. Or, to put it another way, had I done so, I might have acknowledged its presence by talking about it in detail or at least by making some reference to it, rather than simply leaving me to notice it for myself.

And then, as Harry talks on about the East Riding he had known as a boy, I remember him having told me over our tea that the reason he hadn't stayed on for what he called 'the Ball proper' was because he hadn't wanted to go alone, it being the year that his wife had died. My mind wanders again to the Ball, and to the fact I'd spent the whole of it with Richard. As far as I can remember, we'd made a fairly good night of it, the two of us together; I'd been almost happy as we wandered around in our drunkenness, feeling excited about the summer that was to come, and about being free from things for a time. I focus back in on Harry's voice for a moment, hearing him talk of how his father had taken him running at Little Switzerland as soon as he was old enough, and how, when Harry had started to compete, he'd been there to see him win every race, whatever the weather and no matter how far he had to drive to wherever it was taking place. More images of the Ball begin to flit in front of my eyes, one after the other, and it is as they do so that I realise that despite what he'd said about not having stayed on, I saw him later on that night, I am certain of it.

My realisation is, I think, prompted by my recollection of Richard having made a joke about what he was wearing, something about him

being so much of a 'Yorkshire tight-wad' that he hadn't even stretched to black tie. I can't remember with any clarity the visual context in which I'd seen Harry, not at that stage. I remember Richard's joke though, probably because I'd thought to myself that Richard himself was far more obsessed with money than any Yorkshireman I'd ever met, and I'd said so, and we'd ended up arguing about it. In any case, I know Harry was there, and I can't think why he would have told me so specifically that he wasn't, it hardly being likely he'd have forgotten a night like that, particularly given the photograph that must have been hanging on his wall for at least the previous decade.

I begin to tune back in to the pattern of his speech, intending to take the next opportunity that arises to interject and ask him again about the Ball, wondering whether perhaps I've misunderstood him, but being almost certain at the same time that I haven't, when I become aware that he has stopped talking altogether and is staring right at me.

'Alex?' he says, and I realise he has asked me a question. 'You must forgive me if I'm being intrusive,' he continues. 'And you need not speak of it if it will distress you to do so.' I smile, not having any idea what he's talking about, and he is encouraged by this and carries on. 'I heard of his death at the time of course, but I didn't know you then, not in the sense that I do now. Not, at any rate, well enough to write and offer my condolences, if you understand. It was about five years ago, I think?'

When I understand that he is talking about my father I am caught off guard and I start to tell him about the shock of it, and how at first I had wondered whether perhaps he shouldn't have been driving at his age, but that when it came to it, his innocence was proved beyond doubt. I start to tell Harry about the funeral, and how it rained throughout, but I stop when I get to the part about standing at the graveside under my umbrella afterwards thinking I was alone only to look up and see that a handful of people had gathered at the side of the church. It took me some time to work out who they were but eventu-

ally I recognised one of them, and then another, and realised they had been neighbours of ours from the village at the time of the accident, and that they'd come to watch the burial of Dr Death, as they'd sometimes referred to him in the years that followed when they thought neither my mother nor I was listening. Remembering the humiliation I felt the first time I overheard them calling my father this, knowing it wasn't true, and knowing how angry it would have made him if he'd heard them himself, I get no further than that with the telling of my story, finding it is too much, after all, to talk of it.

'We live by death's negligence,' Harry says, mistaking my sudden silence for grief rather than shame. '"Men may rise on stepping-stones of their dead selves to higher things,"' he continues, '"But who shall so forecast the years and find in a loss a gain to match?"' I become aware that I am beginning to feel slightly sick, and uncomfortably hot. Because I want him to stop talking, I smile and thank him, and I say that I would like to go back to my room.

'Of course, Alex,' he says, standing with me. 'Of course, I am sorry. And there is no need to thank me for the things I said; they are not my words. But there is consolation in them, I think, of a kind. You are right though, perhaps we have spoken enough for today. I am sorry if I touched on a subject I should not have done.'

'No,' I say, 'of course not,' and I turn to leave, but as I do my eye is caught by Rachel's face looking out at me from the photograph on Harry's wall. Without meaning to, I hesitate just long enough for him to notice me looking at her, and then I say to him, quite simply, that I remember having seen him that night, long after the Ball had started.

He takes off his glasses and begins to clean them, and I think it is the way he performs this ritual, methodically, slowly, carefully, showing no apparent intention of responding to what I've just said, that makes me lose patience. I look once more at Rachel staring back at me, and decide I've had enough of waiting, and that it's time, finally, to talk about the little book of Browning.

'Of course,' I say. 'I almost forgot. I've read the poems you asked me to.'

'Good,' he says quickly, not looking up from what he's doing. 'And how did you find them?'

'I'm sorry?'

'I said how did you find them?'

When I don't answer he glances up, but only briefly, and I can read nothing in his face before he lowers it again.

'It was the book itself that interested me, Harry, in actual fact, rather than its contents.'

'Yes?' he says, his head still lowered to his task.

'You said in your letter you'd found it among some things of Rachel's.'

Only then does he stop, putting his glasses back on and looking at me.

'And?'

'And I have a question for you,' I reply, sitting down again and leaning right back in my chair, resuming only when he sits down as well. 'It's just that she was reading it, that's all, the month we came to visit you. I remember the cover you see. And the smell. She read to me from it, as a matter of fact, one night in our apartment. So when I opened the parcel you sent I recognised it straight away.'

'Right,' Harry says. 'I'm not quite sure I—'

'I know it's the same book, Harry. I know it is. But what I don't know is this. When exactly did you take it from her?'

I can see his jaw clenching and unclenching as he looks at me but he doesn't answer.

'You see, I don't remember her being away from me that day we came to Oxford. Apart from when she went down to the lake after dinner. You will understand my difficulty, I think.'

'Yes, Alex, I do.'

He is silent then for at least a minute, and when eventually he

speaks, it isn't to answer my question, but to say instead, 'I believe the time has come for us to have that conversation.'

'What conversation? We don't need to have a conversation. You just need to tell me. When did you take it from her?'

'It's not quite so straightforward, Alex. You see—'

'Oh come on, Harry. I think it is. Was it before she died?'

'Alex. Please,' and he stands again, suddenly, folding his arms in front of himself. 'There are some things I have to tell you. Lots of things in fact. But before I can begin, I'm afraid there is more reading to be done.'

And then, to my amazement, he reaches over and takes something from the bookshelf and hands it to me, saying, 'Tomorrow afternoon then, Alex. It's late now, and dinner this evening will be the usual sort of affair so we shan't have a chance to speak. Perhaps you could come a little earlier for tea tomorrow though, so we have plenty of time. Two o'clock, I think.'

I look down and see that what he has given me is a large padded envelope, taped up around the top and with something heavy inside. 'I'm sorry, Harry,' I say, incredulous at his suggestion. 'You don't seem to understand what I mean, not exactly.' I know that my voice is shaking, but I know also that I can't control my breathing enough to make it stop, and when I try to give the envelope back to him he shakes his head and doesn't take it.

'What, Alex?' he asks. 'What is it that I don't understand?'

'Why did you ask me to come here, Harry? Why won't you answer my question about the bloody book? Why did you say you found it among her things?'

'Alex—'

'What things, Harry? I know you lied to me in that letter. Do you seriously think I'm going to sit through dinner again making small talk with virtual strangers while you decide how to answer me?'

'Alex,' he says again. 'I think it is you, if I may say so, who has not

entirely understood the situation. The decision of how I am going to answer your question was one I took a long time ago. I have simply been waiting until you asked it. And now that you have, there are a few more things you must see before I begin my story, that is all. I am trying to give you the best chance of comprehending the sequence of events I will describe. It's important, Alex, that things are revealed to you in the right order, so you may see them as I have done.'

Feeling that I'm completely losing control of the situation, I hear myself telling him I'm finding his approach at best bizarre, and at worst deeply disrespectful to Rachel, and then I feel a resurgence in my stomach of the nausea that has been always there since the moment I discovered, sitting on the ground beside the policeman who would arrest me, that she was dead.

'Are we not beyond that point, Harry?' I ask him. 'Are we not beyond it yet?'

'What point is that, Alex? Are we not beyond what point?' and I see that he is angry also, at the same time as appearing to be genuinely confused by my question.

'Beyond the point of discussing the relative merits of one narrative structure over another. For god's sake, Harry, don't you see? Rachel's death was the end of a life, not the beginning of a fucking story.'

And then Harry looks at his pocket watch and walks over to the door, shaking his head as he goes. When he gets there and turns to face me it takes him a moment or two to catch his breath before he speaks.

'You are right, Alex, of course you are. And I am sorry for you in your loss, you must know that by now. It's just that the particular story I have to tell you is one that began a long time before Rachel died, a very long time in fact. And no matter how angry you feel, you must accept that I can say no more until you have read the things I've given you. It is best that you do so alone, and at your own pace.' And he sighs. 'Do not doubt the loss I suffered on the night that Rachel died. She was as a daughter to me, your wife.'

And then he reaches forward and holds the door open before saying, his voice grown quiet now, 'I very much hope that will be something you come to see for yourself when you hear the things that I will speak of.'

I think it was because I was so surprised by what he'd just said, and because I was too bewildered to argue any more, that I did as he asked and went away. When I left his room I was holding against my chest the envelope that he'd given me, and as I walked down his staircase I heard him call out, 'Six forty-five this evening then, as usual. Goodbye, Alex. And do make sure you find the time to read its contents before you go to sleep tonight. All of it. It is important that you do so.'

'I'll take you through to your father, sir,' the nurse said. 'I am so sorry we couldn't. It was too late sir. It was twice in the air ambulance. It was a helicopter. It was the fastest they could have got him here. Twice they tried, and then on the table. His heart.'

I stopped her then and said there was no need to explain, that a doctor had taken me into a side room as soon as I'd arrived and told me everything there was to tell about my father's death.

And this is what I would have told Harry when he'd asked me about it, if I'd been able to; this was the scene that came back to me as I walked away from his room that afternoon.

I would have told him that the doctor was almost as old as my father had been, and that he'd sat right back in his chair and kept his arms folded all the way through our conversation, as though he was afraid I might cry, or reach out to touch him, if he were to do otherwise. I heard very little of what he said to me, this doctor, my thoughts drifting instead to the helicopter rising above the fields of Hampshire and backing away towards Portsmouth. I imagined the pilot glancing down and seeing a line of traffic stretching out beneath him, and I imagined the police becoming smaller and smaller until they were

indistinguishable from anybody else, their cars like any other but for their position pointing inwards in a ring around the burnt mess of my father's car. And I realised then that there would have been nobody in the helicopter that afternoon who actually knew my father, who could have held his hand in theirs and recognised the weight of it, the particular softness of his knuckles against their skin and the warmth of it where it lay. And nor would there have been anyone to miss him when he hadn't come home for lunch that day, or anyone to wonder where he was. No one who would even have known that he was driving that way, on his own, with nothing in the car but the bag of potatoes he'd just picked up from the farm shop.

As soon as my secretary had finally summoned up the courage to interrupt my meeting and to announce that the transport police had telephoned three times in the previous hour, I called them straight back and was told there had been an accident. When I said it would take me at least two hours to get there, no matter how fast I drove, they said not to hurry, and that the doctors would wait for me. And then they said it again. They would wait until I got there. 'Don't worry, sir. They can do that for you.' I made the mistake of assuming this meant he would still be alive when I arrived, and it wasn't until later on that afternoon that I discovered my father had died just after I'd set off on my journey. The doctor explained that sometimes they said this to people who were driving to the bedside of a dying relative. 'It's safer that way,' he said. 'Nobody rushes if we tell them that; nobody drives too fast.'

He would never have known what had happened to him, the doctor said. He could never have survived. He became unconscious almost on impact. Seconds, only. No more than that. It was almost certain that he wouldn't have felt any kind of pain. 'Often the best way,' he said. And then he was up, and out of his seat, and grabbing my hand on his way out and shaking it, too hard, too fast.

And because I hadn't got there any sooner, there was nobody there

with my father when they switched off the machines and detached him from every kind of wire and drip and sack of fluid hanging from a stand and cleared away the blood such as they could and covered him in a blanket, a cotton blanket, white, with little holes all over it, the kind of blanket you might expect to see a baby in except it was big enough to cover the whole of his body, leaving him there, lying on a metal bed, quite on his own, right in the middle of the room.

Which is how I find him when the nurse has walked me along the empty corridors for what seems like an age, all the time staying just ahead of me and turning back to speak, the rubber soles of her shoes squeaking with every step like the laughter of children who know they shouldn't be laughing. At first I can't get into the room she's taken me to. There are screens placed in front of the door, screens of fabric stretched across a metal frame, hinged into separate panels on top of wheeled feet. She directs me to step behind them. 'You'll find your way, sir. Behind there. That's it.' But the space is too narrow for me to turn in and, from where I am standing, I can't get sufficient purchase on the handle of the door to open it. By the time she has stepped forward and wheeled away the screens so I can reach the door handle properly, my hands are shaking so much that she has to do it for me. I think she will come in with me but instead she closes the door behind me and we are alone together, my father and I. The lights have been switched off, and I look across to where he lies and as I see the familiar shape of him rising still under the blanket the room and everything in it disappears suddenly and for a second or two I can see nothing, only whiteness, and there is a kind of a roaring in my ears. When I can see again, I find that I am standing beside him and I have taken his hand from underneath the blanket and am holding it in my own. I look down at his face and see that the whole of his head has been strapped into some kind of a brace, giant screws on either side clamping his jaw together more tightly than it should be so that he looks as though he has been tortured rather than cared for. I place his hand on his chest

and walk around to the other side of the bed and when I get there I remember the nurse telling me that it would perhaps be best if I didn't look at that part of his head.

I am ashamed to say that I walked away from him then, over to the other side of the room, and I was sick into the sink that I found there and I ran the tap and washed it away and I didn't tell the nurse later on that I'd done it. And then I went back to my father, on the other side this time, and I held his hand again and I realised that the reason his face was the colour of cold ash was because he had not one drop of blood left in him. His hand was too cold, and too heavy, and I leaned over his body and laid my head on his chest and I longed for it to rise and fall but it didn't so I lifted up my head and kissed him once, on his forehead, and then I said goodbye.

The thing that seemed cruellest as I stood with him that afternoon was the violence of his injuries. They told me a week or so later that his neck had been broken and his skull fractured in twenty places. Six of his ribs had been smashed, and all the bones of both his arms had been rendered into pieces. Technically, his death had occurred when his heart stopped for the third time, with the shock of it, but there was never any chance, they said, not from the moment of impact. It seemed somehow unfair that a man as gentle as my father once had been should ever have known what it was to have suffered such violence himself.

When I went back to the nurses' desk in the reception area I found the woman who had walked me to my father's room and I thanked her, and then I asked her to thank the doctors on my behalf for what they had done. She handed me a folder of leaflets on bereavement counselling, and lists and lists of the things I would have to do in the months ahead. She held my hands in hers and said 'I am so sorry,' and I thought we had finished and I would be able to leave without having shed so much as a single tear in front of anyone. But then at the last she said, 'Oh, and there's me almost forgetting to give you these,' and

she reached down beneath her desk and passed me a plastic bag. 'His shoes sir. And his watch and his wallet. There wasn't anything else.'

Before that summer, the one with Robbie and the medicine cabinet and our foolish game gone wrong, he would pick me up and run around the garden with me, hurling me up towards the sky and laughing as though something extraordinary had happened when all it was was that the last of his patients had left for the afternoon and he had come to find me in my room and taken me outside for what he called my Runaround. And sometimes we would throw a ball to one another and my mother would call from the sitting room not to hit the wisteria it had only just been planted and don't get him dirty it's not his bathnight tonight you know it's not. And then we would stop and he would go to the pub for his Justahalf, the drink he would never explain, the drink I knew I would choose as soon as I was old enough to go with him. And my mother would take me upstairs and wash the grass stains from my feet, and then she would put me to bed. And as I fell asleep on those cool summer nights, the windows open and a lamp burning in the corner of my room, I would sometimes hear my father's feet crunch across the gravel on the drive and he would laugh as he came in and my mother and he would fall to their supper, silently.

Sometimes, when he was with a patient, the sound of his laughter would drift from his consulting room. It would echo around the house in the quietness of the afternoon so that whatever I was doing, submerged under a pile of cushions on my bed reading a story, or lying on the floor of the playroom whittling a stick, or sitting at the kitchen table colouring in a picture, I would hear it and stop and wonder when it would be time for tea, or whether Robbie might come soon and ring on the bell and run with me into the garden to play.

And on one of those afternoons when Robbie had come, when

we were inside rather than out because it was raining, we were playing together in my bedroom, just above my father's consulting room, and because of that we could hear him quite clearly, on and off, as we played. 'Why does he laugh so much anyway?' Robbie asked me, pushing me off the window seat and jumping on top of me and punching me on my arm. 'Is it medicine do you think? Do you think he takes medicine or summink, your dad?' And that was how it had begun, this plan of ours, or of mine, I can never remember which of us it was who thought of it first: to take the key from my mother's bedside table while she had her afternoon sleep and to creep through the house past the door of his consulting room to the special room next to the pantry that I was on no account ever allowed to enter, and to unlock his dispensing cabinet and see if we could find it, this medicine, this medicine that might make Robbie laugh as much as my father did.

There was a moment in my mother's bedroom, just after Robbie and I had tiptoed to the head of her bed and he was leaning over to take the key, when I caught the scent of the night stocks from where they stood in a vase on her dressing table. As I did so, I remembered going into the garden with my father to watch him cut them, and how I had felt when we brought them in and my father had given them to her, and the look on her face, and I thought to myself then that we shouldn't be doing what we were doing, Robbie and I, because it would make her unhappy. But he had the key in his hand suddenly and we were running down the corridor and I could hardly breathe I was so excited and then it was too late.

Sometimes in my memory my father's laugh will sound still, suddenly, unexpectedly, incongruously, catching me unawares and stopping my breath in my chest and sending a pain sharp into the middle of my heart so that I think I might die with it. It was the kind of laugh that began as a chuckle and grew as his torso started to shake and grew

again as his head fell back so that he had to pause and say Ye Gods
Man and gasp two short breaths before starting all over again, slap-
ping his thigh and roaring with it, his face red and shiny with tears so
that my mother, if she was there, would start to laugh as well despite
the fact she always looked as though she didn't really want to, and she
would say Oh Love stop please, stop you're making my tummy ache.

14

I went back to my room and lay on my bed, drifting for a while between memories and dreams and the weight of them, and I woke with just enough time to get to the Old Bursary for drinks, so it wasn't until after dinner that I was able to turn to the parcel Harry had given me that afternoon. The meal had taken longer than usual and I'd stayed on afterwards for coffee only to find myself stuck in an interminable conversation with a visiting historian who was determined to talk about his research in more detail than I was really able to follow. I didn't manage to make my excuses until around half past eleven, when I went straight back to my room and sat at the desk. I peeled away the tape and pulled out what was inside and as soon as I saw it I realised it wasn't the first time I'd done so. It was a document wallet, in heavy black leather with zips around the sides. I opened it and looked at the first of the pieces of paper that I found there, and I remembered where I'd seen it before.

It was the one I'd found for Evie on the night I got back to my apartment after Rachel's murder, the one she'd asked me to courier to

her the next morning. That night, having listened to her phone mes-
sage, I'd tried Rachel's desk drawers only to discover they were locked
and then I'd looked again on the bookshelves and found that it had
been there all along. I'd unzipped it straight away of course, to see
what was inside. I don't think I formulated any particular opinion, at
the time, as to there being anything suspicious about what I was being
asked to do. It was Evie, after all. I was just curious, there was nothing
more to it than that, and so I'd opened it and leafed through the first
few pages of its contents. What I found there would have allayed even
the faintest sense of unease, had I felt anything of the sort. There was
nothing other than some old essays, that was all, and when I'd looked
at a few of them, and turned the page to find a reading list on Robert
Browning with Harry's name at the bottom of it, I'd zipped the wal-
let back up and made the call to the courier. That they were essays of
Rachel's from her Oxford days was clear enough; the overly bold hand
and the colour of the ink in which they'd been written suggested as
much, and if I needed any further confirmation, it was provided by
the dates at the top of each page and the presence of the initials 'R.C.'.
And so, assuming Evie wanted them as a keepsake of her goddaugh-
ter, I'd done as she asked and thought nothing further of it.

Sitting last month in a pool of lamplight in that little College
room, I took all of the papers out of the wallet and placed them on
the desk in front of me, realising there must be more to it than I'd
first assumed, and wondering how it had ended up in Harry's posses-
sion. At first, it really did seem to be just a pile of Rachel's old essays.
'"There she stands/ As if alive." (My Last Duchess). Examine Brown-
ing's perverseness.' was followed by one with a longer title strung
along the top: '"Love, you saw me gather men and women,/ Live or
dead or fashioned by my fancy,/ Enter each and all, and use their
service," (One Word More). Discuss Browning's use of the dramatic
monologue.' I flicked through a few more until I reached the fifth or
the sixth: '". . . he played with the curious and the special, they never

submerged him, and it was a sign of his robustness that he could play to the end." (Henry James on Browning). Discuss.' I stopped there and looked back through the ones I'd already seen, noticing that they were all dated either May or June of 1994, the summer term of our second year. I read a little further into each of the essays I'd looked at so far, but there really seemed to be nothing of any particular interest in the text that followed the titles. It wasn't until I reached the seventh or the eighth one that I paused in my reading. I looked at the title a second time, 'Robert Browning: Wife Killer?' and then I skimmed over the script below. What struck me straight away, apart from the somewhat macabre tone, and relative brevity, of the question that had been set, was that the whole of the essay was in pencil, rather than Rachel's purple ink, and the handwriting was completely different.

The other essays had been written in the broad and flourishing script that Rachel had cultivated as a student. By the time I got to know her again later on, after Richard's wedding, her handwriting had softened into an almost ordinary cursive, and although the overall effect was still markedly more artistic than my own, she'd begun to use black ink, rather than purple. But the pencilled writing I was looking at now was in neither of those styles. It was tiny, cramped and scrawling, and the whole of the text seemed to run down the page in one continuous paragraph. I looked at it again and again, knowing I'd seen something like it once before, and then all at once I was there again, on that afternoon in the summer term of my first year when I'd followed Rachel and Anthony and Cissy around the quad, running after them to catch the piece of paper that Rachel had dropped and picking it up having assumed it was hers only to see the very same handwriting I was looking at now. I looked at the top of the essay I held in my hand, 'Robert Browning: Wife Killer?' and I saw that the initials 'A.T.' had been squeezed in next to the title, so faint as to be barely legible.

I hadn't read this far through the contents of the document wallet when I received Evie's message asking me to courier it to her. This time though, pulling my chair further into the glow of the lamplight

so I could see Anthony's essay more clearly, I carried on reading, turning over page after page, trying as best as I could to decipher his writing. The next few essays seemed also to have been written by him, and I was about to give up and put everything away again, thinking that I would need Harry's help to understand the meaning of what I was looking at, when suddenly I noticed that there was something more than a little familiar about the text I was partway through. Looking back again to the essays of Rachel's that had gone before, I quickly realised that, apart from 'Robert Browning: Wife Killer?', every one of Anthony's essays had a replica in Rachel's hand, and that each of the pairs of texts was identical to one another, word for every single word.

That in itself was puzzling enough, but then I turned over the final page of the last of Anthony's versions of the essays, and what I saw next made me feel not only confused but also suddenly sick, with a rush of something like panic passing through the whole of my body, as though I was being pulled through deep water, my mouth open and my lungs filling with it. I looked at the letter that lay there and whilst I didn't understand what it meant, or how it might have come to have been written, I realised that it was somehow immensely important, and that if I'd only carried on reading that night in my apartment in London, I would have found this letter and I could have taken it to someone and shown it to them, and that if I had, the ensuing weeks would almost certainly have taken a different course.

WORCESTER COLLEGE
6 JUNE 1994

DEAR HARRY,

> *She had*
> *A heart – how shall I say? – too soon made glad,*
> *Too easily impressed; she liked whate'er*
> *She looked on, and her looks went everywhere.*

> *Sir, 'twas all one! My favour at her breast,*
> *The dropping of the daylight in the West . . .*

WAS YOUR WIFE A SLAPPER HAZZER? COULDN'T HANDLE
IT, COULD YOU? YOU WILL SLEEP EASY IN YOUR BED ONLY
IF YOU CONFESS YOUR CRIME.

I AM A WELL-WISHER

I turned over the next page, and the next, the sickness growing
in my stomach as I saw that the letter was the first of three. Each of
them was dated a week apart from one another and they were all laid
out in an identical fashion, being typed rather than handwritten, and
I looked more closely and saw that they were photocopies rather than
originals. The second letter was in a tone that was somehow more
menacing than the first, and it seemed to contain a kind of a threat.

WORCESTER COLLEGE
13 JUNE 1994

DEAR HARRY,

> *Oh sir, she smiled, no doubt,*
> *Whene'er I passed her; but who passed without*
> *Much the same smile? This grew; I gave commands;*
> *Then all smiles stopped together.*

SO DID YOU DO IT YOURSELF OR DID YOU GET SOMEONE
ELSE TO DO YOUR DIRTY WORK FOR YOU? THAT IS THE
ONLY PUZZLE THAT REMAINS TO US HARRY. WE'RE CLOS-
ING IN ON YOU.

I AM A WELL-WISHER

The third letter was perhaps even more threatening, and the other thing that made it stand out from the other two was the fact that the quotation it contained was one I had read only a few days before, on the first evening of my stay in College.

WORCESTER COLLEGE
20 JUNE 1994

DEAR HARRY,

> *That moment she was mine, mine, fair,*
> *Perfectly pure and good: I found*
> *A thing to do, and all her hair*
> *In one long yellow string I wound*
> *Three times her little throat around,*
> *And strangled her. No pain felt she;*
> *I am quite sure she felt no pain.*

WERE YOU ANGRY WITH HER HARRY? IS THAT WHY YOU DID IT? IT'S NOT YOUR SECRET ANY MORE HARRY. YOU SEE, WE KNOW EVERYTHING. AND WE MEAN, EVERY-THING.

I AM A WELL-WISHER

As soon as I've read this final letter various options present themselves to me. I sit and turn each one over a few times, feeling slightly dizzy as I try to work out what to do. I delay for no more than a moment or two before I grab the papers from the table and shove them back into the wallet, running from the room and throwing myself down the stairs as fast as I can and out into the night, dashing through the passageway to the quad and taking a course straight across the middle of it. I notice as I run that the snow has begun to melt slightly so that

the lawns are beginning to emerge in patches that show up as smudges of brown in the light of the moon. As I run up the steps on the other side it occurs to me that Harry might not even be there at this time of the night, and that I should perhaps go first to the porter's lodge to check, and, if necessary, to demand his home address.

In the end there is no need. I take the stairs up to Harry's rooms two at a time and when I get there, my chest heaving from the cold and the exertion, I bang on his outer door as hard as I can. I stand back and wait and when after a time I have heard nothing I bang again, harder this time, and for longer.

I am still banging when I hear his voice calling out, 'I'm coming, I'm coming. Please, wait a moment.' And then suddenly he is there, a dressing gown wrapped tight around him and high about his neck, his hair dishevelled and his eyes staring. 'You have read the letters then,' he says, standing back as though he is afraid of me. And when I nod in response, he opens the door a little wider and gestures to me to come inside.

The story Harry began to tell me that night as we sat by the fire in his rooms was, in the end, not so very complicated. It was a sad tale, and a tawdry one, but it could not be said to have followed a narrative path that was, when it came to it, anything other than fairly direct. He warned me that it would take some time in the telling, and that I would have to be patient with him, since it was not one story but many, woven together. Other than that, he had only one caveat before he began, only one reservation about the jigsaw he was about to lay out: he told me right at the start that although he was going to describe a sequence of events which he believed to have culminated in Rachel's murder, he could not claim that his was anything approaching an authorized version. There were questions that remained unanswered, and problems that remained unsolved. Perhaps the biggest flaw of all, he said, was the absence of more than one of the protagonists of the piece, which meant that what I was about to learn would have, for the time being at least, to remain no more than a theory, and one which I

would have to take from him on trust; he hadn't found a way of corroborating it, and nor could he see that he'd be able to.

He apologised for the way he'd gone about things. He knew I had found my visit thus far somewhat bewildering, and he was aware that he might have arranged the whole thing more satisfactorily from my perspective. But until he'd had an opportunity to observe me in situ, as it were, in the way that he'd been able to over the previous few days, until he had watched my reaction to some of the things he had told me, or shown me, or asked me to read, he had been more than a little uncertain of my own role in the proceedings.

His intention on inviting me to Oxford had therefore been, first, to discover how much I knew of the events concerned and whether I had had any greater involvement in them than that of which he was already aware; and then, depending on what had been established in answer to those questions, either to tell me the whole of the tale or to withhold it. He said that he had satisfied himself that I knew very little of it, if anything at all, and could now be almost certain that the entirety of the story he was therefore about to reveal was known only to himself, to Evie, and to Anthony. On my becoming part of that circle of confidants, he wanted me to be absolutely clear that what I chose to do with the information was entirely at my discretion.

'We are none of us blameless in this sorry affair, Alex. We are some of us less culpable than others, but not one of us can avoid a share of the burden of responsibility for what happened to Rachel. Not one. I would be grateful if you would hear me out, and listen to my conclusions before you make a decision about what to do. After that, I recognise I can have no further hold on you. It will be in your gift, Alex, when you know the whole of it.'

'What, Harry?' I asked him. 'What will be in my gift?' He sat back into the sofa then and raised his glasses to his forehead and frowned at me, as though I failed to keep up with what he was saying. 'Our salvation, Alex,' he said. 'Our salvation. Or, if you so wish it, our damnation.

You must decide whether to conceal our story, or to disclose it, and in so doing, you must be our judge.' And then, having poured us each a glass of whisky from the bottle that stood on the mantelpiece, he began.

He'd received the first of the three letters at the end of Sixth Week in the summer term of my second year. His wife had died just before Christmas. Because her death had happened during the vacation, he'd been able to keep it relatively private, arranging for the briefest of notices to be put on one of the boards outside the porter's lodge, announcing that he would not be resuming his college duties, nor his teaching timetable, until the start of the summer term, and noting the address of the hospice to which donations could be sent should anyone wish to make one.

As he told me this I remembered having seen the notice, and having listened to the English students talking about it in the Buttery bar once or twice. I'd overheard them gossiping in a half-hearted sort of a way about how Harry's wife had died, and wondering if it was suicide, or if she'd been murdered by a jilted lover. They'd moaned about how much time he'd had off already, saying that they now understood the frequency of his absences the previous term, unexplained at the time but clearly, with hindsight, relating to what must have been hospital visits, surgery, chemotherapy, but that all the same, it was they who had had to do with graduate students instead, stepping in at the last minute and never having the slightest idea what they were talking about. I was surprised by the way they spoke about him and his wife. Harry had always been someone they'd talked of with something approaching adulation, even awe, and the conversations that I overheard in the bar at around that time seemed remarkable to me in the light of this; there was something in their speculation that was, if not quite salacious, then certainly disrespectful, and that would have been more understandable had its target been a tutor who was less well-liked.

Harry had come back at the start of the summer term to find that Rachel and Anthony and Cissy had all three elected to study Robert Browning as their Special Author, which meant that they would together attend a tutorial with him every week for the whole of that summer term. At the end of that time, over the vacation, each of them would write a dissertation on the poet's work, which would be submitted as their Special Paper for Finals. He was not displeased about this, though he was perhaps a little surprised by the uniformity of their decision. It was not unprecedented to have three students studying the same author for their Special Paper, but it was unusual. At any rate, when looked at in the round, he regarded it as a welcome surprise: they were a group whose company he found stimulating, even convivial, and the intensity of the dynamic between them, which had been apparent from the start, was something for which he came to be grateful, in that it provided him with some distraction in those early weeks after his return from a dark and desolate winter.

Fairly soon though, this was a dynamic that crossed a line from the merely intense to the almost wild, and one that he realised early on would have to be carefully managed in order that the right balance might be struck. They had an energy in their discourse, the three of them, which he knew from the start was something that could either serve to assist them in their learning, or hinder them even to the point of obstructing it. The discussions they had each week were extraordinary in their creativity, and in their combativeness, and the ideas that were thrown out in those sessions developed into something quite original, startling even. He couldn't say that it was any one of them that was responsible for this; it was by their union that it was generated. While the debate would reach its most fevered pitch in the exchanges that took place between Rachel and Anthony, each of them throwing quotes across the room at one another like cricket balls, Cissy was nonetheless a constant part of the dialogue, just in a different way.

'It wasn't that she was any less brilliant,' Harry said. 'On the con-
trary, I think that if she'd stayed, she might even have exceeded the
potential either one of them displayed. Her written work was her forte
though, from the start. It was there that she was really herself. Careful,
analytical. On another level altogether from the others. She was older
than them, you see. She'd already started a course in the US and given
it up halfway through to come over here instead. But she was almost
too careful initially, too controlling. It took the whole of the first year
to get her to let go, to be comfortable with the idea of being spontane-
ous. To take risks with her ideas, rather than always seeing things in
black and white.'

I thought to myself then that I'd known plenty of people like that
at Worcester, remembering Richard's frequent observation that most
of our fellow law students were such pedants they'd end up as tax law-
yers or parliamentary draftsmen, though he usually only made it after
one of them had torn him to pieces for having too few precedents at
his fingertips in support of what he'd considered to be an otherwise
brilliant argument.

'We see it from time to time,' Harry carried on, 'in some of our
first-year students. They will arrive so well-read you know they're in
abject terror of something. It usually turns out to be one of their par-
ents, or both of them. In Cissy's case, she'd treated her first reading list
like a contract, rather than a guide. There was nothing wrong in that,
of course, although it meant that while the others read everything
they'd neglected to before coming up, she started on literary theory,
the sort of material most of them never even get to. And it actually
held her back for a while, this relentless pursuit of perfection, leading
as it so often does to a formulaic kind of blandness,' Harry said. 'But
we got there in the end, with careful encouragement and a few chats
at the end of her first year when she didn't get the results she wanted
and I told her she wasn't being adventurous enough.

'By the time it came to the Browning tutorials she'd got the knack

of it, and she was able to take things less seriously, and not to think so much in terms of right and wrong. She gave as good as the other two from then on. But she did it always in her own way, and of course, however much she had adapted to our method of doing things, there was always the fact of where she came from. "Our little American friend", Anthony called her when he was building up to one of his more withering put-downs. She would sit bolt upright on the sofa, her head turned a little to one side, watching the other two tearing into one another. She'd said to me once, the year before, that she thought we ought to spend less time talking and more time writing, and I would watch her sometimes and wonder whether her reticence was because she was still sceptical about this. But then she would come out with something, right at the end of an argument; something she'd gleaned from a piece of secondary literature the other two hadn't even heard of, and she'd finish it with a killer blow, just like that. It wasn't reticence at all, you see; she'd been listening all the way through, storing things up and preparing her point, so that when it came out, there was rarely any answer to it. Her written work stayed much as it had been though, and I suppose I couldn't fault it. It was just an approach I wasn't accustomed to. Slightly overassertive, perhaps, and a little laboured. Pedantic even. Like a—' and he stopped, looking embarrassed.

'Like a lawyer, you mean,' I finished for him.

'Yes, actually, that was what I was going to say. Her father was one, of course; perhaps that was where she got it from. I should apologise though, for my slip. A kinder way to describe her style would be to say it was simply too cumbersome. Even leaden. Rachel and Anthony were, how shall I say it, more playful with their dialogue, and easier with their knowledge. It was a kind of game for them, though they took it none the less seriously. They were able to be freer with their ideas, that was all, and to be jocund with books, rather than always seeing them as something rule-bound.'

In any case, he said, as the early weeks of the term went by, he was

nothing short of delighted with their progress. Their commitment to the Special Paper meant they were able to take in a range of material far beyond the confines of their subject, their studies even approaching at times what he considered to be academia in the widest sense of the word. Because they each seemed to be working as hard as one another on the days that passed between the tutorials, he was able to push them in their reading, and in their thinking, and consequently their debates each week became something he looked forward to a great deal.

Despite all of this, and notwithstanding their brilliance, there was the occasional incident which made him question whether they were approaching things in exactly the way he would have wished them to. He had detected, once or twice, an increased flippancy in their behaviour which, had he dwelt on it for any length of time, would have concerned him, and which, looking back, perhaps should have done so. He sometimes had a sense, and it was nothing more than that really, just the slightest feeling, that what lay behind the intellectual meteor showers he was witnessing each week was nothing more than a planned exercise, and one from which he was excluded. It was almost as though the three of them were putting on a charade and, rather than engaging in any really serious way with the task in hand, were merely playing with him, trying to provoke him to question them more closely, knowing all the while that he would not.

One such incident took place early on in the term, perhaps even in the second or third tutorial. At the end of the previous week's session he had set them a question from an old Finals paper, something fairly straightforward on Browning's use of the dramatic monologue, as far as he could remember. It was Anthony's turn to read out his essay and he sat deep in the armchair, his head lying back and the pages held up in front of his face. The girls sat side by side on the sofa, as they always did. 'Just here,' Harry said, 'where I am sitting now,' and, rubbing each of his hands on the fabric that stretched away either side of him, he

looked up and met my gaze. He looked away again immediately and stared for some time into the fire before carrying on, his voice quieter than before.

'I remember Rachel taking her shoes off that day, and tucking her feet up beneath herself. And then she stretched out her legs and put them in Cissy's lap. She did that sometimes.' I shut my eyes then against the tears that I felt forming, and I stopped listening. When I tuned back in, it was to hear Harry explaining something about Browning's use of the first-person narrator, and as he saw only incomprehension in my face, he shook his head and told me it wasn't important, and he apologised. In any case, Anthony had gone about answering the question in the way he usually did, straying so far from the topic that Harry may as well not have given him a question in the first place. 'But it was all to the point, Alex. That was the thing,' he carried on. 'It just wasn't what I had expected to hear. But he always made a case for its relevance, an unassailable one, whatever it was that he had written about. It was Conrad that day, I think. *Heart of Darkness*, if I recollect. The debt the modernists owed to Browning. Not that it hadn't been said before, of course it had. But not quite like that. The girls were on to him straight away, as soon as he had finished, both of them this time. They leaned so far forward from their seats to argue they were almost sitting in his lap,' Harry said. 'Rachel actually stood up on the sofa then to make her point, throwing her arms about and jumping up and down until I said, "That's enough, Miss Cardanine, I think you will find that you are sufficiently well served by your natural eloquence to launch your sallies with equal efficacy from a seated position, don't you agree?"'

Of course he'd regretted his words as soon as he'd spoken them, realising they would pick up on this mode of address he had chosen and use it for the rest of the afternoon, and there would be nothing he could do about it. And that was exactly what they did, Miss-Cardanining and Mr-Trelissicking and Ms-Craiging one another with a hilarity they

hardly bothered to mask, though the force of their arguments suffered not a bit for their new frivolity. So fluid was the fight that day he half suspected they might have rehearsed it, there being in the speed of their parrying something almost too quick; something too slick for him to believe it was spontaneous. But since their most rapid-fire debate came in response to his own questions, the rate by which his admiration for them increased was easily matched by the speed with which any doubts he might have had about their integrity were quelled.

At the end of the session that day he had asked Anthony to give him the piece of work he had read from, only to be met with something along the lines of, 'Actually I won't, if you don't mind. Wasn't one of my best,' or some such nonsense to the effect that Anthony was refusing to hand in his essay to be formally marked. Harry assumed it was a joke and had kept his hand out, waiting for the essay, but Anthony said it again, and, as he did so, one of the girls had laughed. It was Rachel, he rather thought, or at least it was until Cissy had nudged her and told her to shut up, and that was the point at which he thought something odd might be going on. All at once he felt exhausted by the whole thing and, losing interest suddenly in their little game, he stepped forward and placed his hand on the essay Anthony was holding under one arm, intending to take it from him and see the three of them out without discussing it further. He felt worn out, all patience with them and their ebullience gone. Their antics seemed to him suddenly like those of unruly children instead of second-year undergraduates, and he realised that not only was it the end of the day but also the end of the week, and that another weekend lay ahead of him with nobody but himself for company.

He pulled sharply on the pieces of paper and, catching Anthony off his guard, found that he had them in his hand. He had opened the door and was about to say goodbye when he registered that there was something more than surprise on Anthony's face, something, in fact, almost like dismay. He looked down at the pages he was holding

to see that rather than the tiny cramped and pencilled handwriting he was expecting to find there, what he was looking at was nothing at all. He was holding three or four sheets of A4 paper, sure enough, but when he turned them over again and again, shuffling through them once more just to be sure, he saw that every single one was entirely blank.

He tried to work out what was going on, and to understand what he'd just witnessed as he'd sat watching Anthony's eyes move across the pages in front of him, listening, or so he'd thought, to the man apparently reading out his essay. And then, all at once, Anthony started to speak.

'I'm sorry, Harry, I mean, I'd written it, you know. But then,' and his voice trailed off to nothing.

'But then what, Anthony? What happened?'

'Well, OK. I suppose I'll have to explain. It's not what it seems, Harry, really it's not. I sat there in my room, right? It was early, you know, this morning, and it'd been a hard one, you know. I'd been up all night really, working on it. Wanted to make it perfect, Harry.'

And Harry turned to see the girls smiling at one another and shaking their heads and he said, 'Don't trouble yourself to explain, Anthony. Just go,' and he handed the pages to him and stood back to let them leave the room. It was Rachel who spoke then, telling him he shouldn't take it so personally, that Anthony really had written the essay, but that he'd been so tired when he'd finished that he'd made a pot of coffee to wake himself up and at the last minute he'd knocked it over, the whole thing, and it had completely soaked the essay and there was no way of retrieving it, and when the girls had gone to get him for the tutorial they'd found him in a total state and told him just to recite it off the top of his head, he'd spent long enough writing it he must have memorised half of it already, and so that was what he'd done, and it had worked hadn't it, and what could Harry actually say was wrong with it?

'Absolutely nothing, was there Harry? He's brilliant isn't he? He just is,' Rachel said, staring at Harry and daring him to question her.

'That's not quite the point, Rachel,' he said. 'There's a little more to it than that, don't you think?'

'Like what, Harry?' she said, smiling. 'Like what?'

'Well. There are other questions to be considered, I think. There is, for example, the question of respect, wouldn't you agree?'

'Of respect?' she said, raising her eyebrows and opening her eyes wide. 'Respect for what, Harry?'

'For the way we do things here, Rachel. For the system that we follow, such as it is.' But then he stopped, realising that what he had meant to say, what he had actually wanted to say but hadn't, was 'For me, Rachel. Respect for me and for the time I spent this afternoon listening to Anthony, thinking that he was reading from a script, believing the image he presented to me. And all the while I was the only one who didn't know what was going on.'

'Oh come on, Harry,' she said, her voice softer, and her face chastened, a little. 'You know that isn't important. Not really. And anyway, that's not the Harry we all adore, is it?' and she looked at the others quickly before turning back and placing a hand on his arm. 'You know what, Harry Gardner? I'd never have thought of you as the sort of man who'd fall back on the idea of a system. You're far too interesting for that.'

'You might say so, Rachel,' Harry responded, irritated by the way she was speaking to him. 'But you will one day learn, perhaps, that the ability to at least show a modicum of respect for a system isn't such a terrible thing to cultivate.'

'But it wasn't his fault,' she replied straight away. 'You heard what he said. You know he's done the work. So it's alright then, isn't it?'

Harry looked at her face then and realised she wasn't going to let it drop. Finding himself unable to summon up the energy to contradict her reasoning, he agreed to put his objections aside. As the

three of them turned to go Anthony stretched out his arm towards Harry, smiling his lopsided smile and saying, 'No hard feelings eh, mate?' and before Harry could stop himself he was shaking his hand and smiling back at him, admitting to himself, albeit reluctantly, that what Rachel had said was true: it mattered little that Anthony had written nothing down. What mattered more was that he had read the texts so closely, and had engaged with them in a way that was, as far as Harry could tell, entirely original. What bothered him though, looking at the three of them smiling at the joke they had played, and, he suspected, at the fact that they'd got away with it, wasn't the question of Anthony's commitment to his studies, nor of his grasp of his material. Instead, he said, it was the duplicity of the thing that unsettled him. That, and the fact that they were all three of them in on it and had clearly found it amusing to tease him in the way that they had.

After they'd gone, it was Rachel's voice he heard floating back up the stairs to where he stood. 'I told you,' she said, still laughing. 'I told you he'd let it go if you pulled it off well enough. He loves us.' And then her voice faded a little as they reached the bottom of the stairs, so that he had to lean forward to be able to make out the end of her sentence. 'As far as Harry's concerned,' she carried on, 'we three can do no wrong.'

He closed the door then and went to stand by the window, watching them walking straight out across the quad instead of going round it and, when the porter appeared on the terrace and called out to them, quickening their pace and carrying on right to the other side, ignoring the man's request that they step away from the grass immediately. And he said to me, almost apologetically, that as he'd stood there watching, he decided there was something he hadn't quite liked in the way Rachel had spoken when she'd thought she was out of earshot. He had detected something jubilant, even crowing, in her tone, and he almost wished he hadn't heard it.

Still, there was little point in making any more of what had hap-

pened than he'd done already, and he quite forgot the whole thing until the middle of term, when, being given cause to be concerned once more, he wondered whether perhaps he should have taken a firmer stance after all, simply as a matter of principle. The difficulties that arose this time were not, he said, within the tutorial room, but outside it. If anything, their work had begun to improve yet further when he began to receive reports from Haddon about some bizarre episodes involving the three of them, episodes in relation to which Haddon had felt obliged to take disciplinary action.

There were no more than two or three occasions on which Harry was called in to see Haddon about them. The first time, Haddon had received a call from the porter one morning to say that he'd seen something on his night rounds he thought Haddon ought to know about. It had started innocuously enough, the porter told him, when he'd had a call from one of the Fellows whose bedroom overlooked the quad. The man had been woken by shouts, and when the porter went to investigate he found the three of them playing French cricket. He chased them off immediately, but not before they'd tried to argue that it wasn't so late, only one in the morning. And when he told them they shouldn't be on the grass anyway, no matter what time of the day or night it was, they ran away then, leaving the racquet behind and completely ignoring him when he shouted after them to come back and fetch it.

That in itself wouldn't have been worth a report to Haddon, not on its own, so he'd gone back to his lodge and simply logged it in his record. Later on though, on his three a.m. rounds, he'd found them again. He'd been on his way back from the north-west side of the lake when suddenly the silence was broken by a splash, and a stifled scream, and he picked up his pace and walked on and saw them swimming out towards the middle. He shouted at them to get out but they pretended they hadn't heard him, submerging themselves in the water and bursting back up again once or twice before heading towards the

other side. He ran round and caught them as they reached the tip of the eastern shore and were clambering out, and he saw that all three of them were naked. They stood there shivering as he hollered at them and shone a torch in their faces to make sure they were who he thought they were, and from their responses to his questions it was clear they were drunk. He told them to get back to their rooms and they went off across the lawns, howling with laughter and stumbling and tripping as they went. The punishment Haddon gave them for this was relatively minor; they were required to spend the following Sunday clearing the stretch of undergrowth that ran alongside the boundary between the college and the canal, bagging up the litter that had been thrown there from passing boats and making the route more accessible by cutting back some of the brambles and transporting all of the debris to the compost heap over by the orchard.

The second incident had some overlap, in that it was the porter again who had reported it to Haddon one morning, but this time the man had been quite distressed by his experience, rather than simply annoyed. It had happened later in that same week when, once more on his night rounds, he'd been tracking the edge of the playing fields and heard music coming from the direction of the Pavilion. Only faintly though, so he wasn't completely sure he hadn't imagined it. There were no lights on, as far as he could see, and when he reached the building and stepped up into the porch, everything seemed to be normal. But as he turned to step back down to the grass, he noticed something draped over the railing. He shone his torch on it and saw that it was a stocking, and then he trod on something soft and reached down and picked up another. And then he heard the very definite sound of a laugh coming from inside, just one, followed by a sudden burst of music and a woman's voice saying, 'Oh for god's sake, Anthony, shut up,' and he knew it was them again.

He went straight in and held up his torch and there they were, Rachel and Cissy, both undressed and lying on the floor beside one

another, covering their eyes with their hands and telling him to switch that bloody thing off you're blinding us. There was a crash from behind them, and a thud outside, and he stepped back out again and went to the side of the building to see Anthony running away across the playing fields. 'Loser,' Cissy shouted from inside. 'You're a loser Trelissick, you know that. Face the fucking music.' Having gone back inside and told the girls to get dressed and clear everything up and go back to their rooms, he'd left them to it and returned to the lodge, disgusted by their behaviour. Seeing them like that had been one thing, he'd told Haddon, but it was what he found the next morning that really upset him. When he'd gone back to the Pavilion at about six a.m. he wasn't expecting it to be perfect, but nor did he think he'd find it strewn with cigarette stubs, empty bottles, candles melted directly onto the floorboards, chocolate wrappers and tissues everywhere across the room. Not only that, he said, but they hadn't even bothered to take their CD player with them, just leaving it there with a stack of CDs beside it. When Haddon heard what they'd done, he ordered the three of them to report to him at six o'clock every morning for a fortnight and barred them from drinking in the Buttery bar for the same period.

On those first two occasions Harry had argued their corner, framing their antics as the exuberance of youth rather than anything more sinister or alarming, and it was because he had pleaded for a softer line to be taken that they'd received only the punishments that they had. But where Haddon backed down both those times, he hadn't even consulted Harry the third time, simply writing him a letter after the event and attaching a copy of the memo the three of them had been sent about their punishment: each of them had received a hefty fine and a warning that a repeat of any such behaviour would lead to a suspension from College for a period of such significance it would threaten their academic performance in the long term. Harry told Haddon he thought he'd gone completely over the top, given what had actually been complained about this

time, but Haddon said he was treating all of the incidents cumu-
latively; since Harry's softly-softly tactics clearly weren't getting
the message across, he had decided it was time to draw a line. It
seemed that a student who lived on the same staircase as Rachel and
Cissy had complained to Haddon that he'd been kept awake for four
nights in a row by music coming from the set of rooms that the two
women shared. The first time, apparently, when the man had asked
them to, they'd turned it down, but after that, they had stopped even
answering their door when he knocked, Anthony and Cissy calling
out from inside that he should leave them alone, they were busy, and
hadn't he ever heard of having fun and why didn't he act his age for
a change. By the end of the week he was too tired to concentrate, and
with only a fortnight left until his exams, he'd approached Haddon
and demanded that he do something.

His complaint, innocuous though it might have seemed, had been
made in a manner that Haddon said he couldn't ignore if he was to
maintain credibility in his role as Dean. The student in question was
clearly in some distress, and he'd told Haddon he didn't want to go
into details, but that if something wasn't done about the noise there
were plenty of other things he could start complaining about. When
Haddon asked him what he meant by that, the man said it didn't mat-
ter, he didn't want to get any more involved than he had to and it was
a free country and Rachel and Cissy could do what they liked with
whoever they liked whenever they liked. None of that bothered him;
it was just the noise. It was keeping him awake, and after almost a
week without sleep he felt like he was cracking up. He assured Had-
don he wasn't suggesting anything illegal was happening, but there
were things he had seen that he wished he hadn't. He'd made what
Haddon had interpreted to be oblique references to their behaviour
having some sexually threatening elements to it, and that was enough
for Haddon: something of the same offensiveness had characterised
all of their escapades, and the situation had to be nipped in the bud if

the college was to avoid the sort of publicity that would be attracted if a firm line wasn't taken.

Harry himself didn't raise the topic with them, nor did he mention the matter of the fine, preferring not to disturb the equilibrium that had grown up between what he had come to think of as their little group of four. As far as he knew, they were entirely unaware of his involvement in any decisions that had or had not been made regarding their punishments. And he was relieved when things inside the tutorial room continued much as they had done before, if in a slightly more subdued fashion. After a couple of weeks he noticed that the edge seemed to have gone from their wildness, and he interpreted this to mean that some kind of balance was being restored. He found himself thinking that by not having spoken to them of their misdemeanours he had been kind, and that they probably felt some degree of gratitude towards him for the lightness of touch he had shown by not referring to the affair.

But then, on the Friday of Sixth Week, he'd come out of Evensong and dropped into the porter's lodge as he always did, wanting to check his pigeonhole before going for sherry with the Provost. He marked the way he'd been addressed on the envelope as unusual straight away, noticing that his name had been typed in the bold capitals of some kind of faculty communication, but with the Esq. placed after his surname that only his students, and particular colleagues, bothered to use. His curiosity making him impatient, he opened it as he stood there, but on seeing what it contained he went straight back to his rooms to look at it again in privacy. In the end he missed sherry altogether, only just getting to Hall in time to eat. He found himself unable to, though, when the food was put in front of him, such was his shock, and his upset.

He knew, of course, that the letter had to have come either from Cissy, or Rachel, or Anthony, but there was nothing about it that suggested it was from more than one person, and he couldn't decide

which one of them to suspect. He told himself he had a week in which to think about what to do, given that their next tutorial wasn't due to take place until the following Friday afternoon. By the end of the weekend, he'd convinced himself that he wasn't completely certain after all that it had come from one of them. The particular choice of Browning poem was so crushingly obvious as to be almost entirely lacking in imagination, and he could hardly believe that students of their ability would have made it. Any number of people would have known that they were studying Browning, and anyone could have written the letters, knowing that the three of them would have been the first to be suspected.

That, in the end, was Harry's undoing. He had thought too much of them, and not enough of himself. He had been blinded by his desire to think well of them and, if he was entirely honest, by his admiration for their youthfulness. At any rate, by the time their next tutorial came round the following Friday, he had done precisely nothing about it, only biding his time and telling himself that the most sensible course of action was to wait and see whether it was a one-off before approaching Haddon about it, a course of action he knew would lead inevitably to some sort of a confrontation with one or all of them.

He realised almost as soon as the tutorial began that he'd made a serious mistake. The atmosphere that afternoon was almost unbearable in its half-repressed hostility, in the barely restrained ferocity with which they spoke to one another, and to him. Something between the three of them had changed. He was baffled by it, and frightened. A link had been broken, a connection destroyed, and he didn't see that it was within his power to restore it, being quite certain that such mediation was beyond him. The three of them seemed suddenly to have gone outside his sphere of influence. Some kind of schism had occurred, and one that had nothing to do with him. That much was obvious, but what he couldn't work out was which way the dividing

lines had been drawn. There was an anger circulating between them, he could think of no other way of describing it, and when it came to the end of the tutorial, he was, for the first time, relieved to close the door behind them.

When he reached the porter's lodge after Evensong he wasn't surprised, somehow, to find a second letter waiting for him. He noticed that although it was still signed off as if it had been written by only one of them, 'I AM A WELL-WISHER', the rest of it suggested that the signatory wasn't working alone. Again, he was surprised by what he described as the laziness of the choice of text, the excerpt having been taken from slightly further on in the same poem, and by the cheapness of the language of the threat. There was something almost careless in the turn of its phrases, and he found that puzzling from three of the brightest students he'd ever taught. Again, he had managed to convince himself by the end of the weekend that there would be no sense in going to Haddon. It was almost the end of term, they were clearly struggling with some sort of difficulty between themselves, and he couldn't see any real risk in giving the situation a chance to settle of its own accord. He knew also that as soon as he reported the matter it would in all probability be the final straw for them, for the rest of term at least.

'I could see clearly what that would mean. And I simply wasn't prepared to do that to them. They would have lost so much more than they even knew they were risking, the three of them. Of course they did come to lose so much more than that in the end, all of them. We all did, I know that now, Alex. So much more than I could have imagined. At the same time though, I somehow thought that if I let things lie, they would come to realise the error of their ways. That they would be able to approach me, and to apologise, if I only gave them the space.' But he also knew that there was more to his reluctance than this. 'To tell you the truth, Alex,' he said to me, 'I suppose I was scared. I was afraid of what it was that they were trying to do to me.'

By the end of that weekend he'd resolved to think of a way of confronting them himself, and of negotiating some kind of a truce. He considered for a day or two how he might bring it up at the next tutorial, deciding that he would simply present them with the letters and set out for them precisely what the consequences would be were they unable to explain themselves satisfactorily.

The tutorial the following Friday was the final one of the summer term, which meant that it would be the last time he would be seeing them before they went off for the vacation to write up their dissertations. Their titles had been chosen weeks ago, and they all knew what they were doing by then. In the ordinary course of events, this last session wouldn't have been one in which any new ground would be broken; rather, it was an opportunity to recapitulate, to consolidate, and to make sure of the way that lay ahead. But he was amazed when, ten minutes into their allotted hour, only Anthony had turned up. Neither of them had spoken a word, only sitting and waiting for the others to arrive, when Anthony suddenly laughed and looked at him as though nothing out of the ordinary had happened, his eyebrows creasing together in his customary frown as he said, 'They're not coming, Harry, you know that, don't you?'

Without knowing why, but being aware that he was feeling suddenly angry with Anthony, and with all of them, Harry said, 'There is no need for you to stay, Mr Trelissick. You may see yourself out. I think you will agree it is better that way.'

Anthony laughed once more, smiling his lopsided smile and saying, 'Mr Trelissick? Not that again, Harry. Come on, don't be a spoiler. I've got questions for you, loads of them.'

But Harry insisted, finding himself barely able to look Anthony in the eye, and when he had gone, he spent what remained of the afternoon in his armchair, the outer door closed and the rest of his teaching for the afternoon cancelled, trying to think through what to do next, but knowing deep down that he would do nothing until after

Evensong, when he would go to the lodge to fetch the letter that he was almost certain would be waiting in his pigeonhole.

When he opened it and saw the extract that had been chosen, sensing the new note of violence that had crept into the correspondence, he walked back to his rooms to collect the other two letters and then he went straight across the quad and started knocking on Haddon's door, not stopping until he got a response.

Within minutes of Harry handing him the letters and telling him who he thought had sent them, Haddon went over to Hall, where dinner had already started, and he called Rachel, Anthony and Cissy out to the front and told them they were to report to him at nine the following morning. He wouldn't ordinarily have given them any notice of the interviews but for the fact that the following day was a Saturday, and it fell technically after the end of term. Even though the three of them were likely to be staying up for the Commemoration Ball that was to be held that night, it would be difficult to track them down if they left early for the summer vacation. Haddon decided against calling them in straight away, since he wanted some time to talk with Harry in order to make a plan. He took the precaution, though, of issuing the three of them with the sternest of threats and making it clear that their attendance at his rooms the following morning was compulsory, and that a failure to present themselves would lead to their immediate and permanent exclusion from College.

Harry came clean with Haddon that evening. He told him everything about the letters, and about the change in the dynamic between the three of them. He also made the suggestion that, in his opinion, the letters had been the work of all three of them acting together. He hadn't managed a particularly convincing rationale for the tardiness with which he'd informed Haddon, finding himself unable to explain the particular bond that had arisen in those tutorials, and Haddon

was generous to a fault in his avoidance of any kind of comment on the reluctance Harry had shown to punish the three of them earlier in the term.

After he and Harry had talked it through, Haddon announced that his intention was that they should each interview one of the three, simultaneously, in separate rooms, and then swap and do the same again before moving on to the other. 'We shall find them out, Harry, you'll see. It won't be difficult,' he said the next morning, walking with Harry back to his rooms after breakfast and setting up a desk and a chair in a side room off the drawing room. Harry's suggestion that such tactics were hardly necessary was met with derision by Haddon, though in the end he was proved to be right about this, if nothing else. His protest having been dismissed, Harry went through with the exercise as Haddon had dictated he should, taking Cissy into the side room while Rachel waited in the corridor and Haddon set to work on Anthony in the drawing room. Harry realised fairly quickly that he wasn't up to the task. All that Cissy would say was that first, because the actual sending of the letters had been nothing to do with her, she didn't need to go into any more detail; that second, if necessary, she would contact her father, who, she reminded him, was a federal attorney in Washington DC, and who would be more than happy to fly over and represent her should Haddon wish to pursue the ridiculous line he was taking; and that third, she also wanted it noted for the record that since she regarded Haddon's behaviour in Hall the night before as threatening, she would be taking that up with the Provost as a separate matter. Harry found himself apologising to her on Haddon's behalf, and was at a loss as to how to progress when Haddon knocked on the door and called them both through to the drawing room. He was standing there with Anthony beside him, and when Rachel came in from the corridor where she had been waiting, he spoke to them all together.

Anthony had, it seemed, confessed to sending the letters entirely of

his own volition. He took complete responsibility for the situation as a whole, and, Haddon went on, he had accepted that this meant he would be sent down from the university, given the warning he'd received earlier in the term. As Haddon spoke, Anthony looked at the floor, and although Harry couldn't be sure, he appeared to be crying. He noticed Rachel and Cissy looking at one another a couple of times, and although he wasn't quite able to interpret their gaze, they seemed shocked by the turn of events that was occurring. Shocked, he said, but also relieved. And then he drew things to a close and sent them on their way, telling Rachel and Cissy as they left that he didn't feel it necessary to remind them that they should still consider themselves to be on notice of the strongest possible disciplinary action should he hear of any further misdemeanours on their part before they left for the vacation, suggesting at the last that they might like to keep a particularly low profile that night at the Ball if they valued their places at the university. Rachel didn't react in the slightest when he said this, but Harry saw Cissy shaking her head as she left, and, although he couldn't quite be sure, he thought he heard her utter the word 'jerk' under her breath as she did so. Haddon missed this, having started to discuss with Anthony the arrangements for his departure, telling him he had to be out of College by two o'clock that afternoon, that there was no reason for him to linger beyond that time, and that all of his university identity cards and keys and passes should be returned to the lodge in an envelope marked for Haddon's attention. 'We certainly do not want to see you here tonight, Mr Trelissick. I will, of course, notify security that you are not to be admitted to the Ball under any circumstances, so I shouldn't try to come back if I were you.' Anthony raised his eyes from the floor only after Haddon stopped speaking, and when he did it was to look at Harry rather than Haddon. As Harry met his gaze he saw that he had been right, and that Anthony was crying, and when Harry put out a hand to shake his, Anthony kept his arms folded across his chest, smiling through his tears and saying nothing before turning and walking from the room.

Harry couldn't leave it at that. Not after the time he'd spent with Anthony, and not without at least trying to articulate how sorry he was that it had come to this, and to acknowledge the strength of his admiration for Anthony's ability, despite what had happened. And so, after he and Haddon had had what Haddon insisted on calling a 'debrief', he'd gone and fetched a book of poetry from his shelves that he thought he might give to Anthony as a parting gesture, and he'd walked over to see if he was still in his rooms.

Anthony had almost finished packing when Harry arrived, and when he opened his door in response to Harry's knock, he seemed surprised to see him. He let him in but didn't stop what he was doing, carrying on shoving things into bags and emptying file after file of papers into a bin liner. 'There's nothing to say, Harry, is there?' he said. 'Only that I'm sorry. Of course I am. I'm really really sorry. I can't explain. I think you may as well go.' Harry didn't know how to respond. He felt sure there was more to it than the version of events that Anthony had presented to Haddon. Instead of answering any of Haddon's carefully prepared questions, he'd apparently given a brief statement to the effect that he had become jealous of Harry's complacency, of the life that he had, and at the same time he'd become convinced of his own mediocrity in those tutorials, feeling more beaten down by Rachel and Cissy each time they met, and more and more certain that he would only fail where they would succeed. And this had become a kind of a madness for him, spiralling into something approaching hatred for the girls, and for Harry. He had felt angry, and he hadn't known how to channel that anger. 'Look at me,' he said to Harry that afternoon in his room, brushing away more tears. 'What was I thinking, turning up here, trying to fit in? Trying to make my way with people like them? With people like you?' Harry tried to interrupt, and to contradict his line of reasoning, but Anthony carried on, his speech quickening and his voice sounding almost strangulated as he described how everything had got completely out of hand and,

without really knowing what he was doing, he'd sent the first letter. He had wanted to hurt Harry, and it seemed clear to him that the memory of his wife was the easiest way to do it. After that, Anthony said, there had been no turning back. He'd set a course that would lead only to self-destruction, he'd known that at the time, and there had been nothing he could do to stop himself.

Harry was puzzled, feeling certain there was something about Anthony's explanation that didn't ring true. Realising he wouldn't be able to communicate with him properly, not that afternoon at any rate, he'd handed him the book of poetry and said that he wished him the best and would like him to understand that he was forgiven. And then he left him there, still throwing things into bags and tearing down posters from the walls. As he walked away down the corridor he felt that he had failed Anthony somehow, more than he had ever failed anyone in his whole life. The only thing he could compare it with, that sense of failure in relation to another human being, was the way he'd felt on the day his wife had died, when he'd walked away from the hospice thinking that if he'd only done something, anything, differently, she would perhaps have been able to pull through.

He went back to his rooms and sat beside the window in the afternoon sun. He drank some tea, looking down on the quad below and watching the preparations taking place for the Ball that night. Some students dragged a table to the bottom corner of the quad and rigged up a film projector, and the chefs from the kitchen positioned a hog roast on the terrace outside Hall. As he watched, he thought about the fact that, had his wife still been alive, he would have brought her to the Ball. He sat and read for a couple of hours, not really taking anything in, and then he packed up his things and closed the curtains and locked up his rooms and left. He made his way to the Provost's rose garden, feeling obliged, despite the events of the afternoon, to make a brief appearance at the drinks party that was being thrown there before the Ball proper, though he did wonder, as he walked along

the terrace, about abandoning the thing altogether and going straight home.

He did his duty at the party in a kind of a haze so that he wasn't entirely aware of what was going on around him, or whom he was talking to, or who it was that was taking so many photographs. When he did finally leave for the evening, he stopped in at the lodge and saw that a bulky envelope with Haddon's name on it had been placed on the side ready for collection, and he realised that Anthony had gone. And then he looked in his own pigeonhole and saw that Anthony had also left behind the book of poetry Harry had given him. There was no note with it, nothing, just the book, so he took it and put it in his briefcase and walked out of College along the red carpet that had been laid there.

That, then, was how things stood at about six o'clock in the evening on the 21 June 1994, an hour or so before the gates were due to open on the Casablanca Ball.

16

The first Harry knew of there being anything amiss at the Ball was when he received a telephone call from Haddon shortly before two o'clock in the morning. He'd been fast asleep for hours in his house on the Woodstock Road. Although he'd taken to sleeping in his college rooms more frequently since his wife's death, he had stayed away that night because of the Ball. Haddon told him it was urgent, and that he should come straight to his cottage when he arrived. He would say no more on the telephone, other than that on no account should Harry mention it to anybody he might bump into on his way.

When he got to the college gates, Harry had some difficulty persuading the team of Moroccan security guards who had been hired for the night to let him in without a ticket, and in the end he had to ask them to call through to Haddon. The first thing that struck Harry about Haddon when he arrived to meet him was that he had undergone an almost total transformation, so that he looked not at all like himself. As Dean, Haddon's role that night was what it always was at

a college ball: that of superintendent of a team of students who spent the night working as stewards, their recompense taking the form of a free ticket. This was a job I had done myself in my first year without too much trouble, and I'd actually quite enjoyed the opportunity it gave me to experience the event without having properly to engage in it. Being unable to afford a ticket once more, and remembering how little effort it had required, I'd volunteered again and managed to persuade Richard to join me. Our job was to keep the gardens as clear of rubbish as possible throughout the night, and to watch for any kind of trouble, intervening where sensible or, if a situation looked as though it would escalate, contacting Haddon on one of the walkie-talkies he'd given us so that he could co-ordinate an appropriate response and bring in the outside security team if necessary.

That night differed from my previous experience in one regard only. The Ball Committee had written to Haddon to explain that an entire cast for the film had been assembled, each of its members picked either from the Senior Common Room, or from among the students themselves, and that the only part they hadn't managed to fill was that of Captain Louis Renault. All that this notional cast had to do was look the part, the letter said; to meet and greet and be generally charming or villainous as the script dictated, in the broadest possible sense. Their letter was obsequious enough to have persuaded Haddon that he should allow the committee to hire costumes for him and his team so that we could carry out our work dressed as gendarmerie, with Haddon being fully made up to play the role of our leader, Renault. Haddon told Harry he'd accepted their invitation with some reluctance, though Harry said to me that as the night went on, Haddon seemed to be entering into his role with an enthusiasm that suggested otherwise.

And so Harry was met at the gates not by Haddon dressed in his customary three-piece tweed, brown brogues below and a deerstalker on top if the occasion so demanded it, but instead as a captain of the

French military police, circa 1942, and one whose knee-high leather boots were a little too tight for him, whose pillbox hat was a little too small, and whose hands, clad in tiny white gloves, held a whistle that was a little on the shiny side. So transfixed was Harry by the false moustache that was plastered across Haddon's face, it took him a moment or two to realise the man was furious with him for having 'given the game away, dammit'. He told me that Haddon had muttered expletives under his breath all the way back across the quad, the two of them dodging groups of drunken students and saying no thank you to cigarette girls and palm readers, and the thought had occurred to Harry that they could have drawn considerably less attention to themselves by walking, rather than running, and by looking as if they were enjoying themselves rather than making for the scene of a crime. And he was right, they could have done, for of course that was when Richard and I had seen him and had our argument about what he was wearing, and whether, as a Yorkshireman, he was a tight-wad.

When they got inside the cottage Haddon let rip, calling Harry an idiot and asking him why he couldn't just have let himself in through a back gate. By that stage, Harry said, he was completely disorientated. Not only had he been woken suddenly from a deep sleep, he'd also just walked though some extraordinary scenes with Haddon waving an imitation pistol in his face every now and again. The college had become another place entirely and its transformation was bewildering. He hadn't been able to get to sleep after supper that evening, having been quite unsettled by what had happened with the letters, and feeling desperately sad about Anthony and how he had failed him. When he'd finally managed it, the sleep he fell into was so deep that the telephone had already gone to answerphone by the time he heard it, so that he was woken in the end by Haddon's voice shouting at him to get up and answer the bloody phone.

All of these things together had made it possible for him to take quite some time to notice that Haddon and he were not alone in the

drawing room. Partway through the argument they were having about the merits or otherwise of his having done what Haddon described as 'involving the security chaps in the whole thing', he looked across to the other side of the room and saw Anthony sitting on the floor in front of the bookcases, one eye blackened and blood smeared across his chin. He was staring wide-eyed and angry at something behind Harry, and when Harry turned and followed his gaze he saw Cissy sitting there, her face also smeared with blood. As far as he could see, she didn't appear to be quite as badly hurt as Anthony. She was sitting on a chair, rather than on the floor, and instead of being hunched over in the way that Anthony was, she was bolt upright, staring back at him defiantly. He was thinking to himself that there was something else about her that didn't look quite right, something he couldn't place, beyond the blood on her face, and then he realised suddenly that it was just that he'd never seen her wearing a dress before, that was all. And that made him think about Rachel, and he was just beginning to look around the room for her when Haddon said, 'She's in the John Radcliffe, Harry. It may surprise you to know that at this precise point in time, a decision is being taken about whether it is necessary for your star student to have her stomach pumped, or whether she's vomited enough of the alcohol out of her system for it to be safe to leave her as she is.' Anthony laughed suddenly as Haddon said this, and looked as though he was about to speak, but Cissy shook her head at him and he said nothing.

'On the advice of her friends I have telephoned her godmother. Although,' he said, looking over at Anthony and back again at Cissy, 'the term "friends" would seem, at this stage, to be something of a misnomer. Our business is not with her, Harry. Not tonight anyway.' And then he turned to Cissy and Anthony. 'You two. You know the form. There's a reasonable chance we can keep this as college business if you stay where you are for the next ten minutes.' And then he ran over and charged down the narrow staircase and Harry heard him

locking the front door to his cottage. He emerged back into the room again and said, putting the key in his pocket, 'There are windows without locks on this floor but I wouldn't recommend it. There's quite a drop. Just bear this in mind, the pair of you: I haven't worked out what happened yet but I'm almost there, and the police would have no hesitation in arresting both of you on the strength of what I've got so far. To leave the university without a degree is one thing, but to do so with a criminal record would make life more than a little difficult. It's your call, but I'm sure as hell I know what I'd do in your position. Ten minutes. We'll be back. Harry, come this way.' And he went over and opened the French doors and led Harry out into the secret garden, walking over to the low wall on the other side.

Standing there in the dark with the sound of fireworks going off on the playing fields, and the noise of a big band starting up beneath them on the lawns that led down to the lake, Haddon told Harry what had happened. About an hour or so previously, he and Towneley, who he'd appointed as his adjutant officer for the night, had been standing in exactly the same spot as he and Harry were now. They'd been carrying out their hourly check-in on their walkie-talkies with each of us gendarmes when they'd seen a woman emerge from the bushes into the light thrown by the fire pit on the southern edge of the lake and reel in an uncertain fashion towards the water. They had both instinctively made as if to run towards the steps down from the garden but had drawn back as she'd righted herself and carried on walking. They'd laughed to one another and, their checking-in completed, Towneley had lit for them each a slim cigar, 'in character', so he said, and they'd leaned on the wall and watched the Ball unfold beneath them. The woman they'd seen a moment or two beforehand had drifted into view again, much closer to them now, seemingly no longer able to keep herself upright. She fell onto the lawn in front of the plane tree and the whole of her body started to convulse, as though she was vomiting, or crying, or both. Towneley laughed at first, but when she'd carried

on convulsing, over and over, eventually collapsing to the ground and becoming entirely still, Haddon gave his command and Towneley ran, climbing over the old iron gate in the wall and slipping and sliding down the steps that were built into it and going over to where she lay. He sat her up on the grass and gave her some water from a flask he was carrying, and Haddon said that from where he stood he could see Towneley stroking her back and wiping her face with a handkerchief. They talked to one another, Towneley and the woman, and Haddon assumed everything was under control and was going back inside when he heard his walkie-talkie crackling and he answered it.

'She's in a mess,' Towneley told him. 'I can handle it. Think I'm going to get her to the JR, the amount she says she's drunk. Not exaggerating as far as I can tell, and she says she's been vomiting constantly for the last half an hour or so. But that's not why I'm calling you. She says there's something going on behind the Pavilion. She specifically said you, Haddon. Said there was something you'd be interested in. I think you'd better get down there.' And so Haddon, wondering who the woman was and what she was talking about, went inside and ran downstairs and let himself out of the front door of his cottage, walking back under the passageway beneath the secret garden and out across the lawns. It was only when he passed Towneley on the way that he was able to take a close enough look to see that the woman he was by now carrying in his arms was Rachel. He knew then that Anthony had made his way back into College somehow, and that it was him Rachel had seen behind the Pavilion. But what he hadn't anticipated, he said, was quite what he'd discover when he got there.

My recollection of the early part of the Ball was fairly clear. Richard and I had received orders to report, dressed in our gendarme costumes, outside the front door of Haddon's cottage at the south corner of the quad, at what he'd referred to in his memo to us all as '1800

hours'. 'Jesus,' Richard said as we walked across the quad, him trying unsuccessfully to make his hat stay on his head and me attempting, with equal ineptitude, to make my plastic rifle swing behind me rather than in front. 'Haddon's dream this, isn't it, Petersen? I propose we're on the case for an hour, tops, and then we knock off for the night. Not sure I can take much more of it than that. Won't be missed anyway. Talk about overstaffing,' he said, pointing his rifle at the crowd of gendarmes that awaited us. He gave up on his hat and tucked it beneath his arm. We both agreed we'd take a fairly relaxed approach to the night that lay ahead. That was the day I'd received Harry's letter telling me I could stay up in College for the vacation, and I think it was because of that that I felt a certain freedom from things, knowing I wouldn't be going home to my father after all.

There were at least twenty gendarmes standing outside Haddon's cottage when we got there, which Richard and I agreed was about ten too many, each of us attributing the numbers to Haddon's tendency towards megalomania rather than any real need. I'd looked at the circulation list at the top of Haddon's memo earlier that afternoon and realised I knew most of the team. The only one who didn't show in the end, as was revealed when Haddon went through the roll call, sounding just like a schoolteacher, was Anthony. 'Trelissick,' Haddon said, rushing down the list. When he was met with silence he shook his head as if annoyed, muttering to himself, 'Of course not. My mistake,' before carrying on to the end of the list and starting to bark out his orders. I think he was actually striding up and down on the grass in front of us as he spoke, if I remember correctly, stopping every now and again to click his heels together, and Richard leaned across to me and pointed out that hadn't he got the wrong end of the stick and had he actually seen the film and didn't he know Renault was a Frenchie not a Kraut? And then we were off, and the hog roast was smoking, and the quad was suddenly full of people taking photos of one another and drinking champagne.

We went through the passageway under Haddon's secret garden

and strolled across the lawns towards the lake. Richard, even though he was walking right next to me, took to radioing me on my walkie-talkie every time he saw a woman he liked the look of, reporting their location by reference to the hands of a clock. Exactly an hour later, and with a military precision of which even Haddon would have been proud, he announced that he had picked up and disposed of no fewer than three empty beer cans and that we had, therefore, done enough to pay our way. It was then that we started to drink in a serious fashion, depositing our hats and rifles in the cloakroom and sketching out a quick calculation to work out precisely how much we'd have to get through to make our tickets worth what they would have been had we paid for them. After standing in the Heineken tent and doing what Richard referred to as starting gently, with no more than a couple of pints, we stopped outside the fortune teller's tent and said alright, why not, at least it would be amusing. I chose not to discover my future, standing instead at the back and watching Richard being told by the woman who sat opposite him, holding his hand and stroking his palm, that he'd become a wealthy man, but not a happy one. 'Good good,' he said to the laughter that broke out around him. 'That's the way I like it.' The lights were low in that little tent and it was overcrowded, and the clouds of some kind of incense that the woman was burning made it even more difficult to see properly, but I was fairly sure I spotted Anthony standing in the shadows at the back of the crowd on the other side of the table. I raised a hand in greeting, but I never found out whether it was actually him or not; whoever it was failed to acknowledge me, only pulling their gendarme's hat lower on their head and slipping suddenly out of the tent.

I hauled Richard out eventually and we wandered around for a bit before going to the Buttery bar, converted for the night into Rick's Bar. 'Oh good,' he said, once we were on to our third martini. 'Some titty action at last,' and I looked up at the stage to see what he was talking about. I recognised Rachel immediately; I had seen her at black tie

events before, and although she wore more make-up than usual, and her hair was set in a style that was new to me, the transition she had undergone was not so very startling. But when I saw Cissy I did a double-take, and my recognition of her was delayed, just for a second or two. I think it was largely because I'd never seen her wearing a dress before. It wasn't that there was anything awkward about the way she did it; on the contrary, it was a look that seemed effortless, at the same time as being very strange. Richard and I compared notes later on and agreed that the only other time we'd seen her out of her customary shorts and deck shoes, jacket and scarf on top, was the week earlier in the term when her father had visited from the US. She'd appeared with him in Hall on the Monday morning and Richard had choked on his cereal when we saw her standing there in little fitted trousers, patent leather ballet pumps and a much smarter version of one of her jackets, all buttoned up and piped around the edges, just like the tiny blazer I'd worn when I was sent away to school. Her hair was smarter that day too, the fringe swept back into a quiff and standing slightly proud, so that her scar was clearly visible. And her nails, as I noticed when I stood next to her at the tea urn, were bright red and shiny. She'd taken him everywhere with her that week; to Hall for breakfast, to the Buttery bar for lunch, and even to lectures, or so we heard from Towneley. They didn't show up at dinner though, and it was said that he'd taken her out every night to meet people he had connections with in Oxford, and that on the last night of his visit he'd driven her to Le Manoir to stay with him in his suite before he flew home again. And then, as soon as he had gone, her shorts came out once more, her hair flopped back down over her scar, and her nails were no longer red.

'Bit sad that, don't you think,' Richard had observed at the time. 'Like taking your daddy to school with you.' I disagreed and said so, wondering to myself what it would be like to have a father who was capable of taking such a ready pride in my achievements in the way that hers was, or even to be aware of them, which would have been a start.

That night in Rick's Bar her transformation was on another scale
entirely. The scar was hidden again, her hair slicked down on her head
in waves, and her face, as Rachel's, was painted like a wartime glam-
our girl's. Their dresses were worn so close and cut so low they were
barely there; covered in sequins and catching the light, Rachel's clung
black to the whiteness of her skin and Cissy's was a coating of silver,
daubed across her tan. They stood face to face, so near to one another
they were almost touching. They shared a single microphone and as
the piano player began to play they turned and said hello to their audi-
ence and then they faced each other again and started to sing.

> You must remember this,
> A kiss is just a kiss,
> A sigh is just a sigh . . .

They swayed slightly from side to side, placing their hands on each
other's bodies.

> The fundamental things apply
> As time goes by . . .

The room began collectively to whistle, and to clap, and as they sang
on, Rachel drew Cissy into her.

> Moonlight and love songs
> Never out of date.
> Hearts full of passion,
> Jealousy and hate . . .

One of the waiters walked over then and passed a note up to
Cissy and she broke away and left Rachel to sing on alone, glanc-
ing at it briefly before turning to the front and looking out amongst

the tables, frowning and shielding her eyes against the light. Then she folded it in two and tucked it in the top of her dress and took Rachel's hand in hers.

> It's still the same old story,
> A fight for love and glory,
> A case of do or die . . .

By the end of the song they had put the microphone to one side and were kissing and someone was whistling and the piano player played on without them. I was surprised, I suppose, at the same time as not being surprised at all, having heard the rumours that I'd heard about Rachel's parties. And then, as people called out for more, Haddon was at the door and marching up to the front and saying something to Rachel and Cissy and they were laughing at him, and at one another, and then he said something else and they stopped laughing and left the stage and went over to the bar, the room booing and hissing as Haddon marched out again.

We wandered fairly aimlessly after that, Richard and I, taking a turn on the Ferris wheel before sitting down beside the fire pit and pulling on a hookah together by the light of the flames. We had quite a good conversation as we sat there, the two of us, and for the first time he actually told me about his childhood, and we compared notes on what it was like being brought up as an only child, in the countryside, and how it had been for the both of us, being sent away to school. I'd drunk so much by then that I was almost on the point of telling him about Robbie, and I think I probably would have done so were it not for the fact that Towneley had appeared suddenly and thrown himself down on the rug beside us and asked whether either of us had scored yet.

After he'd gone again, and we'd found ourselves some food and spent a bit of time in the comedy tent, Richard said we ought to

check on the seamstress's room, and so it was that when the first of Haddon's emergency calls came crackling through my walkie-talkie, we were perched together on a single chair in the corridor at the back of the ladies' cloakroom, craning our necks to see through the tiny window that had been left open and watching one woman after another strip to their underwear whilst repair jobs were carried out on dresses torn by dancing, or falling from bumper cars, or, as Richard put it, 'overenthusiastic shagging in the bushes'. Because Richard told me not to be an idiot, and didn't I realise we were about to get our first actual full-frontal, and because I was drunk enough by then to do whatever he told me to, I ignored Haddon's call and turned the volume on my walkie-talkie right down, despite the fact that Haddon's request for urgent assistance was being directed specifically to me rather than as a general Mayday, and was being broadcast only on my channel. As I leaned forward to see through the window more clearly, I heard the faint crackle start up again and could just make out Haddon's voice. His speech was broken by his own panting and by the sound of him stumbling, or running, and he said something that sounded like, 'Petersen where the bloody hell are you? Come in. Come in. Pavilion. Now. Urgent.' And then I lost my footing and because Richard and I were actually on the floor when the next call came through, to Richard's walkie-talkie this time, and because we had fallen so awkwardly on top of one another that neither of us could move, and because suddenly there was a woman standing over us calling us perverts and saddos and losers and telling us to fuck off, we ignored that call as well, even though by now Haddon was swearing into his walkie-talkie and demanding that Richard find me and that both of us make our way to the Pavilion as quickly as we could. Richard stood then, pulling me up from the ground and saying, 'Martinis. Titty bar. Tout de fucking suite,' before heading back along the terrace, stopping only to throw his walkie-talkie into the nearest bin.

I did the same, of course, so that instead of running to Haddon's side we fell into a corner of Rick's Bar and spent most of the rest of the night in there, drinking ourselves not quite into oblivion, stepping outside every now and again for some air and a stroll across the quad to see if anything interesting was happening. Had we done as Haddon had commanded us to, and gone instead to the Pavilion and made our way round to the back as Harry told me that Haddon himself had done, our view would have been partly obscured by the bushes and partly by the darkness, but we would nevertheless just have been able to see Anthony, his gendarme's trousers pulled down as far as the top of his gendarme's boots and his hat and rifle thrown to one side, lying on top of Cissy with one hand across her mouth and the other trying again and again to pull her knickers far enough away from her body to be able to rape her.

Haddon told Harry that he'd chosen the wrong side of the Pavilion at first, so that he couldn't get through the bushes to where they were lying and he'd had to run back out to the front and all the way round again to the other side. This, I realised as I sat listening to the tale unfold in Harry's room earlier this month, was almost certainly the point at which Haddon had tried to use his walkie-talkie to get through to me, and then to Richard, shortly before we'd thrown ours in the bin and gone to Rick's Bar. Having failed to raise either of us, he'd reached the other side of the Pavilion and pushed his way frantically through the bushes, but by the time he got to them it was Cissy who was on top of Anthony and she was punching him, hard, again and again, right in his face. Anthony was barely moving, just lying there and seemingly allowing himself to be thrashed. Cissy was going about her work quietly, Haddon told Harry, and that surprised him. He would have expected a woman finding herself in such a situation to be screaming, and loudly. Instead, she was speaking in a low voice as she punched

him, and although he couldn't quite be sure, it sounded as though she might even have been laughing as well.

'I think that's enough, don't you?' Haddon said, and she stopped and looked round at him and he could see that she had been punched in the face also, and that there was blood running from her mouth and down her chin. She stared at Haddon for a moment or two, saying nothing, and then Anthony began to moan beneath her and shake his head and Haddon realised it was quite possible that his passivity in the face of Cissy's assault had been due to unconsciousness, rather than acquiescence. He went towards them and Cissy climbed from Anthony and helped Haddon get him up. She stood and watched as Haddon retrieved Anthony's hat from the bushes, holding him steady while Haddon put it on and made sure it was pushed right down on his forehead, and, once Anthony had pulled his trousers up, the three of them walked slowly back across the lawns.

'No no, we're quite alright thank you,' Haddon said, smiling, each time someone offered assistance or enquired after the gendarme they were supporting between them, whose head was drooping forward and whose face was entirely hidden by his hat. 'Drunk and disorderly while on duty, that's all. Utter insubordination. Off to confine him to barracks I think, bread and water for a few days. I daresay that'll do the trick. No no, absolutely no problem at all. We're quite alright. Good night, good night. Thank you. Good night.'

Haddon told Harry as they stood in the secret garden that he'd been able to get nothing out of Anthony or Cissy since they'd reached his cottage, despite having questioned them for almost half an hour. He asked Harry if he wouldn't mind having a go himself, suggesting that a different approach might be enough to get them talking. Harry went back inside and did his best, but it was clear that neither of them had anything to say, and, not having Haddon's zeal for interrogation, he gave up fairly quickly and asked them instead whether they had any views on how things might be dealt with. Again, they didn't say a

great deal, and the only thing Harry could be certain of was that neither of them seemed to have any desire to press charges against the other. He went back outside and told Haddon he'd made no progress beyond that which Haddon had already achieved. Haddon thanked him and said that although he was completely baffled by the impasse they had reached, it lent itself very much to his preferred course of action, which was to keep the whole matter between the four of them. He told Harry how he'd tried without success to call for backup from his team of stewards and was relieved about his failure, given the need to keep the situation under wraps. Rachel would be too drunk to remember encountering Towneley, and Haddon could very easily tell Towneley, who he described as being hardly the sharpest tool in the box, that he'd found no one behind the Pavilion. Anthony had agreed to go, this time for good, and seemed to understand that any further return to College would lead to criminal charges. At the very least, he said, they'd be able to get him for breaking and entering, if they could only find out how he'd got in. Cissy seemed to be minded to return to the US as soon as possible and to remain there, and apart from the balance of the fees that were payable for the rest of her course, her absence would represent no great loss in any quarter but for the Boat Club.

Harry tried to disagree at this point, telling Haddon that Cissy had shown considerable promise, particularly in recent months, and that her departure would not be seen as insignificant when it came to the college publishing its Finals results a year down the line, but Haddon brushed this off, telling Harry that he really had lost the ability to be in any way objective about his students. It was then that Harry remembered Rachel, and he told Haddon that he thought he ought to go to the hospital to check up on her. Haddon said he didn't see that this was necessary, and that her godmother would be there by now and that Rachel wasn't really involved in the situation anyway, not properly. Harry said that he would go all the same, and Haddon

responded that that was all very well, but if she should recall having asked Towneley to send Haddon to the Pavilion, it was essential that Harry keep as closely as possible to the story they'd agreed and tell her only that Haddon had gone, as requested, but that he'd found nothing of any particular interest when he got there.

When they came back inside from the secret garden Cissy was pacing up and down the room, looking at her watch and shaking her head, her face set hard and sullen and the blood drying on it. They asked her one more time if she intended to press charges of any description against Anthony. She looked at them both, and then back at Anthony, and she laughed. 'You know what?' she said. 'He's not worth it. None of you are.' Haddon asked her then if she'd be prepared to sign something to that effect before she left, at which point she simply held her hand out to him and said, 'You're a jerk, Haddon. Give me your keys. Unless you want my dad to file for false imprisonment.' He did as she asked, but only after he'd said that the story must go no further than the four of them, and that meant that neither of them were to tell Rachel about what had happened, otherwise he'd have no choice but to invoke the most draconian of disciplinary proceedings against them. Harry thought he saw Cissy's face change when Haddon said Rachel's name but she hung her head before he could read the look properly, and when she raised it again to speak, whatever it was had gone. 'You really have no idea about Rachel Cardanine do you Haddon. No fucking idea at all. Like I said,' she carried on, 'you're a jerk,' and she took the keys and looked at them all in turn before saying to Anthony, 'So long then,' and walking down the stairs to let herself out of the cottage.

By the following morning she'd gone, and as the letter she left in Haddon's pigeonhole said, she had no intention of coming back. As for Anthony, he'd got up and made as if to follow her, but Haddon had said 'I don't think so, Mr Trelissick, not on your own,' and he'd asked Harry to join him in escorting Anthony from the premises. After

Anthony had refused medical attention, and declined to answer Haddon's question about how he'd managed to break through the security cordon, they'd walked him out of college.

Anthony thus dealt with, Harry shook hands with Haddon and took a taxi to the John Radcliffe. When he arrived in Rachel's room he was surprised to find her sitting up in bed quite happily reading a magazine. 'For god's sake, Harry, Towneley totally overreacted and quite frankly I was too tired to argue with him by that point. They've been terribly nice to me here, really, considering there was nothing actually wrong with me,' she said, putting the magazine down on the bedside table. 'I just wanted a rest. I can go now that you're here. Somebody has to take me home that's all. I told them you'd probably show up at some stage. You'll just have to pretend for the moment that you're my dad if you don't mind. It's only the nurse, she'll never know. Just sign the forms they give you and we can get the hell out of here. Alright?' Through a combination of his own exhaustion and the fact that there seemed to be nothing obviously the matter with her, Harry agreed to do what she'd asked. 'But what about Evie?' he said, puzzled, as she pulled the screen across in front of her and started to get dressed. 'Has she been here?'

'Oh. Evie,' Rachel said. 'Now there's a thing.' She didn't say anything else for a moment or two until, emerging from behind the screen, she turned her back to Harry and held her hair up on top of her head and said, 'Do me up would you?' And it was as he was in the process of working out how to hook Rachel's dress back together again that he heard her say, 'She's been here alright, Harry. Stayed for a while actually. But she's gone back to London now. In actual fact, it seems I have something of a problem.' He fastened the last of the hooks and she turned, shaking her hair back down around her face and saying, looking at him, 'You see, Evie and I have had a little bit of a falling-out.' And then she smiled and carried on, 'I'm afraid I'm going to need your help.'

17

hortly after describing this scene in the hospital Harry paused
for the first time since he'd begun his story. He sat forward in
his chair and rubbed his eyes and said that if I didn't mind, he
would very much like to get some rest, and he hoped I would under-
stand that all the talking was taking its toll.

He pulled out his pocket watch and looked at it before snapping
it shut and saying, 'A few hours, Alex, that's all I ask of you. There is
much more to come, a great deal in fact, and, not being as fortunate as
you in your youthfulness, I fear I will not last the course without some
respite from it now.'

I had, I think, been so completely absorbed in his story that it took
me a moment or two to realise what he was suggesting. My initial
reaction was one of amazement, and, feeling the same anger that I
had felt on his insisting I read the Browning letters before he began,
I was on the point of telling him he had to carry on, that he couldn't
stop, not then. But when I looked at him across the room he seemed
suddenly older then than he had been before, almost as though he had

shrunken into himself somehow. It was clear that he was exhausted, and so, it occurred to me, was I. Seeing from my own watch that it was past four o'clock in the morning, and that there was some sense in his suggestion, I did as he asked me and left him, having agreed that I would return at noon.

I walked straight out across the middle of the quad, and as I made my way back to my room I ran through the very last part of Harry's story, the part he had related to me immediately before telling me he needed a break.

According to what Rachel had said to Harry that night in the John Radcliffe, as soon as Evie had received Haddon's telephone call, she went straight to the hospital and severed her ties with her god-daughter. It was to be several years before they were reconciled, Harry had said, although at the time Rachel told him that it would only be for a couple of months, saying, 'She'll get over it. She's always threat-ening to cut me off without a penny. Has been since I was about fif-teen, actually.'

Haddon had told Evie about the other things that had happened earlier in the term, and in particular the fine that Rachel had incurred by way of punishment for her misdemeanours. 'There was absolutely no need for him to have told her about that. Don't you see, Harry? I mean, she would never have known if he hadn't gone and opened his big mouth. Like I said,' she carried on, and Harry said he remem-bered being struck by that phrase, recalling it to have been a favourite of Cissy's and realising how close the two of them must have been to have absorbed one another's language in this way, 'she'll get over it. But not for the rest of this summer apparently. I can't go back to Chelsea, that's for sure. And I'm completely broke after that fine so I can't rent a place for myself now. Not with college bills as well. I've got no choice Harry. Unless you help me I'll have to give up the course and move back to London and get a job or something. Until she snaps out of it.'

Harry told me that he'd had no idea whatsoever that Evie would go through with this threat to cut Rachel off. As he understood it, the woman might as well be Rachel's mother, and he'd assumed that somebody in that position just wouldn't do that sort of a thing to someone for whom she'd apparently assumed parental responsibility so early on in their life. What Evie eventually ended up doing, by disowning Rachel for far longer than Rachel had thought she would, was, Harry said, to threaten her chances of finishing her degree, a fate that Harry couldn't imagine anybody wanting to bring on someone they cared for even a little.

When I reached the staircase to my room I realised how cold I had become, just in the time it had taken me to walk back across the quad. I ran up the stairs, two at a time, and when I was inside, and had closed the door behind me, I got straight into bed in my clothes. In the sudden heat of the room I felt flushed, and nauseous, not just in my stomach but in my limbs as well, as though not only my mind but my body also was drifting apart from itself into pieces with the effort of trying to keep up with Harry's story. I must have fallen asleep as soon as I lay down, and I suppose I'd been passing in and out of consciousness for a few hours or so when I woke suddenly from a dream. Images from it lingered in a way that meant there was no point trying to sleep again, so I got up and opened the window and breathed in as deeply as I was able to, filling my chest with air so cold it hurt. There was a silence like none other I had ever experienced, almost as though the cold had frozen the atmosphere into something solid and thick, so that even if there had been any movement round about, or noise being made somewhere, it would not have been able to travel to my window until that air was melted.

I leaned a little further out and listened to the silence, turning my head so that I could see across the lawns towards the lake. I pictured Towneley striding across them with Rachel in his arms on the night of the Ball and I tried to work out what Richard and I had been doing at that point. I recalled us disgracing ourselves outside the seamstress's

room and ignoring Haddon's Mayday call, before throwing our walkie-talkies away and taking ourselves off to huddle in the corner of Rick's Bar, completely oblivious to the events that were unfolding not so very far away from us, and as I did so I had a sudden urge to speak to him and tell him everything and ask him to tell me in return what to do. I took out my phone and brought his number up, my thumb hovering over the button to call him as I considered what exactly I would say, and how he might respond.

I put my phone back in my pocket in the end without having made the call; Richard, of course, knew precisely nothing of what Harry had told me, nothing whatsoever, and even if I could at that point have managed to string together a coherent explanation of what I'd learned so far, I thought it unlikely he'd do anything other than tell me to get a grip and go straight back to London. He'd sent me a fairly terse email back when I'd written and told him about accepting Harry's invitation, saying it wasn't, in his opinion, the most sensible decision I'd ever made, not by a long shot, and that he and Lucinda both felt I should start to think seriously about their idea of my moving to New York, sooner rather than later, if not immediately. He said that I really ought to start getting used to the idea that the police were doing their job and would get there eventually, and I would be better off, however painful it might be, looking to the future and making something of it, rather than consigning myself to a life spent dwelling always on the past. I knew that he'd said what he'd said with nothing other than my best interests in mind, and that underneath his dogmatism lay only affection, coupled with a genuine concern for my well-being. But at the same time I was shocked by his lack of patience, and by the complacency with which he assumed that the police would come up with anything more than they'd done already.

I knew, when it came down to it, that there was only one person I could speak to about what was going on, and that was Evie. She was the only person who could answer the questions that had started to

flit through my mind as I stood there looking out into the night, questions about the document wallet full of essays and letters, and about the call she'd made asking me to courier it to her on the night I got back to London, and only she could tell me what had passed between her and Rachel at the John Radcliffe after Rachel had been taken there by Towneley, and why she had reacted in such an extreme way to Haddon's phone call.

I called her number in Tokyo and went straight through to her answerphone, twice, leaving a message the second time saying that I was in Oxford at the invitation of Harry Gardner and would appreciate it if she could telephone straight back and clarify for me a few of the things he'd told me about Rachel. Then I walked over to the computer room in the Nuffield Building to send her an email as well, asking her to explain exactly why she hadn't discussed the contents of the document wallet with me at the time, and why she hadn't handed it straight over to the police when I'd couriered it to her. In the end I suggested also that it was perhaps appropriate that this information should be made known to them now, writing further that I had a feeling Harry would be telling me a lot more that was new to me and wondering, therefore, whether she might like to get there first, so to speak.

It wasn't until I began to type, my fingers punching out my questions on the keys, that I became aware how angry I was with her for keeping things from me, and how upset I was about the fact that Rachel had never found a way to tell me herself. I finished my email by referring to what Harry had said about Evie visiting Rachel in the John Radcliffe on the night of the Casablanca Ball and cutting her off, and I said to Evie that I'd appreciate it if she could tell me her side of the story. Finding by the time I pressed the send button that my breathing had grown shallow, I walked quickly from the room and stood in the building's porchway in the morning sunlight, trying to feel more measured about the situation.

I had no sense of where it was that Harry was going with his story,

nor of how he would unravel it and put it back together again into what he had described as a theory about Rachel's death. Nor was I at all sure that speaking to Evie was going to help me, not in any specific way. I was simply aware that there were things she might have disclosed to me but hadn't, and I didn't feel at all comfortable about her having kept them from me. Hating the powerlessness that I felt then as I looked out across the lawns towards the lake, I tried to tell myself that Harry had said quite clearly that he would take some time to get through everything, and that since I had agreed to hear him out before making any kind of decision about what to do, I should attempt to relax and let things take their shape, and that if I was able to, my perception and understanding of what was to come would be all the better for it.

As I reminded myself of this agreement Harry had persuaded me to enter into, it struck me that the position I was in was, in many respects, no different to the one I always encountered at the start of a new piece of litigation, and that things would be bound to improve. The sense I usually had at that point, of being surrounded by a mass of seemingly unrelated issues moving too fast for me to be able to clutch hold of even one of them, was something I had disliked intensely the first few times I experienced it. It wasn't until I'd seen a number of cases through to trial and out the other side that I got used to it, coming instead to feel a strange kind of certainty that against whatever odds I was confronting, a narrative would eventually be constructed and lowered successfully into place on top of what had seemed at the outset to be a foundation of facts shifting so constantly about one another that they would not bear the weight of it.

But it was an analogy that gave me no comfort, despite its promise of eventual clarity. I had no team of eager juniors waiting to retrieve unopened files and read them for me, or to go off to libraries and research seemingly unanswerable questions. There were no rows of night secretaries ready to take our Dictaphones and type up our find-

ings into letters listing issues to be addressed and documents to be requested, and there would be no team meetings held late at night, analysing and strategising and formulating plans of attack. I was all alone with only Harry as my guide, and if I could be said to have a client of any description, there was only Rachel, staring out at me from the photograph on Harry's wall and unable to issue me with any instructions whatsoever.

I walked slowly back across the lawns and when I got to my room I ran myself a bath and lowered myself into it, feeling a kind of bleakness as the steam clouded around me. Once I was dressed again, sitting on the chair by my window, I began to think seriously for the first time about abandoning the whole thing and walking over to the police station on St Aldates. I reached inside my jacket pocket to check my phone only to realise I'd left it in the computer room. I ran over and found it but Evie hadn't called, and because I was sure she must have picked up my message by then, I logged on to the computer. The email that was waiting for me was a single block of prose, seemingly written with the same angry haste that had inspired my own.

Alex I can hardly believe you're there with Harry Gardner. I'm not really sure why I'm even bothering to reply to your email but I can't talk to you now I'm going to a party and no I can't miss it, not for you or anyone so don't call. What you wrote was extremely insulting. Fine, I can see you might be frustrated with me for having kept things from you but it was for your own sake. There are things about Rachel you're better off not knowing. And anyway if you'd thought about things sensibly for even one minute you'd realise I'd never have been allowed to leave the country and relocate to Tokyo if the police hadn't been 100% content about the fact I'd told them everything. I'd proceed very carefully with Harry if I were you. In fact on second thoughts I'd just forget about him and get back to London and get on with your life. Why you've

decided to trust him is completely beyond me. You know nothing about him Alex, nothing at all. For god's sake, he's feeding you a pack of lies. Either that or he's really never clocked Rachel's habit of keeping things from people, him included. Let's just take one little example shall we, just one – what Harry said about me visiting Rachel in hospital on the night of that ball just wasn't true. I was never there. Yes, Haddon called and told me she was there, and that she'd spent most of that term devoting herself to the task of finding as many dissolute ways as possible to fritter away the allowance I was giving her. I was sick to the back teeth with her by that point Alex, really fed up. After all I'd done for her. I phoned the JR and they told me she was in absolutely no danger whatsoever – they put me through to her and we spoke, briefly, and that was the end of it. I never went there and I have no idea why he told you I did. This is hard for me Alex, really hard. Of course there are things I could have told you but I've made a judgement call, and not just for my own sake but for yours as well. For goodness' sake Alex get a grip. Get some perspective. Get back to London. I don't really see why we have to speak but if that's what you want then fine. I'm out tonight though, all night, so don't call until tomorrow.

I switched off the computer and tried her number at the same time. When I got her answerphone I hung up and walked down the corridor and out into the open air, my breath coming even more rapidly than before.

I left the Nuffield Building with the intention of going straight over to Harry's rooms and confronting him, but instead I made for the lake. As I came to the place where I had found Rachel's body I felt a sudden rush of anger towards Harry, and hatred towards Evie. It took me by surprise and I began to run, half sobbing and half howling as I went, not stopping until I reached the far side of the playing fields. I sat on the ground then and waited until I had cried myself out. When it passed, eventually, I felt only irritation with myself for having lost control like that, and I stood and walked back and forth for a while, trying to clear my head.

I thought about the firmness with which Evie had written. Either she was completely secure in her position, knowing there was nothing I could discover that would alter it, or she was a very good liar, and, having something worth hiding, had chosen to brazen things out in an attempt to destabilise my view of Harry to the point where I would give up on him and go back to London. I felt nothing but disdain for her then, and for the way she'd assumed she could so easily steer me from my chosen course of action.

She had, of course, made an entirely unjustified assumption in questioning my having decided to trust him, since I'd done nothing of the sort; the only decision I'd taken was to listen to him, which is a very different thing altogether. But what she'd said about there being no truth in his tale did have an impact on the way I regarded him, of course it did. When eventually I walked back round the lake, making for his rooms again, I reflected on the fact that if Evie really hadn't been at the hospital, then Harry was either as gullible as she'd suggested he might be, and had fallen for a story Rachel had made up, or he had made up the story himself and was, as Evie had put forward in the alternative, telling me lies. But even if I did believe Evie's version of events instead of his, there was something about Harry's behaviour that made me hold back from agreeing with either of her readings of it. Whatever was going on was more complicated than that, I knew it was. When he had begun his tale in the middle of the night he'd come clean about having invited me to Oxford on false pretences, and he'd offered an explanation for what he'd done. I had agreed to listen until he'd finished, and that was what I intended to do. He'd made no secret of the fact that he was executing a plan he'd drawn up before my arrival, and that what he had begun was a series of revelations of a long and complex nature. What Evie was proposing about my leaving was unthinkable: that he was playing some kind of a game was clear, but if there was one thing I was certain of it was that I wanted to watch him at it a little longer.

Whilst Evie's email had in no way altered my resolve to stay, it did, I suppose, mark the point at which I drew back somewhat from Harry's tale and my feelings began to shift into a new territory, becoming somehow harder than they'd been before, and colder also, so that they resembled something I can only describe as a fairly straightforward sort of scepticism. Harry had made no claim that the version of events he was relating to me was an authorized one, and I had learned enough from the cases I'd conducted over the years to know that the narrative he had begun, the one that Evie had already splintered apart by telling

me she hadn't been at the hospital, would be likely to fracture further as it continued. And I knew it was probable that it would do so in ways I couldn't foresee, so that an as yet unheard testimony might be given that would turn everything on its head, or so that the characters themselves might begin to move at will up or down the table of dramatis personae that Harry had drawn up, stepping altogether from the positions they had been allocated to allow other characters, previously considered altogether too minor for inclusion, to take their place.

It was with a kind of resigned anticipation of that happening that I walked up the stairs to his rooms and knocked on the door and took my seat opposite him, deciding as I did so that I would say nothing of Evie's email, and that instead I would wait and see how he went about explaining things further. He asked me if I would like something to eat with my tea before he began again, seeing as it was lunchtime, and when I said yes, he went off into his side room to prepare it. I sat back in my chair and as I listened to him moving about, clattering a knife on a plate and opening and closing the door of his fridge, I allowed my mind to become a blank canvas once more, ready for him to take his brushes to it.

Harry came back through with some cheese and biscuits on a tray, and once he had poured me a cup of tea, he began to talk. He said he hadn't really thought very carefully, in those early stages, about precisely what he was taking on when he cleared the grant of Rachel's vacation accommodation, gratis, after the end of that summer term. He certainly couldn't have predicted she'd end up as a lodger in his house on the Woodstock Road for the whole of her third year and longer. Evie had written to her at the end of August and said she had no intention of assisting her financially throughout the autumn, and it became apparent to Rachel that she would have ongoing difficulties funding her third year. Her scholarship helped, but when she

told Harry towards the end of September that she was looking for a job, and that the only way she could carry on with her course would be to do her studying in the evenings, he'd stepped in and offered her the attic flat in his house, saying he'd been meaning to find a lodger and hadn't done so and she may as well have it for the time being. Those were the reasons that he gave her, and they were true as far as they went. But he knew his offer was motivated also by his own loneliness, and by the emptiness there was in that house now that he lived in it alone.

He invited her up to see the place, so she could be sure, and over tea in his kitchen he set out for her, on and off, the way he lived then, so that she would know how best to live around him. He told her the hours that he kept, and who she might expect to see there; when it was that the cleaning lady came and what it was that she did as well as a myriad other domestic details he thought Rachel would need to know. He made it clear from the start that he'd accept no payment from her, telling her that in many ways he regarded what she was doing by moving in as a kind of favour to him, since she'd be keeping that part of the house lived in and looked after. He hadn't wanted to make her feel in any way obliged to him, but nor had he been able to see a way of avoiding mentioning that he'd had a job persuading Haddon of the wisdom of what he was doing. He told her he'd talked Haddon round by saying he'd keep an eye on her, so to speak, and would ensure that she was aware that the college's expectations of her academic performance were high, and that it would be in her interests if she could see a way of meeting them, or, if at all possible, exceeding them.

Rachel hadn't said a great deal in response, but she'd seemed to take on board what he was saying. He thought it best, while he was at it, to outline a few of the things he'd prefer her not to engage in; parties, loud music, that sort of thing. And although, as far as he had been able to make out, she wasn't involved with anyone in particular, or at least not in any serious fashion, he'd decided to be safe rather

than sorry, given some of the things she seemed to have been caught up in the previous term, and to add in passing that he'd prefer it if she didn't have overnight guests. He'd been a little surprised when she'd mentioned something about there being someone who might visit her, every now and again, and would that be alright. He responded by saying yes, of course, occasionally, if it really wasn't possible for them to stay elsewhere, but it was to be understood that her priority should be affairs of the mind, rather than those of the heart, at least for the immediate future. He wondered afterwards whether he'd been a little draconian about it, but he felt on balance that what he'd said was no more than fair, under the circumstances, and that even if there was someone who'd seemed to be important, it wouldn't have been more than a fling of some sort, and one that would in all likelihood have petered out sooner or later, in the way that student flings did.

Once the term was underway they'd retreated from one another slightly, getting on with their own lives and their own work in the way that he'd expected them to. Harry dined in Hall most evenings and Rachel seemed quite content with her own company, working away at the top of the house. Having settled into a pattern of sorts, they didn't see a great deal of each other; the attic flat was almost self-contained, and he'd given her a front-door key when she'd moved in. But he liked the idea that she was up there, and he liked the sounds that she made, singing to herself in the bath, or thudding back down to the floor after a headstand, or clattering pots and pans in the kitchen. And sometimes she would drop in on him in the evenings to say hello, if she was lonely herself, and they would sit by his fire and talk about a poem that was troubling her, or a novel she couldn't navigate a way through. He said that he wondered occasionally if she was only humouring him by having these conversations, and they were perhaps an attempt to repay him somehow for what he'd done, but she really did seem at ease as they sat there talking, in a way that she hadn't been at any point during the previous year. She came to see him more frequently

as time went by, and in the summer term she took to doing her revision in his garden, on the other side of the lawn from where he sat reading, so that sometimes he would bring out a jug of lemonade and she would take a break and tell him what she'd been working on, running through her ideas for an essay, or suggesting something she'd come across that he might like to write an article about.

Initially he had been fairly confident that Evie would see sense, and he'd even telephoned her himself on one occasion to try to reason with her and ask her whether she hadn't perhaps overreacted. He'd tried to make light of the situation at first, saying they weren't in a Fielding novel were they, and didn't she think she'd made her point well enough, and wasn't it time to let bygones be bygones? What really shocked him about the conversation wasn't so much what she'd said as how she'd said it, and the anger that he sensed when she told him to mind his own business and that if he actually knew what Rachel was capable of he wouldn't be questioning the situation. There was something almost like hatred in her voice, so he'd given up in the end, and besides, Rachel seemed perfectly satisfied with the arrangement they'd come to. Her work maintained a steady improvement throughout the year, so that nobody was surprised, least of all him, when she got her First and the British Academy funding that she needed in order to stay on as a postgraduate.

And that, Harry said, was that, for a number of years at least. It was inevitable that he should be Rachel's supervisor for her MPhil, and it wasn't until she moved to London to study for her doctorate that she finally did what he described as 'making the break'. The teaching post that came with the PhD funding meant she was more than capable of supporting herself from then on. They kept in fairly close contact in the years that followed and he tracked her progress with pleasure, taking a certain degree of pride in her achievements. The two of them met from time to time in the British Library, at least once a month or more. If he was up in London for his research, or for any other reason, they

would have coffee there together, or lunch if he was making a whole day of it. She'd told him that she'd renewed her acquaintance with me, having known me at Worcester, and that she had been surprised to find herself falling in love. She'd explained that it was because we'd married so quickly that she hadn't had time to even think of inviting anyone to the ceremony apart from Richard and Lucinda, who were our witnesses, and Evie of course. He was a little hurt, but he knew that he had no reason to be, and he'd told her he understood, and that instead she must allow him to invite us to dine on High Table as soon as we were able to, in celebration. She'd sent him photographs of the day and written to him all about it, telling him of her happiness. It was a happiness he shared, not having a daughter of his own. And he was pleased when she'd told him that her marriage had been a catalyst for a reconciliation with Evie, to the extent that their relationship had become one that could at least be described as functional, and some-times even cordial.

That was the way of things by the early summer of this year. For a number of years he'd thought nothing of Anthony, or of Cissy, or of what had happened on the night of the Casablanca Ball. He wasn't par-ticularly surprised not to have heard anything of Anthony in all that time, it being the case with most of the students he'd ever had to send down from the university, and certainly with those who had brought their disgrace on themselves so completely in the way that Anthony had done. He assumed that perhaps he had relocated abroad, there being such a comprehensive silence about him, even from his closest contemporaries. It was rumoured once or twice that he'd graduated from another university and managed to reinvent himself somewhere in the US, but Harry had avoided looking too closely into it. Rachel never spoke of him and Harry never pressed her to, and he had almost begun to forget Anthony altogether until one day in late May, just a few weeks before the night of Rachel's murder.

He'd been sitting one morning at his favourite desk in the Rare

Books and Music Room, one of the quieter reading rooms in the British Library and the one that he and Rachel preferred to work in. He was checking his pocket watch every now and again and wondering how much longer it would be until she signalled to him that she was ready to take a break. He looked once or twice across the room to where she sat reading, a strand of hair falling across the book in front of her and the frown flickering on her face that was always there when she was concentrating. And that was when he'd become aware somehow of another presence, of someone else intruding on his gaze.

He scanned the room about him feeling suddenly uncomfortable and not knowing why and then he saw him out of the corner of his eye. He stared, and then he stared some more, trying to make sure it really was Anthony who was standing there watching Rachel. He looked over at Rachel and back at Anthony, checking it was definitely Rachel who was the object of Anthony's gaze and becoming certain also as he did so that she was entirely unaware of her observer. And then she looked up and mouthed the word 'coffee' to him, a smile on her face and her eyebrows raised in expectation. Harry stood from his seat, feeling sure that Rachel must also have seen Anthony by now, but when he turned around to point him out, he'd completely disappeared.

Harry didn't raise the issue with Rachel over coffee that day. The opportunity simply didn't arise, and he decided afterwards that if she'd known Anthony was in the library she'd have said something to him about it, and if she wasn't aware of his presence, he didn't see that it was necessary to alert her to it, telling himself it must be a one-off, a coincidence, or that it hadn't been Anthony after all, just someone who looked like him. But when exactly the same thing happened the following week, and the week after that, and still Rachel said nothing, he decided, reluctantly, to approach Anthony and initiate a conversation in order to find out what was going on.

In the end it was done for him. It happened one day in early June, as he stood queuing in the main café of the British Library, the one

that sits up behind the King's Library in the atrium as you come in from the Euston Road. Rachel had cancelled on him at the last minute and he was all alone, thinking about Anthony, and about how strange the situation was. Even though he wasn't absolutely sure whether Anthony had been aware of his own presence in the reading room at any stage, he'd somehow known from the first moment he'd caught sight of him that an actual meeting was inevitable. Despite this, when finally it occurred, it took him entirely by surprise.

The first thing he heard as he stood there in the queue was a laugh. It reminded him of the way Anthony had laughed in his tutorials with Cissy and Rachel, and he decided straight away he must be daydreaming, so intently had he been thinking about Anthony and what he would say to him if they spoke. It was a soft low laugh that he heard, and one that seemed to come from right behind him, almost as though the person whose laugh he had summoned up was so close they could have been leaning their head on his shoulder. And then he slowly became aware that the laugh was real rather than daydreamed, and he turned to see Anthony standing there smiling his old lopsided smile, his eyebrows creased together slightly to give his face its familiar air of puzzlement. And then Anthony said something that had never occurred to Harry as a possibility in any of the conversations he had imagined them having.

'Come round to mine for coffee instead. I'm just across the road, won't take us five minutes.'

'I'm sorry? I'm not sure I— Ah! Anthony, isn't it? Anthony Trelissick?' and he knew as soon as he'd spoken that Anthony would see right through his feint.

'Give me a break, Harry. I know you've been watching me. I need to talk to you that's all. And I don't want to do it here. Come on, I've thought it all through. Trust me.'

And when he turned and made for the door Harry followed him, just as Anthony seemed to have known he would. As they left the

library and walked across the courtyard, Anthony jumping up the steps two by two ahead of him, Harry paused for just a moment to consider what it was that he was doing, so that he had to jog slightly to catch Anthony up as he went out on to the street. When he reached the street himself, he found Anthony had disappeared amongst the crowd. Harry thought he'd lost him altogether but suddenly he was there again, standing on the other side of the road and holding one hand in the air, waving.

He crossed over to join him and it began suddenly to rain. It was the kind of rain that falls only in summer, heavy and driving and warm, and the air was full of it before Harry realised he'd left his umbrella, along with the rest of his belongings, on the counter in the café. There was nothing he could do, he decided, except to carry on jogging after Anthony, who by now was dodging taxis and buses and slipping quickly down an alleyway that took them south from the main road and brought them out at the back of a redbrick mansion block. Anthony stopped and stood there, looking back at Harry as he caught up and reached him. 'Blue plaque,' he called out through the rain, turning and pointing up at the wall of the block they stood beside. 'You'll like this, Harry. Paul Nash no less. Paul flipping Nash. On my flipping wall. What do you reckon to that?' and he jumped up the steps in front of where they stood. They passed through a door and down a narrow staircase and crossed some sort of a courtyard, but because they were moving so fast, and because it was raining so hard, Harry saw little other than that it was filled with ferns, and trees of a tropical nature, these last trembling under the weight of the water falling on their branches. Then they were standing in front of a low green door and shaking the rain from their clothes, and Anthony was fumbling with his keys and they were inside.

Harry told me that the only word he could think of as the two of them stood there looking at one another, the only word that seemed halfway suitable to describe Anthony's kitchen, was 'forlorn'.

'This always happens in the summertime. Can't be helped,' Anthony said, wafting ineffectually at the pair of flies that floated in a drugged and hazy fashion in the centre of the room. 'And it gets damp, you know, being the lower ground floor and that. Can't be helped either.' He handed Harry a tea towel, telling him to dry his hair with it, and he took off his shoes and stuffed them with newspaper. He did the same for Harry, lining both pairs up side by side in the hall and telling Harry to take a seat at the kitchen table. It wasn't so much the flies circling above them as they sat that morning, and nor was it the damp that he could almost feel on his face as he looked about at the papers curling on the table and the pictures creasing in their frames. It wasn't those things that made the word forlorn come into Harry's mind, so much as the fact that nothing in the room looked to have been moved for several months, or perhaps longer. It was as though it was all in aspic, Harry thought to himself. Aspic, or something harder.

I know the café Harry was referring to, the one in the British Library where Anthony made his approach that day. I went there once, after Rachel died. It was one of the weekends that fell between my return from Oxford and the start of my sabbatical. During that time, from the Monday to the Friday of every week that passed, I was hardly aware of the memory of her, or of the two of us, finding it possible to lose myself in my work. She had a habit of creeping back into my mind at the weekends though. She was there as soon as I woke on a Saturday morning and when eventually I opened my eyes I would be surprised to find myself alone in the bed, having felt such a strong sense of her presence.

Not having anything better to do, and wanting to know more about the life she'd led while I was at work, I started to seek out the places she'd talked about. I sat on the benches in Bloomsbury squares where she said she had eaten her lunch, and I swam in the open-air pool at

the top of Endell Street. There was a café in a bookshop on Bury Place where I began to read the weekend papers, and I even went to a recitation one Saturday evening at the Poetry Library on the South Bank.

And then there was the British Library. One Saturday morning, a few months after she was killed, instead of lying in bed having one of our imaginary conversations, I walked down the canal to where the towpath stopped just north of King's Cross and I strolled along the Euston Road to have a look at it. I think I had intended even to go so far as registering for a reader's card, meaning to make it a regular trip in the hope I might find a project to embark on, something to research. When it came to it I had only to go as far as the atrium, and to sit in the café for a while, to realise it wouldn't help me. I'd stood first and gazed at the King's Library stacked up against acres of glass and then I'd wandered through to look at the exhibition of maps. After that, I went and found a postcard to send to Harry before walking up a few flights of stairs to buy myself a coffee. I sat down and watched people eating, and talking, and laughing, and I started to feel the kind of anger that I felt quite often at that stage, in those situations. I sat for a while longer, until I became aware that I was staring at someone without meaning to, and that they were staring back at me, and I realised I ought to leave. And as I walked back down the stairs I wished I had accepted one of Rachel's invitations to meet her there for lunch, instead of always saying that I hadn't the time, not during the working week; that I had my hourly targets to meet, and that lunchtimes, if they were for anyone, were for clients. 'Always your work,' she said once. 'It wouldn't kill you you know, to slack off a bit from time to time. See the real world for a change.' I think I pointed out then that the British Library was hardly the best place to do it, and she hadn't asked me again.

When I asked her one day why she went there rather than the library at UCL, she said she just preferred it sometimes. It wasn't only that she needed to look things up; it was also the being there,

in amongst strangers. A change of scene, she explained, that was all. She'd never said much about meeting Harry there. I knew from the steady stream of postcards that arrived that they were in touch, and I knew they saw one another from time to time. But as with so many things about Rachel, the degree of intimacy they shared and the level of involvement he'd had in her life, as well as the responsibility he'd taken for her well-being at Oxford, were things she didn't talk of, and consequently, things I only found out about after her death. And although Evie has come to be someone I think of as a woman so much mistaken about so many things, she'd been correct when she'd written in her email from Tokyo that her god-daughter had a tendency to keep things to herself. I knew already that Rachel was someone who was capable of small deceits, having closed the drawers she would leave ajar after working at my desk in my absence, never saying a word to me about the fact that she'd looked in them. And if any of what Harry has told me is true, I see now that she was capable of larger ones also. I have not, however, seen fit to judge her for that tendency she had, given the fact she grew up with someone like Evie in charge of her.

Sitting in Harry's room that afternoon and looking at him spreading a piece of bread with butter and taking another slice of cheese for himself from the plate he'd prepared for us both, I wondered if he had any idea that I'd been the other half of what he'd surmised to have been no more than a student fling, the one he'd encouraged Rachel to break off at the end of the summer vacation we'd spent together in College. As I watched him chewing on his food and dabbing occasionally at his mouth with his napkin, I pictured him sitting in his kitchen and setting out the terms and conditions of her gratis occupancy of his attic flat and I hated him then. I hated him for having imposed his embargo on our relationship. I hated him for what he had done to her, and for what he had done to me.

She told me once, when I asked her to, why she had dropped me so suddenly at the start of that Michaelmas term, and I realised as I thought about what Harry had said that her account fitted almost exactly with his own.

We had talked of it, she and I, on the morning after Richard and Lucinda's wedding when we'd woken together in my apartment. I brought the subject up, after we'd eaten our breakfast and had gone back to bed again. We were talking about that summer vacation we'd spent together in College, recreating for one another our memories of the conversations we'd had each evening on our strolls around the lake. We'd compared our recollection of that first time we kissed, lying on the grass in the middle of the night in Haddon's secret garden, and I told her then that that was the moment at which I'd fallen in love with her, properly. She laughed at me a little when I said that, and I put my hand over her mouth to stop her and I told her I was being quite serious, and that, as a matter of fact, I'd been in love with her ever since.

'How could you have been?' she said. 'How could you have been in love with me all that time? We didn't even see each other, Alex. And you'd never really known me anyway, not properly. What, you mean you remained chaste for me always? Pining away in Islington with only your heron for company?'

And I laughed too then, saying that of course there had been other women, on and off. And yes, I had walked with them on Highbury Fields and there had been moonlight in the trees and my hands in their hair while I kissed them and I had taken them home sometimes and listened as they told me about themselves after we'd slept together, and I would offer them breakfast before they went, promising to call them again sometime. And when she asked me whether I'd called them like I'd said I would, these other women, I told her I'd done so only rarely, and I described for her the emptiness I would feel as they talked, these women, and how each time it had happened I would have

a sense of wanting to be elsewhere, and that it was almost as though the person whose body was moving against mine wasn't really there, so entirely were my thoughts turned in another direction. And then I asked her about why she had dropped me at the end of the summer.

'What happened?' I said, taking her face in my hands as we lay entwined together in the sheets. And then I said it again, 'What happened?' and I looked her right in the eyes and brought my head closer to hers. 'You never said, not really.' She drew away from me then, lying back on the pillow and placing her hands over her mouth and closing her eyes as I carried on. 'It was horrible, you know, what you did to me. I couldn't understand it. Not after the way we'd been together, not after that summer.'

The weeks that followed the kiss had been extraordinary for me. When I'd gone to see Haddon the next morning, as he'd ordered me to when he'd stormed from his French doors in the middle of the night and thrown us out of his garden, I was worried he might spoil things for us, but when I got there he just wanted what he called 'a quiet word', making a series of inscrutable comments about the sort of company I was keeping. Nothing of what he said meant a great deal to me and I'd taken very little notice; I was just relieved he wasn't going to be heavy-handed. And then he went the next day anyway, somewhere abroad for his own vacation, so I didn't see him again until October. After that, there had been hardly anyone else around that was known to either Rachel or me. Most of the other rooms were let out to summer schools or visiting academics, so that we were in our own world, somehow. The flow of our togetherness was interrupted by no one, and we made the college our own and devoted ourselves to one another entirely.

That was how things were until the last ten days or so of September, when the air began to turn and she started to cut herself adrift in ways so tiny I managed to persuade myself they weren't happening, until one day, just before the beginning of term, when we stood at Oxford station waiting for her train and she took her hand from mine

and told me it was over. It was crowded that day on the platform, and noisy, so that when she said it would be a good idea if we stopped seeing one another, I thought for a moment I had misheard her. But then, when I tried to take her hand again she repeated herself and carried on, saying, 'It should never have happened should it, Alex, you and I? We were simply thrown together by circumstance, wouldn't you say? And I suppose we were both lonely, that was all.'

She didn't really seem to be speaking with complete conviction, and it was almost as though she was acting out a part she'd learned, hesitating slightly over her words and smiling strangely, in a way I'd never seen her smile before. I tried to talk her out of it, asking her why and saying she was wrong, she must be out of her mind, we were happy, we should talk, she could tell me if there was something I needed to do differently. But she said simply that there was nothing to talk about, and that since we'd never been friends before the summer anyway there was no need to see one another again was there, not really. Her own friends would be coming back in a day or two for the new term, and so would mine, and there was our work to think about, and it was just a summer fling, and I was completely overreacting.

I was stunned, and said so, recalling for her some of the things she had told me in the mornings when we had woken together that month, but she said don't be an idiot and didn't I realise I sounded like a teenager. And it was then that I told her I loved her, and she stopped speaking and started to cry, silently. She wasn't shaking or sobbing or making any noise at all; she was just standing there, still as a stone, the tears falling slowly down her cheeks. She made no attempt to brush them off, just letting them land and staring at me. Eventually, unable to stand it any longer, I reached out towards her face, but she took my hands in hers, gently, and moved them away from her, pushing me back and telling me never to say anything like that to her again, and that she was sorry, she really was, but there were things that had happened, things she couldn't explain, things she hoped I would never

know, and that all of them together meant she had to be on her own, without distraction for a time, to focus on her work, and she really had no choice, and it would be better for both of us if we didn't speak of it again. After I'd stood staring back at her for a while, unable to understand clearly what was going on and wishing desperately that it wasn't happening, I realised there was nothing I could say that would make her change her mind and I said goodbye and walked away and left her there, standing on the platform waiting for her train.

I hadn't really seen her again after that, not to speak to. Richard came back and did his best to shake me out of it, which helped, and I supposed that that was what she'd meant about our friends coming back and us returning to the lives we'd lived before the summer. I was puzzled though, by the fact that the people I'd thought of as her friends hadn't come back, and that she'd removed herself so completely from college life, not even living on site any more.

That morning in bed in my apartment, the morning after Richard's wedding, when I asked her to tell me what had really happened, and why she'd broken things off in the way that she had, she said she couldn't remember, not exactly, and please could we talk about something else, and I said no, it mattered to me, and I began to recall for her, in as much detail as I was able to, the things we'd said to one another on the station platform that day. And she stopped me halfway through saying please, that was enough, and of course she remembered, she just didn't want to talk about it, and I looked at her where she lay on the other side of the bed, staring up at the ceiling, and I saw a tear running down her cheek.

'I can't explain, Alex, I can't. I'm sorry, I should go.' She started to get up, reaching for her clothes.

'Why?' I said. 'Why do you have to go all of a sudden just because I asked you to talk about that?'

'Do you want me to stay?' she said, sitting back down on the edge of the bed and looking at me, puzzled.

'Of course I want you to stay. Of course I do,' I said, and she got back under the covers again and I told her it didn't matter, we didn't have to talk about it if she really didn't want to, it was such a long time ago, all that did matter was that we were together again and of course she shouldn't go for god's sake, I'd only just got her back and as far as I was concerned I wasn't going to let her out of my sight again for quite some time, if ever.

'What do you mean, ever?' she'd said, quietly, burrowing her face into my neck and wrapping herself around me.

'I love you, Rachel,' I said. 'I've told you that and I mean it. I don't care what happened then. I really don't care, whatever it was. It isn't important, not any more. I just don't want you to leave me again, please.'

She said alright, I'll stay, but there are things I won't be able to talk about, you have to understand that. And she put her face up to mine and stared right into my eyes and said, 'Alex, this is the thing. There are some stories that can never be told. And you shouldn't say you love me because you can't, not properly. You don't even know me, and you wouldn't if you did, really you wouldn't.' But I told her then that I saw things differently from her, and that it was my belief that one could never really know another person anyway, not completely. I said I was fairly certain I was capable of loving someone without question, and that was what I understood to be the meaning of unconditional love. 'You mean you're saying you love me unconditionally now, Alex? Are you crazy?' she asked, smiling through her tears. And I said yes, I supposed that was what I was saying, but that it was all getting a bit complicated and philosophical for me and I was just very glad to have her back, having lost her once already. 'Prove it to me,' she said then. 'Prove it to me that you love me unconditionally.'

'How?' I asked. 'How should I prove it?' and because she buried her face into my chest and pressed her mouth right up against me as she spoke, so that I couldn't see her any more and nor could I make out

her reply, I pulled her head back away from me which meant that we were looking right into one another's eyes when she said, for a second time, 'Marry me, Alex. Prove it by marrying me.'

Much later on, when the evening had fallen and she said 'Let us go then, you and I,' and led me out on to the balcony, she told me that it really should have been me who had proposed, and so I did.

And that is a scene that comes back to me sometimes, the two of us out there against an evening sky that burned with a low red sun, her face looking down at me where I knelt on the ground in front of her, her expression utterly unguarded for one of the very few times I would ever see it so. It is a scene I have replayed for myself endlessly, taking it carefully from the store I have of such scenes, and wondering as I do so about the wisdom of looking at it, or at any of them, such is the sorrow that will follow. And sometimes this scene will show itself to me unannounced, emerging from the tapestry of my grief that is there when I wake in the mornings and find, as I sometimes do, that I have become trapped in a frame of sadness which has been constructed around me in my sleep, so that there can be no escaping from it. And when this happens I can only watch, feeling the shuttles rattle above me and underneath me and the threads run back and forth beneath my skin until pictures start to emerge, hundreds of them in turn. Each one takes its shape gradually at the beginning, and then, at the last, becomes suddenly, rapidly, clear before being replaced a moment or two later by another. At first, I will notice only that one colour of thread, red perhaps, is emerging from the warp of my skin more frequently than any other and forming itself into nubbly patches here and there, dotted across my torso. And then a different colour will do the same, and I am trying to read these patches and make sense of them and I cannot until the moment when everything begins to move too quickly for me to be able to keep up and there we are,

running hand in hand on a Sunday morning across the lawns in front of Kenwood House, caught by the rain without coats or umbrellas and neither of us caring in the slightest, and Rachel's hair is wet like pelt and when we reach the trees I stop and pull her into me and kiss the water from her face. And then we disappear, and instead I am watching us walk out across Camber Sands and squeeze ourselves onto a rug too small for all the things we've brought with us for our picnic, the picnic which is to be the last of the summer in which we were reunited. It was a weekend that fell a fortnight or so after Richard and Lucinda's wedding, still hot enough to swim in the sea, or at least to paddle. After we had dried ourselves and eaten our lunch we'd tried, each of us, to paint a watercolour with the set I'd given Rachel as a gift that morning. We'd been silent for an hour or so, sitting side by side and sketching first, Rachel saying she knew I didn't want to bother with that bit but I must, that's what the book I'd given her with the box of paints said we had to do. And then, later on, when I told her I'd finished my painting, she looked across at what I'd done and she looked out to sea once more and back at my picture again and said, Alex I think you might be colour-blind have you ever had a test?

It takes almost nothing these days, just one tiny thing really and I am with her, falling and tumbling and drowning in the memory of her.

She is everywhere for me, without compass or restraint.

The rain came in early that day on Camber Sands, and as we walked back to the car, her hand held fast in mine and her steps falling more rapidly than my own so that we might keep a pace together, I looked back once and saw our footprints strung across the blank canvas of the beach, marking out our separate rhythms in a cursive falling there, carefree on the wetness of the sand.

So lost am I in my thoughts it takes me a moment or two to realise Harry is no longer sitting on the sofa opposite me, and I think perhaps he has gone out and left me on my own. But then I hear him moving about in the other room, clearing up from our lunch and making more tea. I look at the photos hanging on the walls and I wonder about the ones Rachel had sent him, the ones of the day we were married. When he comes back in I ask if he will show me them and he looks surprised, standing still in the middle of the room as though uncertain. But then he puts the teapot down and walks over and starts rooting around among the pine cones and postcards that are lined up in front of his books. Apparently finding nothing there, he removes one after the other of the invitations that stand there also and stacks them neatly on the floor beside him so he can look in some of the box files they were hiding. I am beginning to think he is playing with me, and has no intention of actually showing me the photographs, but at last he finds them and walks back towards me. Before he relinquishes his hold on them though, and just as I am about to take them from

him, he says that while he doesn't mind me looking at them, he would prefer it if I did so on the understanding that he would like them back when I have finished. He can arrange for copies to be made, of course, but he would like to keep the originals, if I have no objection. Because of the anger I feel when he says these things, anger at his controlling fumbling attempts to negotiate terms as to his release of these images of Rachel, I do not reply. Instead I lower my arm and leave him holding the photographs out in front of him and I sit back in my chair, shaking my head involuntarily, repulsed by what he's tried to do.

Eventually, and appearing to have become as embarrassed as I hoped he would, he hands them over. I look at them with more haste than I would have liked to, my frustration and irritation being so intense that it actually feels as though it is coursing like boiling water up and down the inside of my arms and across my chest and I want, suddenly, to punch him. I have to flick through them only once to know I have seen them all before and have them almost by heart, so familiar are they. All of them were taken on the day we were married and are either copies of ones from our own album, or of the ones that I found when, in the week before I visited Harry, I'd finally opened the envelope of photographs that Evie gave me in the police station on the day after Rachel was murdered. And so I hand them straight back to him, noticing as I do so that I am unable to stop my hand from shaking.

'And the letter?' I say, my voice so clipped I feel as though I have hit him rather than spoken. 'Or do you require a written agreement of some sort prior to your releasing it?'

'I'm sorry, Alex, really, I am so sorry,' and he almost jumps back over to the bookcase and as he starts to open and close the files again, sifting through the papers inside, I can see that his hands are shaking also and he is become hunched over, like an old man, and I realise I have upset him and I am ashamed for the cruelty I have shown. Of course, when I read the letter he hands me, I find it contains nothing

that is not already known to me, being simply a description of the
tiny ceremony we held in the register office, and of Rachel's dress, of
how handsome she thought I looked, and of the menu we chose for
the lunch we had with Richard and Lucinda afterwards. And I under-
stand then that Harry's reluctance to share these things, the letter and
the photographs, is born not from a desire to keep anything back from
me, but rather from a fear that I might take away all that remains to
him of Rachel. My anger softens and instead, I feel only pity. But while
I have calmed down, it seems that he has not. He takes the letter from
me and tries to fold it back into its envelope but he can't make it fit. It
drops from his hands and shoots under the sofa and as I lean forward,
meaning to retrieve it for him, he flinches, so I sit back and leave him
to it. When finally he has found it, and put it away on the shelf, he
takes his place on the sofa once more and pulls a handkerchief from
his breast pocket and starts to wipe both his eyes with it, over and
over, and we sit for some time in silence, neither of us making any
mention of the fact that he is weeping.

Eventually he puts his handkerchief back in his pocket and he
coughs, once or twice. He stands and pours us some tea and says he
will begin again from where we left off, returning to Anthony's Judd
Street kitchen, and as he starts to speak we are there once more, the flies
circling above him where he sits and the pictures curling on the walls.

'Did you really think I'd written them on my own, Harry?' Anthony
said, standing over Harry where he sat at the kitchen table, still
attempting to dry his hair with Anthony's tea towel. 'I mean, "My Last
Duchess", for god's sake. Bit of an obvious choice, isn't it?' he carried
on, pulling up a chair as he spoke and sitting down opposite Harry.
'And such a girl's choice. You could have credited me with a slightly
more finely honed imagination than that, couldn't you?' and Harry
thought suddenly about getting up and leaving there and then, unsure

he wanted to hear what Anthony was about to tell him. He stayed though, and that was how he found out the letters had been Rachel's idea, in the beginning.

Just as I am beginning to settle into Harry's story again, sitting back in my chair and following, in a grim kind of a way, the soft rhythms of his voice, he stops suddenly, almost as soon as he has begun. He says nothing, simply staring into the fire and looking very much as though he is going to cry again. When I ask him if he is alright he looks up and he raises his eyebrows as though he is surprised to see me there, as though he has been thinking about something else entirely.

'I am quite alright, Alex, yes. It is just that it will be difficult for me to tell you these things, that is all. If I were to be frank, I would have to say that I would rather not be the bearer of any of this tale, let alone this particular part of it. But that much, I suppose, is obvious to you by now. As it is I have begun, and I must carry on. I would simply ask that you be patient with me.'

I nodded and he continued, but for the next few hours, as he picked a route back and forth through the events Anthony had related to him during the first part of his visit to Judd Street, it was in so awkward a manner, and by way of a narrative so shot through with digressions and periphrases, and so crowded with ellipses and euphemisms, that I found it difficult to follow what he was saying with any degree of clarity, however hard I tried. It was, I think, both the fact that I'd upset him just before he began, as well as the very obvious ill ease he felt about having to relate events that would not show Rachel in a guise with which I would be familiar, that accounted for his awkwardness. I did my best to follow him, though I suppose I must bear some responsibility for having done so without a great deal of success. Were Harry to have been a client I was preparing for cross-examination I would have been able to interject at will, to question and to challenge. Or, alternatively, were his to have been the voice of an opposition witness, speaking to me from the pages of a written statement, I would

have been able to scrawl exclamation marks in the margin, sticking Post-it notes full of questions all over the pages so that someone else more junior than me could take them away and draft a letter seeking further particulars, thus eliciting the information I knew was being kept from me.

But instead I could only wait, storing away the facts as they were parcelled out and hoping to be able to piece them together later on. That I also contributed to the somewhat shoddy quality of the resulting narrative is something I would be the first to acknowledge; my frustration was so intense I sometimes found myself losing concentration altogether and drifting off, filling in the gaps that Harry was leaving, all too aware as I did so of the dangers inherent in such an approach. When he'd finished his attempt, and we had broken once more so that we could each of us change for dinner, I went back to my room and telephoned Evie, just as I had warned her I would. It was during that call that she told me her version of the same events, amongst other things, and only afterwards was I able to construct any sort of a cohesive picture for myself from the glimpses Harry had given me of the circumstances in which the letters had been written, the letters purporting to blackmail him for the murder of his wife.

I'd said nothing to Harry about Evie's email, nor did I see any reason to tell him it was my intention to speak with her. He'd revealed to me that afternoon that Evie knew at least as much as he did of the events surrounding the writing of the letters, and also that the two of them shared a common source for their knowledge. It seemed that Anthony had contacted her on the day he was sent down. After he'd confessed to Haddon, taking sole responsibility both for writing and sending the letters to Harry, he'd packed up his rooms and gone, leaving behind him the book Harry had given him as a parting gesture. And almost as soon as the wicket door had closed behind him, he'd found a phonebox and made a call to Evie. I knew very little at that stage of what kind of relationship, if any, had existed between Evie and

Anthony. I already had a sense that their paths would have crossed on and off, Anthony having been so often a guest at the weekend parties Rachel had apparently thrown in Evie's house at Chelsea. And then of course, playing at the back of my mind, there was the photograph on the parking ticket, the one that had been taken years later, a few weeks before Rachel's murder. But it wasn't until the following day that Harry would explain why Evie and Anthony were still in touch by the time of that photograph, and reveal what lay behind that May morning meeting outside the library where Rachel did her work.

When Anthony had spoken with Evie on the afternoon he'd been told to pack his things and go for good, he'd broken down and told her everything, so distraught was he at what had happened over the previous few weeks. Where Harry had been reticent with me in the telling of the tale, Evie, when I telephoned her, had relished it, seeming to take a strange kind of pleasure in conveying the most sordid of its details to me, and doing so with such visceral clarity that it was almost as though I had been there myself.

My call to Tokyo was answered straight away, but it was a man's voice that greeted me rather than Evie's. When I asked to speak to her he muttered a few expletives before passing me on and from the drowsiness in her voice I gathered I had woken them up. I apologised to her, saying I'd given no thought to the time difference and asking when I could call back, but she told me that she'd rather get it over and done with there and then. She said she'd thought things through since sending her email and had decided that, while of course it was none of her business how I wanted to spend my time, or to waste it, she wanted to make it clear that if I insisted on staying in Oxford with Harry Gardner I had to understand she had no intention of keeping up a running commentary on whatever else he was going to tell me. She was happy to speak now, briefly, but after that I was on my own. And then she added, reminding me quite how nasty she could be, that she couldn't help observing that if I'd acquainted myself rather better

with my wife than I had done, it perhaps wouldn't be necessary for me to go around the place bothering people about things that had happened such an awfully long time ago.

'Evie,' I said in response, determined not to rise to her goading, 'shall we talk or are you just going to carry on insulting me?' and she said right, fine, let's talk. And then she yawned, slowly, and told me to get on with it.

I said there were a number of things I wanted to ask her about, but that it might perhaps be best to start with the letters that had been inside the document wallet she'd made me courier to her. I said Harry had told me a certain amount about them already, and that he had described for me, in a manner of speaking, the way he understood them to have been written. I explained that whilst he'd clearly given me as full an account as he was able to, I would be grateful if she would tell me a little bit more about it, knowing as I did that she and Anthony had discussed it on the day he'd been sent down. 'Why of course, Alex, why ever not?' she said, and I noticed at once that there was no longer any drowsiness in her voice; what I heard there instead was a strange kind of excitement, and an energy that was distinctly vindictive.

She began by saying that she'd warned me in her email about the wisdom of asking too many questions, and that she would proceed only if I was quite certain that was what I wanted. And then, when I said nothing, she told me that the phone call she'd received from Anthony, the one that he'd made immediately after leaving Worcester on the day he'd been sent down, was something she would never forget, such was his distress and his anger about what had happened. The way he'd been later on that same afternoon was no less raw and unrestrained, when she'd met with him in her office and asked him to tell her everything again so that she could be quite clear in her understanding of the part Rachel had played in the events he was describing. And that was an affect that she managed to recreate for me in her retelling, even from such a distance and from such a time removed.

Once she started to talk there was no stopping her, despite the reluctance she'd professed to at the outset, so that by the time we came to the end of our conversation I saw from my watch I had missed dinner altogether. Realising that if I hurried, I might still be able to find Harry at dessert, I jogged across the quad and straight up the steps on the other side. But when I reached the top I slowed my pace and walked back and forth along the terrace a few times, wanting to sort the facts as Evie had described them into some sort of order in my own mind. It was my intention to place them one by one alongside Harry's, these facts of hers, so that I could test the links between them and find the ones which held most fast, and most true. I placed those of the resulting sequences of images and statements that were sufficiently coincident for my task on top of one another, as though they were drawings sketched on separate pieces of tracing paper, and then I moved them up and down and back and forth, turning them over and over to see if I could find a position whereby they could be aligned with one another closely enough to form what I considered to be a cohesive, single, image. If Harry had given me a page torn from a children's puzzle book, then Evie had taken a pencil and scored in the lines between each of his dots, so that as I reached the end of the terrace for the last time and made my way down the narrow set of steps that led to the room where dessert was being held, something like a composite version was beginning to emerge, and I knew that with a little more time and left to its own devices, what I was looking at would become clear enough for me to feel almost as though I had been a voyeur on the events, if not quite a participant in them.

I opened the low oak door at the end of the corridor and found that dessert had only just begun. All I'd really missed was the procession out of Hall and the stroll along the terrace, each of the guests and Fellows who had been sitting on High Table clutching their linen napkins and following Harry as he would have led them towards the room that I stood looking into. It took a moment or two for my eyes to

adjust after the brightness of the lights in the corridor, but eventually I made him out through the glow of the candles that had been placed everywhere, and the soft flickers of the fire he sat beside. As he saw me he stood, gesturing that I should make my way towards the one empty place that remained. It was with some relief that I became aware that the people I would be joining were so deeply engrossed in one another that I'd be unlikely to have to contribute to their conversation. The seats were arranged in little groups of three around the room, loosely forming a large circle, with tiny walnut tables in front of each group, but to describe it thus would be to suggest a greater degree of order than was conveyed by the scene I looked on as I sat and took the plate that Harry handed me. If the layout of the furniture was designed to imply a kind of clumsy chaos, then so was the content of the large table that sat just beyond this gathering. It was covered with silver bowls and plates and platters piled with fruit so ripe that some of it was dripping, a little. Pomegranate seeds spilt deep crimson, landing on peaches that sat in a curious perfection beneath them, the juice running slowly down each yellow globe until it slipped, at the last, onto the tabletop's sheen and sat in a glistening pool. Everything seemed to glow amber in the half-light of the fire, and the darkness of the panelling, combined with the complete absence of any electric light, made that low-ceilinged room seem crowded, almost suffocating. I loosened my tie and took the first of the decanters that was passed to me and poured myself a crystal beaker full of something dark and sweet and I sat back, breathing in its heavy scent as deeply as I could before beginning to drink.

Every evening thus far, when we have come through to this little room after dinner, I have seen only the surface of things, so involved have I been each time, albeit reluctantly, in the conversations forced upon me. Tonight though I am able to observe things more closely and I notice there is more of a system than I have been aware of hitherto. When I arrived Harry had still been checking the seating plan

he'd drawn up on the back of an envelope during dinner, making sure everyone was in the right place and talking to the people they were supposed to be talking to. And now we are all settled, he stands every once in a while and nods to one of the other Fellows. His chosen assistant, thus selected, rises as soon as he is able to extricate himself without offence from the conversation in which he has been engaged. He steps forward to the large table and takes, according to the way in which he has interpreted Harry's nod, either a decanter, or a bowl of fruit. He carries it over to one of the little groups of three and offers them its contents before replacing it on the table and returning to his seat, easing seamlessly back into the conversation. Before too long, Harry is on his feet again, nodding and signalling once more, so that none of the guests have to trouble themselves for an instant and neither are their plates ever empty nor their glasses unfilled. They are, in this way, almost continually waited on by one or other of their hosts, disturbed only when it is necessary to encourage them with the politest of reminders that they might like to pass a decanter to their left or to their right, should they have forgotten to do so.

This is a rhythm that is disturbed only once on this particular evening, when a man appears from a door cut so unobtrusively from the panelling that until he opens it I haven't even realised it is there. He nods at Harry before moving briskly across to the table and setting down a plate of papaya with quarters of lime. After this, he circles the room once, replacing a candle that has burned too far down, and picking up a stray grape from the floor where it has fallen. And then he is gone and we are become once more an orrery suspended, this little circle of guests, with Harry a dark star somewhere at our outer reaches ensuring we are always static, that our glasses are turned from gold to purple and back again, and watching us wipe juices sticky from our chins as he observes the liaisons he has engendered taking place all around him.

This is the scene that surrounds me in this little room, the dark-

ness only held off by the fire and the occasional glint of a candle's flame flashing back from a piece of silver as I sink further into my chair and allow the wine to settle in my veins. And this is the point at which I summon for myself once more the pieces of tracing paper that are Harry and Evie's stories, drawing them out from the back of my mind where they have continued unaided in the task of aligning themselves so that I might see for myself the scenes they depict. And with the lull of conversation ebbing and flowing round about, the events that they describe start to materialise before me, faintly at first and then more clearly, and I watch, mesmerised, as Anthony and Rachel and Cissy between them dream up the idea of writing Harry a series of anonymous letters accusing him of murder.

It started as a joke. Just the sort of thing the three of them were always coming up with on the afternoons they spent hidden away together in the set of rooms Rachel and Cissy shared. They would schedule them in, these lost afternoons, as they came to call them, maybe once a week or so. They'd take it in turns to buy in provisions, bottles of vodka and packets of multicoloured gold-tipped cocktail cigarettes from the tobacconist on The High, each of them having purchased an ivory cigarette holder on Rachel's instructions. And so it was that they would close the outer door of the set and strip naked and begin to drink, and to smoke, and to talk. It was very pretentious, Anthony said, and he, perhaps more than any of them, was aware at the time that it was just one big Oxford cliché. But that was why he liked it so much, in a way. He felt he finally belonged, on those afternoons they spent together behaving like Oxford students. That he had at last been accepted into that world.

It would depend on what day of the week it was, and on how much vodka they'd been able to afford from the kitty they'd built up, but quite often the afternoon would stretch into the evening, and on into

the night, and if Rachel and Cissy had nothing in the fridge Anthony would be sent out under cover of darkness for a takeaway, and if they got too cold finally, in the middle of the night, they would take baths and wrap themselves up in duvets and carry on drinking.

There were very few rules in that commune of theirs. The first was with regard to its membership which, they agreed right at the start, would be forever restricted just to the three of them. 'Whatever happens,' Anthony recalled Rachel saying as they toasted their union on the first day of its formation. And they must never tell anyone what they did on their lost afternoons, Rachel saying once more, 'Whatever happens,' and Cissy saying it back again, making the other two repeat it with her as though they were boy scouts sitting around a campfire swearing a secret pact, so that he'd half expected one of the girls to bring out a penknife and demand he draw a drop of blood and mingle it with theirs.

Beyond that there was only the sex to be legislated on, and that was something Rachel and Cissy seemed to have worked out between themselves in advance, announcing to Anthony in that first meeting that he could look all he liked but he couldn't touch, whatever happened. He could touch himself, of course, and they seemed quite keen that he should do that, but he was never to touch either of them, and he would never be invited to join in. So he stuck to the rules and only watched, bringing himself off again and again as he sat in Rachel's armchair and gazed at the two of them making love to one another, always in the manner of a performance rather than an act of real intimacy. He found it fairly unbearable most of the time, having to stay just away from the bed they lay on, or to sit just apart from them on the floor, but when he'd tried to raise the issue with them and suggest it might be time to revise their agreement, they'd told him he could take it or leave it, and that if he couldn't handle it he could just walk away there and then. And so he'd stayed, and carried on watching, and in a strange kind of a way he'd come to find

it more manageable each time, once he'd accepted he was only ever to be an observer.

And then, one day in late May, half an hour or so into one of their lost afternoons when the sex was yet to come and they had only just started to drink, they all three of them went through to Rachel's bedroom and he and Cissy were watching her undress when she said, 'Why do you think he's so obsessed with Browning anyway?' and that was how it started.

They talked about Harry all afternoon, in an idle kind of a way. They came around again to the poems eventually, and Cissy said something about Harry's wife, and brought up the rumours that had been circulating about how it couldn't have been cancer, it must have been a lover, or suicide, or something.

'What d'you mean, "or something"?' Rachel said. 'D'you mean murder? You think he murdered her?'

'Oh for god's sake, Rach, why don't you shut up,' Cissy replied. 'Of course he didn't.'

'But why not? It happens doesn't it? People do do that sort of thing you know. And that,' Rachel carried on, running one hand lazily over Cissy's breasts and back again, and then trailing her fingers over her stomach and letting them rest there for a minute before moving her hand further down, so that Anthony began to listen less carefully to their conversation, 'would explain the Browning.'

They'd talked about it again the next time they met, and Rachel seemed to have become quite enthralled by the idea. And when one afternoon they had all three of them agreed in their drunkenness that it was quite possible, if not probable even, that Harry had murdered his wife, she'd said it: 'I think we should send him a letter. Test him out, you know. See if we can get a rise. It'd be fun, don't you think?' And they had laughed about the idea and flicked through some poems and read them to one another, hideously drunk, and when they had found poem after poem suited to their task, Anthony fetched a piece

of paper from Rachel's desk and sketched the letters out there and then.

They'd struggled over how to sign them off, choosing and rejecting first one name and then another from the poems. 'We'll find something perfect in *The Ring and the Book*, I know we will,' Anthony said, picking up Rachel's copy.

'Fuck off, Anthony. You're trying to be cleverer than you actually are, as usual,' Cissy said. 'Forget it. It's fucking boring and fucking long and I'm the only one of us who's ever going to read it. Let's just make something up.'

And that was when one of them had come up with 'A Well-Wisher'. They'd all toyed with the idea of translating it, preferably into something with a literary twist. 'How about Ben Volio?' Anthony suggested. 'You know, Shakespeare, but make it into two names.' Cissy had objected though, telling him not to be an idiot, they wanted a baddie not a goodie, someone really evil, not some kind of Mr Nice Guy. 'Don't be so simplistic, Cissy,' he'd responded. 'People can be both, you know. They can be bad and good at the same time. I mean, it could be argued, for example, in R and J—'

'No,' Rachel said then. 'No they can't. Most people are only one or the other. I mean it. Some people are all bad, whichever way you look at them. However many times you give them another chance, they'll fuck you over. Even if they say they love you.'

He'd argued it out with her for a while, but when Cissy joined in he'd backed off and left them to it. Until, that was, they'd started to say some really ridiculous things to one another, and the whole thing had descended into an actual fight, and he'd had no choice but to step in and break it up and tell Rachel to stop crying, neither of them were trying to fuck her over. They were her friends, he told her. And they were having fun, that was all. She'd calmed down then, all of them had, and they'd decided to stick with 'A Well-Wisher' and leave it at that.

'Three weeks left till the end of term,' he'd said. 'We'll send the first

one at the end of this week, after we've had our tute with him on Friday, and we'll see what happens. If he doesn't take the bait we'll carry on sending them, one a week, until he does.'

'Alright,' Rachel said. 'We'll crack him, you'll see,' and she lay back on her bed and Cissy climbed on top of her.

'Who's going to actually send them though?' Cissy asked, later on. 'I'm sure as hell not going to. My dad would kill me if we got found out.'

'Oh come on,' Rachel said. 'Don't be a chicken Ciss.' And that was when Anthony had put his proposition to them. He would type up the letters in the computer room so they couldn't be traced, and he'd send them, but only if they agreed to give him something in return. 'Oh my god Anthony you sleaze!' Rachel said. 'I can't believe you think we'd actually fall for that!'

'Why not?' Anthony replied. 'What's so unappealing about the idea of actually letting me fuck one of you anyway? It's not like you don't know me well enough by now is it?'

Rachel and Cissy began to laugh at him then. 'Know you well enough?' Rachel said, gasping for breath. 'Ciss, he thinks it's because we don't know him well enough! Can you believe that?' And Cissy joined in, telling Anthony to take a long look at himself in a mirror next time he found himself in front of one, and the two of them carried on laughing until, he said, they were actually almost screeching with it. He hated them both at that moment, really hated them. But then suddenly Cissy stopped laughing and said, 'OK. Let's do it. It's only a fuck, after all.'

'No it's not, Ciss,' Rachel said, half laughing, half horrified. 'God, you're so—' and she broke off there, getting up from the bed and walking over to the other side of the room.

'What? Rachel, what? I'm so what?'

'So. I don't know. So immoral,' Rachel said, and she wasn't laughing any more.

'Rachel,' Cissy said, sitting up in the bed, mock-passion on her face

and her hands clasped in front of her chest. 'I never knew you cared, darling heart!' and she got up and ran over to Rachel and kissed her for a while before stopping suddenly and saying, 'Cut!' She pushed her away and walked back to the bed and lay down before carrying on. 'You know what, honey, who cares,' and she turned her head and announced to Anthony, 'You're on, kiddo. But the letters were your idea if anyone ever finds out about them, right? Not my problem, OK?'

'OK,' Anthony said, and he got up from his chair and started to walk towards her.

'Oh for god's sake not now you funny little northerner!' Rachel said, walking back to the bed and climbing into it. She lifted the covers over her and Cissy, placing her hands on Cissy's face and looking her right in the eyes. 'When shall we let him, Ciss? When?'

And that was when they agreed that if, and only if, Anthony sent all three of the letters, and if, and only if, he got away with it, they'd meet him behind the Pavilion at midnight on the night of the Casablanca Ball and give him his reward. 'Outside?' Anthony said, desperately wanting to get into bed with the two of them there and then. 'Why outside?' he asked.

'Why not?' Rachel said. 'Have you never had sex en plein air Anthony?' she carried on. 'You're so boring. He's so boring isn't he Ciss. So fucking boring,' and she turned to Cissy and pulled her down under the covers and with the sound of the supper bell ringing out across the quad, Anthony sat back down in his chair and watched the shapes of their bodies moving under the duvet and that was when he decided that he would send the letters after all, whatever happened.

The girls had backed out pretty much straight away, just as he'd expected them to. So that when he told them he'd gone ahead and put the first of the letters into Harry's pigeonhole they were furious. They swore they'd never speak to him again, and didn't he realise

how much shit they'd got themselves into already that term, and what
had he been thinking and it was only ever a stupid joke and what the
hell was he going to do about it now? He'd tried to calm them down,
telling them it didn't matter, it was only one, and Harry would never
know who it was from, not for definite, and he was hardly the sort to
confront them anyway, and they should just forget it.

They weren't convinced, and the tutorial that Friday had been
awful for him. He was amazed the two of them had even shown up.
They'd refused to acknowledge him all week apart from one morning
after breakfast when they'd waited for him outside Hall and marched
him down to the lake and told him he had to go to Harry and confess
and stop it all and make it alright. 'OK,' he'd said. 'OK. How about you
give me what you promised me first, and then I will?' They'd looked at
one another, he said, and then they'd laughed at him. 'Grow up little
boy,' Cissy told him, and she'd started to walk away. Rachel had stayed
for a minute or two longer, saying she was sorry about it all, but he
should really get a grip now and sort it out, and she couldn't help him
if he wasn't able to help himself.

Anthony said that she'd sounded just like his mother had when
he was a child and he'd done something wrong to get her attention
and she told him off and he hated her for it. And it was because of the
way that he'd felt, then, that instead of going to make his amends with
Harry, and putting a stop to the whole thing, he'd gone to the lodge on
the way to dinner and put the second of the letters in Harry's pigeon-
hole. Of course, when he told Cissy and Rachel, that was it. They froze
him out completely and he'd spent the week alone, feeling as though
he was going slightly insane. He was completely at a loss as to what to
do with himself, and what to do about the letters. And then, when nei-
ther Cissy nor Rachel showed up for the last tutorial, and even Harry
had rejected him and sent him away without so much as looking at
him, he decided he may as well see it through to the end and send
the final letter. After Haddon had called the three of them out of Hall

and Rachel and Cissy found out that he'd sent that one as well, they'd stood with him on the terrace after Haddon had gone and told him he was on his own. They would deny everything, they said. There was no way of tracing their involvement, and if it came to it, it was their word against his. 'Safety in numbers,' Cissy said, and it was because Anthony knew that she was right that he'd owned up the next morning, almost before Haddon had started to speak.

He said to Harry that when he'd stood in Haddon's study that morning and been told he was going to be sent down, he'd realised that his world as he knew it was over, and he'd found himself unable to shake the hand that Harry offered him. He'd lost everything, and he'd been too devastated at that point even to feel angry with Rachel and Cissy about what had happened. It was Harry's visit to his rooms that'd been the final straw, though, and that was when he'd decided to do what he did next. Harry's forgiveness, he said, and his gift of the book of poetry, had somehow made him angry where he hadn't been, and Harry's kindness in the face of his own cruelty had shown him a clear and final glimpse of what he was about to lose. And so, as he stood on Gloucester Green waiting for the bus that would take him back to Manchester, he used up the last of his cash by making a telephone call to Evie, and, in his anger, telling her everything.

When I made my call to Evie in Tokyo and woke her from her sleep, she in her turn told me everything that Anthony had told her in the course of his call from Gloucester Green, and in the conversation the two of them had had later on that afternoon, when they'd met in her office at the Ashmolean and talked it all through once more. And when she had told it all to me, she reached the end of her contribution to my understanding of events. That was the moment when the lines that were scored on her tracing paper faded suddenly, when a man's voice called out and interrupted our conversation, saying would she come back to bed now and hadn't she been on the phone for long enough and she said yes, alright, I'm coming. She finished by saying

that she didn't see that we needed to speak again, repeating her previous admonishments with regard to my being in Oxford and telling me again to get back to London and get on with things and leave the police to it, saying that nothing Harry could tell me would bring Rachel back. She said at the last that she was leaving Tokyo the following day anyhow, and had no idea how long she'd be away, so there was no point in calling her again in the immediate future.

'Don't worry, Evie,' I said. 'I'll find you if I have to, wherever you are,' and she laughed and told me that there was really no need to threaten her, she had nothing to hide, and that I could carry on playing detectives with Harry if I wanted to but as far as she was concerned she could think of better ways to spend her time. And then the line went dead and I realised she'd hung up without my having asked her about the photograph on the parking ticket, and about what exactly she'd been doing with Anthony and Rachel that day outside the British Library. As I got ready to go and see if I was still in time to find Harry at dessert, I resolved to ask him about it before he got very much further in his tale.

Earlier on that afternoon, at about the point in the story where Evie's rendition of the events in question had come to a halt, Harry's own narration had come good again, so to speak. Having got through the sequence of events that he had found it so awkward to talk about, he'd become a better storyteller once more, so that instead of dots, he gave me images and dialogue and wove a fuller clearer picture in the way he'd done before. He reminded me that when Anthony had approached him in the British Library and taken him back to his Judd Street flat, he himself had still been of the understanding that Evie had disowned Rachel on the night of the Casablanca Ball as a direct result of Haddon's phone call. However, when he sat in Anthony's kitchen and Anthony began to tell him about standing in the phone box on Gloucester Green on the afternoon he'd been sent down, he realised that the conversation Anthony was about to describe was, in all prob-

ability, what had lain behind Evie's rejection of Rachel, rather than Haddon's phone call to her later that night.

Evie had persuaded Anthony to stay where he was until she got there, she was coming straight away, and when he'd pointed out that he was in a bus station and that there was really no need, he'd just wanted her to know, that was all, she'd given him directions to her office at the Ashmolean and said that she'd arrange for him to be let in, telling him to go there and wait until she arrived. So he did as she asked, and when she got there he gave her the document wallet he'd kept with the photocopies he'd made of the letters, and some other things he had wanted her to see.

'What other things?' Harry had asked him then.

'Oh. Just the Browning essays, you know.'

'The Browning essays?' Harry replied. 'What essays?'

'You didn't know about that, Harry? I thought you must have.'

And when Harry said he had no idea what he was talking about, Anthony told him that he'd written every single one of Rachel's Browning essays for her, week by week, in addition to the ones he'd written for himself, and that she'd copied them into her own hand before the tutorials began each time, so that there was no risk of Harry finding out about it.

Harry told me that this was perhaps the thing that had shocked him most that day in Anthony's Judd Street kitchen, rather than anything Anthony had said about the sort of things the three of them had done together, or about Rachel and Cissy being lovers, or about the way they had been so cruel about him in their gossiping. 'They were young,' Harry said to me. 'And she was very young. And her life, you know. What she'd grown up with. Or without, rather.' But the cheating had saddened him. To think that she'd sat each week and read essays to him that were not her own, and that he'd never had so much as an inkling that it was happening. 'Why did she do it?' he said in his confusion to Anthony, remembering how her work had improved the

following year, when she was working entirely alone. 'There was no reason,' Anthony explained. 'She was just too lazy, that was all, and I was just too willing.' And it was only then that Harry realised that every single thing Rachel had told him that night in the hospital, and throughout the summer that followed, had been founded on a series of untruths. He felt a bitter anger then but checked it straight away; he wasn't entirely sure he'd understood Anthony correctly, nor could he bring himself to really believe what he was hearing.

When Anthony had handed over the document wallet to Evie, and when he'd told her everything that had happened, and when she'd made him go over it again and again, so that she could have every last detail, she had been, he said to Harry, incandescent with rage. She'd asked Anthony to stay in her office and wait until she came back, and she'd gone straight over to College and found Rachel and told her she wasn't welcome in Chelsea that summer, and nor would she ever be. And, she'd said, as far as money was concerned, Rachel was hence-forth to make her own way in the world.

'After all I've done for her,' she said to Anthony when she got back. She'd been gone for almost an hour, and because he hadn't known what else to do with himself he'd ended up idly rifling through the drawers of her desk and guessing her password before flicking through the emails in her inbox. He was wondering what he'd been thinking, agreeing to sit and wait for her like that, and he'd been on the point of giving up and leaving when suddenly she was there, slamming the door behind her and throwing her keys on the desk. He was surprised by the intensity of her reaction. If he'd thought for a moment that she would actually cut Rachel off in the way that she had, he would never have told her. He knew he'd made a colossal error of judgement, and one for which he was truly sorry. 'I barely knew the woman at that stage,' he said to Harry, as though in explanation. 'I'd met her once or twice, that was all, at Rachel's parties in Chelsea sometimes, the morning after, you know, over breakfast, when we were all on our

best behaviour and Evie was grilling us about our work, demanding to know our plans for the future.' What he hadn't realised was that Evie was also on her best behaviour on those occasions, and that rather than the lovely maternal figure she had presented to them all, he described her as becoming, that day in Oxford, 'a bitch from hell'. 'When push came to shove, she just turned into a really nasty woman. I thought she was like, you know, Rachel's kind of replacement mum or something. And I didn't think someone's mum would do something like that. My mum was always a bit of a nightmare but nothing like that. Took me straight back in when I got home to Manchester. No questions asked. And I'd been sent down from Oxford fucking University for god's sake.'

As Harry sat there listening to Anthony, he realised that by the time Rachel had gone to the Ball that night, Evie had already passed her judgement. He ran through the events in his mind, only half listening to Anthony, and he tried as best he could to piece it all together. Having done so, the thought occurred to him that it was quite possible that the whole episode of Rachel convincing Towneley she was so inebriated as to need hospitalisation was nothing more than a scheme, and that she'd thought far enough ahead to know that all she'd have to do, when it came to it, was to ask Harry to arrange for the college to help her in some way, thereby solving her problem. He was completely amazed by what Anthony had told him, and when he remembered the way she'd turned her back that night in the hospital, lifting up her hair and asking him to do up her dress, he felt like a fool. It was as though the floor had shifted beneath him that day in Judd Street, and as if the walls had moved from their place as Anthony spoke, repositioning his understanding of their history. Partway through their conversation he'd had another sudden memory of Rachel, in the weeks leading up to her Finals. He pictured her lying on her back in his garden reading a book and reaching out to take the glass of lemonade he'd poured for her, without so much as looking at him, and at that moment of recollection,

the nonchalance he'd read at the time as being born from the ease of their companionship became something entirely different.

'I am sorry to say this, Alex, but I did become angry with her then. I did. Very angry indeed. Not for long, not at all, but it would be dishonest of me to pretend otherwise,' and he looked away, scratching the back of his neck and coughing once or twice before carrying on.

He said that his anger passed almost immediately, and he found himself only saddened by what he'd discovered, deeply so. And even then he'd forgiven her straight away. She had always struck him as embodying a strange combination of immense vulnerability and excessive resilience. There was about her, he said, a toughness. He told me then how he had come in from the library one day in the Michaelmas term of her third year. He'd been standing at the bottom of the stairs, taking off his coat and his hat, when he heard her voice and realised she'd left her door open by accident. She was speaking to herself loudly enough for him to be able to make out what it was that she was saying, over and over, 'Rachel fucking Cardanine you are such an idiot get a fucking grip. Idiot. For god's sake. Idiot, idiot fucking idiot,' and so on, so that he froze where he stood and waited until he heard her door close before he moved again, not wanting her to know that he'd been listening. And he often wondered, as he sat in his garden watching her revising, a book held up in the air above her face to protect her from the sun, or when he heard her singing in the bath or reciting a sonnet to herself when she thought he couldn't hear, what it was that had made her so angry with herself. In the years that followed, observing the almost desperate competitiveness with which she built her academic career, he'd carried on wondering what had given her this need always to push herself. And he'd assumed it must have had something to do with the fact she'd lost her parents and had had to make do with Evie instead. That was how he'd explained her behaviour to himself that afternoon in Anthony's kitchen: given the fact that she had been brought up by someone like that, and in the

light of the parameters within which she'd been forced to operate for most of her life, he concluded that he should feel only compassion towards her, rather than any kind of anger. There was disappointment in his step as he'd made his way back to the library to collect his things and begin the journey home, of course there was. But none of the anger he'd felt at first, or, if any of it did remain, it was only slight, and already subsiding.

Sitting on the train to Oxford later that day, he'd thought through Anthony's version of what had happened at the Ball. When Evie had come back from seeing Rachel, and when Anthony had answered all her questions, she'd told him it was too late in the day for him to set off for Manchester, he wouldn't get there until the middle of the night. She'd insisted he let her put him up in a hotel, and he'd obeyed her once more. She'd taken him to the Randolph and checked him in, saying she'd collect him the next morning and drive him back to London, seeing as she would be going that way herself, and it would be no trouble for her to drop him off at Euston. It was, she said, the least she could do after what Rachel had done to him.

But that was where he'd drawn the line, telling her it was one thing to put him up for the night, and yes, he was so shattered he couldn't face travelling back straight away, but he could make his own plans in the morning, he wasn't a kid.

'Of course,' she said. 'Of course, I'm sorry. I didn't mean to patronise you, Anthony. Don't take offence for goodness' sake.' And she left him then, telling him to stay in touch and to let her know how things went when he got home to his mum.

After she'd gone he left his things in his room and went straight out for a walk. Wandering aimlessly around town, he became more and more frustrated about what had happened, imagining Cissy and Rachel getting ready for the Ball in the set of rooms they shared, and he started to formulate a plan. He knew a way into College that would, in all probability, have been overlooked by the security team, and he still had his

gendarme's costume. He went back to the hotel at about seven o'clock and changed before making his way down to his chosen entry point. He got in without any trouble and experienced only a couple of moments when he thought someone might have recognised him. On both occasions he'd simply pulled his hat further down on his head and slipped into the shadows. Having managed to keep to himself for long enough, he went to Rick's Bar at the time his ball programme told him Rachel and Cissy would be doing their cabaret. He stood by the door and gave one of the waiters a note, asking them to pass it up to the girls and pretending it was an invitation to let an admirer buy them a drink. And then he left the bar, hoping they'd fall for it.

It wasn't the first time he'd forged Towneley's handwriting. He'd lost his key one day and had had to go to the lodge to sign out a spare. Noticing Towneley's signature above his own, he'd found himself copying it over and over, idly, while he stood waiting for the porter to find the right key. Immediately afterwards he'd gone to the Buttery to buy some bread and margarine, and when he got there, he'd realised two things simultaneously: one, he had no cash on him; and two, the person behind the counter was someone he'd never seen before. Without really thinking about what he was doing, he'd signed for his things on account, using Towneley's signature instead of his own, and it had passed without comment. He didn't do it that often, he said, and only ever for smallish items, but every now and again, if he was running out of money, he'd repeat the performance in reliance on the fact that Towneley was so wealthy himself he'd never check his Buttery accounts when they came through at the end of each term. And as for the likelihood of Cissy and Rachel allowing themselves to be lured to the Pavilion by Towneley on the night of the Ball, he knew it was a long shot, but he also knew they'd be fairly drunk by the time they got his note, and something Cissy had said on the last of the lost afternoons made him think she'd had a fling with Towneley fairly recently and liked it. He was pretty sure that if she took the bait, Rachel would

probably follow. He was prepared for it not to work, he said, thinking they might see through the idea of Towneley asking them to come to the same spot they'd arranged for their own assignation, but it was the only plan he could come up with and so he'd given it a go, writing in Towneley's hand that he'd be waiting for them behind the Pavilion and could 'give them a taste of paradise' if they chose to accept his invitation. An hour or so later on, having filled his pockets with food from the stands that had been set up everywhere, and having built up a stash of free cigarettes and miniatures from the women wandering around handing them out by the trayful, he walked down to the lake and round to the playing fields and hid himself behind the clapboard building that stood there, settling down to wait, finally able to relax now that there was no longer any risk of being seen. It was shortly after midnight that he heard the two of them pushing their way through the bushes.

'He's not here Ciss,' he heard Rachel whispering.

'Let's wait for him though,' Cissy replied. 'I want to tell him what a little idiot he is before we go tell Haddon he's back.'

And he'd known then that the game was up. He watched them standing there, picking twigs from one another's hair and brushing themselves down, and he weighed up the choice between staying hidden, or revealing himself. He'd waited a little longer until they'd moved about a bit in the clearing and were standing close enough for him to be able to smell them, when Cissy suddenly said to Rachel, 'What a stupid cock,' and Rachel replied, 'I know. But can you believe he's actually stupid enough to think we'd fall for it?'

'Oh yeah,' Cissy said. 'Anthony stupid Trelissick. Stupid stupid stupid,' and she pulled Rachel towards her and they started to kiss, until she broke off and carried on, 'You know what though?'

'What?'

'Would have been quite nice if it had been Towneley, don't you think? En plein air and a threesome? Huh? Don't you think?'

Rachel pulled away from her then, moving back towards the bushes they'd emerged from. 'Jesus Ciss. No I don't actually. Sometimes I just don't get you.'

'Come on honey. Lighten up! I'm joking,' and Cissy went towards her and tried to kiss her again but Rachel pushed her away and Cissy said it once more. 'I'm joking. Rach. You know how I feel about you, come on.' They began to argue then, but because their voices had dropped just a little too low for Anthony to hear them properly, he gave up trying and came out from his hiding place. He'd meant to surprise them but he stepped on a twig and broke it and Cissy swung round and when she saw him she laughed and said, 'At long last. You are such a little loser,' and that was when he stood forward and punched her, hard, right in the face.

He hadn't really known what he was doing, he said to Harry. He hadn't even had a plan, as such, of what he would do if they actually came in answer to his note. He certainly hadn't intended to attack them, and when it came to it he'd acted entirely on impulse, angered by what they'd said about him, and tipped over the edge by Cissy's greeting.

It could have been either one of them, it just so happened that she was standing closest to him when he lashed out, knocking her to the ground and falling heavily on top of her and finding himself instantly aroused by the sensation of having injured her. Looking back later on he realised Rachel could very well have screamed for help, and that if she had, someone would undoubtedly have come running. Or she could probably have had a good chance of pulling him off Cissy, who, having been momentarily knocked out by the force of his blow, was by now putting up a fairly good fight from where she lay beneath him. But for a reason he'd never quite worked out, Rachel only stood and watched as he held Cissy down with a combination of the weight of his body on hers and the pressure of one of his hands covering her face and pushing her head into the ground, while he undid his trousers

with the other. When Cissy bit him, so that he pulled his hand away from her mouth for just a second, she shouted Rachel's name.

Anthony flipped his head up and looked at Rachel but she did nothing, just standing there with her arms folded and half a smile on her face. 'Go for it Ciss,' she said, quietly, and Anthony said she looked very much as though she might have been crying at the same time as smiling. 'It's only a fuck after all, isn't that what you said?' and she turned and disappeared into the shadows, leaving them there in the clearing.

His memory of what happened next, he'd told Harry, wasn't entirely clear. He was on top of Cissy, and then he wasn't, and then he came round to see Haddon looking down at him where he lay, and then he was being walked back across the lawns by the two of them and Haddon was throwing cold water on his face and hauling him into a chair in his study and questioning him. And then Harry was there, and then he wasn't, and then he was being told that it was all over for him, again, and Haddon and Harry were walking him to the college gates and leaving him to stand on his own on the flagstone path wishing very much that he was inside instead, and that things had turned out differently.

20

As I sat by the fire during dessert on what turned out to be the last night of my winter visit, watching Harry direct his fellow hosts again and again, I replayed these scenes for myself, as well as the lost afternoons that Rachel had spent with Cissy and Anthony. When the evening was finally over and I stood to go, I became aware that I had drunk more frequently than I should have done from the decanters that had been passed to me. Harry seemed to notice also, so that when I reached the top of the stairs and stood on the terrace, swaying slightly, I found that he was by my side placing a hand under my right elbow and gently holding me steady and saying he thought it best that we carried on our conversation in the morning. When I nodded, realising that any kind of concentration was entirely beyond me, he offered to accompany me back to my room, saying he was sure that the guests would be very well looked after by the staff in the Upper Senior Common Room when they got there for their coffee and their Armagnac, and that there was really no need for him to go with them. Nor did I object, once we'd gone down the steps from the

terrace and had started to walk around the quad, when he held my elbow a little more firmly, righting me once or twice when I slipped in the ice that had started to form on the path. The fresh air helped, and because I was already feeling much better by the time we reached the other side and went through into the Pump Quad, when he asked if I'd mind waiting while he let himself into the Buttery to fetch some milk for his tea in the morning I said no, of course not, go ahead.

In an attempt to sober up I decided to read everything on the notice-board in that little courtyard. Having performed this exercise once, and then once more just to make sure, I thought I must have managed it, but I found when I turned to look at what was written across the wall behind me that it hadn't really made a great deal of difference. Harry was taking his time to get his milk, so I tried to focus with par-ticular attention on what it was that I was looking at, narrowing my eyes and staring intently at the Boat Club results that were sprawled in a chalked graffiti, everywhere it seemed. There appeared to be more of them than I remembered there having been when I was a student, and looking more closely I saw that, in fact, hardly any of the old ones had ever been erased. As far as I could tell in my slightly drunken state, and in the semi-darkness of the Pump Quad, the more recent results had simply been chalked over the top with every year that had passed, so that I was looking at a kind of kaleidoscope of letters and num-bers and lists of names strung out beneath sketches of pastel-coloured flags, weaving one amongst the other. Where the records from earlier years had faded with time, the later ones stood out more clearly, but still, my attempt to focus on them in order to steady myself turned out to be a hopeless one and by the time Harry came back I felt more, rather than less drunk, and I had even started to think that one of the flags I was staring at was actually fluttering in the breeze.

I told Harry I was quite alright to go back on my own, and that I didn't know what had come over me and that it must just have been the heat of the fire, and the length of the day, and the things we had

been talking of. Noticing a flush in his cheeks and a strange brightness playing in his eyes I wondered if he also had drunk too much. But as he strode off around the quad with his gown billowing out behind him, his face tilted slightly upwards as though sniffing for a scent, he looked to be doing so in a perfectly sober fashion and, having watched him take the steps on the other side two at a time, I went back to my staircase feeling quite ashamed of myself.

I slept fitfully that night, waking every now and again from strange dreams that I could remember nothing of, not specifically, having the sense only that I had been distressed by them. When I got up I had a dull pain behind my eyes and it was with a heavy head that I walked into Harry's room and sat down in his armchair for what was to be the last time that I did so before I returned to London. I was grateful for the mug of coffee he handed me, and despite the urgency of my desire to hear the rest of his story, it would be dishonest of me to say that I had not wished, slightly, that he could have begun with a little less alacrity than he did.

But he'd clearly slept better than I, and he launched with renewed vigour straight in from where he'd left off. All at once we had begun again, and Harry was talking about the fact that Anthony had told him that, all things considered, he'd got over the whole thing quite quickly at first. On the day he'd been sent down, after he'd packed up his room and Harry had been to visit him, he'd left College for what he really thought would be the last time, and he'd made the telephone call to Evie which led to her checking him into the Randolph for the night.

When he went to leave the following morning, he found that she'd paid his bill in advance, just as she'd said she would, and she'd left him a letter as well. Or at least, that was what he assumed it was until his train pulled out of Euston later on and he opened it and found a bundle of fifty-pound notes inside. There were ten of them in all, and

he told Harry it had made him feel a little sordid in a way, as though he'd been paid off somehow, for something. He'd even thought about how he could get it back to her, imagining that if he'd opened it while he was still with her he might have thrown it down on the ground and told her he was worth more than that. But he'd kept it, giving it to his mum at the end of the summer for putting him up and for asking him no questions and for loving him in the way that she did.

It was, he said, probably the hardest summer of his life, and he'd sunk into what he called a fairly dangerous depression. But eventually he'd found a job working for his mum's boyfriend's company and he spent the evenings in town with his old schoolfriends, drinking beer rather than vodka and keeping all his clothes on while he did it, or instead, just staying at home with his mum, doing nothing in particular and liking it. When in the following September her boyfriend offered him a traineeship with his company he took it, absorbing himself in his work. He became an IT geek, he told Harry, finding that his mum's boyfriend had been right about what he had called Anthony's 'aptitude' for programming. There was something satisfying in writing scripts and eradicating flaws and seeing something follow his commands so obediently, and he found a strange kind of beauty in this new language he was learning to parse. By the time he finished his training he'd achieved a kind of stability in his life, and when he found himself in need of a change of scene and with no real ties to speak of, he'd taken up the offer of a programming job in Tucson, Arizona. It was an escape of a kind, and the relocation package he'd negotiated was almost ridiculous. He'd gone there with no real plans for his future beyond an intention of working hard and saving as much as possible. The experience of moving there and discovering an entirely new world was so absorbing that it wasn't until he'd been there for just over a year that he found himself beginning to dwell again on what had happened.

It started with a woman in a bar, on a night when he was lonely.

She asked him what part of England he came from and when he said Manchester, she asked him if he'd ever lived anywhere else and he said yes, he'd lived in Oxford once. There was something about this woman, and the conversation they had, which brought it all back to him, and vividly, so that over the next few days he'd thought of little other than Rachel and Cissy, and about what he had lost on the day he'd been sent down from Oxford.

He told Harry that when he started to look online he'd been able to find virtually nothing on Cissy, whereas when it came to Rachel, the internet was heaving with her. Her photo on the English department website came up straight away and when he looked at his computer screen and saw her looking back at him, one eye half covered by the strand of hair that fell across it and the beginnings of a smile on her face, it was the start, he said, of what quite quickly became an obsession. He was perfectly aware he could probably have ended up becoming fixated with either of them; it was just that Rachel was everywhere he looked, and Cissy wasn't.

Initially he'd been jealous, of course he had. It wasn't as though Rachel had done what she'd always said she would and made it at Oxford, but she'd got her post at UCL, and from the pages of entries that followed, it was clear she was already developing a strong profile in her field. 'It could have been me,' he said to Harry. 'In fact it probably would have been, wouldn't it?' It was easy to start ordering back copies of her articles, and sending for details of the conferences she'd be speaking at, or the lecture programmes she was running, and the more he did of that kind of thing, the more he had a sense almost that they were getting to know one another again, having simply lost touch for a while. In the end any jealousy that he'd felt was transformed into a straightforward admiration for what she had achieved. He told Harry that he'd come to feel fond of her again, in the way that he'd done before.

It was inevitable that he would try at some point to resume contact

with her. He was aware that she might at first be reluctant to rekindle any kind of friendship, and that he would have to take it slowly. But he hadn't anticipated quite how bluntly she would respond. The first letter he sent was returned, unopened. He looked in the envelope she'd put it in to see if she'd given some sort of explanation, or justification, but there was nothing other than a compliments slip on which were written the words, 'Please don't write again, Anthony.' 'She hadn't even bothered to sign it,' he told Harry. 'That was bad enough. But what really got to me was the fact that it was one of those compliments slips with all her details set out at the top, all her qualifications, everything.' It was seeing the 'Dr' that was printed before her name, he said, that had made him jealous all over again, and angry.

He took the English department number from the slip and telephoned with a story about being a friend who had lost her email address, saying he needed to send through something personal so he couldn't use the department one. At first the woman laughed at him and said of course she couldn't give out a personal address, but then he said he had a flight to catch, and he'd try again another time, and he chatted to her for five minutes or so, dropping enough little details about Rachel's life into the conversation for the woman to think that he was sufficiently bona fide to be given the email address after all. He took the precaution of setting up an internet identity that couldn't be traced, and he sent his first email the next day, signing himself off as BEN VOLIO, knowing she'd recognise that as the name they'd argued about using for the letters they'd written to Harry. He asked her to give him a chance, and he attached a PDF of the letter she'd returned, telling her that reading it was the least she could do if their friendship had ever meant anything to her.

He waited a few days, but eventually he realised that he should interpret her silence as a further rebuke. He'd installed some monitoring software on his laptop before sending the email, and he knew she'd opened it, and knew how many times she'd looked at it, and for

how long she'd done so each time. He got over his upset after a week or so, he said, and decided to give her one final chance, taking a fairly soft approach so as not to scare her off. He forwarded the previous email to her and wrote at the top that he wasn't sure whether she'd got it the last time, but just in case she had and was ignoring him, he thought it was only fair to point out that he didn't think it was really on just to blank him in that way, after all they'd shared, and he'd be grateful if she'd at least reply, just once. He finished by saying he'd completely understand if she didn't want to, and if he'd heard nothing within a week he'd back off and wouldn't write again.

That hadn't worked either, but he knew he'd drawn her in more successfully this time: he could see that she'd looked at the email a few times a day over the following week, for a good quarter of an hour or more each time. And so he wrote again, abandoning his former restraint and telling her she was being a bitch and she should grow up and snap out of it and just pick up the phone and call him. Again she hadn't responded, and again the frequency with which she'd looked at the email increased, as did the length of time she'd spent doing so on each occasion.

He realised as soon as he sent the next email that he'd crossed a line, but he'd been drinking and hadn't been able to help himself. He told Harry that he'd been sitting in his office one night after an evening spent cruising the bars of Tucson with very little success, and he looked at the clock on his laptop and realised she'd probably just be walking to work in London. He pictured her strolling through Bloomsbury with her bag of books and he closed his eyes and imagined her giving her lectures, and going to the canteen for her lunch. He wondered who she'd have sat with, and then he started to think about what she'd do when she got home that night, and who she'd be doing it with. And that was why, he said, he'd ended up writing a few things he probably shouldn't have, and finished by telling her that if she didn't start replying to his emails he'd have to write to her depart-

ment head instead and tell him that she'd copied his Browning essays that summer term. He was pretty sure this would do the trick, this little threat, innocuous though it might seem at first. He was almost certain she'd have used the content of those essays for her dissertation that summer, and that it would have been a pretty big part of her having got a First in the end, which in turn would have secured her funding for her MPhil and led ultimately to her PhD and her departmental post. He said that she would realise, as he had, that he was therefore in a position to expose her as a fraud.

He received a reply straight away. He told Harry she'd completely overreacted, telling him she regarded his communications as harassment, and that she'd go straight to the police if she ever heard from him again. She said she trusted he'd agree that they stood in positions of equal strength in regard to the damage they could do to one another's lives by any such revelation of their shared histories. She would, she said, take his silence as an indication that he'd seen sense. And so, he told Harry, he had.

It wasn't just the content of her email that had snapped him out of what he called his 'brief spell of insanity'. Just after the email had come, and at the precise moment at which he was reading it for a third time and trying to decide what to do, his mum's boyfriend had called from Manchester with the news that she was ill, properly ill, and that Anthony should come home if he could, that night if possible. He'd suddenly realised how very stupid he'd been, and how close he had come to making the same kind of mistake he'd made in Oxford. And because he'd decided there and then that he didn't want to throw his life away a second time just because of Rachel Cardanine, he'd done as she asked and resolved not to contact her again, deleting all trace of their correspondence from his laptop and leaving for the UK the following day.

His mum had been pretty much fine in the end. Her recovery had been made against the odds, though, and he was glad he'd been there

to nurse her through it. By never having taken more than a couple of days off in all the time he'd been in Tucson, he'd built up enough leave to be able to stay for the whole of the month that followed. When it came to going back, he decided against it. He told Harry he'd been scared by how strange his behaviour had become, attributing the whole episode to the soullessness of the life he'd been living, and the lack of any real connections in Tucson. So he'd based himself back in Manchester, not far from his mum, and started to work alongside her boyfriend again, settling fairly soon into some kind of normality.

Things had continued in much the same vein for some time, and he was fairly sure they would have continued to do so were it not for the fact that he'd bumped into Evie the following September. He'd been seconded to Edinburgh on a short-term contract, just for a fortnight, and he'd gone out one evening to while away a few hours before he went to sleep. Intending to see a film, or perhaps a play, he'd dropped into a bar first for a drink. He was standing waiting to be served when he caught a scent in the air that was familiar to him and had looked at the back of the head of the woman in front of him and thought suddenly that it was Rachel. He was about to tap her on the shoulder when she'd turned and looked him in the eye and said, 'Anthony. Oh my god,' and he'd seen Evie staring back at him, looking just as surprised as he was.

They'd had a drink together, and, both of them being in the same position, with time to spare and an expense account to burn, one drink had turned into another, and another, and they arranged to meet again the following evening. On that first evening, Anthony said, they'd run through the events of that summer and Evie told him she'd pretty much patched everything up with Rachel, and he told her in return that he'd lost touch with her god-daughter and he was fine with that, things having moved on in the way that they had. They'd briefly compared notes on how well Rachel was doing at UCL, and how it had all worked out for Anthony in the end, and how the whole

thing was in the dim and distant past now and there was no need to rake over it endlessly, was there? By the following evening, each of them seemed to be in agreement that they'd avoid that topic of conversation and stick to the present instead, and they found that the time passed quickly enough without either of them having to stray much further than the trials of travelling with their work, and the projects by which their lives were being consumed at the time, or the films they had seen, or the holidays they'd have liked to have taken had they only been able to find the space in their diaries.

On the third night, when she asked him if he'd like to have dinner with her and suggested trying the dining room of her hotel, Anthony wasn't at all surprised to hear her asking him up to her room afterwards, saying it didn't have to be complicated: she was lonely, she wanted sex; he was there, and she thought he probably did too. Of course, Anthony had said to her, why not. And he told Harry it had been easy enough to do what she'd asked, and that he found that with the lights off, and his eyes half closed, he was able to imagine it was someone else, so that when she'd invited him back the next night, and the next, he hadn't been able to see any reason to turn her down.

Their affair had continued in a desultory kind of a way over the following few years; they had, in a slightly non-committal fashion, and invariably at Evie's behest, started to co-ordinate their travel plans where possible, spending the occasional fortnight sharing a hotel room at the expense of either one of their employers. Once they'd started, it seemed simple enough to carry on. Evie professed not to mind in the slightest about the fact he had a girlfriend, and the arrangement suited him, providing a welcome distraction from his more than ordinary home life. When in the spring of 2006 the opportunity came for him to take up a post in London he'd accepted it, wanting an excuse to make the break from the woman he was by then living with in Manchester. Evie had tried to persuade him to live nearer to her in Chelsea and he'd been tempted, liking that part of town. But then at the

last moment he was offered the long loan of a flat on Judd Street that belonged to someone he knew through his work. He'd taken it straight away, telling Evie it made more sense for him to do that and be based around Euston rather than living in west London as she'd suggested, since he'd be going back up and down to Manchester to visit his mum and it would save him hours of travelling time.

It was only in the spring of 2007, once he had settled fairly comfortably into his London life, he said, seeing a little less of Evie with every month that passed and finding satisfaction instead in the beds of other, much younger, women, that Evie had broached the subject of Rachel again. He'd agreed to stay over one weekend in Chelsea and she'd said over breakfast, with what Anthony told Harry was more than a hint of bitterness in her voice, that he may as well pop into the British Library to see if he could find her, given that he lived so close to where she worked these days, and that he ought to really, if only to offer his congratulations.

'What for?' he said, amused by Evie's woefully unsuccessful attempt to cover up her jealousy of her god-daughter even after all this time, and genuinely puzzled as to what it was that he should be congratulating her for.

'Oh, Anthony, my love, my dove,' Evie said, smiling. 'Surely you've heard? It was last December for goodness' sake. Rachel is married.'

'Christ,' Anthony replied. 'Who the fuck to?'

'You mean you really don't know? Why, to Alex Petersen of course.'

He hadn't heard, he told Harry, nor had he managed to hide his shock, agreeing with Evie's observation that, whilst it was odd that someone like Rachel had chosen to marry a lawyer, it was no surprise that she should have engineered a situation that would place so few demands on her at the same time as providing the material comforts she'd never be able to obtain for herself as an academic.

Harry had apologised when he'd told me this, saying that he didn't for one moment want to cause me any offence but that it was his inten-

tion to give me as full a picture as possible of the story that Anthony had told him, and of the way in which he had told it, and I said of course, there was no need to apologise, I'd been perfectly aware at the time that there would be few people who understood the relationship that Rachel and I had enjoyed, and that at times I had even found myself wondering why she loved me quite as much as she seemed to.

Harry continued, telling me that Anthony had apparently done nothing about what Evie had told him until just after Easter. When he got off the train back from Manchester after the holiday weekend he walked back towards Judd Street and found himself stopping in front of the British Library. He stood outside its gates and gazed at its entrance, wondering where Rachel and I would have spent our Easter holiday, and when she'd be coming back, and it was when he'd unpacked his things that he did it, for the first time in such a long time, tapping her name out on the keyboard and seeing entry after entry come up, just like they had so long ago in Tucson. It was so easy, he said, to catch up on everything she'd been doing, and so strange to think he was living so close to where she worked. It was some time still before he went into the library to see if she was there, having to travel to Edinburgh again on business, and he found in the meantime that it was enough just to look at her pictures on the internet and think about what he'd say if he did see her, and to wonder how he might approach her. When Evie asked him a few days later, jokingly, whether he'd been to the library yet, he laughed it off and told her to grow up and act her age and that it was all behind him, she knew it was, and she'd believed him.

And then one day in early May he'd made what he described as a terrible mistake. He'd been staying in the Chelsea house for the Bank Holiday weekend and had taken his chance on the Sunday morning, when Evie had gone to the gym. He'd spent an hour or so flicking through a few of the pictures of Rachel he'd been able to find online, and then he'd scanned the pages of some online journals and other

people's Facebook sites for more before reading a few of her internet articles and catching up on the various blogs she posted. When he'd finished he switched off Evie's computer and went for a run to try to clear his mind. So successfully had he done so that he'd forgotten about it by the time he got back, and it wasn't until later on, when he heard her key in the lock, that he remembered what he'd done and realised he'd forgotten to clear his browsing history. He didn't have a chance to cover his tracks before he left that evening but there was nothing he could do about it. He told himself it would be fine, she'd never check anyway, and he didn't know what he was worrying about. But of course she did check, and she telephoned him a couple of hours after he'd gone to bed, saying he'd better get back over there and damn quick and explain himself.

He did as she asked and they had a furious row. Evie called him a stalker, saying he should make up his mind whether he loved her or her god-daughter, and couldn't he at least have kept his nasty habits to his own bloody computer. He shouted back at her that she was insane, what did she mean, love her, he'd never said he loved her, he'd just given her what she wanted and it had only ever been about sex. She cried when he said that, and then, to his amazement, so did he. They opened a bottle of wine, and then another, and he told her almost everything then, about the emails he'd sent from Tucson, and about how Rachel had responded. Evie grilled him at first, asking him if he was sure he'd told her everything and what had he actually written to make her react like that? Anthony said he couldn't remember exactly, it seemed like a long time ago now, but it definitely wasn't as bad as Rachel had made out, and when he started to cry again Evie accepted what he'd said and consoled him, saying he shouldn't take it so much to heart. She told him Rachel always had been a bit melodramatic, coming home from school in the holidays with pathetic little stories about being bullied, or teachers being unkind to her, that were clearly invented just to get some attention. Evie held him and let him cry

some more, saying she knew he was growing away from her, and she knew it had only ever been about sex, and that it was coming to the point where their paths would stop crossing in the way that they had, and she understood that. But she said that he was her concern whether he liked it or not, and that she was worried about him, and that he had to find a way to sort himself out and work out why it was still happening. She said he should look at his life and see what a success he'd made of it, and he should just forget what had happened in Oxford, and that he'd achieved just as much as Rachel had but in different ways, and in different places, and he should let it go and make his own way in the world.

And when he tried to say it wasn't really anything serious she told him she knew he'd browsed online for Rachel for more than two hours that morning and that someone would have to be properly insane to want to look at pictures of her god-daughter for that long and they laughed, the two of them, and he came out with it then, saying that he was jealous, and a little bit angry still. He told Evie that all he really wanted from Rachel was an apology for what had happened, and that that was all he'd ever really wanted when he was doing the same thing in Tucson. He simply wanted Rachel to tell him, face to face, that she understood what it meant to him to have lost the chances that she'd taken instead of him, and to agree that she was just as much to blame as he was for the events of that summer term. And he told Evie that he knew he'd never get them back, the opportunities he'd lost, and that he'd probably never be able to completely overcome the sense of shame he felt about it all, but if Rachel would only talk to him, and recognise the part she had played in him being sent down, it would somehow release him from the hold that she had on him still.

Evie said then that she completely understood, and that she'd help him. By the following weekend she'd asked Rachel out for lunch and put it to her. She'd gone back to Anthony and said it had been an unmitigated disaster, that Rachel had stormed out of the restaurant

having asked Evie whether she had any idea that it was a psychopath she was talking about, and did she have any idea what a fool she was making of herself hanging around with someone like Anthony Trelissick, and having told her that she'd go to the police about both of them if Evie brought it up again since she clearly didn't realise what he was capable of. Evie asked him then whether he was absolutely sure he'd told her everything about the emails he'd sent, and when he said yes, and reminded her that she herself had called Rachel 'melodramatic', she said alright, of course, and she promised Anthony she'd try again, saying she'd had an idea about how to bring Rachel round. And though he never quite got to the bottom of what it was that Evie had done to persuade her, a day or so later she reported that Rachel was considering the idea, and that she'd agreed to come up with some terms and conditions for a meeting.

And so it was that Anthony found himself standing outside the British Library at eight o'clock one morning in mid-May, waiting with Evie for Rachel's car to appear. She'd said that she would only meet Anthony if Evie was there as well, and that she'd pick them both up at that exact spot and take them somewhere of her choosing, and that they mustn't be late since it was a red route. In the end it was Rachel who was late, by more than twenty minutes, so that by the time she'd arrived Evie had grown impatient and was at the espresso bar just along the road. She told Anthony later on that when she'd heard her mobile phone ring and had seen Rachel's name come up at exactly the same time that she'd also heard the frantic honking of a car horn, she'd known it wasn't going to work. And she was right, leaving her coffee on the bar and running back along the road to find that Anthony was already sitting in the front seat and Rachel was very, very angry. She was so angry, in fact, about Evie not being there and about Anthony getting in the car and sitting right beside her, that as soon as Evie opened the back door and started to get in herself, she'd told them both to get straight out again and forget it.

They did as she said and stood by the side of the road and watched as she pushed her way into the line of rush-hour traffic, jabbing at the horn in anger.

As Harry told me this part of Anthony's story, sitting across the room from me on the last day of my visit, I'd reached into my jacket pocket and felt for the parking ticket that had been stuffed down the back of Rachel's desk. It was still there where I'd put it when I rushed from my apartment to catch the train to Oxford, and as I heard Harry telling me about the events depicted in the photograph, I left it where it was, rubbing it between my fingers once or twice before taking my hand back out again and thinking to myself, not for the first time, that if only Rachel had been able to tell me any of it, I could have protected her.

By later on that evening, Anthony told Harry, Rachel had apologised to Evie and agreed to consider another meeting, but over the next few days she'd started to become evasive about the whole thing and Anthony had gone off the idea, telling Evie it was all a bit ridiculously cloak and dagger and they should just leave it. But having seen her in her car that morning, and for such a brief moment, he wanted to see her again, so he went to the library the very next day and looked out for her, and when she arrived he melted into the queue behind her and followed her to the reading room, standing back in the shadows and gazing at her while she worked. It had only been for about ten minutes, he said, the first time, and when she hadn't so much as noticed him, he'd convinced himself it wouldn't hurt to do it again a couple of days later, and then just once more after that. And of course it had become a habit, and one that was no trouble to him, finding it quite easy to convince his boss that he could just as well work from home in the mornings for the rest of the month, his diary being almost entirely empty of client meetings.

He said to Harry that by going to the library each day and watching her, he was simply building up the courage to speak to her, and he was comfortable there was nothing odd about his behaviour. He decided that he'd relied on Evie for long enough, and that he was perfectly capable of sorting it all out on his own, and that in any case he didn't see that it was for Rachel to dictate the terms of their meeting. He had made what he described as a completely straightforward plan to approach her one day and just ask her to have coffee with him, as if it was the most normal thing in the world. Catch her unawares, he said to Harry. Take her off guard, you know. And in a public place, where she couldn't very well cause a scene. But then one morning, standing with his back against the furthest wall of the Rare Books and Music Room wondering if he should make his move, he'd scanned the room once or twice and back again and had found himself, to his amazement, looking at Harry. As he watched, almost unable to believe his eyes, he saw Rachel raise her head and smile at Harry, and he saw the two of them gather up their books and leave the reading room together.

He'd said nothing to Evie by that stage about having been to the library and it had been his intention to keep it that way, but when the following week he'd seen Harry sitting there again watching Rachel, he hadn't been able to help himself and it had somehow slipped out over dinner that night, such was his fascination with the situation. 'Harry bloody Gardner,' he began, 'would you believe it!' and then he realised what he'd said, and of course he had to explain what he'd been doing in the library, and Evie and he had the same awful argument all over again.

'And what did you decide to do this time,' Harry asked him, 'you and Evie?'

'We decided we had to try again,' Anthony said. 'Of course we did. But however much we talked it through, and however many ways we found of looking at the situation, we kept coming up against the same problem.'

'And which problem was that?' Harry asked, sensing what was coming and hoping he was mistaken.

'The problem we kept coming up against, Harry, the problem we couldn't find a way round, no matter how hard we tried, was what we could do about Rachel.'

'What do you mean, what you could do about Rachel?'

'How we could bring her round, that's what. How we could make her agree to meet me, and how we could get her to apologise.'

'I see. And what did you decide, in the end?'

'Ah,' Anthony said, leaning across the kitchen table towards Harry, his face crinkling into its familiar half-smile, half-frown. 'That, Harry, is where you come in. Or at least, I very much hope it is.'

And when Harry sat back in his chair and raised his glasses onto his forehead and crossed his arms Anthony stood and said, looking down at him, 'You see, Harry, this is the thing. Evie and I need your help,' and then he smiled his old lopsided smile. 'We need you to make Rachel see things as we see them. We need you to make her change her mind.'

Harry was reluctant to get involved at first. Anthony said he'd completely understand if he turned them down, and that he more than anyone was aware that the whole thing was a little absurd, but he and Evie had decided it was worth a try, thinking it likely that Harry would be able to talk Rachel into some kind of meeting where they had failed. He spoke with a wheedling tone that morning in Judd Street, and Harry was bewildered by the constant switching from the fragile pleas of a man desperate for resolution, to an excessive and almost self-indulgent openness about matters that were extremely distasteful. It was obvious Anthony had suffered unduly for something that had not been entirely his fault and that, for whatever reason, his life was still being affected by it, but Harry knew that he couldn't right a

wrong, not at this stage, and that nobody could really help Anthony except himself.

It was thinking once more of Rachel that made him agree in the end. Thinking of Rachel, and of what she might stand to lose if he didn't intervene. Despite Anthony's assurances that he was over it, and that it was only because he'd seen Harry in the British Library that he'd thought it was worth one last try, Harry was disturbed by the things Anthony had told him, and deeply so. While he couldn't see Anthony going through with his threats to expose Rachel's plagiarism, and while no real damage would be done even if he did, not now, it was clearly desirable that such an outcome should be avoided. If a way could be found of helping him to move on sufficiently for him to fade once more from their lives, Harry could see no harm in trying to make it happen. Indeed, he considered himself duty-bound to do so, feeling an enormous degree of responsibility for how things had ended up: Anthony was right that Rachel's career had not been disadvantaged by her long association with Harry, and he knew that if he and Haddon had only managed to get to the nub of the matter at the end of that summer term, everything might have turned out very differently for Anthony.

He decided in the end it was just a conversation that needed to take place between two adults about events that had happened a very long time ago, and it struck him on the train back to Oxford that it didn't have to be any more complicated than that. The plan he devised was straightforward. He settled on the idea of a dinner in Oxford to which everyone could be invited and over which he would preside. The more he thought about it, the more obvious it seemed that this was, in fact, the only sensible solution. Sitting in a taxi up to his house on the Woodstock Road, he resolved to discuss things with Rachel when he was next in London. When he got into College the following morning he sent the briefest of notes to Anthony to that effect and a postcard to Rachel saying he'd be back in town on

Monday, sooner than he'd expected, and if the weather was fine and she had the time, why didn't they go for a stroll on the river? Unless he heard otherwise, he would wait for her in the British Library courtyard at noon.

'Let's see the Dalí,' she said the minute they met, tugging at the sleeve of his jacket like a child, so that he felt the cruelty of what he was going to do. 'It's on at Tate Modern,' she carried on, pulling at his sleeve again. 'You'll love it, I promise,' and she started to walk away, only stopping when she realised he wasn't following her.

'What?' she said, puzzled. 'What is it? Come on. We'll wander down to the river like you said. Bloomsbury, Covent Garden, Waterloo Bridge. It'll be lovely. Come on Harry don't be grumpy, it's a completely gorgeous day,' and she was pulling him across the courtyard and they were walking and because he couldn't think how to begin he didn't, letting her turn the conversation whichever way she wanted until they were on the bridge and had stopped to look at the views on either side.

'I can never make up my mind which one I prefer,' she said, turning first one way and then the other. 'Never never never.'

'St Paul's,' he said. 'Surely.' And then, realising he couldn't leave it any longer, he began. 'Rachel—'

'But there are so many cranes always,' she said, looking back that way. 'I'm not sure they need as many as that, not all the time. Imagine if there weren't any. It would be so beautiful wouldn't it?'

'Rachel—'

'You're right,' she said, looking west again before saying, reluctantly, 'I always think I ought to prefer this one. But isn't it just too obvious? Big Ben. Isn't it Harry?' and she turned back to look at him. She swept her hair back from her face with both hands, squinting at him in the sunlight. 'Are you alright?'

'Yes, I'm alright, but there's something I have to tell you, I'm afraid.'

'What do you mean you're afraid?' she said. 'Afraid of what?' and she laughed. 'Has someone died, Harry?' and when he shook his head she laughed again. 'Can't be that awful then can it? Out with it, and stop looking so gloomy for goodness' sake.'

'I mean I'm afraid you might not want to hear it, that's all,' he said. 'But there we are,' and he took her arm in his and steered them both around to face the South Bank and started to walk with her across the rest of the bridge, not wanting to look her in the eye.

'I have spoken with Anthony Trelissick,' he said. She stopped walking immediately and he turned and saw her face set against the clouds that blocked out the sun towards Westminster and for a moment, he wished he hadn't said anything after all.

'Anthony Trelissick?' she said, looking as though Harry had actually struck her. 'Are you insane Harry? What the hell right do you think you have—'

'Rachel. Please don't be angry until you have heard what I have to say.'

'Of course I'm bloody well angry, Harry. What's going on? What's bloody well going on?'

She stood there with her arms folded, staring wildly at him, and she was on the point of speaking again when he said, 'Rachel. Reserve your judgement, please. At least until you've listened to me. I think you owe me that much, if nothing else.'

She looked amazed, but didn't say a word, so he pressed on in the face of her silence. They started to walk again and he described how he had gone to Anthony's flat. He said that he was only speaking to her about it because Anthony had asked him to, and then he began to tell her everything he'd learned while he was there.

She said nothing while he told his tale. It wasn't until some time after he had finished that she spoke again, and even then she did it

so quietly she was almost whispering. They'd reached the other side of the bridge and had walked down the steps and were standing by the railings in front of the National Theatre, looking out at the river. 'Oh, Harry,' she said, staring blankly at the water. Her eyes were open slightly wider than before, as though she were a sleepwalker, or had seen a ghost. 'I am so sorry.' And she half stumbled over to one of the benches behind them and sat down, wrapping her arms around herself and leaning forwards. 'I am so sorry,' she said again, and then she was silent, so he stood beside her and waited.

Eventually she sat back up. 'I'm not sure you'll ever know how grateful I am for the things you've done for me,' and she shivered slightly, despite the sun that fell on her. 'All of them. And I'm not sure you could ever imagine what it meant, to have your help when I did.'

She was crying now, choosing her words slowly and speaking so quietly that Harry had to sit down beside her on the bench and lean in towards her to hear properly. 'And I don't think I can even begin to explain myself, for the things I did. And for the way I was. I wouldn't be able to. I'd have no idea how.'

'Please, Rachel,' he said, but she shook her head and carried on.

'Will you forgive me, Harry? I mean, can you?'

'Of course I can forgive you.' She sighed and wiped her eyes, and he reached in his jacket pocket for his handkerchief. 'But Rachel, really, it's more important that we have what we do, the two of us. What we've built up, over the years. It was a long time ago, all of this. I do think you need to think about Anthony, though,' he said, holding out his handkerchief to her. 'For fairness's sake, if nothing else,' and then he saw again a flash of the anger Anthony had described.

She pushed his outstretched hand away and stood from the bench. 'Fairness! What has this got to do with fairness? He's a psychopath, Harry. You think he told you everything? You really think he told you all the disgusting things he wrote in those emails? Do you?' and people started to look at her and look away again, embarrassed.

'Rachel. Come on. You're upset. You're not thinking clearly. Please sit down,' and when she did, he continued. 'Anthony is a damaged man. And you had no small part to play in—'

'Harry for god's sake,' she said, standing again. 'We're all damaged aren't we? Even just a little bit? Christ. But we don't all go around the place sending filthy stalker letters and behaving like some kind of nutter. Why didn't you tell me you'd seen him watching me in the bloody library? Why?'

'I didn't think,' he said. 'I didn't know. I couldn't be sure it was him.'

But he could see that she wasn't listening, and he watched her walk back over to the railings and lean against them, putting her head in her hands. When he went and stood beside her and placed a hand on her back, she shrugged it off straight away.

'The past is the past, Rachel. And neither of us can rewrite it. But what we can do is try to make amends. That's all he wants and that's all I'm suggesting.'

'An apology? Jesus. You really think that's all he wants?'

'I do, yes. And I think you'll find that an apology can be a very powerful thing, in actual fact, for the person who has been wronged.'

Rachel laughed and shook her head and sighed, pushing herself away from the railings as he continued. 'I'm sorry if you think I've gone too far already but, really, I'd be grateful if you'd look at things from my perspective. When he took me there that day and told me those things I had my entire understanding of a past turned upside down and inside out. So you will have to forgive me, Rachel, if you think that by listening to him I have betrayed some kind of trust. We are all capable of such errors of judgement, I think, as a betrayal of trust, wouldn't you agree?'

'Fine. Emotional blackmail. I get it.'

'Rachel. I'm not doing that. I am simply saying that I think we can find a way to resolve things, and I also happen to think it's in your interest that we do so.'

She sighed again and they stood for a time in silence, looking out at the water. When a river taxi went past he tried to defuse things by asking her if she'd ever taken one and she said no, she preferred to walk. He said he hadn't either, and when she asked him why not, he took advantage of the ground he seemed to have made and explained that he'd always suffered from terrible seasickness. He told her then about a day trip he'd taken once, as a child, with his parents and his cousins. The sea had been flat, he said. As flat as a saucer of milk. And still he'd been sick, which meant they'd all had to come back early. He hadn't been on a boat again for years after that, and even then it was only one that was moored on the Thames for a party and it had happened all over again.

'Dirty British coaster,' Rachel said, suddenly, and he was puzzled until he looked and saw the tug that was shuddering past in front of them.

'With a salt-caked smoke stack,' he replied, finishing the line for her, glad that something seemed to have shifted, and that everything might be alright after all.

'OK then, Harry,' she said. 'What exactly did you have in mind?'

'Shall we walk again?'

'Oh. Well if that's all you're after, no problem,' she said, and he laughed a little at her joke, and as they made their way underneath the trees it was with the sound of seagulls wheeling that he set out his plan. She'd become distressed again once she'd heard it, almost immediately, and they'd argued quite heatedly as they walked, until he realised he wouldn't be able to persuade her otherwise and they had come to a compromise.

She said that the conversation that had to happen was to be, as she understood it, between her and Anthony, and nobody else. Not Harry, and certainly not Evie. On this she was intractable: it was Anthony who was demanding the whole thing, and she'd already made her amends with Evie, some time ago now, and if Harry meant what he

said about forgiving her, then she'd made them with him also. Evie and Harry were only involved because she and Anthony hadn't managed to sort it out, and while she recognised it was very kind of them to help and that each of them had her and Anthony's best interests at heart, there really was no need for them to listen to the actual conversation. He gave in to her arguments but insisted on retaining some of his original idea, saying why didn't she and Alex finally come to dine on High Table, and why didn't they do it on Midsummer Night? That way they could stay on and make a weekend of it, and she'd be able to fit in a meeting with Anthony while she was there.

She seemed reluctant at first, and when finally she agreed, it was almost as though she was doing so only because she'd used up all her energy in fighting her way out of a group reconciliation. 'Alright,' she said, 'why not,' and as they walked on further Harry asked her what she thought she would do about arranging the actual meeting, where it might take place and when. But she'd been evasive in her response, saying it didn't really matter to him did it? She seemed to have accepted at face value his assurances that she was forgiven, and she told him, with her former self-confidence restored, 'This is what will happen, Harry. Give me Anthony's address and I'll write to him and sort it out directly. Alex and I will come to dinner with you on the Thursday evening and we'll all have a perfectly nice time. It will be good for Alex to meet you properly now we're married, and then Anthony and I will meet at some point over the weekend. And that,' she carried on, 'will be that. But Harry,' and she stopped walking and put her hand on his arm and looked at him and he saw there were tears forming in her eyes once more. 'There's absolutely no need for Alex to know about any of this. You must be quite clear about that, all of you. You see I love him, and he loves me, and none of this is relevant to him, and it would only hurt him if he found out. I haven't had to tell him yet. And I don't want to.'

By now the tears were running fast down her face; again he held out his handkerchief to her, and again she pushed it away.

'He's given me something I thought I'd never have, Harry. Never. He's given me something uncomplicated, and loving, and he's made me happy in a way I didn't know was possible. So if you really are doing this for my benefit, I'd be grateful if you could leave him out of it. I'm not asking you for anything else, Harry. Not any more. Just this. Just do this one thing for me, Harry, please.'

When Harry told me about the conversation he and Rachel had had that day on the riverbank, I knew then that whatever else I might come to discover about her didn't matter, and that none of the things I'd learned so far mattered either. I was sure that she had loved me, and I had come to a better understanding of the ways in which she'd done so. As I stared into the fire thinking about her, and how desperately she had wanted to keep these things from me so that I wouldn't be hurt by them, Harry made an observation about how, to his mind, mourning the absence of a person was a little like falling in love with them again. I realised he was talking about himself, rather than me, and of his own wife, rather than of Rachel. What he said next, though, made me think he might have been reading my thoughts.

'I think what I mean is this, Alex,' he said, interpreting my silence for a lack of understanding. 'If you were to ask me to tell you about the ways in which we loved one another, I am not sure I would be able to, not really.' And then he was silent, and I thought that was all he

was going to say, but instead he continued, insistently, as though I had asked him a question he was determined to answer, however difficult it might be. 'I think I would have to say, rather, that it was in the quiet unfolding of our lives that we did so, she and I. It was more, perhaps, a question of being understood.' He was looking away from me then, speaking so quietly it was almost as if I wasn't there in the room with him, and I realised he'd been asking himself this question and considering his answer to it for some time, and that he was going to tell me something of his deliberations whether I wanted him to or not.

'She would let me board the train to London before her, whenever we took it together,' he said, sighing. 'She wouldn't get on until she knew that I was settled. I always had to sit facing the direction we were travelling in, you see, regardless of how busy the carriages might be, or how long it might take me to find a place. Regardless of how many people I might annoy. She would hover on the platform, moving along the outside of the train as I moved along its inside, until she was sure I had taken my seat, and then she would come and find a place as near to me as possible. It didn't much matter if we couldn't sit exactly side by side, you see. It mattered more to her that I was not out of sorts at the beginning of a journey. I asked her once if she minded the whole rigmarole and she said that she didn't. I wasn't sure whether to believe her,' he said, smiling at the thought. 'And then one day I saw her through the window of the train. Just when I'd found my place, and had asked someone to move all of their bags even though there were two seats opposite that were free where I could quite easily have sat. I looked through the window to wave to her that she could come in and I saw her standing there on the platform. I saw her before she could see me, that was the thing. Because her lips were moving I thought perhaps she was engaged in a conversation but I could see no one near her, and then I realised she was talking to herself. And when she raised her eyebrows and put her hands on her hips and heaved out a great sigh I realised she was fuming, Alex, do you see, quite liter-

ally fuming with frustration.' And then he paused again, as though he was waiting for me to respond, but I could think of nothing to say. 'I suppose,' he carried on, eventually, 'that was one of the ways in which I knew that she loved me. The fact that she lied to me like that, and pretended it didn't bother her in the slightest, that ridiculous little habit of mine. She never said, not once. And now there is no one to do that for me, when I take the train to London. There is nobody there to pretend they do not mind my absurdities, great and small.'

We both of us sat quietly then, looking into the fire. I thought Harry might ask me to tell him something in return of the ways in which Rachel and I had loved one another but he didn't, and I'm not sure I would have done even if he'd asked. But I did think to myself that I might have described for him how I would wake sometimes in the mornings to find her looking at me. She would smile, and I would see in her eyes something like relief, and she would say, 'Where were you, Alex? Where have you been in your dreaming?' And then, when I folded her into me and closed my eyes again she would say 'It doesn't matter. It doesn't matter. You're back you're back wherever you've been,' and she would fall asleep again herself, tight in my arms, sometimes for so long I would have to wake her and when I did she would say, as though it had been me that had been keeping us there, 'Let's get up, let's do something. Now, this minute before the day is gone,' and so we would.

Sometimes, though, she would change her mind and we would stay where we were and make love, sleepily, and I would bring breakfast back to bed and draw the panels across, both the ones in the bedroom wall and the outer glass itself, so that there was no distinction between the outside and the in, and we would sit, and eat, and talk about all the things we might do together later on. Afterwards we would put the breakfast things on the floor and lie back down again and talk some more, sometimes for hours, the duvet pulled up under our chins and the two of us resting back on piles of pillows, nestling against one

another. 'Like a couple of stowaways huddling together for warmth,' she'd said one Saturday in late October as she lay with her head resting in the crook of my arm and the length of her stretched out alongside me, and the air was cold and there was a breeze so strong it lifted things from surfaces and rattled at the lampshades so that the whole of the room was moving and we seemed to be the only still things in it.

On some of those mornings we talked of serious things and secret hopes, and on other mornings we talked of nothing very important at all, simply sharing some of the thousands of inconsequential fleeting thoughts that go to make up what might be called a consciousness. She spoke rarely of the past, not in any lingering fashion, and she volunteered nothing of what Harry had told me, nor anything about her childhood. 'Had we but world enough, and time,' was all she would say when I asked her once about what it had been like to grow up with Evie, and why there was so much tension between them. Nor would she tell me that morning what she meant by the phrase she had used, or where it came from, just turning away and lying on her side. Eventually I turned and lay that way also and said I was sorry for asking and she turned back and smiled at me and I no more understood that smile than I understood what she'd said; it was a smile that shut me out, one that invited no further questions.

I had learned something of the language of smiles from my mother. She'd sat me down at the beginning of one of my first holidays home from school and told me that she'd made up names for all of her smiles, in the way that one might have names for tempests out at sea or for winds across a desert. She taught me these names, one after another, showing me the smiles that went with them and waiting until I understood each one, and what it would mean about the way she was feeling were I to see it on her face. She said she was teaching me them so that when I came home from school in the holidays I would be able to read her more easily. Like a book, she said, so that our absences from one another would hardly matter. She told me that

if I tried ever so hard to remember, we would be able to rub along together like stones on a river bed, she and I, despite those separations we'd had to endure. And when it came to the end for her, years later, I remembered them still, so that it didn't matter when she had no energy to speak at the last: I sat by her bedside holding her hand and when she smiled at me, I knew what she was trying to tell me and I told her the same thing back.

I came to learn Rachel's smiles also. The one I loved the most, or at least, the one that made me happiest to see, was one that she smiled more often than the one I'd come to think of as her 'cease and desist' smile, but still no more than occasionally, and even then it was only ever by accident that she did so. There was a sweetness in it that sometimes stayed for days, and when I saw it there I knew it meant that she had, for a time, decided to believe me when I said I loved her. 'Despite everything, Alex?' she would say, frowning. 'Despite absolutely everything?'

'Despite what?' I would reply, completely at a loss to know what she was talking about. 'Despite everything what?' and I would laugh, and she would smile that smile and come forward and kiss me and say, 'It doesn't matter, Alex. It doesn't matter what. I know you do really. I know that you really do.'

I suppose it came to be a way we had between us, Rachel and I, of talking so rarely of the past. She intruded infrequently upon my own, although I think I would have become happier, in time, for us to have discussed it. I did try to tell her about Robbie once, on one of the weekend mornings when we lingered in bed, but I'm not sure I was very successful in my attempt. We'd eaten some fruit, and drunk some coffee, and then we lay back down again, and she reached over and took my hand, placing it on her chest and closing her eyes. I watched her chest gently rise and gently fall, and watched my hand move with it, and neither of us said anything for a while until she moved again, wriggling around a bit and making herself comfortable, curling her head against my neck once, and then into my shoulder and away again, pulling my

arm out from underneath her back and resting my hand on her chest again, like it had been before. And then she said, 'Tell me something,' and I said, 'What?' and she said, 'Anything. Anything at all.'

'Like what?' I asked.

'Really, Alex, anything,' she said. 'Just something. Tell me a story. Tell me something I don't know. Tell me something you've never told me before.'

And that was when, without intending to, and without knowing quite why I was doing so, I found myself starting to tell her about Robbie and me, and about our accident and about what had happened afterwards. I told her everything, slowly and particularly, and in a way that I had never told anyone before, not even when I was away at school and we all swapped stories about our fathers after lights out. That morning, as I talked on and on in our bed, Rachel said nothing, not a word, and I think the way she listened so carefully led me to believe that she didn't mind me telling her, and that she wasn't going to judge me. And so I carried on, and on, and told her everything there was to tell.

After I'd finished, still she said nothing, and I saw that my hand was rising and falling on her chest with a regularity that meant her breathing had settled into the rhythm of sleep. I don't think I minded terribly at first. In fact I don't think I minded at all until later on that afternoon, when she had gone out and I was standing in the kitchen making some tea, alone, and the thought occurred to me that she had in all probability fallen asleep as soon as I'd started to speak, and that this momentous occasion, the occasion on which I had finally told somebody the biggest secret I had ever kept, had gone entirely unwitnessed, so that my story remained unknown by anyone but me.

Harry asked me about none of these things, and so I stayed silent until, soon enough, he carried on from where he'd left off. Soon after his

meeting with Rachel on the South Bank Anthony had called briefly to say that he'd got Rachel's letter and everything had been arranged, but when Harry asked him what exactly the plan was, he'd been cagey at first, and then suddenly said he had to go. He told Harry not to worry, it'd all be fine, and he thanked him again for his help and the line went dead and he was gone. Rachel had been just as reluctant to tell Harry what was actually going to happen, and this vagueness as to the precise arrangements for their meeting had concerned Harry on three counts. He was slightly uncertain as to whether to trust her to go through with her promise to meet Anthony. And he wasn't entirely comfortable with the idea of Anthony coming into contact with Rachel again, in that he still had some lingering doubts about what he referred to as Anthony's 'hold on reality', and his tendency, on occasions, to resort to violence as a way of expressing his feelings. And third, he said, there was Anthony's own indecision and general unreliability. Despite all they'd done to bring about the meeting, it had failed once before, and might fail again, and Anthony himself might be the cause of that if he decided at the last minute not to show up, rendering the whole exercise redundant and leaving Rachel exposed still to the threat of whatever he might choose to do in the future in terms of embarrassing her professionally.

He had woken one morning in a panic, remembering Rachel's outburst on the South Bank about Anthony and wondering whether she really had been overreacting, as he'd thought she was, or whether he should have taken her more seriously. In an attempt to allay his concerns on all of the points that were worrying him, and having no one else to turn to, he telephoned Evie a day or so later and they met to talk things through. He told me that although the meeting had been fine, he'd come away with a sense that he'd failed, somehow, to communicate to her the precise nature of his reservations. She'd been pretty savage with him when he attempted it, calling him a fool and saying that he always had been a little precious about Rachel, and a

little unbalanced in his assessment of her abilities, which were, when it came down to it, no more remarkable than anyone else's in her field, and didn't he know that she was married to a Worcester lawyer now and wasn't it time he stopped following her around like a puppy? Anthony just wanted Rachel to say sorry, Evie said, that was all. He'd got over his crush on her years ago, it wasn't about that any more, there was nothing malign in his fascination. He was a perfectly normal human being, she said. 'I mean, Harry, he works in IT for goodness' sake!' she said. 'How much more normal can you get?' He was just aggrieved, she said, and whilst she had to agree that he had, in the past, occasionally let that sense of grievance get the better of him, it was all over now, couldn't Harry see that? Harry tried to explain to Evie that his concerns lacked the specificity with which she was imputing them, and that it was just that there had been something about the way Anthony was that day in Judd Street, something slightly peculiar in the light behind his eyes. But when it became apparent that Evie would give him no quarter, he'd let it drop.

And then he raised the question of whether one of them might lose heart at the last and falter in their resolve, leaving them no further on than they were already, and he suggested that his and Evie's presence might, on that score, be no bad thing. Evie told him he was being over the top, but she caved in in the end, looking in her diary and saying that she was due to take a visit to the collection at the Ashmolean, and she might as well do it that weekend as any other, and there would be bound to be some kind of fund-raiser on the Thursday she could get involved in as a cover story so Rachel didn't get uptight about her being there. She couldn't promise anything, not in any definite way, but she'd do her best. Harry thanked her, and suggested they kept in fairly close contact over the weekend, and could he have her mobile number?

In the end, he found that he was able to set his reservations on one side. In addition to Evie's opinion, there was his own assessment of

Anthony, whose story he had, after all, heard first hand, and there was also the fact that he was in a position to be able to maintain a greater degree of objectivity about the situation than Rachel was, being less caught up in it than her. And so it was that the plan had been laid, and Rachel and I had driven to Oxford on the afternoon of Thursday 21 June at about the same time that Anthony and Evie would have been making an identical journey. And so it was also that I was the only one of our number who was entirely ignorant of what lay ahead.

Harry said that it was at about two o'clock on that Thursday afternoon that Anthony had telephoned him again. He was in his rooms when the call came, sorting through some examination papers. It sounded from the background noise as though Anthony was calling on his mobile, but when Harry heard a series of beeps and the line went dead, he realised he was using a payphone. When Anthony called back a moment later, he told Harry straight away that he was due to meet Rachel at midnight, down by the side of the lake.

'She said I had no choice. Take it or leave it. So I took it.'

'But why there? And why then?'

'She doesn't want Petersen to know, that's why. Stick to each other like limpets, those two. She's just going to run down and see me and yeah, I mean that's fine with me. I mean, it's happening isn't it. That's what matters. He won't know anything if we do it like this, she can just leave him for five minutes or something and we can talk.'

'By the lake?' Harry said. 'Can you not meet in town tomorrow or something? Isn't that a slightly unorthodox way—'

'That's Rachel for you, Harry. Anyhow, it's fine. Actually I quite like it. Just like old times eh?'

'And what about Evie?' Harry asked. 'Have you told Evie what you're doing?'

'No I haven't. And no I'm not going to. Why should I?'

'Why shouldn't you?

'She's given me so much grief about the whole thing, Harry. She's already fed me a pile of bullshit about some fund-raiser she's going to at the museum so she's just coincidentaly going to be in Oxford. I mean, I know she hates those things. She's always complaining about them. It's such a lame excuse. She just wants to be hanging around finding out what's going on. She's giving me a lift, that's alright, but that's as far as it goes. She'll just have to live with it, I'm not getting into that. I wasn't going to tell you either but I thought Rachel would have told you anyway and, well, you know, I'm grateful. I mean, thank you. I'm glad it's happening.'

'Of course,' Harry said. 'Of course. You are welcome. I just hope it will bring about a resolution to things, I really do.'

And Anthony laughed and said he was sure it would work out, one way or another, and then suddenly he said he had to go. Just before he did, Harry said he'd appreciate a chat in the next day or so, just so he knew how it had gone, and they agreed to meet in his college rooms the following morning for coffee.

Harry carried on with his story, reminding me that he had invited Rachel and me to his rooms for 6.15 so that we could leave our things there and borrow a spare gown or two if we hadn't brought our own, and have a glass of wine with him before going over to drinks in the Old Bursary. I remembered as he spoke that neither of us had had coats that summer night, and there was only Rachel's bag in the end, and that she'd insisted on taking it to dinner with her, and had still had it with her when she'd gone down to the lake, and the police had never been able to find it.

At about five o'clock, Harry said, just as he was getting out some wine glasses and checking the Chablis was in the fridge, he decided he ought to let Evie know what was going on, having told her that he would. He didn't see why Anthony's reluctance to communicate with her should prevent him from doing so, and he felt at that moment

that he needed her support. He tried her mobile but it went straight to voicemail, and looking at the clock he realised that there was just enough time for him to walk over to the Ashmolean and see if he could find her in her department. He sat at his desk and wrote her a note, passing on exactly what Anthony had told him, intending to leave it with her secretary if she wasn't in her office when he got there.

He added a bit more to the note, writing that he hoped Evie would be able to slip away from the fund-raiser before it was over, and why didn't she come into College and wander down in the direction of the lake at about that time, just to keep an eye on them. He'd written a postscript giving her directions for the secret garden and telling her that Haddon was definitely coming to dine on High Table and wouldn't be in his cottage, and why didn't she slip into the secret garden at about half past eleven? Haddon never locked his door when he was at dinner, Harry wrote, and he always stayed late at coffee afterwards, so she could easily hide herself away to watch from there and slip back out of College again without anyone knowing. He told her he intended to pop up to the Old Library after dinner and watch the events unfold from up there, so he'd give her a quick call on her mobile once he'd seen Rachel setting off towards the lake. He walked over to the Ashmolean but he hadn't been able to find Evie, so he'd pushed the note under her door, almost certain she'd leave her things in there before the fund-raiser.

By about ten past six he was waiting in his rooms for us to arrive when he had a last-minute panic about whether she would actually get the note, and he tried her mobile again. It was switched on this time but it rang and rang and he heard us coming up the staircase and there we were, trying on gowns for size, and he was pouring us our Chablis and the evening had begun. There wasn't the opportunity for him to talk to Rachel in private, and he didn't dare raise the subject in my hearing after what she'd made him promise on the South Bank. It was odd that evening over dinner, he said, picking up little signs in her

behaviour that might have given her away had Anthony not already told him what had been arranged. She was excited somehow, even a little nervous, and Harry saw her looking at her watch again and again and checking her mobile under the table on more than one occasion. He noticed also her insistence that she had to take her bag with her to dinner, rather than leave it in his rooms, and he could only think that this had something to do with what was inside, something he'd discovered by accident when we'd arrived and he'd taken it through to his side room only to drop it and see the little book of Browning fall out.

Everything went as planned, he said, when he managed after dinner to go up to the Old Library without our realising. We'd said our goodbyes and he told us he had to go back to his rooms for something. As soon as our backs were turned, he slipped up the spiral staircase. He was half sure at that point that Rachel would waver, it having seemed that we'd been about to let ourselves out of College, but a few minutes later, standing by the window, he saw her walking down the side of the quad. He pulled his phone from his pocket to call Evie only to find that there wasn't a signal in the Old Library. He knew it wasn't essential, but all the same, he was annoyed at finding himself confronted by this little problem, and so he did the first thing that came into his head and picked up the lamp from the table in front of him and switched it on and off a couple of times, thinking that Evie might be looking up towards the library windows. There was no way someone that far away would actually have been able to see him flashing the lamp, but he did it anyway, for his own satisfaction.

He was amazed when he saw a light flashing in response from somewhere in the direction of the secret garden, although it looked to be coming from slightly beyond that point and further towards the lake. And he was even more amazed a moment or two later to see a second light, closer this time, flashing in what he thought must be the secret garden. He was confused then, and a little scared, until he real-

ised that the first light must have been some kind of trick played on him by his own eyes, caused by nothing other than a reflection of his own lamp in the glass he stood in front of, and that the second light must have been Evie after all.

Just after the lights stopped flashing, Harry saw the porter emerge from the alcove beneath the library. He watched him stand on the quad's north terrace looking about himself for a moment or two and glancing up at the clock before carrying on along the terrace, disappearing into staircase number 6 and embarking on his night-time rounds. Everything seemed now to be going ahead in the way Harry had hoped it would and it was with a slight sense of relief that he walked back down the spiral staircase, thinking that it would all be over and done with before too long. Having passed me sitting in the shadows where I had dozed off while waiting for Rachel, he'd walked out on to the terrace and headed towards his rooms to fetch his things, intending to watch from his window for Rachel coming back up from the lake. And that, of course, was the moment that he heard her scream and he knew that something had gone wrong after all and that she and Anthony must be having some kind of a fight. He found himself frozen to the spot with the shock of it, absolutely unable to move, or even to think, and then he saw me running and stumbling down the steps and he turned his head slightly to see the figure, who he realised must be Evie, running up the quad and passing me on the steps and disappearing towards the entrance to the college, the whole thing taking no more than a minute at most.

When Harry felt the sensation of strength coming back into his legs, he stumbled back along the terrace and went straight to the lodge to report what he'd seen and to tell the porter that there was something going on down by the lake. But when he got there he found the place empty. Then he remembered seeing the porter setting off on his rounds and realised that he would have heard the scream as well and would have run to see what was going on. He felt certain

that between the two of us, the porter and I would have been able to break up the fight, or whatever it was that was happening. He thought of what Haddon had told him about Anthony attacking Cissy on the night of the Ball and he was concerned, not being at all confident that Rachel would share Cissy's aptitude for self-defence. But at no stage did he actually think that anything serious could have happened, given that I would have reached her so quickly and would have been able to intervene.

At that point, Harry told me, he realised he had a number of options. He could either go down to the lake and see what he could do to help, or he could go back to his rooms and watch from his window, or he could simply go home and wait. He was annoyed with Evie for having run off like that, since she must have known he'd want to talk to her and find out what she'd seen. And he was rueful about the fact that things seemed to have gone wrong, feeling for Rachel and knowing she'd have had an awful lot of explaining to do when I'd got there and broken up whatever was happening. In the end, concluding that he would be of no use to anybody if he stayed, he decided to go home, so exhausted that he was barely able to put one foot in front of the other as he walked over to Gloucester Green to find a taxi, trying Evie's phone one more time only to hear it ring and ring again.

That was his understanding of events when finally he managed to drift off to sleep that night, hoping he'd be able to make more sense of things in the morning. He felt so tired that he set his alarm a little later than usual, but he'd only been asleep for a few hours when he was woken by the sound of a loud and repeated banging and his bell being rung over and over. He fell from his bed and wrapped his dressing gown around him and staggered across to his bedroom window and when he looked out and saw the police car that was parked in his drive he knew that Rachel had been hurt. There was a pain behind his eyes suddenly, as though the brightest of lights was being shone in them, and his stomach felt as though it was dropping to the floor, all in a

piece. As he walked slowly from his bedroom and made his way down the stairs he realised that he had to make up his mind what he would and wouldn't say in the statement he was about to give, and that in so deciding, he would be formulating a version of events that he would have to stick to for good, whatever happened.

He couldn't understand why the officers wouldn't tell him exactly what had happened to Rachel. When he asked, they would say only that she'd been involved in an incident, and when he asked again, they said nothing. And so he began, resolving as he answered the first of their questions that he'd give them only the barest of facts as they might have presented themselves to him had he actually known nothing of Rachel's plan to meet Anthony beside the lake, or of Evie's presence in the secret garden, or any of the details of the histories the four of them shared. He closed his eyes slightly against the brightness of the lights in his kitchen and tried to imagine it was me he was talking to, rather than the tape recorder the police had brought with them, and that he was choosing his words as carefully as he was only in order to keep the promise he'd made to Rachel that I should know nothing of what had passed between her and Anthony, rather than through any desire to mislead. And he said that of course, at that stage, he had no reason to think that Rachel had come to any serious harm, supposing instead that she and Anthony had had, at the worst, some sort of a fight.

It is difficult to portray with any accuracy how I felt as Harry described the little ways in which he'd attempted to justify his decisions. It was revulsion, I think, that I sensed most strongly in myself; a revulsion born of anger, and shock, and dismay, and sadness. And those things seared through me almost physically, so that once or twice the room seemed to swim about us and there was a moment when Harry's words became distorted, as though I was listening to him underwater, his voice booming and warped and looping in my

head before everything settled again and his speech returned to normal and I heard him saying he'd had little difficulty in giving his statement, in that the police were just asking a series of straightforward questions, and it struck me then that he had no idea at all of the impact that his words were having on me, so wrapped up was he in this narrative he had constructed, and so intent was he on the telling of it, having found at last a listener.

He continued to describe, coldly and calmly, the night he'd spent sitting in his kitchen committing perjury, and he finished by telling me that because they'd accepted his answers so readily, he'd become quite comfortable by the end of it and offered them a cup of tea, saying they must be even more exhausted than he was. They said no thank you though, and when he saw one of them making a note of the fact he'd offered, it occurred to him he probably shouldn't have done so.

While giving that initial statement had been easy enough, he said, the interview he'd been required to attend later that morning had been a more difficult affair altogether. A couple of officers had called at his house at about eight o'clock and asked him to come down to the station, saying it wouldn't take long, they just had a few routine questions. And it was on the way there that they had announced, almost in passing, that Rachel had been murdered.

22

They began his interview by reading his statement back to him and he sat, silent and hardly breathing, unable to believe what was happening. He was horrified by the series of untruths he found himself listening to, but even in his confusion he knew his brief and knew he had to stick to it, whatever happened. He got through it in the end, but not without experiencing considerable problems in dealing with one or two things in particular. The first real challenge was with regard to the question of why he'd changed his mind about going back to his rooms to collect his things, and why he'd gone up to the library instead. 'A poet, you say?' the first policeman asked him. 'And which poet might that be?' And of course, Harry said, he'd answered without thinking, wishing immediately that he hadn't referred to Browning, feeling he'd given something away just by saying that. And then, when they pressed him further about why he'd felt it necessary to look up the answer to Rachel's question at nearly midnight, rather than leaving it until the morning, he really did get in a bit of a mess. Thinking on his feet and feeling a sudden sweat breaking out across

his chest and under his arms, hoping it wasn't also appearing on his forehead, he told them he'd been quite irked by Rachel's apparent surprise at his not having had the answer to her question at his fingertips, and that they'd had a little spat about it actually, over dinner, and she'd laughed at him for it, even though she knew how sensitive he was to the assumptions people were making, quite unfounded assumptions, about his memory not being as sharp as it might be. He almost came unstuck again when it came to thinking of a response to their enquiries as to what Rachel's question about Browning had been, and he really didn't know what to say when they asked, several times, about this spat with Rachel, and whether he could suggest who else at the dinner table might have heard it, since they hadn't managed to find anyone.

And then, of course, there was the postcard he'd said he was going to write and drop in to our hotel in the morning. 'We've got one of our officers up at your house looking for it now, Mr Gardner,' they said, after someone had interrupted the interview and put a note on the table. 'Only thing is, they can't find it. Any chance you could tell us where it is, this postcard?' Harry said he felt quite sick at that point, considering for a moment whether to say he'd written a note instead, on some paper that he'd found in the library, and that he'd dropped it round to our hotel on the way home. But he realised immediately how pointless that would be, given that they'd have searched there also, so he simply said he'd been too tired in the end and had left it until the morning, but that he hadn't thought there was much point when it came to it, not after the police had been to see him. 'But you found your answer, Mr Gardner, did you?' they asked him next, and when Harry wavered, they pulled out the tape of his previous interview and played it back to him, and he heard his own voice speaking to him from the early hours saying yes, he had found his answer. And when they had turned off the tape and looked at him, he had to say no, now that he thought about it, he couldn't for the life of him recall what it had been.

And as if those things hadn't been difficult enough, there was the question to be dealt with of why, on hearing the scream and seeing me stumble down the steps and seeing the figure running past me as I'd fallen, he'd decided to go home. Why hadn't he gone to his rooms, or to the lake to see what was happening? He got through it by telling them that Rachel and I were no longer students, and whatever we might or might not have been doing after dinner, running around the college or not running around the college, had not been his business. He said he'd decided it was entirely possible at that stage that the running figure had simply been a late-night jogger, and that the scream had come from outside the college walls rather than in, but that it had been sufficiently distracting for him to have forgotten what it was he'd been going to his rooms to collect, and because of that he had just decided to go home, and that was all there was to it.

They'd let him go in the end and he'd had no more trouble from them, supposing to himself that if they'd seemed a little aggressive in their questioning, and if they'd been a little sceptical of his story, they'd only treated him in the way they treated everyone they interviewed, finding it a successful method for filtering those who had committed a crime from those who had not.

By the time the interview was over, he'd begun to feel extremely unwell; he was unsteady on his legs and faint with exhaustion, appalled by what was happening. Such had been the need to focus his mind on the questions he was being asked, it was his body that reacted instead and registered the shock he'd felt when the police told him Rachel was dead. At that moment, he said, everything had slowed down suddenly, as if the car they were in was sliding by on thick grease, unable properly to move, even though he could see from the speed at which things were passing by outside the window that they had not, and they were not. Having been shown out of the interview room, he left the police station feeling so disturbed that he wondered, just briefly, whether he was dreaming, trapped in some kind of suspended nightmare, and

when he got back to his rooms in College he was unable to do anything other than sit without moving in his armchair, clinging to the hope that Anthony would stick to their arrangement to meet for coffee that morning.

In the end there was no knock on his door, and no telephone call either, and when the clock struck noon he telephoned Evie again. He got through this time and asked if they could meet, saying he thought it best they didn't speak on the phone. She told him to come to her office at the Ashmolean and as he walked over he felt a certain sense of relief at the thought that he was about to find out what had actually happened, and what she'd seen from the secret garden. Only, Evie told him when he arrived, she hadn't seen anything at all, for the simple reason that she hadn't been there.

Harry said she was barely able to string a coherent sentence together at first. When he told her he'd seen her running back up the quad from the secret garden, and when he asked why she hadn't at least telephoned him afterwards to tell him what had happened, she said she had no idea what he was talking about.

'But you know about Rachel?' he asked, feeling totally confused by what he was hearing.

'Of course I fucking know,' she replied, almost shouting at him. 'Alex phoned me from the police station. That was bad enough, having to hear it from Alex fucking Petersen, but you do realise what I had to do afterwards don't you?'

'No,' Harry said. 'No I don't.'

'Who do you fucking think identified her fucking body, Harry? Do you have any idea what that was like for me?'

'Evie. I'm so—'

'I don't suppose you know either that the last time I had to identify a body was twenty-five fucking years ago and it was Rachel's fucking mother. Christ, Harry. You shouldn't be bothering me with your stupid questions, not now.'

'Right,' Harry said, his breathing shallow and his heart racing in his chest. But still she hadn't finished.

'So unless you've got something useful to tell me like where the hell that little shit Anthony is I'd be grateful if you could just piss off and leave me alone.'

'Right,' he said again. 'That's exactly what I was hoping you'd be able to tell me.'

And then he listened, stunned, as she claimed never to have found the note he'd put under her office door, and said that at no point during the previous evening, nor during the night, had she realised he'd been trying to contact her. She'd either been in the bath, she said, or she'd had her phone switched to silent, for example during the speeches at the fund-raiser.

'Quite frankly,' she said, 'I'd had enough of the whole thing by the time the party started and I decided to leave the lot of you to your own devices, come what may.'

'Come what may?' Harry repeated back at her, hardly believing what he was hearing.

'Fuck you Harry Gardner. Don't even think about trying to make me feel responsible for what's happened. Alright? It was out of my hands. Wasn't ever in them as a matter of fact, so you can drop the bullshit. God knows I'm feeling bad enough already, can't you see that?' And when he said yes, of course he could see that, but he still didn't understand how she'd spent the rest of the evening, and what she'd been doing later on when she hadn't answered the phone call he'd made from his taxi home, she really did shout.

'For christ's sake Harry. It's none of your fucking business.'

'Alright,' Harry said, 'Alright. But what are we going to do about Anthony?'

She calmed down a bit then, and told him she hadn't tried Anthony's phone, and she didn't think it was such a clever idea to do so now, and nor had he tried to call hers. She was going to just wait, that was

all, and in her opinion, Harry should do the same. Harry told her in response that he'd arranged to meet Anthony that morning but he hadn't shown up, and that he really didn't know what to do next.

'Nothing, Harry,' she said. 'You do nothing at all. We wait, and we see. That's all we can do.' And then she stood and walked to the door and held it open, turning back to him and saying, 'I'm sorry to have to say this to you, Harry, but I'd like you to leave now, and I mean right now. She's dead, and nothing you or I can do will change that. We stand only to lose by sticking our necks out any further than we have done already. I think we both know what's happened, and as far as I'm concerned, there really is nothing else to say. You have my email address, I think. If you have any real need to contact me, use it.'

It was as he walked back over to Worcester from the Ashmolean trying to digest what Evie had told him that things felt as though they were really beginning to unravel. He went back to his rooms and spent the rest of the day in a daze, sitting in his armchair looking down on the quad and hoping in a vague sort of a way that Anthony might yet turn up, listening for his tread on the staircase at the same time as knowing he wouldn't hear it. And then he went home and slept, returning the next morning to wait. He said he hadn't really admitted that was what he was doing at first, convincing himself that despite it being a Saturday, when he would normally have gone to the farmers' market, or walked out to a pub for lunch, it was better to go to his rooms and start to sort through his things for the summer vacation, discarding the papers he no longer required and perhaps even marking a few of the Finals scripts that had come. It was only when my call was put through that he realised he'd been hoping Anthony would make an appearance, his heart jumping and a wave of adrenalin running across the inside of his chest as he realised he had no idea what to say to him, or where he should begin.

The porter told him that the caller he was about to put through was a former student who hadn't given his name, and when Harry

heard my voice on the line instead of Anthony's, he was shocked, and completely thrown by my proposal that we should meet. It was a meeting he found excruciating in the extreme, he said, and one of the most difficult conversations he'd ever had in his life. Still, as far as he could tell, it passed without incident. Wearied by the anxiety it gave rise to, he left my hotel and went back to College and almost fell into the Senior Common Room for his lunch, taking a seat on his own and staring into space. Before long the table was filling up, and he looked across to see Haddon sitting down opposite him. He nodded, and made it clear he wasn't interested in having a conversation. The two of them had already spoken earlier that morning, having bumped into one another in the quad, and he hadn't been particularly surprised by the line Haddon seemed to be taking. The tone in which he'd spoken, Harry said, bordered almost on the sensationalist, as though he was discussing an episode of a murder mystery series for the television rather than the death of a former student.

As he waited for his next course to arrive, Harry listened on and off to the conversation Haddon was having with the junior colleague beside him, feeling fairly irritated by the fact that he seemed to be continuing in the same vein. He'd been about to lean across the table and tell Haddon that the way he was talking about Rachel was disrespectful, and reprehensible, when he heard Evie's name mentioned and kept quiet. He'd missed the very beginning of the conversation but from what he could make out, it seemed that Haddon had just come from coffee with a colleague, the History of Art Fellow, who'd been at the Ashmolean fund-raiser the previous evening and had reported seeing Evie there.

'Oh yes,' he heard Haddon say, 'had my own run-ins with her in my time. Bit of a vixen if you get my drift,' he said to the junior colleague, whose eyes, Harry said, widened at the thought of whatever it was that she might be about to hear. And then it was Harry's eyes that widened, as Haddon went on to say that Evie had apparently been at the party at

the Ashmolean, and had listened to the speeches and stayed for a short while afterwards, but that just when Haddon's informant had been on the point of approaching her, she'd left the room suddenly, and in the company of a man rather younger than herself. 'Poor show really,' Haddon said, smiling back at the junior colleague and luxuriating in the attention she was paying him. 'Someone in her position. Should have stayed on in my opinion. Talked to the other donors, pressed a bit of flesh. Had other things on her mind though, what?'

And that was the point at which Harry began to realise he was facing the situation very much on his own. Not only had Anthony disappeared without trace, but if Haddon's report was to be believed, Evie and Anthony had been at the party at the Ashmolean but had left well before the end, which meant they would both have had plenty of time to change and be in College before midnight. Given those things, his realisation that she very probably had been in the secret garden after all, and that it had been her he'd seen running up the side of the quad, left him without a great deal in the way of options when it came to answering the question of why it was that she was lying to him, and what it was that she was trying to hide.

Harry asked himself that question again and again in the months that followed. He thought once or twice during the summer that he might be going insane. He passed his time largely alone, in Oxford, spending day after day in his college rooms ruminating obsessively on what had happened and failing to come up with any kind of idea of what he could do about it. He'd thought of contacting me right from the start, but however many times he considered it he simply couldn't imagine how he would begin to tell me what he knew. And he assumed that my reaction would be to go straight to the police, which was something he wanted very much to avoid given that it would inevitably result in his being treated as a suspect and charged with having given false

evidence. His certainty of his own innocence had provided him with the justification for deciding against that course of action, but even that was something he had come to doubt, in a slightly fantastical way. When the police had begun their reconstructions he'd watched each one from the window of his rooms overlooking the quad. They would wait until the sky was as clear as it had been on the night of Rachel's murder, and then, when the moon was just at the right height, a team of actors would take to the stage and it would begin. He said he couldn't help but stay and look, and that at first he'd found it uncanny, how perfectly it was done each time, how little deviation there was from the events as he remembered them. But then one night as he'd stood at his window watching, he'd realised the scene that was being played out was essentially one of which he was the only scriptwriter, and from that point on he'd started to wonder, on and off, whether he had perhaps made the whole thing up, or imagined the events altogether.

He'd taken to travelling to London only when the air cooled again and he realised it was mid-September, forcing himself to go back to the British Library despite what had happened, recognising the need to stabilise his life in some way and thinking that the resumption of his once familiar routine might be the best approach to take. He had, of course, found his first visit overwhelmingly difficult, and had taken to using another reading room, being unable to feel comfortable in the one in which he and Rachel had so often worked together. And he had, on a couple of occasions, found himself crossing over the Euston Road to stand outside Anthony's Judd Street flat, just on the other side of the street. He did this for no more than half an hour or so at a time, perhaps longer, hoping to catch a glimpse of him. But he saw nothing, and had no word from him either, until the telephone calls began.

It was at the very end of September that they started. To his growing sense of unease a pattern quickly developed whereby, at about the same time each afternoon, the lodge would put through a call to his

room, telling him that the caller had declined to give his name. He would take the call only to hear the sound of a busy street for a minute or two before a series of pips signalled that the caller's money had run out. And then there was nothing until the same time the following day. He had felt certain, he said, that it was Anthony, and he found himself almost longing for the next call to come, thinking that perhaps that would be the occasion on which Anthony would actually speak to him. He'd thought once or twice about asking the police to trace these calls, but had realised that if he was going to do that, he may as well tell them everything, and, this being a course he had already decided against, he could see no way of asking for their assistance.

He told me that the preparations for Rachel's memorial service in October had provided a certain solace, in that he was able at least to feel that he was of some use to me. And as the date we had fixed for the service drew closer, and Anthony still hadn't replied to the invitation, he'd somehow known then that he'd never see him again. He'd allowed himself to hope that Anthony might just show up unannounced, but as far as he was aware, he hadn't. When I'd mentioned early on during my visit that I thought I'd seen someone who looked like him slipping in at the back of Chapel after the start of the service, he'd wondered at first whether I might have been right, but had decided on balance it was unlikely even he would have done something quite so brazen.

In any case, after that, the phone calls stopped altogether. He missed them, he said, these little silences, and after a couple of weeks he started to worry, and to fear that something awful might have happened. It was a thought he'd entertained right from the start in a non-specific sort of a way: the possibility that Anthony might be so filled with remorse for whatever it was that he'd done on the night that Rachel died that he would no longer have been able to live with himself, and that that might explain his disappearance. His fears were confirmed, he said, in as much as they could be, when he received a telephone call from the Metropolitan Police

in mid-November asking him to attend Holborn Police Station for an interview about a missing person. He had panicked at first, of course, thinking that the police had caught up with him and had spotted some kind of a link between Anthony and Rachel, but to his amazement, after the first ten minutes of the interview had passed, it became apparent that the Metropolitan Police and the police in Oxford had made no connection whatsoever between the two cases, and he had stopped panicking.

The officer told him that one of Anthony's neighbours had alerted the police to the fact that there was a strong and unpleasant smell coming from his Judd Street flat, and that he hadn't been seen entering or leaving the property for some time. As was normally the first step that was taken in such cases, they'd forced an entry. Finding the place empty and obviously unused for some time, and that the smell was caused by nothing more sinister than festering refuse in the unemptied kitchen bin, they'd filed the case as non-urgent and started a series of routine checks. His employers told them he'd handed in his notice in early June. His colleagues had thought nothing of the fact that they hadn't heard from him; Anthony had never been particularly sociable with any of them, and had mentioned that he was taking some time off to go travelling. Checks on his passport had revealed that it hadn't been used at all in the previous six months and they had assumed he was simply elsewhere in the country, preparing for his travels. But when they had contacted his mother a couple of weeks later, she'd told them that she hadn't heard from him since July and that she was becoming more and more concerned about him. He'd written her a letter saying he needed some time alone, and that she knew how much he loved her but he hoped she would understand that he would appreciate it very much if she didn't try to contact him, or to find him, and that she mustn't worry about him, nor should she let anyone know that she'd heard from him. She was beside herself, she said, and had been on the point of contacting the police when

they had called anyway, and so she'd told them about Anthony's letter, despite him having asked her not to.

And then the policeman had smiled at Harry across the table and said, 'Quite a little letter-writer this Anthony was, by the looks of things,' and he handed Harry an envelope. It seemed that Anthony had left it on the kitchen table in his flat. It was addressed to Harry at Worcester and had a first-class stamp on it. They'd opened it at the time but had filed it away, finding there was nothing particularly remarkable about it. But in recent weeks, he said, Anthony's mother had started to give them what he described as 'a bit of gyp', so they'd reopened the investigation. They'd found the letter to Harry on the file and thought they may as well get him in for a chat to see if he could help them before they put the matter away again.

The officer said that at this stage they were ruling nothing in, nor were they ruling anything out. Anthony had closed all his bank accounts and no trace of him could be found in the UK, or at least not without further expenditure of a kind that wasn't being contemplated. The decision had been taken to draw a line under things for now, there being no reason to treat his disappearance as anything other than what the policeman called 'a voluntary'. Harry said that it had struck him as odd, this missing-persons terminology, making him think only of summer evenings when he'd left Chapel after Evensong to the sounds of the organist's improvisation soaring around the quad, and for a moment he had thought he was close to tears at the sadness of it all. Realising that to expose his emotion at that point would be more than a little unwise, he had bitten his tongue to stop himself, before looking down to read the letter.

He was relieved and disappointed in equal measure to see that it provided nothing by way of explanation. It contained not a single clue, being simply an invitation to Harry to come to the flat and take whatever books he'd like to have, since Anthony was going travelling for some time and didn't know when he would return. The policeman

said that it was clear that Anthony had simply forgotten to post it, and once Harry had told him that he was sorry but he really couldn't help him, the man had offered to walk him round to the flat so that he could take some of the books before Anthony's mother came down to collect everything the following week. 'Only if it's no trouble,' Harry said, and so they walked over to Judd Street to see what they could find.

The flat, Harry said, was cleaner than he'd expected it to be, and there was none of the fetid smell the policeman had described. 'Had it done professionally,' the man explained. 'The neighbours, you know.' But there were still a couple of flies circling in the kitchen, and when the policeman opened the door through to Anthony's study, saying that that was where the bookshelves were, Harry said that they were met with a sight that disgusted him. A couple of flies had obviously been trapped in that room also, and had multiplied, so that there were thirty or forty of them circling in a cloud in the middle of the room and the floor was littered with tiny blue-black bodies. 'Like a scene from a Hitchcock film,' Harry said to me. 'It really was grotesque.' And then, as the policeman started to swat at the cloud above his head, and to open the windows and waft as many of them outside as possible before going back to the kitchen to fetch a dustpan and brush, Harry looked across the room and saw the little book of Browning sitting in the middle of Anthony's otherwise empty desk. He realised then that the whole thing had been planned to happen in exactly this way, and that Anthony had intended for him to come here in the company of a policeman and to find this book, the book that Harry had seen fall from Rachel's bag in his rooms on the night of her murder.

He made a show of going over to the bookshelves and selecting a few volumes, browsing quite calmly as though nothing out of the ordinary had happened, and then he walked over to the desk and said to the policeman, with what he hoped was just the right degree of nonchalance in his voice, 'Ah. Robert Browning. One of my all-time

favourites,' before picking it up and adding it to the ones he had taken from the shelves.

It wasn't until he was on the train home that evening that he'd taken the book from his bag. It fell open at 'Porphyria's Lover', and he held it closer and saw what he thought was the tiniest trace of blood on the corner of the page, putting it away again almost immediately, such was his sorrow, and his fear, and his confusion about what he should do next.

By then it was mid-November, and the tale he was soon to tell me was beginning to take shape more clearly in his mind. Over the following fortnight he'd thought hard about whether to contact me, or whether to go straight to the police, but in the end he had decided to invite me to Oxford and tell me his story, using the feint of having found some things of Rachel's that he thought I might like to have.

'So, Alex,' he said, getting up out of his chair and walking over to the window. 'There it is. We have talked and talked and I think I have told you everything I know. I would like now to begin to draw some conclusions, if I may.'

Before he started he made more tea and fetched crumpets from the fridge, and as he put them on skewers on the fire I thought of Rachel, and of her interview, and I wished very much that she was there with us, to hear what it was that Harry was about to tell me.

He began by saying that although at times he still felt completely bewildered by the picture he was looking at, seeing only ill-formed shapes emerging from shadows and disappearing again, he had been aware from the start that the truth most probably lay in what was the simplest explanation for the murder: that Anthony had lost his temper with Rachel that night and had bludgeoned her to death and escaped from College somehow, and that Evie, watching from the secret garden, had run away and denied all knowledge of the whole thing, feeling herself to be culpable in some way. The only variation which he thought possible was that Anthony had intended to kill her

all along, and that Evie had assisted him somehow, and was equally guilty, which was why she was still denying her presence in the secret garden that night. That she had been there, despite her protestations to the contrary, was a fact that had been elevated almost to the status of an objective truth for Harry when he'd overheard Haddon's report of seeing her leaving the Ashmolean party in the company of a young man. His visit to Judd Street a couple of weeks ago, when he'd found the book of Browning that he was sure Rachel had been carrying with her when she'd gone down to the lake, had confirmed his suspicions; it was clear to him that Anthony must have found it in her bag and taken it back to London with him, and that by leaving the letter where the police would be sure to find it and contact Harry, he was somehow seeking to taunt him with the fact he had been her killer, knowing what the consequences would be for Harry were he to reveal his suspicions to the police, having kept them to himself for so long.

He said he'd only ever really faced one barrier in his attempt to prove this hypothesis, given his certainty that the figure running past me on the steps had been Evie, and that was the question of how Anthony had made his escape from the college gardens immediately after he had killed Rachel. That Anthony had been in College at some point that day was something Harry and I both knew, or could at least be almost certain of, having seen his pseudonym in the Visitors Book. Harry had presumed its cryptic nature had confounded the police and that they must have attributed it to a prankster and neglected to consider it further. But as to how he had got away from the scene of his crime that night, that had bothered Harry quite considerably. The police had made much of the security cordon that the college had put in place five years previously, and he hadn't been able to understand how Anthony's departure could have gone unnoticed. I recalled as Harry said this that my suggestions to the detectives that they should perhaps widen their search beyond the running figure

had been met each time with the response that all the other exits had been covered by CCTV, that they had eliminated from their enquiries almost everyone who'd been recorded entering or leaving the college by those routes during the forty-eight hours preceding and following Rachel's murder, and that there was no other way out. And they were right, Harry said: given the height of the walls, and the spikes and broken glass that had been placed along the tops of them, apart from the one low wall that ran beside the south-west side of the lake and followed the line of the canal, there was really no other way. He had been several times to look at the route that Anthony would have had to have taken to get out via the canal. He had seen how far he would have had to fall before hitting the water, and, having considered the dangers that would have been involved in attempting such a thing in darkness, he'd decided that it just wasn't probable he would have risked it, even if he'd been able to push through the trees and bushes forming a natural barrier between the path and the wall.

That left open the possibility that Anthony had not in fact been there at all, Harry said, and that it had actually been Evie who had waited by the lake and murdered Rachel. But then, at the end of our second tea together, when I told him about what the porter had said about the old gate at the back of the playing fields, he'd thought he had his answer at last. Having resolved to investigate it further he had sent me away for the day on my long walk across Boars Hill and through Wytham Woods, and my visit to the Ashmolean. His story about being in London all day had been a ruse, nothing more than that. He said that what the porter had told me was correct; it had been twenty years or more since the gate had been closed off, and although it had still been in use when Harry had arrived at the college to take up his Fellowship, it wasn't long afterwards that the paths had been rerouted. Because he had given no thought to it since then, and wasn't able to recall its exact location, the first thing he had done, having ascertained from the porter that I had set off on my walk as he'd told

me to, was to go up to the Old Library and look at the plans of the college from that time.

When it came to it, Harry said, it had been almost impossible to get to, and apparently the porter had been absolutely right when he'd told me that unless one knew what one was looking for, one simply would never have found it. Harry had made his way down to the playing fields and walked across to their far side. He'd paced back and forth for some time, he said, and had decided on what he thought might be the right spot, but he could see no way through the undergrowth, none whatsoever. He'd been about to give up and was wondering whether he should go and let himself into one of the gardeners' sheds and borrow an axe and simply start hacking his way through the bushes at random, such was his frustration, when suddenly he'd seen a gap in the branches and stepped into it, covering his face with his hands as best he could and pushing and pushing until his foot made contact with something hard and he lowered his hands from his face to see that he was staring at a brick wall. He'd edged along to his left, branches sticking into his back and tearing at his coat, until finally he came to the gate. Standing with his face jammed up against the wood in front of him and a cluster of rusted-up old chains and padlocks pressing uncomfortably into his stomach, he realised how irrational he had been to think Anthony could have done this thing, and quite how absurd his expedition was: all the police would have had to do was walk the boundary from the outside in order to see the gate from the street. His endeavour had been nothing but the wildest of goose chases, he said, and on returning to his rooms and taking the debris from his hair and seeing that he had torn his coat in a couple of places, he felt more than a little foolish for having thought he could succeed where others had failed. Regardless of this unanswered question, Harry said, the fact that Anthony really did seem to have gone missing was, in his opinion, yet further confirmation of his guilt. Whether he had absconded

abroad, or whether he had done as Harry thought possible and killed himself, was neither here nor there in terms of Harry's suspicions. As for Evie, he said, he still hadn't got to the bottom of why she was denying that she'd been there, unless it was the case that she had assisted in Rachel's murder. He said he'd heard nothing from her since she'd sent him away from her office in the Ashmolean the day after Rachel was killed, until one day shortly before her departure for Tokyo when she'd telephoned him and said she was leaving and had something she wanted to give him and could he come and collect it from the museum since it wasn't really something she could leave in the porter's lodge.

He'd gone over straight away, thinking they might speak and he might ask her whether she'd heard from Anthony. But when he got there he found her secretary waiting for him instead. She'd handed him a parcel and said no, Evie had left no message. He'd walked back to his rooms and opened it to see the document wallet full of the Browning essays, and the letters. He said that as far as he'd been able to work out, Anthony had given it to Evie on the day of the Casablanca Ball and she'd kept it. I was able to tell Harry then that I believed I had had my own part to play in his story, in a way that had escaped his knowledge, describing for him how I had followed Evie's instructions on the night I'd got back to London and found the document wallet and couriered it to her, and we worked out together that there could have been any number of occasions on which Evie might have given the letters and the essays to Rachel in the years that had passed since the Casablanca Ball, and that they could well have been on the shelves of my apartment ever since the day she'd moved in. We talked a little more about this question, and Harry suggested in the end that he thought the letters may have been the route by which Evie had finally persuaded Rachel to acquiesce to the idea of meeting Anthony, by giving Rachel this folder and by making her feel so guilty about what she'd done that she'd given in.

Either way, Harry said, his experience of opening the document wallet and reading its contents had been an extremely painful one, as he imagined it had been for me also, and he thought it best that I dispose of it now, depending of course on what I decided to do with the information he was giving me.

'What do you mean?' I asked him. 'What do you mean, depending on what I decide to do?'

And then Harry rubbed his eyes and, stretching his arms above his head, laid himself out on the sofa. He said nothing for a minute or two, just lying there, and I was beginning to think he'd fallen asleep when he swung his legs up and over onto the floor and sat back up and looked at me, saying, 'This is what I mean, Alex. What I have told you is only a version of events, nothing more than that. And I have not been able, on my own, to decide whether to disclose that version, or to continue to conceal it—'

'You really think there's any question?' I broke in, finding it impossible to believe he was persisting in the idea that there was room for doubt. 'You do realise what you're proposing? You understand—'

'Alex,' he said, standing up. 'Don't mistake me for a fool. Of course I understand. And of course I know that even by my proposition I am made criminal. I just don't think the decision is a straightforward one, not at this stage.'

'In what way, Harry? In what way exactly is it not straightforward?'

'A condemnation as ready as the one you seem to be suggesting would be ill-conceived, Alex, in my opinion, that is all. To leap so quickly to judgement would, I think, be to deny something of the complexity of the situation. You have the luxury of choice here, don't you see?'

'No, Harry, I don't as a matter of fact. There's nothing complicated about it. You've lied to me all along. Even your letter was full of lies. Why should I listen to you now?'

'I have lied, you are right. I can't dispute that charge, and nor have

I tried to. There were reasons at the time for my doing as I did, and I've explained them to you. I lied having been lied to, and I am asking you now to see beyond that. I'm not proud of the decision I took when the police came and knocked on my door. On the contrary, these last few days we've spent together, I have shown you my deepest shame. Until I invited you here, until you came and let me tell you the whole of it, it has sat heavily with me, this secret I have kept. I promised Rachel I would keep her story to myself, and that is what I did,' he said, taking a step towards me and carrying on, beginning to rush his words together as though struggling to keep up with what he was trying to say. 'That moment on the river when she turned to me, right at the end of our conversation, she was crying, Alex. She had tears running down her face and she begged me, do you see? She begged me to make sure you didn't find out. It was the only thing she cared about by that stage. None of the rest of us really mattered to her any more, I don't think. Not really. Not Evie, not me. Not even Anthony. She was angry with him, of course. She was angry with all of us. But you could see it in her face, quite apart from what she was saying. You could see that there was only you.'

And then he slowed down again, stepping back away from me and speaking more quietly.

'She told me you loved her. She told me you'd made her happy, and you'd given her something she thought she'd never find. And she asked me to let that be, that love there was between the two of you, and to protect it, so that it could grow undisturbed in its innocence, just as it had been. And that is what I tried to do, Alex. That was my aim when first I lied. That was all she asked of me that afternoon, do you see, nothing more. In doing as I did from that point on, my thoughts were only of protecting her, Alex, and protecting you also. I took the path I took that night in my interview with the best of intentions, you must see that.'

'And then?'

'And then, having done so, I continued on it, but only because I had been left there all alone, and could find no other route. Don't think I haven't dwelt on how I could have done things differently. Don't think I haven't lain awake at night these last months thinking through every step I took, even from the moment the three of them walked through my door for the first time, so many years ago. And don't think I didn't see, for every step, the other I might have taken instead.

'I have made a series of errors of judgement. I was kind where I should have been firm, and harsh where I should have shown only compassion. I tried always to be fair, Alex. But I did not ask questions where I should have done, and I listened to others where I should have heard only Rachel, and what she was trying to tell me that day on the South Bank: that she was afraid of Anthony, and had good reason to be. And when, at the last, I hesitated about the plan that had been put in place, and I woke one day in a panic, thinking I might be mistaken about Anthony after all, I failed her again by seeking counsel in Evie about what had been planned, rather than keeping my own and confronting my doubts. And then suddenly it was Midsummer Night, and there you both were, knocking on my door. I'd had a sense that afternoon that things were slipping from my grasp, and that people were beginning to withdraw, and to withhold things from me. But events began to move too fast, and in directions I could not fathom. I tried, Alex. I tried to keep hold of it all, to stay in control. I did what I could. But then—'

'But then what?'

And, when he said nothing,

'Well, what?'

'But then it was too late,' he said, quietly, and as he spoke the words he was unable even to look at me.

'And that was when you began to tell your lies, to cover up what you had done. And now, what? You're asking me to tell them with you?'

'I lied to the police that night in the belief that Rachel was alive,

Alex. Injured, perhaps, yes. But alive. And in the belief also that I had made her a promise, and that by staying silent, I was keeping it.'

'And then? When they told you what had happened?'

Harry paused then and didn't answer. He sat down again, hunching forwards on the sofa and wrapping his arms around himself as though he was cold, and when he did speak again, the pauses he left between his sentences were so long I kept thinking he had finished.

'Alex,' he began, and he sat back up, keeping his arms wrapped around himself even more tightly than before. 'I am asking you to forgive me, and to help me. The project I embarked upon when I agreed to Anthony's request has failed, and it has done so catastrophically. I am left with the worst kind of despair. I have passed my story on to you in the hope that you will share with me the burden of deciding what to do with it. It is, in many ways, more yours than it is mine. You're hardly even a character in it for large swathes of the narrative, but you and Rachel loved one another a great deal, and of that I am very conscious. You are now in possession of what may be the key to the mystery of her death, and I don't seek to stand in your way if you choose to divulge it to those who may be able to solve that mystery. I am simply proposing that you think a little longer, at least, before you reach your decision.'

I said nothing, my head spinning, not at all sure how to respond. And then I told him, as calmly as I could, 'I'm afraid I don't see it like you do, Harry. I just don't.'

'Of course, Alex. And you have every right not to. That was the risk I took when I invited you here.'

He stood again and walked over to the window and leaned against the frame, with his back towards me. I thought he was looking down on the quad, but then the light changed and fell differently for a moment and I caught his reflection in the glass and saw that he had caught mine also and was looking right at me. 'As I said when I began, the question of whether the tale is to have a conclusion is one that you

must answer. It is for you to decide whether we shall remain as inno-
cents, Evie and Anthony and I, or whether we shall each in our own
way be condemned for whatever parts we have played in Rachel's mur-
der. We can, I think, be almost sure that Anthony killed her, and for
myself, I believe there is little to be gained by a further telling of the
tale. The scent of a hare is fresh and strong when you put her up, but
the longer she runs the more it fades. I can see no great advantage in
the protracted and painful exercise that would have to be undertaken
to establish his guilt, if indeed it is possible to do so conclusively, given
his absence.'

And then he was silent for a time, and the light changed again and
I could no longer see the image of his face.

'There is this need in us always, isn't there, Alex, to find everything
out, and to judge, so that there may be some final atonement for what
has passed. The mistake we can so easily make, all of us, is to assume
that if we achieve those things, then we will have our solace. All I am
asking you to do is to be quite sure, before you reach a decision, that
this need cannot be met some other way. That we cannot seek expia-
tion by another route. When you have thought further on it, you may
come to agree with me that we can close the book and let things lie.
Alternatively, you may wish to see it published, in order that others
may read it, and in order that its villains might be punished.'

He turned from the window and walked across the room towards
me. 'I would suggest, if I may, that you go and get some rest, or perhaps
take a walk and think things through. I will do the same, and would
be grateful if you could come back later on this afternoon, at half past
three or thereabouts, and let me know what you have decided. Alter-
natively, should you find you need longer to make up your mind, you
might be so kind as to tell me what point you have reached in your
deliberations. Goodbye, Alex,' he said, holding the door open for me.
'And thank you for keeping to your agreement to hear me out. I am
grateful.'

23

I had walked halfway down the stairs when I felt suddenly dizzy. I
fell forwards, grabbing on to the rail and sitting down as quickly
as I could, thinking I was about to faint. I felt none of the things
one might have expected me to feel on leaving Harry's room that day. I
remember wanting to weep as I sat there, or at least thinking that was
what I ought to be doing, and that perhaps I should even be crying
in the way I did from time to time as a boy, heaving out sobs so great
that I'd often wondered in my childish way whether it was possible to
drown myself with my own tears.

Instead I felt only a kind of numbness, and when I realised after
a while that my dizziness had passed, I stood and walked back to my
room and climbed fully clothed under the covers of my bed. A few
hours later I woke suddenly from a dream. My shirt was soaked with
sweat and my skin was running with it, and I was hot and cold at the
same time and the room was swimming around me. I got up, and
undressed, rubbing myself dry with a towel before taking the last of
the clean things that were left in my bag and putting them on.

I had been dreaming of my mother, and it struck me as I stood beside the window, looking out across the lawns, that it was the first time I had dreamed of someone other than Rachel since the night of her murder. The dream was one that recurred frequently after my mother died and I went to Oxford and had only my father to stay with during the holidays. In the dream I am floating in the air, completely enclosed in a bubble. The bubble is somehow flimsy, and soft, and not quite transparent but clear enough for me to be able to see through it. And I notice that there is another bubble floating next to my own, made of the same material but slightly bigger than mine. I become aware that there is someone inside it, and as I press my face against the fabric I see that it is my mother, and at that moment she sees me also, and we reach out our hands towards one another as we float, but we cannot touch one another, and although we try again and again, it isn't possible and we drift away from one another and I call out to her but then she is gone and I am alone and it is as though she was never there.

I put all of my things in my bag and look around the room to make sure I have left nothing and I go straight over to Harry's rooms for half past three. I stand and wait for some time before I see the note that is tucked between the door and the frame. It is addressed to me, from Harry, and it says that he has gone for a walk and why don't I meet him beside the lake instead; there is something he would like to show me. I walk back down his staircase and I stop at the spot on the terrace where he said he'd stood and watched me stumbling down the steps on the night of Rachel's murder. I look up towards the Old Library windows, and back at the quad, and I see that the snow has begun to melt much faster now and that large swathes of green are beginning to show through where the sun has fallen on it, and I wonder why Harry wants to meet me by the lake rather than in his rooms. And at about that moment, a thought that has been formulating itself in a tentative kind of a way throughout the whole of my visit, the seed of which

was perhaps planted when Harry sent me the little book of Browning, crystallises into something firmer, and I feel as though someone has shaken me, hard, on the shoulder, or clapped me on the back.

Of course, the fact that Harry himself is the only authority for any of the information that he has given to me was something of which I was aware from the start of his tale, when he sat by the fire and told me that what he was about to relate was a version of events, and nothing more. But such was my absorption, and such was my desire to hear an ending, that I think I paid less attention than I might have done to the fact that so many of the things he said were based on untruths, or on fabrications of his own or others' making. As Harry said to me himself, there was always a reason for the lies that he told. He had to say that he was going to London for the day to make sure I wasn't around to find him searching in vain for the old gate I had reminded him of, but as I stand there I remember the ease with which he had glossed over exactly what he'd done with himself that day, diverting my attention by showing me the photograph of his boyhood self in Trafalgar Square. And then I recall him saying how simple it had been, really, to lie his way through his police interviews and to continue to do so in the months that followed Rachel's death, and I remember also the seeming glibness with which he confessed his dishonesty to me at the close of his story, and I wonder, just for the briefest of moments, whether it is entirely wise of me to go in the growing gloom of a winter's afternoon, at a time when the college has become almost entirely empty, to meet Harry at the place where Rachel was killed. He put to me his theory that Anthony and Evie were in College that night, but the fact remains that if they weren't, then the only other person who could have killed Rachel is Harry himself. He told me he had forgiven Rachel, and that he had come to understand her behaviour, but he told me also how angry he'd felt when he found out the extent to which she had manipulated him. And although he said his anger had passed, it can't have done completely; there must also have been bitterness in

him still, even just a little, knowing that she'd kept so much from him that was known to others, despite the constancy of his kindness.

I begin my walk across the quad towards the passageway beneath the secret garden, making my way towards the lake, and I think about the insistence with which he had presented himself as forever the fable's innocent bystander: gazing at Rachel as she worked in the British Library; watching from the library windows; standing on the terrace; loitering on the pavement outside Anthony's flat hoping for a glimpse of him, and following the reconstructions of the night of the murder from where he sat in his college rooms above the quad. And I reflect on how much at odds this is with what seems actually to be the case: not only did Harry take a leading role in the drama he has produced for me, but he also stood beside the camera from time to time with his megaphone, directing the spectacle we were all of us taking part in.

And then I emerge from the passageway, onto the lawns, and I see him. He is waiting beside the lake with his back towards me, looking out across the water. I walk over to where he is and I stand behind him for a while, keeping as still as I am able to, until finally he becomes aware that I am there and he turns and I am staring at him and he is staring at me and I realise we are both thinking exactly the same thing: each of us is wondering whether the other is a man capable of murder.

I smile at him, and shake my head, and he smiles at me, and neither of us says a word.

A minute or two passes with us standing there like this, each in a silent way, and then he shifts his posture slightly, pointing at the stump of the tree we are next to. I look at it, puzzled, and then I remember that it was once a gently spreading holm oak, and that Richard and I would sit beneath it sometimes at the weekends to read the paper together and skim stones across the lake. Harry leans into it, patting its trunk with his hand and rubbing it as though it were the flank of

a horse, and he tells me that it had to be felled last year, when it was found to be rotten at its core.

The light is fading, and there is the soft sound of a woodpigeon in the trees on the other side of the lake, and Harry bends down towards the ground as if to pick something up and I am once more suddenly, foolishly, afraid, but then I realise he is pointing at something in particular, gesturing to me to bend over also and look at the base of the stump. It seems easier, clad as I am in my winter coat and boots, to kneel on the ground, and so I do and with Harry standing over me, I try to work out what it is that he wants me to see. There appears to be nothing to look at other than snow, until Harry steps forward and brushes some of it away to reveal a tiny plaque with something engraved on it and I read the words, 'Rachel's Worcester', and I shiver slightly against the cold. As I stand back up I notice that a rose has been planted at the base of this broken holm oak, and that it has sent three shoots up around the trunk, trailing itself about. I turn to Harry and he smiles again, and I see that there is a tear running slowly down his cheek. He tells me then that it is an old rose, and that it was found the previous summer in the Provost's garden. He did some research and discovered that it was a variety that had not yet been named, and so it was that the Provost had asked him to choose one. That, he said, was how he came to name it after Rachel, and that was why it was planted beside the lake, so that in the summer months this silent piece of tree will become busy with bees, and clad about with flowers also.

We are both quiet then, and when it seems there is nothing else to be said, I take his hand in mine and I thank him, telling him I will think about the things he has spoken of and I will write to him. I walk back across the lawns to collect my things and start my journey home. I look back only once, just as I reach the top of the lawns, and I see that he is standing exactly where I left him, his hands in his pockets and his hat pulled low on his head, looking out across the water into the evening that is falling all about him.

24

I am standing here on my balcony watching the tail lights of the planes coming into London and I am thinking about the moment when I will start to come in to land this evening in New York. At that point in a flight, just as the pitch of the engine's hum is altered and there are the beginnings of a pull towards earth, I feel an intense awareness of the fact that I am neither in one place nor another, of my being neither here nor there. I suspect that is how I shall always feel now that Rachel has gone: forever suspended, forever now.

I have received the call that tells me my taxi is ten minutes away. I have run through all the things I had to do before leaving and I can't think of anything I might have missed. Preparing to live elsewhere has been a fairly simple process in some ways, although at the last there was a not entirely unexpected hold-up with my immigration, which meant that an entire morning this week was given over to a slightly tense last minute stand-off in the US Embassy. 'The open ended nature of the investigation', as they called it, meant they took some persuading that I should be allowed on to American soil.

Quite possibly the biggest hurdle to my feeling able to go ahead and book my flight, though, which I did only last night in the end, was the question of how I should deal with the information Harry gave me. Of course, with hindsight, I could say that there was never any doubt in my mind about whether I would choose, in his words, to condemn or to forgive; that even as we stood beside the lake saying our last goodbyes I knew it was just a matter of time before I took the train back to Oxford and went to the police station on St Aldates, which is exactly what I did yesterday. But it wasn't quite as simple as that. In the first place, there was the need, as I perceived it, for me to sort the facts into some sort of order in my own mind before I could even so much as consider passing them on to someone else. Being unsure of how exactly I would narrate the whole thing if I were to decide that that was what I was going to do, I was reluctant to proceed until I felt certain I would be able to in a way that left nothing, or as little as possible, to chance. I turned my attention to it then, trying as hard as I could to set aside my own feelings about the events that were being described, and to treat the facts as though somebody else entirely had instructed me to marshal them into an argument. And, after a time, things started to take shape, following the process to which I had become accustomed in my work, whereby a charcoal sketch would transform, gradually, into a line drawing of such razor sharp precision that it could not have been done by any human hand.

But despite all my efforts in this regard, and despite the tenacity I brought to my task, my impression that there was something incomplete about the story grew, so that however many times I rehearsed the events for myself, I had a sense that things were not quite right, and that there was something I should have realised but hadn't. At a certain point, however, it became clear there was nothing further I could do with the information I'd been given, and there were no more connections to be made. I had picked the tale apart and put it together again in as many different ways as I was able to, but still I could iden-

tify no possible conclusion other than the one that had, in essence, already been written.

I'd made a fairly careful note of what Harry had told me, spending the evenings that followed my return from Oxford sitting at Rachel's desk and writing it all out alongside tables and timelines, charts and diagrams. And when I'd done this, I opened the boxes the police had delivered back to me, the ones with all of Rachel's things in, and I went through their contents again, slowly, in case anything seemed different in the light of the information that Harry had provided.

When I went to bed the day before yesterday I was no further on than when I started my task, being both reluctant to erase from my mind the doubt about whether Harry himself might have been involved in Rachel's death, as well as having the persistent sense that there was something staring me in the face that I was still unable to see, despite all my looking.

It's often the way of things that one's problems are solved at a time when one is not making any kind of effort to address one's mind to them, focusing one's attention instead on something else entirely, and then, almost without one realising it something falls into place: a square peg becomes round and fits into its slot, or a balloon is released from its mooring and drifts into an empty sky. Nevertheless, as I stand here on the balcony waiting to go, it strikes me as a little ironic that after all my hard work, my discovery, if I can call it that, was made not by the application of my own intellect to the material before me, nor because there was anything particularly brilliant about my powers of assimilation and analysis, but instead, because of something that Richard, without having any idea of its significance, let slip in the postscript to an email I received when I woke up yesterday morning.

And it was only when I read it that the story which seemed to have petered out came back to life again, so that I left my apartment and caught the train to Oxford, taking with me my notes of Harry's narrative, and the charts and timelines and diagrams I had prepared, as

well as certain items from the boxes of Rachel's things. All of these together will, I think, give the police a head start on the investigation they will begin today. And because it took me such a long time to tell them everything, it wasn't until after midnight that I got home, exhausted by the experience of finally handing everything over to somebody else.

What Richard had written was, he said, something he'd been meaning to tell me but had kept forgetting to mention. The brevity with which he expressed himself made it clear he'd only just remembered to include it at the last moment before pressing the send button, and meant that I had to speak with him before I could really believe he was telling me what I thought he was. What he confirmed for me then turned the narrative Harry had put together, and the equation he had set out as lying behind the choice I had to make between condemnation and forgiveness, completely on its head. It would be fair to say that by that point, at the same time as continually weighing the question of what Harry's own role had really been on the night Rachel died, and whether to believe a word of what he'd said, I was still, on some level, considering his idea of keeping it to ourselves. The statistics I'd dug up on the likelihood of ever finding a missing person gone as long as Anthony, and on the hundreds of young men being lifted every year from railway tracks, made for a persuasive case in favour of Harry's theory that Anthony's name would, at some point, appear in an unobtrusive death notice in the Manchester newspapers. I supposed that Harry would write a piece on him for the college records, and his mother would mourn, and I would write to Evie in Tokyo and tell her, and that would be that. Or, if nothing so dramatic had happened, there was still the question of how Anthony might ever be found. When what that search would entail, in terms of the exposure of the stories that lay behind it, was weighed against the trauma and upset that would be caused should it be a fruitless endeavour, the equation I was left looking at was not in any way attractive.

In the end, the question of whether I should trust Harry or not had no real bearing on my decision to pass his story on. I am quite sure he took no active part in Rachel's murder. Whilst there are some unanswered questions in terms of his version of events, and whilst perhaps there always will be, it is clear to me that the basic instinct by which he operates is one of kindness, and I have concluded that it is not in his nature to be anything other than good, in an essential kind of a way. If Harry is guilty of anything beyond his perjury, it is only of having tried too hard to influence the lives of others. He perhaps cared too much for Rachel, and so became blind to reason, feeling too keenly a desire for reconciliation, and a need for resolution. He is not someone who is capable of doing harm to another, not intentionally. I am quite certain that any involvement he had in Rachel's death could almost be called tangential; whilst it might be said that he stage-managed the performance, there was nothing knowing in the way he went about it.

Or at least, that was what I felt on the train back to London after my visit, having heard his long apology. And I suppose that is how he hoped I would feel, and why he went about telling me things in the way that he did. And it is, on balance, what I would like to be able to conclude. But there are other ways of looking at the decisions that he took, or failed to take. Harry presented his behaviour to me as that of a man seeking resolution, and trying only to be fair, and good, and I believe that is also what he told himself. I am no doctor of the mind, but the day before yesterday, as I was thinking about Harry, and the way he had attempted to justify what he described as a series of errors of judgement, I remembered a newspaper article I read two or three years ago, written by a psychoanalyst, about an experiment. A man was hypnotised and placed in a room full of chairs. He was told the room was empty, and on his being instructed to move from one corner of it to another he was seen to thread his way through the chairs before being led from the room again. When he was questioned about why he had chosen such a circuitous route, his explanations were

many and various: he'd seen a nice picture on the wall he wanted to look at; he'd been distracted by a noise outside. Anything but the real reason, the existence of the chairs.

I don't blame Harry for offering me a falsified rationale for his actions: he is a man, as I am. In all likelihood he had no idea that he was doing it, and he is not unusual in having had to rewrite his history in order to be able to live with himself. That other way of looking at the situation, at his having spoken to Rachel the way he did that day on the South Bank, exacting her agreement to his project, as he called it, would be one that cast his actions as those of someone driven not by fairness, or goodness, or a desire for resolution, but instead by anger, and jealousy, and guilt. Lacking the courage to confront his own mistakes and make his own apology to Anthony, he used Rachel to do it for him. Such a view would render his behaviour irredeemable, on the application of the principle that a man who allows a situation to develop whereby a crime may be committed, who fails to act to prevent it when he might have done, and who afterwards is silent when he could have spoken, is no less culpable than the one who wields the blow: fault may arise by omission, and is not obviated by the absence of intention.

I do not yet know what I think of Harry Gardner. I only know that I am not sorry that my move to New York means I am unlikely ever to see him again. Whatever else might be said of him, he made a game of Rachel's safety, and for that I cannot forgive him.

And then there was Evie. It did not seem to me, in the end, that my visit to the police would give rise to any risk of her being implicated in the crime, despite Harry's suppositions as to her complicity. I didn't tell Harry about the conversation she and I had last week, nor do I think there is any need for me to do so, not now. What I discovered when I spoke to her made it unlikely she'd be in danger of serious condemna-

tion. I'd emailed her in Tokyo with the briefest of messages to the effect that I'd returned from my visit to Oxford, and I had just a few remaining questions, particularly in relation to her fund-raising activities at the Ashmolean in the summer. She began her call to me by saying straight away, and before I could really ask any questions, that when she arrived in my cell on the Friday evening with my bag of clothes, she'd already made a statement about what she was doing on the night of Rachel's murder. She said the reason Harry hadn't told me about it was that he didn't know, and she didn't really see why I had to either, but that if I insisted, she had been at the fund-raiser as planned, but only for the first twenty minutes, at which point she had renewed an acquaintance with an old student of hers who had become rather a success in the banking world. He'd flown over from Tokyo for a long weekend and had come back to Oxford to make a donation to the museum. They had hit it off rather well and given up on the party, going straight back to his hotel room and spending the rest of the evening and the night together. He'd been more than happy to assist the police with their enquiries, as had the staff at his hotel, and her alibi was as sound as they came.

And the note? I asked. Had she really never seen Harry's note, the one that he'd taken over to her office before dinner? Had she really been ignorant of Anthony's plan to meet Rachel beside the lake at midnight? No, she said, she hadn't got it, and nor had she known. She'd assumed, when he'd told her about it later on, that he'd put it in the wrong place and it had been mislaid, or that the cleaners had found it on the floor and, thinking it was rubbish, thrown it away. Either that, she said, or he'd been making the whole thing up about having left it there. In any case, she carried on, she'd been so irritated with the whole situation by then that she almost deliberately hadn't gone up to her office before the function, half suspecting that he might do something of the sort. Having had all she could take of Anthony and his childish needs, and of Rachel and her selfish melodramatics, she'd decided they could all look after themselves.

'But why?' I asked her then. Why hadn't she told the police about any of it, about Anthony and Rachel, and Harry and his plan? How could she just have walked away from the whole situation as though it was nothing to do with her, when surely she must have realised what Anthony had done? She'd stopped me and said it wasn't so simple, really it wasn't. And then, in a calmer, tireder voice, all stridency gone, she explained that when it came to giving her statement, she had panicked. She'd thought only of herself, and of her alibi, and it wasn't until she came through to my cell and saw me sitting across from her on the bed looking, she said, just like a little boy, that she realised she'd made the wrong choice, and that she should have told the police everything.

In the days that followed, Harry had told her the precise details of the plan he said Anthony had kept from her, and she had reached her own conclusions about what must have happened. Having done so, she found herself unable to go back on her decision: nothing would change the fact that Rachel was dead, and however many times she thought about giving another statement, and from whichever angle she considered the idea of telling the truth, she could see only what she stood to lose. She was aware that Anthony was more than capable of turning the story around to frame her, and that was what she described as her sticking point. Of course, she had always suspected what kind of a man he was, but even though she'd known throughout their relationship that to prolong her association with him was at best foolish, and at worst idiotic, at no point had she imagined him to be in any way dangerous, or violent. As I heard her say this, I did consider telling her what Harry said Anthony had done at the Casablanca Ball; about him forging Towneley's signature and about him assaulting Cissy, but I decided instead to see what she had to say, wondering whether she'd known about it all along. It seemed so amazing to me that she could have been involved with Anthony over such a long period of time, and in such an intimate way, without his having disclosed it all to her, or without her having wheedled it out of him. On the other hand, I could see that it was

entirely in line with Harry's portrayal of Anthony's character that he could have withheld it, and I could see also that someone as self-serving as Evie would have been able to remain almost wilfully ignorant. In the end it was apparent from what she said that she really had never known and so I held my silence, being unable to see any purpose that could be served by breaking it.

In any case, Evie had realised eventually that she'd been very wrong in her assessment of what Anthony could be capable of. She saw how easy it would be for him to say that she had manipulated him from the moment he'd been sent down from Oxford and she'd begun to intervene in his life. She thought it quite possible that he would have had little, if any, hesitation in going so far as to portray her as having controlled him even to the point of murdering Rachel, and so she had held back, saying nothing further to anyone.

She couldn't claim to be happy with the way she'd behaved, but as she saw it, happiness didn't come into it. She'd been uncertain about her decision for some time, and was still considering the possibility of rethinking it, of trying to overcome her fear, but then the post in Tokyo had come up. She told me a little more then about the summer that Rachel's mother had died, saying there had been nothing in the coroner's report to suggest that she had not taken her own life that September afternoon on Oxford Street, and that it was her belief that she'd done so. When she read the letter she'd left asking Evie to take care of Rachel, she knew she had no choice but to pull out of the Junior Research Fellowship she'd just been given at Oxford and to put her career on hold for at least a year or two until Rachel was settled, and until they had established a closer rapport. And so, never having wanted children of her own but finding herself suddenly in sole charge of an eight-year-old orphan, she'd gone ahead and given it up, having no idea whatsoever how difficult it would prove to be for her to rebuild the professional relationships she'd abandoned for the sake of the emotional well-being of a child not even her own.

'When Anthony telephoned me that day in June,' she said, 'crying his eyes out because he'd been sent down, and when he told me what she'd done that summer term at Oxford, how carelessly she'd behaved with regard to her own place there, something she'd been lucky enough to have access to only because I'd made those sacrifices for her, I was furious, Alex, I won't pretend otherwise.' And that wasn't even to begin to take into account what Rachel had done to the other two, to Anthony and Cissy, by walking away and leaving them to their fate without owning up to the fact that it had been her idea to write the letters in the first place. When a post as prestigious as the one in Tokyo came up, Evie had no intention of letting Rachel hold her career back in the way she'd done as a child, and so, having been offered the chance of a new life she'd taken it, making pragmatism her virtue and trying to have as few regrets as possible.

I wasn't surprised by what Evie told me; not about her decision to back out of Harry's plan on the night of the murder, nor about her having remained silent when she could have spoken. Those were exactly the sort of things I would have expected of her. Nor was I surprised to discover she had apparently taken no active part in Rachel's death. There was something sinister about her, in that she had at her core a kind of a steeliness which I distrusted instinctively, but I had seen her face at the police station when she came to my cell with my bag, and I had seen her eyes when she'd taken off her sunglasses, and I recognised what I saw there as grief, having known it myself before then. At the same time as knowing she was looking across the room at me with suspicion, I knew there was something else there also: there was compassion for me in my sadness, and some kind of a desire to communicate to me the fact that she knew what it was that I had lost in losing Rachel.

Until the moment I read Richard's email yesterday morning and realised I had no choice but to go forward, it was Rachel herself who was causing me the most difficulty in my deliberations about what

to do. I could see only that the damage that would be done to her memory would be immense, and given the likelihood that so little, if anything, would be gained by going to the police, the trail having grown so cold, I didn't feel at all sure I could bear the responsibility of making public the things I had discovered about her, things that would otherwise remain entirely private. Whilst the regard in which I held her had not altered, I was very aware that there were those who, unlike me, were they to hear of the events that lay behind her death, would be unable to resist the urge to allow their good opinion of her to be undermined, and that by making these events known to them, I would be tarnishing the image she had chosen to present to the world.

There are no two ways about it: I am simply unable to articulate how devastated I am by the things Harry told me, and by the fact she hid them from me. I am so very sorry that when it came to it, and she found herself pushed from all sides into such an intolerable situation by Evie, and by Harry, and by Anthony, she seemed to have been so overwhelmed by her fear of what my response would be if I found out, that she doubted her own belief in me and questioned the constancy of my love for her.

My regret that she kept her silence is something I feel only in the sense that I am quite sure I could have helped her to resolve things, and offered her my protection, if only she had told me what was happening. I have not come to judge her yet, and I don't suppose I ever shall. Although it is quite another Rachel who has emerged from Harry's story, I am, if anything, more certain, rather than less, of how deeply she loved me. And that is more important than anything Harry might have told me.

It was not only the depth of her love of which I became more aware as he told me his tale, but also some idea of what had lain behind the intensity with which she had felt it. This is something which, if I forget it even for an instant, I have only to read again the letter that Evie gave me at the police station to be reminded. I took that letter with me to

Oxford on my winter visit, and I read it more than once in the pauses that arose between the chapters of Harry's tale. It will come with me to New York also, despite my having the words by heart, and I suppose it will be something I keep with me always, in this way. *Dear Evie*, she wrote, and I picture her sitting at her desk and I wonder what I was doing as she picked up her pen to begin; whether I was there in the room with her, having no idea that it was me she was writing about, or whether instead I was out here on the balcony, cutting some herbs for supper, so that if she had glanced up she would have seen me here before she lowered her head and continued with her letter.

> *There is a point, in loving, where want becomes need. Where to have possessed that which one desires is no longer enough, and when one realises that one will never have one's fill of this person, however much one is given.*
>
> *This is what has happened to me, Evie, and, in response to your question last week, this is why I am marrying Alex Petersen. It is because we have come to need one another, he and I, and it is my belief that we always shall. I don't expect you to understand this, knowing that you don't concern your-self with the idea of love, or with the notion that such a thing as a constancy of affection between two people might be pos-sible.*
>
> *You taught me nothing of these things; what I know of them I have learned entirely from Alex, and from the kindness he shows me. At the same time as freeing me from the person I was before I knew him, he has allowed me to become entirely myself, and because of that I am amazed by this new life I am living.*
>
> *Alex is gentle, and quiet, and strong, and steady. He is to me all of the things that no one else has ever been, and his love for me is unconditional. He doesn't question me, and he doesn't*

doubt me, and there is a certainty in the way he behaves towards me which I have come to think of as devotion.

I'm not trying to change your mind about my choice. When I tell you that we love one another, Alex and I, I do so only because that is how it is with us, and how it always will be.

I woke yesterday morning at around five a.m., as I usually do, but instead of trying to go back to sleep I got straight up, knowing I was going to be hard pushed to do everything before leaving today. I put some coffee on while my bath was running and I switched on my computer in a sleepy kind of a way, expecting to find very little of any interest waiting for me. In the last few days I've been receiving regular updates from Richard charting the progress that's been made on the deals I'll be working on when I arrive. He told me he's doing this so I can hit the ground running, as he describes it, but I'm aware he does it also because it provides him with a channel for his excitement about bringing me over, and it allows him to show me what a success he's made of himself already.

When my inbox appeared on the screen I saw he'd made no exception to his daily habit, and nor did there appear to be any seismic shift in the nature of its content. The first two emails I read summarised new terms that had been agreed in the previous few hours, attaching a transaction memo for another deal that had just begun. Because I

heard the coffee boiling over on the stove I didn't open the rest of them straight away, not until I'd made some toast and checked on my bath and had come back through with my breakfast.

What I see when finally I open the very last of them is set out in the most throwaway of postscripts and typed in the hasty breathless style that Richard always uses when he has an anecdote but doesn't really have the time to tell it. As I begin to read it the first time I freeze, unable to process what it is that he has written but knowing that it is somehow of enormous significance.

> PS been meaning to tell you sorry kept forgetting, you'll never guess who I met last week – you'll get used to this, it's a small world over here . . . so the old Yank on the other side of the table says he can't come for closing drinks, has to meet his daughter, daughter's boyfriend, blah blah blah, rushes off to the airport, shows up again an hour or so after the drinks've started – pissed off as hell – she's stood him up. Anyhow, proceeds to get very drunk and tells me the oddest story. Dammit got to run, Lucinda's malfunctioning about the screaming wonders that are MY SONS (CAN YOU BELIEVE IT!!!) – I'll save it for when you get here – turned out his daughter was at Worcester with us that's all, do you remember her, that slightly peculiar American woman who coxed us to victory and promptly disappeared back to the US? Craig, chap's surname was. Can't remember her name though. Something Craig. Safe journey eh? Cheers.

It isn't until I read it a second time that the dominoes of facts I have laid out in my mind over the course of the previous week begin to topple this way and that and something I have known all along without having realised it, so deeply buried has it been, reveals itself to me, rising up from among the rubble I am contemplating. And it is because this memory surfaces when it does, rather than lying dor-

mant forever, that not only do I scald my leg by letting my mug of coffee slip slowly from my hands, my whole body becoming slack with shock, but also that the bath is left to run, so that when I remember it later on, the water has flooded right across my bedroom floor and out into the corridor.

The memory that surfaces is an old one, but none the less vivid for it. It is so vivid in fact that when I close my eyes and watch as Richard and I walk up the steps on to the terrace in front of Hall on a winter morning in our second year, knowing as I sit there in front of my computer what it is that I am about to see next, I experience the sensation that someone has walked into the room behind me and emptied a bucket of ice down my back.

We're on our way to the Old Library to work for a couple of hours before breakfast, there being only ten days left until the mock-exams Haddon has insisted on setting us. We reach the alcove by the porter's lodge and are met by the sight of the Men's Eight, huddled in a pack, their breath steaming against the cold and all of them jumping up and down in preparation for the training run they're about to go on. Richard steps into the lodge to get something and I hear a couple of them mouthing off about the fact that their bloody cox has demanded they get there at six a.m. only to be late herself. Then one of them who has been hovering on the edge of the group keeping a lookout says, 'Here she is, the lovely lady herself, at long bloody last,' and they turn, and so do I, and we all see Cissy Craig running improbably fast up the side of the quad, the hood of her jogging top pulled forward and down, tight around her head, her figure so small she might be a teenage boy. And as they start to sing, 'She'll be coming round the mountain when she comes!' their slow hand-clap keeping time with their voices, she picks up her pace even more and hurtles towards us at an extraordinary speed, her torso thrown so far forward she looks like a sprinter just off the blocks. She is moving so fast she reaches the top of the quad in an instant and takes the whole of the steps in no more than a couple of

strides. Reaching the men waiting in the alcove, she runs straight in amongst them, barely pausing, and the group moves off as one, slipping out through the wicket door to begin their run around the city. I step forward and hold the door open for the last of them and I see them jogging across the road to Gloucester Green, the height of the pack and the proximity to one another with which they're running meaning that the hooded figure seems no longer to be among them.

And then the memory has run its course and I remember watching the CCTV playbacks the police had shown me on the day after Rachel's murder. They'd recited to me, again and again, the precise details of Harry's description of the figure he'd seen hurtling up the side of the quad, the one that I insisted I hadn't seen. And then, when still I said I hadn't, they'd shown me, over and over, the images of the figure slipping out of the door and losing itself among the group of students who were gathered outside. As I turn back to Richard's email once more, I realise that when I'd sat there in the police station, listening to them repeating what Harry had said, and watching the images flicker on the screen in front of me, the reason I'd had the sense throughout the whole experience that I had seen it all before, at some other time, and in some other place, was that, in fact, I had.

And as soon as I realise it was Cissy who Harry saw running up the side of the quad in the minutes after Rachel was murdered, I realise also, from what Richard has said in his email, that because she is alive and well somewhere, it will be possible to find her. I get up from my desk intending to leave for Oxford straight away and to go directly to the police station when I get there, trying to remember as I walk across the room what time the first train leaves from Paddington. But then I decide that I should speak to Richard before I go and find out what else Cissy's father told him during the conversation in which he'd said he'd been stood up at the airport by her and her boyfriend, and what was so odd about the 'oddest story' that the man had told Richard in his drunkenness.

I go back to my desk and pick up my phone and dial Richard's number, but it's Lucinda who answers and when I ask to speak to him she says for god's sake Alex, I mean, hello and it's lovely to hear you and everything, but it's the middle of the night here I thought you were coming tomorrow can't you wait till then? And when I say I'm sorry but it's urgent she holds the phone away from herself and I can hear her soothing one of the twins. When she speaks again she says alright, if you really have to, I'll go and wake him up but I'll have to finish the feed first so can I get him to ring you back?

While I wait I google Cissy Craig, thinking Harry must either have been as gullible as Evie thought he was if he believed Anthony when he said he'd been able to find virtually nothing on her when he'd begun to stalk Rachel online from Arizona, or alternatively, he was simply so ignorant of how the internet worked that he wouldn't have realised how improbable this claim was. And I am angry with myself for not having thought there was something suspicious about this when Harry told me, and for not having realised it was such an obvious lie that it must have meant Anthony was hiding something, something about Cissy. When my search comes back with precisely nothing beyond a few references to some Worcester Boat Club results dating back to the early nineties, I am no longer angry with myself, and instead I am confused, but then Richard calls, and he explains immediately why my search was unsuccessful.

'Yes yes yes. Cissy. Of course. You're right. That's what she was called. Her dad called her something different that's all. By the way can I just say it's bloody the middle of the bloody night Alex? Lu's pretty pissed off actually, and, well, I mean, I'm pretty knackered myself. This is the first night in the last fortnight I've got to sleep before three.'

'Are you sure it's the same person though? It's Cissy you're talking about? Are you sure he's her dad?'

'Alex you're not even listening to me are you? Are you alright?'

'Please just answer my question. Do you really think I'd be asking

you if it didn't matter? Are you sure she's the same person? Rachel's friend? The cox? Why was her dad calling her something different?'

'Yes, Alex, it's the same person, but that isn't what she's called now and the man should know he is her bloody father. Can you please get a grip and let me get back to bed and we can talk about it tomorrow. Oh god. They've both woken up now. Hold on,' and he goes away and I can hear a high-pitched wailing in the background and it sounds as though Richard and Lucinda are having an argument as well.

When he comes back he tells me he has to go and do I have any idea how hard it is for them both, the sleepless nights, the feeding?

'Well no,' I say, 'I don't suppose I do. And I don't suppose I ever will, Richard, will I? Not now.'

'Oh god, Alex, I'm sorry. Can we not talk about this tomorrow though? Are you sure you're alright? Have you been drinking?'

'I'm alright, Richard. And no I haven't been drinking. I just need your help that's all. And I need it now, not tomorrow. I can't explain, sorry. It's just too complicated. I'd be very grateful if you would just do this one thing for me, OK?'

'What one thing?'

'Trust me. That's what. Just trust me. I'm going to ask you some questions. And I want you to believe me when I say it's very, very, important that you try as hard as possible to remember everything this man said to you. In an hour or so I'll be passing it all on to the police. They'll contact him themselves but I need to make sure they know where to start when they get to him.'

Richard doesn't say anything and I think perhaps I have been cut off, but then he is there again.

'Alex, you do realise you're actually being an idiot don't you? A complete idiot. I'm sorry but I'm actually beginning to wonder why I asked you to come. You do know I pretty much staked my reputation on you when I vouched for you being ready for this?'

'And? What? Are you saying you don't want me to come any more?'

'For god's sake. You just don't seem to have made any improvement, psychologically speaking. Listen to yourself. What the hell does Cissy Craig have to do with any of it?'

'It's your call, Richard. Trust me or don't trust me. But make up your mind soon will you? I've got a train to catch. Practically speaking.'

And that was when he gave in, saying that he wouldn't be able to tell me much but that that was hardly surprising, given the conversation had no significance for him whatsoever beyond the quirk of the coincidence that a contemporary from our Oxford days came up. What little he could tell me was enough though, once I'd asked him question after question and he'd drawn on the deepest reserves of his barrister's memory for his answers.

He told me Cissy's father had come back disappointed from the airport having gone there to meet her and her boyfriend. He'd been looking forward to seeing them, and he'd even texted her on his way and told her he'd met up with an old chum of hers from Oxford and he was sure that he could fix it that they could all get together at some point while she was in town. But when he got there the flight had already landed and they were nowhere to be seen, so he came back to the party and carried on drinking. So disappointed was he, Richard said, that he'd drunk a lot more than he should have done and became quite emotional about the whole thing. And when I stopped him then and asked about this boyfriend of Cissy's, and whether he'd said anything about him, anything at all, Richard said oh yes, now he came to think of it, he'd said something about the boyfriend being English, and that he couldn't remember for certain but that he might have said his name was Edward, or Ted, or Benjamin or something, yes, that was it, Ben, no no, wait. Benedict. Benedict Wilson or something. No, not Wilson, some kind of Italian sounding surname. But yes, he'd definitely said he was English.

And when I asked him whether the man had said anything about where the flight had been coming in from he said 'Jesus, Alex, the man

was drunk, we both were, and I was knackered. And I'm even more knackered now.' But then he said, 'Oh. Hang on, OK. I remember.' And when I said 'Well for god's sake, Richard, where?' he said Tucson, Arizona, and it was by way of this last detail that he confirmed for me that Cissy had been in Oxford on the night of Rachel's murder, and that Anthony had been there with her.

I asked him why Cissy's father had been quite so upset about them having cancelled on him and he said that that was where things had become slightly odd, and that he was sorry to say that the two of them really had got quite drunk and he wasn't all that happy to go on the record with it, given what I was intending to do with the information, and why didn't I bloody well ring him myself if I had so many questions and did I want the man's number in Washington DC, which was where he'd gone back to? And then, straight away, he said he was sorry, he was tired, and that the man had said something about having been estranged from his daughter for years, and that she'd come back from Oxford in the nineties and dropped out completely, and that there might have been some drugs involved, and that the next thing she'd done was to take herself off to some kind of a commune in Arizona and do what Richard called 'the whole healing thing'. She'd apparently refused to speak to her father for the entire time that she was there, blaming him for the fact that things had gone so badly wrong for her. Richard said he'd got the impression that the meeting at the airport had been one of many failed attempts at reconciliation, and her father had said he'd be trying again as soon as she decided to start speaking to him. And then he remembered, at the last, that the man had also said something about having been so cut up about the whole thing, and so worried about her being sucked in by some kind of a cult, that he'd had her trailed by a private detective while she was in Arizona. And that when the detective had told him some things about the English boyfriend she was hanging around with, things he wished he'd never known, he'd sent his daughter a letter telling her

these things and begging her to come home but she'd written back saying that was the last straw and he should forget the idea of seeing her again, ever.

Then Richard said he really couldn't tell me anything else, and that he was too tired to even think about where I was heading with it but that I should go to the police if that was what I wanted to do and let them take it from there. He told me to think things through very carefully, given who Cissy's father was and what it would do to my career if I got it wrong. I said thank you, and I'd explain everything when I got there, and that of course I'd think things through, what the fuck else did he think I had been doing for every minute of every day since I'd got back from Oxford. Alright, he said, alright, and I asked him to apologise to Lucinda for me and he said he would, and not to worry too much about her. She was just like that these days, she'd get over it.

As soon as we'd finished speaking I got dressed and made a half-hearted attempt to mop up the bathwater that had spread across my bedroom, and then I stuffed all my papers and charts and timelines and diagrams and notes into a bag, along with a few things from the boxes that the police had returned, and I went downstairs and out on to the New North Road and caught a cab to Paddington.

I knew I wouldn't be able to come up with answers to all of the questions I'd be asked in Oxford when I got there, nor would I be able to give them the name of Rachel's killer, not for sure. But I felt fairly certain that what I could tell them would lead to their being able to solve the mystery of her death. And as the train pulled out of the station, I found a table to myself and did as Richard had felt it necessary to suggest I do, and I thought things through very carefully indeed.

I decided at the beginning of the journey that I would work still on the premise that Evie's alibi would hold fast, and that despite this new

information that had come to light about Cissy, and the impact I considered it to have on almost every aspect of Anthony's story, I would assume also that Harry had told me the truth about his own involvement in the meeting he had persuaded Rachel to attend. I knew that the police would have to set those assumptions aside for the purposes of their investigation, and that they would in all likelihood start from scratch with both Evie and Harry, given the fact that they had lied so comprehensively in their statements. Where the police would be able to revisit both Evie's alibi, and the whole of Harry's version of events as he had described them to me, I could do no such thing. I turned my thoughts instead to Anthony and Cissy, being certain that they had been there, the two of them, and being almost certain also that they had met with Rachel beside the lake, and that this meeting had resulted in her death.

It was clear to me that I wouldn't be able to work out precisely what their respective roles might have been on the night of the murder, and that I wouldn't be able to answer the question of whether Cissy had run up the side of the quad with her hood pulled tight about her face as the piece's primary villain, or merely as an accomplice in Anthony's grand plan. Nor, I realised, would I be able to say with any certainty whatsoever whether the crime they had committed that night was premeditated. I was aware, of course, that it was entirely possible they'd gone to the lake in search of the apology that Anthony said he had so badly needed, and that Cissy had wanted one just as much as he had. And I could see how, in the circumstances and in light of the considerable tension that would have surrounded such a meeting, something could easily have gone wrong, and that Rachel might have said something that could have provoked either one of them into attacking her.

I couldn't think of any concrete suggestions to put to the police as to when it was that Anthony and Cissy had met one another again after they'd both left Oxford; whether perhaps Anthony had moved to Arizona and found Cissy there by chance, bumping into her in a Tucson bar one night, or whether they might even have kept in touch ever

since the night of the Casablanca Ball, so that perhaps he'd moved to Tucson because she was living there, theirs being a friendship that was only disrupted, rather than broken, by the events of that summer term. Either of these things seemed possible, now I knew that the tale Anthony had told Harry was a tapestry woven from half-truths, picked clean of any thread by which she might be glimpsed.

My thoughts came next to the question of Cissy's name, and the fact that Richard was so certain her father had called her something else, which tied in with my being unable to find any trace of her online. Whilst I thought it more than likely that of all the questions the police would face, this would be the easiest to answer, and that it would take no more than a phone call to her father to do so, it bothered me to think that I didn't know. I wondered if she'd had another name at Worcester, a nickname I should have been able to remember, but I couldn't recall one, and I decided instead that unless she'd simply changed her name altogether and the one she used now had no connection whatsoever to her past, the most obvious explanation was that the name 'Cissy' itself had been the nickname, being short for Cecilia, or Alice, or something, and that on leaving Worcester she had reverted to the use of that name, whatever it might be.

I laid out my notes of Harry's story across the train table in front of me, as well as my charts and my diagrams, and I looked at them again, wondering what it was that Cissy would turn out to have been doing since she left Oxford, and what would be discovered, eventually, about how her life tied in with Anthony's. Having read all of these things a couple of times, my mind was flooded with such a multiplicity of options that I was unable to process them in any measured way and turned my thoughts instead to whether I was able to draw any conclusions as to what her motives could have been for killing Rachel, intentionally or otherwise, or, if she'd acted only as Anthony's accomplice, for having condoned what he had done. And if, on the other hand, they had each of them gone to the lake in search of an apology, only for things to go

horribly wrong, then why, I wondered further, would she have felt such a need in the first place to have held Rachel to account in that way?

What Richard had told me about Cissy's father hiring a private detective to trail his own daughter reminded me of the story she'd told Towneley about how she'd got her scar, and I thought then about the two of them, alone together for weeks on the ocean, her wound becoming infected under her bandages, and I wondered what kind of a man he was. And then I remembered her dressing up for him when he came to visit her in Oxford, and how she'd taken him everywhere with her that week, even to her lectures, and how I had read his presence there as a manifestation of the pride he took in his daughter's achievements, and the affection that he felt for her. And I tried to imagine how he might have reacted when she came home from Oxford that June and told him she wouldn't be going back. It made perfect sense to me that she should bear a grudge against Rachel that was equal to the one Anthony had carried with him for so much of his life. Cissy also had lost her degree that Midsummer Night when she had walked out of Haddon's room and caught the plane home to the US, going back to this father who she'd said would kill her if he found out she'd been involved in the writing of the letters, and she also had lost a future that might otherwise have been hers. But still I couldn't quite see how this, without more, would have made her able to lay claim to the same strength of motive as Anthony had had, given the nature of his obsession with Rachel and the strength of his feelings for her.

I began then to look again at what I had brought with me from the boxes of Rachel's things and as I did so, moving them about on the table in front of me, something Evie had said when we last spoke came back to me. I'd barely registered it at the time, it striking me only as a throwaway comment, and one buried in amongst others of the sort I'd come to block out, so derogatory were they about Rachel, and so obviously expressions of the fanciful notions Evie entertained about her on account of the jealousy she still so clearly felt towards her. She'd

said something fairly nasty about my being mistaken if I thought my wife had been some kind of a saint, and didn't I realise that she was, in fact, only capable of thinking of herself, and that she'd hurt plenty of people in her time. And that was when she'd said it: 'That poor little American girl was actually in love with her, Alex, you do know that don't you?' and I'd said nothing in reply.

Of course, I had always known that Rachel and Cissy had shared some physical intimacy; I'd seen them kiss one another on the night of the Ball, on stage in Rick's Bar. But apart from that moment, which was after all part of the cabaret, I had only rumours to go on, and largely those I'd picked up from Richard, via Towneley, about the so-called weekend parties Rachel might or might not have given at the Chelsea house. And then there were the scenes that had been described with varying degrees of specificity by Harry and Evie in their piecemeal retellings of what had only ever been Anthony's version of the 'lost afternoons' that the three of them had apparently spent together. I thought again about what Evie had said, and then, my thoughts returning to Towneley carrying Rachel across the lawns and taking her to hospital, I thought again about Rachel and Cissy on stage in Rick's Bar that night, and other images began to come into my mind. It was when I recalled their presence in the black and white photograph that hung on Harry's wall, Cissy's arm draped lazily across Rachel's shoulders, that I began to look with more urgency through the things I had brought from the boxes the police had returned, and I found the envelope I'd grabbed before running out of the apartment, stuffing it full of as many photos as I could fit in it. I searched among them thinking I might have forgotten it, but there it was all of a sudden, the picture of Rachel standing on the deck of a boat in Turkey, the photo she had cut in two before reconsidering and taping it back together again and keeping it locked away in her desk. And it was only as I sat on the train yesterday and looked more closely at the woman who stood beside her, her head resting on Rachel's shoulder and her arms wrapped around her waist, that I recog-

nised Cissy smiling out at me from underneath her sun hat. As I began to think that there might, after all, have been more to this relationship than I had realised, I put the photograph down and took up instead the love letter, the one the police had brought to me twice in London and asked me to help them with.

It is only a copy that I have, and I recall as I look at it again that the original had been written on airmail paper, and that there had been neither an envelope bearing a postmark, nor a date, an address, or a signature. But I find when I read it this time that I need none of those things to see, clearly, that it could only have been written by Cissy.

> We spoke of love once, you and I, when we fell on the grass and held each other. And I really thought you meant it when you told me that you cared for me.
>
> I found out last night just how wrong I was.
>
> Like I said, I'll never forget you, whatever happens, and I don't think you'll forget me either, not for a long time anyway. You might think now that you will one day, but this much I know for sure: you won't be able to, however hard you try.
>
> So long then. I'm going this afternoon and I won't be coming back. I guess that's the way you wanted it.

The clues in the letter are slight, and will take some explaining to the police, but there is enough for me to be quite certain of its authorship. It is by her use of language that she reveals herself to me, and these glimpses of her that I catch in the text are visible to my eye only because of the particular attention which Harry, in the telling of his tale, paid to words, and the ways people use them. 'Whatever happens' is the phrase that gives me my first hint of Cissy's voice, and as I hear her say it I picture her on one of the earliest of those lost afternoons, making the other two repeat it back to her again and again, this boy-scout mantra with which they sealed their membership of their secret clique.

'*Like I said*' is what she breathes to me next, her voice lifting from the page just loudly enough for me to hear it above the hum of the train as it hurtles, and I remember Harry having told me that Rachel said these words to him in the hospital, on the night of the Casablanca Ball. He said then that he had been struck by her use of the phrase, recalling it to have been a favourite of Cissy's and observing that Rachel's reproduction of it had indicated to him how close the two of them must have been to have absorbed one another's language in this way. And then I hear Cissy saying it also, her voice echoing to me from across the years in the hour or so after she'd been found behind the Pavilion fighting with Anthony, Rachel having informed Haddon of their presence there. I picture again the scene that took place in the aftermath, and I can almost sense the anger with which Cissy used this phrase that night in Haddon's drawing room when she realised it was all over for her. I remember Harry describing her response to the last of Haddon's threats: 'Like I said, you're a jerk,' she'd said, before carrying on, in her American way, 'So long then,' and walking out of his cottage. And then I recall Harry telling me that Haddon had found a letter from her in his pigeonhole the next morning informing him that she was leaving Oxford and wouldn't be coming back, and as I read again the last two sentences of Cissy's letter, '*So long then. I'm going this afternoon and I won't be coming back. I guess that's the way you wanted it*', I realise that she would have written this letter on the same morning that she'd written to Haddon, leaving it in Rachel's pigeonhole and going from Oxford for good.

As the fields shot by and the train neared Oxford, I read the whole of the letter one more time, using a wider lens and going back over the opening once or twice:

> *We spoke of love once, you and I, when we fell on the grass*
> *and held each other. And I really thought you meant it when*
> *you told me that you cared for me.*
> *I found out last night just how wrong I was.*

I thought about what Cissy's experience might have been of the events she referred to as having taken place '*last night*', and I remembered Harry's description of what she'd said to Rachel, and then to Anthony, behind the Pavilion, and the way she and Anthony had fought that night. I turned over this idea of her having been in love with Rachel, really in love, as I had been, and I wondered whether she might have come to hate her enough to have killed her, or to have been an accomplice to her murder, such was the intensity of her passion, and such was the pain she felt, perceiving herself to have been rejected, or wronged, by this woman she had loved, this woman who she thought had loved her back.

I closed my eyes and I saw Anthony hit Cissy to the ground and climb on top of her, and I saw Cissy struggle and bite Anthony's hand and I saw her use the only opportunity that was afforded to her for speech by crying out Rachel's name, and I saw Rachel, standing there watching Cissy being assaulted and calling out her name, and I saw her smile and say through her tears, 'Go for it Ciss. It's only a fuck after all, isn't that what you said?' And I saw what Cissy would have seen from where she lay, Anthony's hand clamped back over her mouth again: I saw Rachel walking from the clearing and leaving Cissy to her fate, and I felt what Cissy would have felt then, on realising she had been abandoned by her lover.

For my own part, that was enough. Of course I didn't know whether Cissy had actually been in love with Rachel as much as it seemed she might have been, nor did I have any sense whether Rachel had ever loved her back, remembering only the awkwardness with which Rachel had responded to my questions in the summer about whether she had kept in touch with Cissy at all since she had left Worcester, and how strange it seemed to me at the time that she had broken off contact altogether in the way that she had. What I did know, though, was that their relationship had been an unusually intense one, and that there had been anger there in Cissy, and that if what her father had told Richard was

true, it was an anger from which she hadn't yet found release. It seemed quite possible to me, therefore, that she might be someone who was still likely, so many years later, to have been able to give that anger a voice only through violence, whether intentionally or otherwise.

I stared out of the window, thinking about Rachel, and about Cissy, and then I thought some more about what would have happened after Rachel had walked away from the Pavilion and been seen by Towneley and Haddon collapsing onto the grass, her body convulsing. And I wondered about how Cissy and Anthony would have felt when Haddon had appeared at the back of the Pavilion, and at what point exactly the two of them would have become fully aware that it was Rachel who had told him of their presence there. That would have been the moment, I realised, that the spell which Rachel had cast on them would have been broken once and for all, and the mystique that it seemed she had held for them would have been shattered beyond repair. For if Cissy and Anthony were in love with Rachel, and if so many of the things that they each of them had done in the two years that they spent together had been done in the hope, if not quite the expectation, that she might love them back, that must have been the point at which they would finally have realised how foolish they'd been to have nursed such hopes in their hearts.

I thought of them going to the tobacconist on The High and asking for the gold-tipped cigarettes she had told them to buy, and of Rachel coming up with the idea of the Browning letters and the other two playing along so readily at first, until only Anthony was left in the game. I thought again of Cissy draping her arm around an unresponsive Rachel on the steps before the Ball, and doing the same on the deck of the boat in Turkey, and I thought once more of Rachel's trusty servant Anthony, fighting in the Buttery bar to protect her honour by punching Richard in the side of the head. And I saw then that there was no other way of looking at it: when Haddon had gone to the Pavilion that Midsummer Night so many years ago, on Rachel's

instructions, he had not only broken up the fight that was taking place between Anthony and Cissy, but he had also released them from the thrall in which Rachel had held them.

As I thought about Rachel walking away from them and collapsing on the grass, I thought also about Haddon and Towneley seeing her there, and Towneley running to her rescue. I wondered then about what Harry had said about the way her body had been convulsing, and that it had been either because she was vomiting, or crying. It seemed obvious, suddenly, that the latter was the case, and that the reason she was sobbing so hard was because she knew that the part she'd been acting out was finally over, and that something she had only ever thought of as a joke had been taken literally, so that all of them in their little group of four, as Harry had come to think of it, were being hurt because of her, and in ways she had never intended. And it was then that I saw things clearly, and realised she'd played the games that she played without meaning to, and only in order to keep her orphaned self apart from the world she saw around her, being too much a prisoner of her own mind, and of her own past, to believe that any of what she encountered there was real. And I saw then also that this love that Cissy, and Anthony, and Harry, had had for her, was of their own invention, and that she had not sought it from them, being a waif who cared for no one, thinking no one would care for her.

I knew even as I thought these things that none of the pieces of information I had collected, nor the ways in which I had attempted to read them and draw them together, could go as far as enabling me to work out what had really taken place beside the lake on the night she was murdered. My role in these proceedings was restricted to that of a gatherer of facts, only listening and observing, collating and transmitting, so that I might enable others to begin to investigate. But regardless of my awareness of the restrictions within which I was operating, I nevertheless found myself imagining what might actually have happened that night beside the lake. And so it was that as we crossed the

last of Oxfordshire, I sketched out a story for myself, and this is how it went: Cissy might have been waiting by the lake behind the plane tree, and Anthony might have been in the secret garden watching for Rachel, and the two flashing lights that Harry had seen from the Old Library window might have been the two of them signalling to one another that Rachel was on her way, so that Anthony would then have slipped down the steps from the secret garden and stood waiting for Rachel to emerge from the passageway beneath. I thought it all through again and again, and I imagined him greeting her, and I imagined the two of them walking across the lawns together, talking, Rachel having no idea that Cissy was there. I saw them reach the plane tree, and I saw Anthony kneeling on the grass and Rachel kneeling beside him, and then I saw Cissy step from the shadows and lift a stone into the air, silently, before bringing it down on Rachel's head for the first time. And then I heard Rachel scream, and I saw Cissy bring down the stone again and again until, at perhaps the fourth blow, I saw Rachel give in and sink forward, her face falling down until it met the grass, and I saw Cissy drop the stone and run back across the lawns and through the passageway and up the side of the quad, the hood of her jogging top pulled down tight on her head, passing me on the steps where I had fallen. I saw Harry standing in shock on the terrace opposite and I saw Anthony, having picked up Rachel's bag and run across the bridge to the Provost's garden and cut through to the playing fields, waiting in the bushes until he could see the porter bending down over me where I knelt with Rachel's head in my hands, and then I saw him tracking his way around the edge of the fields and creeping along to the boundary with the canal and pushing through the bushes before slipping over the wall into the water, leaving no trace by which he might be found.

The train stopped then and we were at Oxford, and I stepped on to the platform into a morning colder than the one I had left behind. I walked quickly from the station concourse and began to make my way up towards the castle mound, heading for St Aldates. I have often

found over the years, largely in the context of my work and particularly when I am engaged with a piece of litigation, that when I am faced with events of enormous significance, or with a factual matrix so dense and complex as to seem almost impenetrable, I focus instead, and completely unintentionally, on some minute detail that apparently carries no great weight whatsoever. And I have always supposed that this tendency stems from no other cause than the fact that to do so is manageable, and reassuring, and comforting, in the face of other, more troubling difficulties.

Yesterday, as it turned out, I made no exception to this habit of mine, for as I started my walk up towards the castle, I began again to think through what Richard had said in his email about Cissy not being called Cissy any more, and her father referring to her by a different name. I had crossed Rewley Road and had walked along Hythe Bridge Street as far as the canal when I saw on my left the trees of the Worcester playing fields, following the line of the towpath, and I wondered whether Harry was in his rooms, sitting alone by his fireside, and whether he was worrying about what I would decide to do. And then I wondered, if he wasn't there, where he was instead, and who he might be with, and I thought that perhaps I should have telephoned him to let him know I was coming.

I had just begun to hope that I wouldn't bump into him by chance when I reached the right-hand turn leading to the castle mound and took it, leaving the environs of Worcester behind me altogether. I knew I'd be able to explain myself quite easily if I did see him, given the suddenness of the discovery that was the catalyst for my journey, but still, I wanted to avoid it, having no desire to speak with him, and knowing how awkward I'd feel if I had to. I reflected then on how that was a sensation I'd felt on more than a couple of occasions during my visit, and I began to wonder whether I'd made myself feel like that each time, or whether it was something in Harry's manner that had brought it about. But then I remembered the night I'd drunk too

much at dessert and I felt my cheeks flush slightly just from thinking about him walking me back across the quad, his hand under my elbow. When I recalled how I'd tried to sober myself up by reading the writing on the wall in the Pump Quad, I realised that not only had this feeling been, on that occasion, one completely of my own making, but also that it was entirely appropriate I should have felt it.

I suppose it was the surfacing of this latent memory of what I had seen there, written on the wall, that made me think again of Richard's email, and of how, not being able to recall Cissy's name, he had referred to her as 'that slightly peculiar American woman who coxed us to victory'. And it was at that moment, just as I was making for the castle mound, that I stopped and turned in my tracks and retraced my steps and walked back up Worcester Street instead, heading for Worcester itself. It wasn't that I'd worked out the name she would have been using instead of Cissy, only that I knew how I could find it out, my mind having been cast back suddenly to the afternoon that Richard and I had stood beside the Isis cheering along with everyone else as she was carried from her boat on the shoulders of her crew. The reason I turned from my course yesterday was because I'd seen her even as I walked, rising into the air above us all, seemingly lifted higher still by the noise of the shouts that rang out over the water and across the fields beyond, the whole of College having shown up to chant the nickname she'd been given by her crew, the name that was printed in block capitals across the back of the T-shirt she was wearing that day, in recognition of the debt she was owed for the skill with which she'd manipulated and harried her men along the river.

Again, I knew this was the kind of detail the police could very well find out for themselves without the slightest trouble, but having felt the hint of satisfaction that came when I realised it was within my grasp, I wanted to be able to present them with what I considered to be the final piece of my jigsaw. And that was why I skirted the college walls one more time, half running up Worcester Street with the

intention of jogging along the terrace once I was inside and following the steps down into the Pump Quad. When I got there, I thought to myself, I would be able to scan the palimpsest that was its walls and find what I had missed in my drunkenness: I would read the display of the nicknames of her crew that summer, knowing that hers would be written there also, right across the top.

But when I rounded the corner where Worcester Street meets Beaumont Street, with the muffled remembered sounds of those riverside chants ringing just too faintly in my ears for me to be able to make them out, I found that it was not to be. Because it was Midwinter Night, the iron gates had been locked shut, so that I couldn't even make my way up the flagstone path that lay beyond them to bang on the huge wooden doors.

It was, I suppose, entirely understandable that this blow would strike me as hard as it did. Things had seemed to be so nearly at an end, and I had thrown myself at the mark that day, fighting to keep inside what wanted to come out. Determined to see things through to a conclusion, I had been determined also to staunch my grieving until my work was over. But I was defeated then, facing those locked gates and the wooden doors that lay beyond them, and that is why I raised one hand and held it against the coldness of the iron and I wept, wishing very much that I might have gone inside and grasped at the thread I knew was waiting for me, tying it to the others I had brought from London, so that I had done my best for Rachel.

I don't know how long I stayed there in front of the gates yesterday. I only know that I realised, eventually, that I wasn't standing up any more but sitting on the ground, slumped against them, and that my hands and my feet were numb with cold. I pulled myself up and began slowly to retrace my steps, making my way up past the castle and turning right at the top of Cornmarket. I headed down the hill to the police station

and when I got there I went with a couple of detectives into an interview room and began to talk. After an hour or so, calls were made to London, and later on, more officers arrived. When I'd finished telling them Harry's story, and my own, I answered as many of their questions as I was able to. And when they'd read all the documents I gave them and looked at the severed photograph also, other calls were made to other people in other countries, and to the Provost of Worcester College to request the opening of his gates, despite it being Midwinter.

And because of the tales that I told, seats on other flights were booked last night, in addition to my own. There is a plane that has taken off already for Tucson, with men and women on board who will be looking for Anthony, and for Cissy, and for the man Cissy's father hired to watch his daughter, on and off, over the years. And there is another that will be on its way to Tokyo, where Evie will be invited to discuss in greater depth the part she played in the drama of her god-daughter's life, and death, and to tell them a little more about her relationship with the young man who, along with the staff of his hotel, had so obligingly given her her alibi. Among the passengers that will, about now, be boarding the flight that is due to land later on today in Washington DC, are those who will question Cissy's father, and in a few hours from now, a train will pull out of Euston bound for Manchester, and for Anthony's mother. At around the same time, a couple of officers will be let in through the gates at Worcester to take some photographs of the names written on the wall in the Pump Quad, and to look through the college archive for the Boat Club reports heralding Cissy as its hero, and to begin again to tread out tracks around the lake and to measure sightlines from the Old Library. And, slightly further north, at the top of the Woodstock Road, a plain-clothed policeman will knock on the door of Harry's house, as happened once before when the leaves were still on the trees and he slept with the contentment of someone who knows not what it is to have the death of another man's wife on his hands.

I have no real sense of what they will discover when they come in

to land and turn to their respective tasks, those detectives in their aero-
planes. I was aware even as I'd started to speak to the police yesterday
that I was simply passing on a version of events, and that mine was no
more authorised than Harry's. I was able to provide only traces and
imaginings, after all, having nothing better to offer. And now, as I can
only stand and wait, I am becoming yet more aware, horribly so in fact,
that there is a chance that what they will learn when they arrive at their
destinations, if indeed they learn anything at all, may add precisely
nothing of any significance to that which they know already. I cannot
avoid confronting the prospect that despite my journey to visit Harry,
and my note-taking, and my sorting of facts and ordering of narratives,
carried out so painstakingly and so late into the night as I sat on my
own at Rachel's desk in the evenings after I returned to London, look-
ing out at the heron and breaking only to walk on to the balcony and
see the moon falling on the water; that despite all this, I will, on their
return, be no further on than I was when the snow began to fall and I
took the train to Oxford. I cannot but think of the possibility that I will,
for all my learning, be found wanting; that I will have failed Rachel, and
wholly so. It might well be the case that what I have provided by way
of a theory, or a collection of possible theories, about her death, will
prove to be nothing more than a house built of surmises and resting on
a foundation made entirely of coincidence, the only concrete shred of
evidence, such as it is, being the tiny spot of what might or might not be
blood on the corner of a page in a book of poetry.

It was, I think, one afternoon on our honeymoon in Florence
that Rachel told me, throwing down a novel in despair so that I
asked her why she'd done so, that a tale whose resolution rests only
on coincidence is one that is hardly worth the telling. Despite the
cold, we were sitting at an outside table of a café, if I remember cor-
rectly, in the Piazza di San Lorenzo, each of us wrapped in blan-
kets and holding our tea while we read, in the hope that our hands
wouldn't freeze. I questioned her conviction, asking her to explain

exactly what she meant, and how exactly she was using the term coincidence, suggesting in return that every piece of knowledge in the whole of the history of time had been acquired by way of a coin- cidence, to some extent, if one went back far enough in searching for its provenance. We argued the idea back and forth for a while, in an easy kind of a way, until eventually I observed that what she was saying was absurd, and that any number of cases in any number of courtrooms across England were being won or lost on an almost daily basis by virtue of facts gleaned by coincidence of one sort or another, and that surely, that was how the most interesting denoue- ments came about. 'Not in fiction darling,' she said, smiling. 'In life, yes. It happens all the time, of course it does. I know all about that. But there are rules when it comes to literature. Hard and fast ones, to be broken at an author's peril.' And she laughed then, and looked in her bag for another book and said she'd run out and why didn't we go across the piazza to the market stalls that were strung along the other side and see if she couldn't find something to read next. 'Of course,' I said, glad to be moving, and we set off towards the piles of second-hand books we'd passed when we arrived.

'But what else is there?' I asked her in the middle of the night just passed, as I lay in the darkness of my room wishing she was there to help me slow my thoughts enough to fall asleep again. 'What else do any of us have to go on, when it comes down to it, other than coincidence?'

I listened for a time to the wake of her silence, imagining what she might have answered, before I carried on.

'Can it not be said,' I asked, 'that we none of us know anything by any other route, really?'

And then, for the first time in all these months, she spoke.

'Hush now, Alex.' She put her hand up to my face and placed a finger on my lips. 'We've talked about that already, haven't we?'

'But I can't—'

'You can't what, Alex?'

'I don't—'

'You don't what? Alex, come on. It's OK come on, come here.'

She moved her hand up and stroked my head, and then she ran the back of her fingers down my cheek, wiping away my tears and licking them from her skin.

'Rachel.'

'Stop talking,' she said. 'Stop thinking even. You're thinking about it all too much, Alex,' and she came closer and stretched her body out beside me, the length of it, rubbing my toes with hers. 'You try so hard always, to work things out. To make things right. Perhaps that's why you're a lawyer, not a writer of novels.' Then she laughed a little, softly, and brought her face to mine and murmured in my ear, 'And perhaps that's why I love you.'

'I'm sorry,' I said, hardly able to breathe for the ache in my heart. 'I'm so sorry, Rachel.'

'Sorry for what?' and she reached her hand up and stroked my head again. 'Come on,' she whispered. 'Let's not talk any more.'

She folded herself into me.

'Just love me, Alex. That's all I want.'

And so I held her, reminding myself of how the clefts and hollows of our bodies fitted together so well, and as our breathing settled into one rhythm, something in me let go and I was able at last to fall asleep.

Harry said to me that I could do with his story what I would. And I am conscious that I can be no more proprietorial about the one I told the police yesterday. They will do with it whatever they see fit, and that is something over which I can have no further control. It's not my story any more, and whilst I am not sure that it ever was, I feel better, some- how, for having given it away to someone else. And just now, as I hear my telephone ringing to tell me my car has arrived, and as I close the balcony door for the last time and go through to the hallway to pick up my suitcase and lock the front door and post the keys back through the letterbox, I am only glad that I no longer have the burden of it.

EPILOGUE

New York, Saturday 21 June 2008

4 A.M.

I wake in the night still, every night. Like all those before me who have loved and lost their love, I enjoy the split-second's grace that is given to grievers when they open their eyes from sleep, a grace afforded to them in the unkindest of ways by the lapse of the conscious mind's recollection of what has happened. As a slate that has been wiped entirely clean, there is for me at that moment no memory of my running towards the lake. Nor of my pausing and thinking there was nothing the matter after all. Nor of my standing then in the light of the moon and realising there was something odd about the position of Rachel's body and starting to run again. Nor of my holding her head in my hands and feeling the weight of it.

Instead, I am all contentment as I turn in the deepness of the dark and stretch out my hand for a warmth that is not there.

A Note on Harry Gardner

As with all of the characters in this work of fiction, Harry is a fictional character.

I am glad that I was taught English A Level by Andrew Dobbin. I am glad also that I studied English Literature with, among others, Edward Wilson and Professor David Bradshaw at Worcester College, Oxford, and with Bernard O'Donoghue at Magdalen College, Oxford.

Those that know Edward, or know of him, will perhaps recognise him as a source from which I drew in creating Harry Gardner. I would like to note that, to the extent that Harry is a character drawn from life, all of the good in him comes from Edward, and from Andrew, David and Bernard. And if Harry can be said to be flawed, then all of his flaws are drawn from my imagination.

Thanks

A number of people helped me with the writing of this book, and I am grateful to all of them for the things that they did. I would especially like to thank Simon Marshall, and Darian Leader. I would also particularly like to thank Simon Trewin, Beth Coates, Clara Womersley, John Glusman, Tori Leventhal, Andrew Dobbin, Edward Wilson, David Bradshaw, Richard Gipps, Mara Carlyle, Andrew Ruhemann, Brendan Wright, Nicholas Mercer, Sarah Addenbrooke, Matthew Brotherton, Rachael McGill, Florence Dollé and Mike Shaw.

A lot of the book was written during a snowbound stay in Worcester College, Oxford in January 2010. I am grateful to Coleen Day, Annie Belz, Vickie Porter, Emma Goodrum, Mark Norman, Peter Brooks, Lance Oliver and Michael Howe for the warmth of the welcome I received, and for the help I was given while I was there.

EVERY CONTACT
LEAVES A TRACE

Elanor Dymott

DISCUSSION QUESTIONS

1. Near the end of the novel Alex says "every piece of knowledge" in the whole of the history of time had been acquired by way of a coincidence, to some extent." Does the novel bear out this assertion?

2. How does Alex's statement that "I can only stand and wait" (p. 392) relate to John Milton's sonnet "On His Blindness," the last line of which reads "They also serve who only stand and wait." In what ways might Alex be seen as a blind man? What does it mean that on the night of the murder Alex's glasses fall from his face?

3. How does nature play a role in the story? For example, what do birds represent in the book? Discuss the possible meanings of the heron on Alex's balcony, or the woodpigeon on p. 155, or the hooting owl at the end of chapter nine.

4. In what ways are facts manipulated by the characters in order to control the actions of others? Consider what Harry tells Alex in chapter fifteen: "You must decide whether to conceal our story, or to disclose it, and in so doing, you must be our judge." How does revealing or concealing facts relate to being a judge?

5. At one point Harry says, "Don't think I didn't see, for every step, the other I might have taken instead." To what extent are these characters in control of their lives? Which characters have the most control, and which the least?

6. Consider the "engagement game," suggested by Lucinda in light of the later "games," played by Anthony, Cissy, and Rachel. What role do games play in the lives of these people and in Rachel's eventual murder?

7. The roles of parent and child come up throughout the novel. In what ways do Harry and Evie play mother and father? What does Harry mean when he says, "Childhood is another country, Alex, and we are none of us as clear in our memories as we like to think"?

8. On p. 13, Adrian says of the waitress, "Makes them feel valued that does, learning their names. Doesn't it, princess?" Discuss how the names of people and things affect the characters in the novel.

9. In chapter ten Rachel and Alex leave a play early. Alex says later that "[t]he stage and the seating and the lighting towers had been taken away and not a trace of them remained: it was as though it had never happened." In what ways is the action in the novel like a play? How do the detectives reenacting the murder play into this theme?

10. The novel's title is based on the founding principle of forensic science: that every criminal leaves some kind of evidence behind, no matter how much care is taken to the contrary. How does this principle relate to the emotional relationships in the novel?

11. Alex comes to learn Rachel's smiles intimately, but he never knows many intimate details of her life until after she is gone. How much must we know about one another in order to love one another? Is Alex's love any less valid for his lack of awareness?

12. Alex remembers an article he had read about an experiment in which a hypnotized man walked through a room full of chairs, oblivious to the chairs' existence. How does this experiment relate to Harry's experience in the novel? To Alex's?